Rook To Strasbourg

Michèle Milano   Michele Olson

Rook to Strasbourg is a work of fiction. All characters are products of the Author's imagination. Any resemblance to persons living or deceased is purely coincidental.

This book or any portion of it may not be used or reproduced in any manner whatsoever, nor stored in a retrieval system, or transmitted in any form or in any means- by electronic, mechanical, photocopying or otherwise without express written permission by the Author.

Copyright © 2024 Michele Milano
All rights reserved

Cover Art: Michèle Milano

I dedicate this book not only to my husband of many decades, without whose unwavering support, this book would never have become a reality, but also, most importantly, to my great, late friend, Co-Author and Franco-Fun PAL, Michele Olson. To you, Miki, the memories of all our laugh and giggle filled adventures into France will forever be in my thoughts and cherished memories! You are dearly missed!

PROLOGUE

The heavy stillness muffled the natural sounds of a damp September's night. A tangible thing, it smothered the calling of the night owls, the whisper of the pines, the river's lapping against the old brick and mortar bridge.

Headlights flashed against the stone and disappeared as the car silently rolled forward, then stopped on the riverbank. It waited there. Seconds ticked by; its headlights extinguished as a river boat passed beneath the arched bridge.

The car's driver watched the teeming deck from the shore. Jubilant laughter trickling up to his ears. The distant music, the festive mood seemed disjointed on such a night. The breeze from the water touched his face through the open window, but failed to cool him, for it too carried the muggy heat. He lit a cigarette, the flame, a brief flicker against an impassive face.

His eyes followed the boat as it cleared the bridge. Obscured from view, he snapped a chrome switch and flooded the car's interior with light. Blinking, he then reached for the papers neatly stacked on the seat next to him. Just once more:

To The Editor:
Kindly print the enclosure in your Sunday edition of the Post. You may verify the information by telephoning the Voiture at the enclosed number . . .

With a rustle, he flipped to the next page and scanned the brief paragraph.

The Officers and the Voyageurs of Voiture NO. 689 are notified of the death of Voyageur Johann Moreau on September 4, 1987. Voyageurs are requested to be present for the Legion Service at Hanson's Funeral Home, Hyattsville, MD at seven this evening. The members of the Voiture extend sincere sympathy to the family.

Emile Slater, Chef de Gare,
Donald Montgomery, Aumonier

"Pawn to Queen's Fourth," he whispered softly, then folded the papers with loving fingers.

The boat vanished around the river's bend as he turned the ignition. The car moved forward, stopping dead center on the ancient bridge.

His heels crushing against the crumbling mortar as he circled the car. Pausing over the trunk, he glanced around, down the river, up both sides of its hilly banks.

The trunk sprang open. Patting the rounded burlap, chuckling, he struggled to free the heavy canvas roll from its cramped prison, then dragged it forward till it slumped over the fender. In a slow, easy movement, he slung the bundle over his shoulder.

The man chuckled again, recalling the futile struggle, the fear in the eyes as his prey fought for breath. Then, the vacant stare as life left the body. Limply, the corpse had toppled to the floor where it lay in a crumpled, lifeless heap.

He staggered to the low bridge wall, his back to the stones and shrugged his shoulders. The burlap roll slipped over into the blackness with only a hint of a splash. Gone.

The man remembered his cigarette and retrieved the glowing butt from the car's ashtray. Then, he leaned against the wall and waited. His gaze on the faint, white foaming bubbles rising to the water's surface.

The river . . .his past, present and future plans, all here, on this bridge and the river below.

But the water flowed on, never ceasing. From the mountains to the plains it journeyed, oblivious to the passage of night or day or to the ages of humankind that lived in this valley. The river, the dark theater of death and birth, his only trusted friend. It never spoke of the past and it never revealed its secrets.

Tonight . . . the man laughed again, a mirthless, hollow sound. *Tonight, the river would be trusted with yet another secret.*

The sound of another boat's engine intruded on the night. He grimaced and tossed the last of his cigarette into the dark water before hurrying away to his car. One more task before the night was through; one last undertaking before the usual, restless sleep . . .

Impassive eyes pinned to the shadowy road before him, the speedometer needle steady as his headlights tunneled though the darkness. The car lurched as the wheels sped over a curb; reaching his destination. A finger touching a visor control and a garage door lifted, allowing his passage.

A thoughtless breeze parted the gauze curtains, as he entered, tapping a muted rhythm against the window sill. Papers crinkled and a singular light fixture rocked gently, flaring its grim glow against the checkered onyx.

Sixteen luminous white soldiers coldly faced their ebony opponents at attention as thin fingers reached for a black pawn, then rescinded. Brushing past the chessboard, with an impatient snort, he crossed the room. Parquet tiles creaking as he shuffled to his destination. Standing picture still, sun-stained hands reached for the mahogany chair.

The open book beckoned from its resting place. He gripped the worn edges of the leather-bound journal. How many volumes lay strewn about the room filled with the same longings? He opened the book and absently caressed the parchment, his depthless stare blankly eyed barges floating upriver. Picking up a fountain pen, his temples pulsed as he fixed his empty gaze on his journal, he knew the Walt Whitman words by heart:

5 September 1987

> *O Captain! My Captain! Our fearful trip is done,*
> *The ship has weather'd every rack the prize we sought is won,*
> *The port is near, the bells I hear, the people all exulting,*
> *While follow eyes the steady keel, the vessel grim and daring;*
> > *But O heart! heart! heart!*
> > *O the bleeding drops of red,*

Where on the deck my Captain lies,
Fallen cold and dead.

    The pen's point bore down on the page and tore it.
    "O Captain, yes, rise up!! Rise up, won't you!!" Shrilling laughter shattered the room's uneasy silence. "Soon, my friend, I promise, we'll meet—soon."
    His caverned eyes narrowed and his mouth parted to a ravenous chuckle as he extracted a video cassette from a drawer. His lips mouthed the black plastic as he walked over to a television. Perhaps, a little entertainment before bed . . . .
    With a practiced calm, he sat perfectly still in the darkness. All was silent again, save for the click of the remote control. The screen became vibrant with the animation of a busy city. The camera's eye panned over the glass and granite bedlam, then rested steadily on a single pedestrian waiting impatiently at a crosswalk. Dark, curly hair tumbled wildly about a red Stetson; the toe of her boot tapping the pavement in six-eight time. Horns blared; tires screeched.
    Swiftly, the camera's hungry eye focused tighter on the woman's face. Her eyes, those unforgettable eyes, bright with confidence beneath the felt hat—the remote clicked again and the face froze. The room painfully quiet, save for the ticking of the video equipment.
    "Such a beautiful face"— the watcher crooned and narrowed his eyes in salacious anticipation. Laughter bubbled obscenely from the dry, crusted lips, as he imagined the feel of that glowing, pliable skin and the expression, on that uncommon, lively, unforgettable face.
    " . . . . *HIS* face," the watcher hissed and the screen went black.

CHAPTER I

    High atop softly wooded slopes piercing the gloomy mist, shards of brilliant crystals sparkle and twinkle from behind the bronzed facade of Heidelberg's castle. A hollow ghost, the Schloss, where deep within its cascading ruins lay the secrets of its violent demise; looming, brooding and waiting in silence above the medieval streets that cling to its pedestal.
    Nightfall seems to flow down from the Odenwald mountains creeping slowly into the ancient river valley. Thousands of street lamps spark and headlights spiral about the pedestrian core as Heidelberg dons its evening cloak. The illuminated Castle suspended in darkness, a dangling flame over the Altstadt.
    Terrace doors are flung open to hundreds of café tables, crowding the cobblestone streets with people, trickling laughter and an overwhelming hum of anonymous voices filtering through the golden halo of the city. For at night, Heidelberg sheds its tourist cocoon and slips into its mysterious, gothic cape.

Paula Giordano tapped her fingertips against her lips as she perused the multicolored nutcracker display. Hundreds of black-painted eyes glazed in perpetual bewilderment— the feeling of the surreal washing over her. Turning away, she checked her wristwatch once again. The fragile second hand clicked: One minute before the hour. ***Time.*** She patted her Stetson firmly in place and headed down the cobblestone alley toward the Alte Brücke, her flat wooden heels slapping the stones in an even-tempered rhythm.

Even at this hour, tourists milled around the old bridge arching high over the Neckar River. Others content to sit on benches along the banks and stare at the wavering lights flickering in the river's reflection. Below, powerful beams from barges and tourist boats sprayed the murky waters with opaque rays.

Fourth bench north of the old bridge. She strained her eyes for the familiar balding head.

He was there. Of course. Never in all the years she'd known him, had he been anywhere else.

"Late again," came the wavering voice in guttural English.

"It's these German watches." Dropping down next to him, she made a show of tapping her watch and lifting it to her ear, pretending to listen. Then, shaking her head in disgust. "They work great in summer, but come autumn, the little birds fly off to the Riviera."

Jorgi's protruding lips cinched tightly together in a smile. "And you, little bird," he softly wondered, "to where do you fly? You and Tony have not yet found one another; am I close?"

She looked away, across the river toward the looming ruins. "Let's just say he never found me; even though I was there starin' him in the face the whole time."

A warm hand slipped over hers and squeezed paternally. "As much as I detest all things French," the old man sighed, "there is one good quote among their droolings: 'To know is to understand, then forgive,'" he whispered in French.

"So, what's to know that I don't already know about?" She rustled in her pocket, extracted an envelope and slid it beneath a larger one next to her. "Anyway, this is all your fault, you old tease, so no lectures, okay?" Impulsively, she threw an arm around the old man and gave him a smothering hug. "Danke, mein Freund."

The affectionate gesture drew disgusted looks from passersby. Flinging her hands emotionally in the air, the American uttered in syrupy French, "Age is irrelevant where love is concerned!"

"Am I to understand that you've given up on your former *career* shall we say?" Jogi interjected, looking directly into her eyes. "To be honest, I never thought you were right for that kind of work. You are, how shall I say it? Far too much of a free spirit, I believe is the expression."

"That's putting it far too kindly, my friend. And, I'm thinkin' that still after all this time, Tony still considers me a mere Rookie. Maybe he's right, after all."

The old man nodded, sliding his hand over hers again. Paula looked off into the distance.

"Though, I must say, your talent for foreign languages is simply stunning."

The American broke her gaze of the river and looked at Jorgi.

"Yes, well, that may be true. I do love languages, but I definitely was not cut out to be a DOD, Department of Defense language instructor for the company— or even a DODDS part time high school teacher back then. And lastly, my latest gig as a greeting card artist in New York . . .talk about a stupid "cover" for my *real* job! I'm *so* glad to be out of it! And, *all* thanks to you, I'm off to a whole new adventure!"

The two laughed heartily. Jorgi reached into a pocket for a handkerchief. Before he finished patting his eyes, the American had vanished. Only the vague tapping of her boots was distinguishable in the night.

"Like a passing comet in the sky," Jorgi murmured and busied himself with buttoning his sweater against the night's chill. He must hurry home. Gerta would worry.

A step clicked on the cobblestones and the old man quickly glanced up.

Already blocks away, inhaling the brisk fresh air, the American eagerly hurried toward the future, oblivious to the crumpled old man slumped against the park bench, eyes bolted wide in disbelief as ivory white hands gently slipped the lids shut.

CHAPTER II

Hordes of young French soldiers clamored through the train, lugging and shuffling duffle bags everywhere. Conductors shouted imminent departure to the scurrying passengers as Paula felt the rush of anticipation she always experienced at the beginning of a journey.

The great wheels screeched as the Heidelberg-Strasbourg line pulled away from the German terminal. Blaring its deafening whistle, it trudged through the stiff morning haze, reflecting bare glimpses of still hidden sunlight upon its forged steel.

In a matter of seconds, it gained momentum, whizzing past the waking suburbs, then speeding through the peaceful Rhine Valley, with only an occasional steeple or castle ruin perched on the softly sloping countryside.

The compartment door flew open.

"C'est bien libre — ces places à coté de vous?" The three soldiers squeezed through the opening, hoping for a vacant seat.

"Oui, oui. Je vous en prie." She gestured to the vacant seats. But, somehow, there wasn't quite enough room, so after trying various balancing tricks with the racks, the soldiers moved on to the next car.

Alone, at last. Paula lay her head back on the vinyl headrest, the events of the past few days, a dizzying collage of lounges and departure schedules. Pleasurably, she laughed out loud at a sudden thought. *Oh, I wish I could trade places with a flea on Tony's lapel. I'd love to catch the expression on his face when he gets my note. Vaya con Dios, amigo: Not with mio.*

"Put him outta ya mind, for crying' out loud!" A stern, wrinkled face flared in her mind. Grandma Marella. "Go on witch yer life, Paoli! Life don't hand out too many apples. A lotta worms, yeah, but not much that shines. You got that?"

Yes, Marella, a fresh start, just like you advised. Illustrating a book on architecture for a famous historian and who knows where from there? When life hands me road apples, I'll make . . .. applesauce?

Yes, and adios to greeting card art. So long, to bland bouquets, balloons and teddy bears. Goodbye to trite maxims and bad poetry.

The American rolled her head sideways and watched the rushing scenery. With the Odenwald fading in the distance, the land leveled out into the Rhine Valleys' rich farmland. Ripening wheat blurred blond in the window, glowing golden in the crisp autumn morning sun. Like a fleeting ghost, the train's shadow skimmed the fertile ground.

Trains. How Paula adored them. Forever would she link romance and intrigue with the coziness of a sleeper and the mystery of a dining car. *Enough daydreams, Paoli girl,* she told herself severely and with a righteous sense of duty, she opened up the tourist guide:

Clinging precariously to the northeastern corner of France, the region of Alsace is perhaps one of the most disputed sections of land in modern day Europe. Due to the intermittent occupations by Germany throughout the ages, the first in —

Bo-r-i-ng — the impatient reader skipped a few pages:

The native Alsatians speak at least two languages now, the most common being French, German, English and of course, their native dialect of Alsace, a product of their combined cultures.

The capital city of Strasbourg straddles the tenuous border between the two countries, a palatinate of the —

Skip — skip — skip . . .

—along the Route du Vin, the famous Wine Route, winding south from Strasbourg. There are five types of wine grown in the region, named after the vines from which they are created. These are: Riesling, Tokay, Pinot Noir . . .

Paula tossed the book onto the seat beside her. *Okay, so I'm not the studious type. I'll just learn about Alsace through experience. And my first lesson, since I'm heading to France...*

A strong waft of sautéing onions and mushrooms assailed her senses. Wriggling her nose, she inhaled the euphoria. Ahhh. Grabbing up her purse, she left her luggage where it was and sniffed her way out into the corridor, following her expert sniffs, she turned left to where the delightful aromas hailed.

After some tight roping, swaying, then lurching into people, compartments and through scattered luggage, the hungry woman stumbled to the last of the hopelessly airtight doors. She yanked the thing open and darted in before it slammed back on her arm.

Her delighted features fell. "Really, what a dump," she mumbled, standing on the sterile white tile.

No one acknowledged her. Waiters ran back and forth between cheap formica tables, carrying trays of tepid coffee in waxed cups alongside generic fried indiscernibles.

So much for romance. Choosing a corner booth, she flagged down a harried attendant as he ran by. "Bitte," she shouted out with all the confidence born of living in the Big Apple. "Ein bratwurst mit pommes frites und café." The waiter paused, the accent throwing him. *German? American?* Catching her eye, he decided against telling her it wasn't his table and scuttled toward the kitchen.

Paula smiled with consummate smugness and turned to the window. She recognized the Black Forest to the east; the ruins of a castle jutted from its mystical, pine covered slopes. Soon the train would turn from its southbound track and head west over the Rhine and enter into France.

In only minutes, "Ein wurst, pommes frites und café. . .Guten appetit." The apron clad server slapped the bill on the table and hastened away.

Murmuring, "Don't let me keep you from your break." She reached for the red plastic bottle and promptly doused the sausage from one end to the other, then the potatoes. Picking up the generous brötchen, Paula panned around the room, a contented grin playing at the corners of her mouth. "Just like home!" Blissfully, she bit into the greasy sandwich.

"Then, you must be American."

The guilty evidence clutched in her fingers; Paula looked up. Gawking.

Totally out of place in the dime store surroundings, the middle-aged Frenchman smiled down at her in a friendly, ironic fashion, as if they shared a common joke. *Wow.* Paula swallowed hard.

The smile widened. "Is this seat free?"

"Uh, well—"

"Ah, but you cannot refuse me, lovely Mademoiselle," the Frenchman continued smoothly as he draped his cashmere coat over the back of the booth. "It is a matter of life and death. You see, I am a jewel thief and that gentleman across the aisle is, ah, pursuing me. But if I sit here—" the Frenchman slid into the other bench — "like so, and we act as if we have been traveling together all along, then we will throw him off the track." Grey-green eyes twinkled with mischief above a charming, boyish grin. "So to speak."

Like Puck, imprisoned in the body of Louis Jourdan.

Captivated, Paula peeked over her shoulder and spotted the unfortunate object of the Frenchman's attention. With the unease of a man obviously not used to traveling alone — probably married with six kids, the passenger pretended to read the Frankfurt news.

Summing him up, Paula thought: *Hm. Male, about thirty- no, forty with shaggy brown hair and a mustache to match. His suit had to come from Wertkauf or some other German discount chain and cut too short. Clashing socks peeped out the tops of scuffed brown imitation "leather" shoes.*

"Actually," Paula corrected in a stage whisper. "You are quite mistaken. That man is KGB." She adopted a mock-Russian accent. "And he has been tailing *me* all around Europe. So, you see, we may be useful to one another."

"Espresso, s'il vous plait! . . .KGB?" The Frenchman continued without missing a beat. He lowered sandy brown eyebrows in mock-concern. "Are you, perhaps, a spy, Mademoiselle?"

"Oh, good heavens, nothing quite so ordinary!" Paula shook her head, trying to resist the smile tickling her lips. "I'm an international merchant, more precisely, a collector of information. A tidbit here, a rumor there, sprinkled with possible scandals everywhere— all soon to be splashed into print. My book is due out any day."

The "jewel thief" rested fine woolen sleeves against the table's edge. "And the KGB, they would not like this?" He wondered.

"That man," she whispered and gestured with her head, "has followed me through all seven continents, from publisher to publisher. London, Moscow, Tokyo . . .He's absolutely desperate for my manuscript."

"Will you go into hiding?" He suggested helpfully. "Or perhaps, you will change your identity?"

"Frankly, I've exhausted my options. I shall hand myself over in Strasbourg — and settle for paperback."

"The "jewel thief" laughed aloud. Paula shushed him. "Shh. We can't let him know we're onto him."

Just then, the brown-haired man rose and left the compartment. "See?" She lifted both hands in defeat. "He'll probably have them abduct me at the border."

"Then, it is I who must come to your rescue," the Frenchman declared. "Mademoiselle, you must sit with me until we have safely crossed into France and save me from the danger of a far less charming table companion."

Paula pretended to reflect upon his offer. "Yes," she pointed out, "but, what if *you're* spotted?"

"Little chance of that." He shrugged slender shoulders. "Always, I wear the disguise on my little capers. And even if I were, never do I carry my plunder. You see, I do not work alone."

"Your wife?" she guessed, reaching over to tap the diamond ring on his left hand with a pointed arch of her brow.

The Frenchman smiled, caught out. "No, Mademoiselle, not my cherished wife. She is . . . how do you Americans say it . . . my respectable front. No, my son, Christian, is my co-conspirator."

Get me his number, cause if he looks anything like you . . . "And you are persuasive enough to lure him from his wife?" she guessed.

"Touché!" He eyed her with a mock reprimand.

"Extremely transparent," Paula agreed with an irrepressible grin. "You're right; I'll have to try harder. Let's see. I could say . . . I suppose he fell into a life of crime to support his wife's extravagant habits, or, he is looking for the perfect jewel to crown her Titian hair."

The Frenchman exploded with laughter. "Mademoiselle, truly, you are a breath of the spring in this musty dining car! I surrender: I know my betters. He has no wife." He studied her a moment more and then, as if making a decision, the elegant gentleman retrieved a leather-bound memo pad from his jacket pocket and jotted down an address. Tearing it from the tiny pad, he added, "have a look for yourself, at Strasbourg's most coveted playboy."

"You mean, *you're* not?" joked Paula as she stared at the proffered white slip, tempted. *Okay, so take the stupid paper, then chuck it later. . . . maybe.*

"Alas, no," the jewel thief sighed, "my wife would not have it."

Just then, the border guard entered the car. Paula realized with astonishment they were already in Kiel, the nondescript suburb bordering France and Germany.

Eyes sparkling in conspiracy, the couple dutifully handed over their passports. The guard glanced over the documents with a bored look, then moved on.

"Well," Paula sighed and gathered up her things. "That's my cue . . ."

"Your cue?" the Frenchman enquired, politely standing himself.

"Yes. Once the border guard checks my counterfeit passport, I have to rendezvous with my contact in the luggage car."

"Most uncomfortable," the Frenchman sympathized. He regarded her with a Louis Jourdan-kind-of-smile and quite suddenly kissed her lightly on both cheeks. *Wow. Oh. Wow.* This close, she detected a faint draft of a masculine cologne mingling with tobacco and the touch of his skin, smooth and newly shaven. Then he backed away, grinning Puckishly. "To quote the great Molière, 'My fair one, let us swear an eternal friendship.' Perhaps, I shall read your book someday."

Paula found her voice. "Who knows?" She stammered, her cheeks pink, but her tone nonchalant. "If they don't catch me first."

Weaving though the hodgepodge of outlying modern suburbs, the train bustled into the central Strasbourg station, poised on the edge of the city's older — and more picturesque center. With a sense of growing excitement, Paula peered through the clattering double doors as she clung to a metal bar for support. A fleeting impression of slate roofs huddled en masse beneath one stupendous spire, Notre Dame, of course. A new start, a new beginning and the perfect place for it.

The doors swung open, the passengers behind her began to push forward and Paula slipped out onto the platform to avoid being shoved.

Europeans! Juggling guidebooks and bags, she rushed headlong though the terminal, scratching through the bottom of her backpack for the hotel's address. *Just great. Doctor Junger was nice enough to write it all down for me and now, I've—*

"MMPH!" Paula plunged headfirst into somebody's steadying arms. The backpack flew, zipper open, raining coins, papers and pencils everywhere. "Oh . . . hell," she swore and squatted down to gather it all up.

"Do excuse me, Mademoiselle," someone apologized in a perfect imitation of a British accent. The Frenchman bent down to help. "I wasn't watching—"

"Well, you should," she flushed, glancing up. "Hard enough carrying around all this stuff without — OHH!" Eyes widened in shock; she snatched away the incriminating passports he clutched in his hand. "A woman can't even travel alone anymore," she muttered, snatching back her passports, then zipping back up the knapsack.

"Here." The stranger politely retrieved her garage sale suitcase— the hinges — sprang open, spilling the contents around their feet, to the delight of a rapidly assembling circle of bystanders. They applauded.

The embarrassed American threw herself down again and started stuffing the mess back into her valise. "Perfect! Just perfect!" She mumbled with a reddened face. "Welcome to France. Knew I should've had that lock fixed!"

"All my fault," the Frenchman gallantly apologized. "Perhaps, if you let me—"

"Hey, do you mind!" She snatched silken lingerie from his hands.

Eyes helpfully curious under a pillbox hat, a blue suited gendarme wandered over. "Is everything okay here, Miss?" He asked in French.

"Yes, Officer." Paula blew the hair from her eyes and glared at the helpful nuisance. "This man is bothering me."

"But—" The Frenchman protested, but too late, for the flustered American had already fled the scene, struggling in the distance with the exit door.

"Shame on you, Christian," the gendarme lightly rebuked, slapping his friend on his back. With a loud laugh, the policeman sauntered on.

Just then, another passenger shoved the Frenchman, pushing him forward.

"EHHH--" Christian stared after the brown haired man, running for the exit, grabbing the door, the American had left swinging. *What sort of people were riding the trains these days, anyway?*

A familiar voice mischievously quoted Molière in his ear. "'What the devil was he doing in that galley?'"

"Papa," Christian shouted, exasperated and smiling at the same time. He kissed his father's cheeks in greeting. "I might have known you were somehow involved. Very well, who is she supposed to be then? Another dancer from the Moulin Rouge, or perhaps a madam on holiday from the red-light district of Amsterdam?"

Grey-green eyes twinkled. "Merely a decoy," Maurice Larsonnier informed his son and sadly shook his head. "I do hope, for his own sake, the poor fellow loses her."

CHAPTER III

"Marella?"

"Who the hell's this?"

Impatiently. "Whaddya mean, who the hell's this? It's Tony. . ." At the pointed silence, he added, "Tony Giordano."

"Oh. You. I ain't got time ta chat witchya; I'm watching' Johnny. He's got on a trapeze artist who went ta school with Nixon, and I don't wanna—"

"So, tape it! This is important!"

"I got betta idea," Marella suggested. "I'll tape you, and watch Jonny live." She started to hang up the phone.

"Wait a minute! If ya don't hang up the phone, I'll . . .I'll give ya five dollars."

She considered that. "I want cash. None of your damn checks."

"Okay, okay. Cash. I only wanna ask ya one question, anyway."

"So! It's your five dollars."

"Where the hell's Paoli?"

"Paoli who?"

Now, he lost his temper. "Whaddya mean, Paoli who?"

"I mean, I know a lotta Paolis. Paoli, who runs da checkout at the market. Paoli who married that Greek bastard who runs the sardine cannery. Then there's that Paoli who lives down on Brook Street. The one who used ta be Paul. I gotta admit, I was skeptical, but he was one ugly man before."

"I mean, *our* Paolina." *Patience. Patience.*

"Why didn't ya say so? You're gettin' a hell of a lotta information for five bucks. She ain't here."

"She ain't here either. We were goin' out for her birthday."

"Sure, you were. Three weeks ago. She got tired-a waitin'."

*Ah, jeez, **three** weeks?* "She ain't at her apartment either. And I hear she quit her job."

"Look, I answered your question and the meter's runnin'. I wanna get back to Johnny and—"

"Ten bucks. Ten bucks and ya tell me where she is."

"I don't know where she is and I wouldn't tell ya anyway. Even if I thought ya had ten bucks."

Suspiciously. "She shackin' up with some bum? You putting' some more-a your crazy ideas in her head?"

"Sure, like she wants ta trade one bum for another. I gotta go now. The trapeze artist gave his seat over to a guy who writes spy books."

"Crap. Whydya waste your time?"

CLICK.

Tony slammed down the phone and reaching a brawny hand into the ripped pocket of a cheap polyester suit, withdrew a plastic wallet that matched his orange tie. The clerk behind the counter smirked at the cowboy embossment. *Where'd ya git that, pardner, the rodeo?*

The small clerk's face molded into a more pleasant expression for the customer produced a platinum credit card. Their eyes met. *Phony smile.* The clerk reached for a pen behind the register.

"You enjoy food?"

But the accent was too much for the preoccupied customer. "Huh? Oh, yeah, yeah. *Actually, it was pretty good.... Love the stuff—but—I'm still freakin' hungry.*

The clerk glanced at the signed receipt, still smiling as he examined the blank "tip" column. He bowed, muttering in Chinese.

"The same to you, pal." The man in the cheap suit snatched his coat and leather cap from the dragon coat rack and bolted out of the restaurant.

"Ah, damn! Should've stayed home." He brushed the sleet from the shoulder of the yellow vinyl, then glanced at his watch. Jeez, freezing' cold. Gettin' too damn old for this garbage. He pulled up the faux fur collar, bracing for the cutting wind. Dessert might've been a good idea.

Immense pagodas rose up over Chinatown, an eerie gold in the orange night skies of the D.C. metropolis.

Egg rolls and that won ton crap sure won't do the job. Better yet, I'll get some real grub when I get to where I'm goin'.

He looked at his watch again. Ten past midnight. Ought to be here any minute now.

Bus number 3 seemed to materialize out of the darkness, racing at a death-defying speed on the shining, wet pavement. It pulled into the deserted stop with a screech of its brakes. "Come on, man! You gettin' in or what? I ain't got all night!"

Filthy city, with filthy people working it. The man with the vinyl coat ruefully chuckled, after all, he was part of the 'filth'. He dropped in three quarters, saying nothing to the driver.

Hm. Third seat on the left. So, okay, I can count. The bus lurched forward, but the seasoned passenger grabbed the side of a seat without so much as a sway. He glanced up to see the driver's sneering expression in the rearview mirror. "Say, watch it, pal, I might just haul you in. Don't tempt me, you got that, brother?"

The driver pulled into the next stop. His eyes in the mirror, assessing the multicolored leather cap, the plastic coat with the fake fur lapels, the orange screaming over a yellow shirt.

"You some pimp for old chicks or somethin'? Cause I ain never seen threads so—mannn— so damned ugly. No sir, I'll behave. Don't want no old chicks you got comin' for me."

The few scattered riders on the darkened bus shuffled their feet and stared out into the night.

The synthesized rhythm seemed to come from nowhere, blasting the silence of the city bus. The rap pounded at the foot of the bus steps, the man in the multicolored cap rolled his eyes.

All passenger's eyes remaining averted to the bleak, wet streets, only one pair blandly stared at the rubber skin cap, the diamond studs lining the earlobes, the shoulder length hair pinned back into a ponytail.

As if entertaining an audience, the man sauntered down the aisle, belting out a few notes to his blaring music. He stopped suddenly, adjusted his 'box' ever so slightly and continued down the aisle.

"What you lookin' at, bro? My fi-ine threads, no doubt." He smoothed his metallic, woven coat down with pride and flung his 'instrument' into the second seat. He sat sideways, his shining ponytail swishing against the dirty glass, and looked the older man up and down.

"Better watch yourself. I wouldn't mess with him." The bus driver broke in. "He might just 'haul you in'."

"OOh-oo." He moved a little closer, and the passenger stared back, unmoved by his mocking words. "He is *way* too old, if you ask me, brother. Out way past his bedtime if you ask me and from the looks of it, he's dressed for Hawaii-Five O!"

Chuckles emanated from all the corners of the bus.

The man in the earrings smiled, then batted his eyes. He slid his arms about the seat's metal rim and cupped his chin in his hands. "You think you cool, brother, don't ya?"

"Beat it, Bud. You're gettin' on my nerves." The passenger in the third seat smoothed the brim of his leather cap. His eyes focused beyond the man with the radio, as if he weren't there.

"Don't be calling' me Bud, I ain'your friend, Elmo." He leaned in closer. "You dig rap, brother?"

"It's crap."

The man with the ponytail reached for his blaster and popped open the cassette deck, while the other passenger extracted an unfiltered cigar from his inside coat pocket.

"Thank you, brother — don' mind if I do." The man in the second seat snatched the cigar mid-air, then shuffled in his pockets and produced a slim, gold lighter. Inhaling deeply, he jammed in another cassette. "You gonna dig this, Grandpa."

The other cringed at the obnoxious beat. "Look, PAL, your ugly face is starting to get to me, so why don't you go rob a store or mug some old broad — better yet, stand in some costume store window. I don't give a damn where you go — just get out of my face." The older man said calmly, without inflection.

The driver glanced through the rearview mirror; his face troubled. "Hey, calm down, man. I don' wan no trouble on my bus! Just shut your faces, man, you got that? Just shut it or I'm callin' the cops on this here radio!"

"Hey, brother, I didn't do nothin': Just mindin' my own business. Listenin' to a little music, that's all, man, just listenin' to a little music—" The man in the metallic coat jumped up as the bus approached the next stop.

"Don't leave on my account, Bud. You were next on my dance card."

"You betta watch yo ass, Pappy," the man with the blaster threatened in a loud voice.

"Cause one of these damn nights, I'm a git ya. I'm gonna slice you up and put you on toast, you hear me — man, you got that??"

"Bon appetit." He turned his head away, staring blankly at the lonely avenue.

The number three bus pulled away from the grimy bus shelter. The man with his 'box' strutted away, shouting angry obscenities to the darkened buildings. Then he stopped abruptly, just as the bus passed him by.

Blue eyes from the third seat back met his. He offered the passenger an obscene gesture and the man in the third seat barely contained his grin. In his pocket, he clutched the cassette, turning it around and around in the palm of his hand. His last assignment. *Thanks, brother.*

He then realized the driver's eyes again watched him, through the tell-tale mirror.

"Bastard," he muttered loudly, feeling suddenly hungry.

CHAPTER IV

The solitary spire of Notre Dame soared above Strasbourg's amber tiled roofs as if to pierce the weightless clouds in the serene autumn skies. The ancient bell struck one and its singular resonance shook the windows lining the cobblestoned streets. The streets themselves seemed to tremble with the bellowing echo, lingering long afterward through the minute maze of alleyways and stucco dwellings.

The old man's cane tapped an uncertain rhythm along the uneven stones. Pausing before a used bookstore to catch his breath, squinting weary eyes through the painful glare of the afternoon sun, and perused the dusty display.

Such a pity to see these old friends mistreated so. Vintage tomes of past exploits and adventures out of mind. Like a forgotten Valhalla, where the heroes sit and sip their mead, and boast of feats only they remember.

A bright red ball bounced against his knee; it startled the old man from his daydream.

"Oh . . . Pardon, Monsieur!" Contrite green eyes appealed to the man in the black overcoat, who steadied himself with an ebony cane. He raised puffy eyebrows to reveal eyes the color of the pastel sky above.

"No bother, little Mademoiselle," he replied in German-accented French. He tipped his hat and bowed to the tiny blonde. With a questioning look, the old man perused her flimsy attire and wrinkling his forehead, added, "Does your Maman know you are out, so dressed in the cold?" He gestured with his free hand to her thin, cotton blouse.

The child's eyes dropped to the ground. "Non, Monsieur," she mumbled.

"Then, off with you, little sweetheart. You don't want to upset your Maman." The old man placed the brown felt fedora on his head as the light footsteps pattered away.

Resuming his difficult stride, the elderly gentleman ventured on down the cramped back street, his goal the forged Fox creaking loudly as it swung back and forth, back and forth over the restaurant's door.

SCREECH-SCREECH-SCREECH!

Near the front window, the Maître D' tried not to cringe at the annoying, disturbance with true Maître D' aplomb.

"Why the hell does he keep staring at me?" Paula muttered. "Can't a woman even sit alone in this country?"

"I'm tell' ya, Pawli, it's an aura. Men are absolutely fascinated by women who ignore 'em. Your kind is the most fa-bidden fruit, and men, bums that they awl . . ."

Yeah-yeah, Marella. I'm a regular apple in the garden of Eden. My hair is so tight, the follicles are snapping like popcorn. And this wool suit is itching me to the bone. My pantyhose has more tributaries than the Amazon and my shoes are shrinking like the dollar.

A whispering violin concerto floated through the hushed restaurant; Paula, oblivious to the glares of fellow patrons, tapped her spoon to the side of her Perrier bottle in accompaniment and took in the beautiful, luxe décor with a satisfied smile.

Placed with a spirit of spontaneity, the table arrangements tried to offset the heaviness of brocade chairs and stiff white linen, but not with any great success, and somehow, Paula found herself smack center in a profusion of potted palms and indoor trees. The skylight directly overhead shedding a waxy, unflattering light upon her lonely self.

The Maître D' smirked as he eyed the impatient American, tapping her heels, cursing sotto voce, as she vainly tried to escape the slap of leafy branches. *Slap!* A branch speared her abundant chignon, tearing at her tender scalp. *Okay, that does it!*

Self-declared, lips pursed, Paula reached into her handbag and produced a sleek Swiss army knife. Sipping her mineral water so-o-o very casually, one hand deftly unfolded the blade. Eyes glancing back and forth over the glass — *Okay, I'm cool.* Smoothing her napkin with one hand as she shifted in her seat, she reached again for the Perrier. *SNAP!* A twelve inch section of branch slipped silently to the carpet. Within that lapse of a second, the knife slipped back into its cache.

The American lowered her glass. Firm fingers grasped her shoulder.

"Fraulein Giordano?"

Paula started guiltily and smothered a cry. "Ja?"

A well-dressed elderly man balancing with a cane wavered over the table.

"Er . . . Herr Doctor Junger?" She managed with a pink face.

"Bitte, forgive my tardiness." Karl Junger felt his way into the opposite seat. "But these legs are not as reliable as they once were."

Good going, Paoli. Toe pushing twig to one side, Paula summoned her wits and reached her hand across the table. "A pleasure to meet you, Herr Junger."

"Ah, but the pleasure is entirely mine, I assure you." The old man smiled graciously and clasped her shaking hand in his own wrinkled fingers. "Not every day a beautiful, young woman comes into my life. Especially, one with a résumé such as you have compiled, my dear."

"Résumé? Oh, yes, my CV. Well, you see, Jorgi tends to over exagg—"

"Not at all, not at all," Junger interrupted. "That is, his letter was extremely complimentary to you, but I found nothing insincere in his words."

Words of the naked truth wavered on her lips. *Oh, what the hell. I'll just have to prove myself.*

A white coated waiter looked down at the couple from above a lofty nose as he offered two leather bound menus. "Perhaps, first, an aperitif?" He suggested in stilted English. "Wine, champagne —" His eyes rested on the American for the slightest fraction of a second — "a Cola?"

The couple exchanged a playful glance.

"Perhaps, my dear, you would like to order for us both," the old historian suggested archly.

"Why, y-e-e-es, I think, I would." Clearing her throat, Paula opened the menu and perused it.

"Hmmm." The waiter began to smirk.

"Let's see. First, we'll start with —" The waiter lost his smirk as the American began rattling off their selections in rapid-fire, unaccented French.

Junger, instead of being offended, was obviously tickled by her performance. And so, never one to disappoint an audience, Paula started hamming it up. Mimicking her grandmother's best glower, she interrogated the astounded waiter as to the freshness of each ingredient, as he assured her in tones growing more and more respectful that Monsieur De Bourchegrave — *whoever the hell he is* — sees to the purchase and selections of everything, from the white asparagus, to the force-fed geese. The waiter hurried off to do her bidding.

"So," Junger said, still chuckling. "Apart from the 'help', how do you find my city?"

"Absolutely charming, magical!" Paula answered at once. "But, very surprising. Most of the time, Strasbourg is totally, positively French. But then, all at once, it seems very, very German."

"Oh, my dear, don't let a native hear you say that," Junger lightly scolded. "Oh, no, no, no! They will stiffen quite righteously and pronounce to you in proud tones, 'Mademoiselle, we are Alsatian first, French second, but, never, *never*, are we German!"
The German's voice faded a trifle; suddenly losing his smile. "Old grudges are never forgotten . . . especially by these proud sons of Alsace."

Blurting out in reply, "Okay, so, why do you stay?" Then, coloring, "Oh, sorry, I didn't mean —"

Junger reached over to pat her hand. "Quite all right," he reassured her. "A reasonable question, demanding a reasonable answer. You are very young, my dear, but someday, you will learn — always in life, there are difficulties. It is the one constant, that one must pay a certain amount of retribution for the simple act of living. In a small way, this book will be my retribution."

Just then, the same waiter returned, followed by another who placed a free standing champagne cooler beside their table. It provided her with a graceful way of changing the subject. "Well, I've never seen a bottle like that. The flowers look hand-painted." Paula leaned closer to peer at the bottle now tipped into her glass.

"Do you recognize the style, by chance?" Junger sat back in his seat, his hands pressed together, lightly tapping his chin.

The artist glanced over the bottle's face with a practiced eye. "I'd say Chagall . . . but on a champagne bottle? Honestly— you *French*!"

The waiter ignored the blunt commentary and departed with a curt bow. "Please, do not direct that accusation toward myself," Herr Junger gently chided with a smile. "I am no more French than you." He lifted his glass and the American followed suit.

"Here is to dreams and the . . ." He paused, tossing her a quizzical look. "And the relish of their fulfillment, ja?"

"So, tell me. How is it you speak such perfect French? And without any trace of an accent? I know your father must be of Italian origins, with a name such as Giordano. Perhaps, your mother is French?"

"Ah, Herr Junger. There, you have stumbled upon a mystery."

"Ach, how so?"

"Well, I'm not sure anyone knows my mother's actual origins. But, that is one of my bucket list challenges that will have to wait a bit longer . . .for when I'll have more time to dig in to that."

Luckily for Paula, the assembly line of food carts interrupted the awkward conversation, as course after course streamed from the kitchen in a continuous wave to their table.

Paula, hardly embarrassed by her ever-voracious appetite, savored every bite: Crudités, patés, things with delicate, flakey crusts filled with something only God and the Chef could recognize, a delectable mint sorbet, sprigged with one leaf somewhere around the fifth course, then, a blur of artistically arranged platters served at alarming rates. Champagne, wine, more Champagne.

All at once, the table seemed to clear of china, but still the couple sat there, loathe to move.

"You have done much for an old man's ego today," Junger told her. His face rippled into a sweet grin. "It has been too many years since I have laughed so. I shall, from now on ignore anything written on the subject of your New York." He held up his hand, as if swearing an oath.

"Well-l-l-l. We're a convenient target. We natives see it as our duty to educate or rather, de-program the masses." Then, once again, they fell into muffled chuckles.

The waiter sniffed as he walked by. "I think, I insulted him," Paula whispered and slid her hand over the old man's quivering knuckles as she leaned forward. "It's my *only* shortcoming," she confided with a sparkle. "But, I do it often."

Junger, frowned in confusion. "What is that, my dear?"

"My foot spends a lot of time in my mouth."

"Oh, dear, the teeth marks must be painful."

They laughed again and Junger wiped away a tear from the corner of his eyes. "Coffee?"

"Lovely. Please."

"Perhaps, you might wish to repair to the powder room?" he suggested.

"She frowned in confusion. "Oh-Why?"

"Well, I've been waiting for the appropriate time to tell you, but—" He gestured to his own greying head. "You have a few errant leaves in your hair."

Paula wilted as she ruffled her fingers through her tight chignon. *Oh, Lord . . .*

"I thought for a while it might be one of those modern hairstyles. But, I can see by your expression, I was wrong."

"Uhhh. Excuse me, then. I will repair to the powder room." Beating a retreat through the swaying trees and stucco arches, Paula followed the pewter sign marked "toilette," pushing through three or four heavy doors, down a musty, marble stairway.

"Finally! I bet you get little tired of all these hallways," she chattered to a chambermaid leaning over a dirty mop. But the woman only stared back with disinterest at the friendly American. "This is a charming establishment through and through," muttered Paula and heaved open the final door.

The sight was a welcome one. Warm colors of rose and jade brightened the mirrored anteroom lined with plush upholstery, where one might indulge in a cigarette . . .. or in gossip concerning the other dinner guests, depending on the company one was keeping.

Heavy stockinged legs stretched out from behind the door: An old woman, dozing with a porcelain plate propped on her apron, the coins piled within, rattling as she snored. The harshness of a difficult life, evident by unwieldy grey hair obscuring perhaps purposefully, her face. Shoes without shape peeped out from under a faded blue housedress.

Paula took comfort in this familiar European sight.

Oh . . . wipe that smug look from that face, Paula Giordano. She stared, suddenly depressed, into the mirror. Tree particles and a few small leaves sprouted here and there around her head. *So, there goes the image.* Easily, she removed the elastic, as the curls tumbled around her shoulders, dropping leaves onto the marble floor.

Mercilessly, she brushed the tangled thicket and then re-examined herself again in the soft light. *Ickkkk. A little champagne and your eyes could pass for the map of Manhattan. The road map, that is.* Raising her chin, she fixed her candid gaze on her face as she turned from side to side. Her expression fell. *Oh, forget it.*

Paula turned around and lifted a hand to open a stall. A prominent, handwritten sign proudly proclaimed the commode "out of order". *Goodness, you'd think in a creme- de-la-creme restaurant, at least, the toilets would flush.*

Well, the other, then. Paula placed her purse on the handy shelf. And began to close the door—

CRASH!!!

THE DOOR HURLED INWARD and the force knocked her against the commode.

"Hey!" Instinctively, she reacted at once, but too late, for the door swung shut, then with maniacal force, flung wide again, catapulting her into the minuscule corner.

"Oomph!" Her cheek smashing into the stone wall as she blinked against the searing pain.

Hands wrenched at her hair and grappled her neck, smearing her face into the cold marble wall.

CHAPTER V

TRAPPED! The victim staying dead still, blind to her attacker, waited for whoever it was to renew the attack. With desperation, her mind prowled the stall for some sort of defense. *My stun gun! In my purse . . .*

"You so much as flinch, and I shall break your neck," the gravelly voice promised in hissing French. The hands tightened around Paula's small neck. With brutal force, they shoved her even deeper into the wall. Her nose and lips pressed with a tearing pain against the unyielding marble.

Oh, God, what'll I do? What'll I do?

So dreadfully near, she felt the attacker's sticky, hot breath on her neck. The rancid odor of stale garlic sickened her.

One hand left her neck; she could discern a rustling, as if someone were going through her purse. *NOW!* She jabbed her elbows at the invisible aggressor in a practiced move, but the huge hand only wrenched her arms together like brittle toothpicks. Then, with an oath, the attacker thrashed her against the wall.

Paula screamed and moaned in pain, but no one heard. The bathroom door slammed. And there she lay, convulsing and shuddering on the cold bathroom floor.

Get up, get up, damn you. Just get up! She could hear Tony's voice as if he were there, in the stall, standing over her and cursing at her in his gruff thunder.

Paula struggled to her feet, then steadied herself against the toilet, her knees giving way as she nearly fell. But with renewed determination, she grabbed the swinging stall door.

Water . . . just splash some water on your face. Wait . . . Her heart thudded unbearably loud. My purse! Oh! She sighed in relief as she spotted the strap under the next stall. *Deep breaths, Paula. Deep breaths.* Her mind was slowly clearing from the panicked fog; the thudding diminishing slightly.

Mechanically without tears, she checked her purse. Francs, gone. Credit cards vanished. Her passports! Paula breathed a sigh of relief as she checked below the hidden compartment. *Yeah, still here.*

*Can't just call the police. I'd be sharing a cell with . . . Who the **hell** was that?* On wobbly feet, she made her way to the sink. From the corner of painful eyes, she spied the empty chair.

I was mugged by a weak, old woman? Ohhhh . . . Paula slid her hand under the turtleneck and massaged the bruising collarbone. *Definitely, not so weak.* The forgotten water flowing into the ceramic sink, sloshed over the sides, dripping onto her skirt. She slapped it shut, bending over wearily, sinking her face into the ice-cold water. Immersed for a few bracing seconds, Paula rose and grabbed one of the plush towels piled next to the silent chair.

Closing her eyes for a few moments, she collected her frightened wits and then faced her reflection. Her face burning with a telltale red splotch. *How the hell am I gonna cover that?* The American brushed her hair again, finagling a casual effect to cover the darkened cheekbone.

Years of training and practice permitted her to keep her emotions in check: *Face calm. Go.*

Karl had busied himself with her portfolio. Intent upon a watercolor of St. Patrick's he barely glanced up, for which she gave a wordless prayer of thanks. The table cleared of plates and platters, while coffee cups waited, carefully stacked away from the canvases.

No hysterics, she ordered herself. *This is your big break. Just play it cool and when you get back to your hotel, you can throw yourself on your bed and cry your brains out. You can even throw up if you want to, but NOT HERE, NOT NOW.*

"Sehr Schön," the East German breathed as he replaced the last of the drawings. "Truly, a unique eye. I am very impressed, Fraulein Giordano." Looking up at her with admiration in his blue eyes, "I sincerely cannot believe my incredibly good fortune to have you as an associate."

"Why, th-thank you, Doctor Junger," she stammered.

Her new employer held up a hand. "Bitte, my dear. I know we Germans are a stuffy lot, but I cannot expect you to follow our example. No, I would be so much more comfortable if you were to call me Karl."

"Karl." She repeated his name. "Thank you, Karl. And I'm Pao-Paula."

"Paula. A lovely name. The feminine form of Paul, which means, I believe, 'little.' Certainly, it does not describe your artistic talent." He played the gentleman and refrained from mentioning her "new" hair style.

The head chef's customary appearance in the grand salon interrupted their conversation. A sublimely handsome face beamed beneath a crisp white chef's hat; the Frenchman bowed with a flourish to muted applause.

"Henri De Bourchegrave," Junger explained. "He owns the restaurant. Maybe a little pompous, but an excellent chef."

"He sure is good-looking." Paula watched as he stopped here and there to make polite, small talk. With a smile, he nodded his dark head at each effusive compliment, yet his manner seemed to say, "but, of course!"

"In fact, I think he's one of the prettiest men I've ever seen!"

Suddenly resembling a mischievous leprechaun, Karl chuckled softly.

"Then, perhaps, you would like to meet our most infamous objet d'art." The German lifted a wrinkled hand before Paula could stop him.

"Oh, no, Karl, I—"

"Ah, Monsieur Junger!" De Bourchegrave exclaimed in French as he responded to the famous German's summons.... Posturing himself between the two diners, shaking the historian's hand. "Yet again, you grace our modest establishment." Dark eyes slid away from the old gentleman and flashed as the Frenchman assessed Paula.

"And you have brought a lovely companion!"

"Why, yes. This is Mademoiselle Giordano from the United States."

De Bourchegrave swept up her hand and bent over the fingers, his warm lips pressing the skin with more than cordial fervor. His breath brushed her, as he murmured an "enchanté".

Now, I know what the salmon felt like at the market this morning, she thought as she shifted ever so slightly away from the ogling Frenchman. *Yuk, breathing heavy: Maybe he's been chasing his sous-chef around in the kitchen.*

De Bourchegrave clasped her hand even more firmly. "An American," he crooned in English, his accent thick. "All the way from America, to sample my Chateaubriand! An honor, indeed!"

"I didn't exactly—"

Overcome with emotion, the French chef kissed her hand again, his lips even more impossibly heated than before. "Ah, and it is Mademoiselle— so, you *are* as free as zee birds in zee trees, n'est-ce pas? So-you must come again," he added. "You must come for an intimate dinner as my personal guest. We close on Thursdays; that would be perfect!"

"I don't think—"

It was Junger to the rescue "And how is your beautiful wife?" The old man naively interjected in French. "Is she here? Surely, you newlyweds are inseparable."

That did the trick. De Bourchegrave's oozing smile stiffened as he released Paula's cramped fingers. "I shall give her your regards," he muttered, feigning an invitation to another table and quickly moved on.

Paula met the German's twinkling eyes. All at once, they burst out in helpless laughter.

"You . . .you, rascal!" She accused.

"Forgive me," Karl apologized with an impish smile. "It is an old man's only pleasure to arrange certain situations and then watch them develop."

Busboys removed linen from the far tables, and the noise of an industrial sized vacuum shattered the dignified silence.

Junger smiled ruefully. "I suppose that is a signal to us, ja?"

"Yes, I guess so." Paula gathered up her purse with hidden relief. His hand gently guided her, gallantly clasping her elbow as they walked out into the bright afternoon sunlight.

"So, I'll study the manuscript for a few days, and then—"

His hand left her arm. She heard the heart-shaking thud as he fell to the street. "Karl!" Paula quickly knelt down. Her own worries evaporated; her anxious eyes searching the confused face. "Karl, are you hurt? Here, let me help you."

The younger companion gently lifted a supporting arm, as they both struggled somewhat to their feet. Junger breathing a withered, "Danke."

Still supporting him, Paula glanced uncertainly right and left.

"You're alright then?" She endeavored to conceal her growing concern, already she felt very fond of this lovely old man.

But as his eyes regained their mysterious twinkle, "One does not arrive at such a ripe old age without the stamina to survive a few light tumbles now and then," he reassured her. "I am as strong as a bull." Then, squeezing her hand, he gestured toward the street.

"Now, off with you. You have an assignment to complete for a very impatient employer." The wavering voice carried a hint of mock reproach.

Impulsively, Paula rested her hands on his narrow shoulders — she could hardly tell where the coat ended and he actually began. Removing his fedora, she pecked him on his forehead. Then, with a soft smile, she popped the hat back where it belonged and added, "Thank you so much for the wonderful afternoon, Karl. I'll call you to set up a meeting in a week, at the most."

Karl, obviously touched by her gesture, bowed reverently. He warmly squeezed her hand again and watched as she went away down the cobblestoned street, as swiftly as if the wind itself swept her from his sight.

"Ouch!" Hissing at the sharp pain, Paula quickly withdrew her fingers from the scarlet blotch. "Damn, that hurts." She leaned against the bureau and peered at the damage. *No good trying to cover it up with more makeup. By morning, it'll be purple; no foundation in the world to cover that, at least, not here, in this room and damned if I will go out in public like this.*

Hm . . . . Tentatively, she brushed her hair forward, just a bit. Her reflection stared back from under a curtain of brunette curls. *Should have one of those cigarette filters . . . No, dah-ling, I'm afraid I'll be out of town, on location. You know that new Zeffirelli film. But, let's do lunch . . .*

"Oh well," Paula chuckled, then, sighing, she tossed the brush. It landed amid the heap of toiletries, knocking over a bottle of moisturizer. The milky white mess dribbled onto a used Kleenex and oozed onto the lipstick blotches and powder smears. Feeling perverse, she ignored the mess and tossed herself onto the bed.

"Fate," she moaned. "Now, I'll HAVE to stay inside and read Karl's book." She eyed the huge white manuscript on the desk. Well, maybe she'd just skim it and pick up the finer points. *Nahh. Fate just handed me a HUGE opportunity!*

I'll really dig in, study and research the local architecture and produce my best artwork! AND I need to channel Tony and watch better my own back! Groaning aloud, Paula reached for the telephone.

The desk answered after two rings. "Bonsoir."

"I don't suppose you've got any ice on the premises."

"Ice, Madame?" The clerk showed no surprise.

She could just imagine exactly what he was thinking: American. "If your refrigerator is not working, Madame, I could send—"

"No, no. I need a bag of ice. For . . . an experiment."

"I see." He didn't, of course, but Paula couldn't tell it from his voice. His singular lack of curiosity could very well earn him a plaque in the Hotelier's Hall of Fame. "Very well, Madame. I'll see what I can do."

"Um, just have it left outside the door."

"Outside the door, Madame?"

"Yes. I'm going to take a shower and I won't be able to hear the knock."

"Very well, Madame."

Well, that's done. Paula hung up the receiver and lay back against the pillow Her lips screwed together in a thoughtful grimace. Not much she could do about the grandmere-from-hell. Or the stolen francs, or the lost credit cards. She considered calling Jorgi . . . Well, maybe a note to his box and forget the phone. He'd probably combine a few German words that wouldn't even be physically possible, much less intelligible.

She sat up and threw her legs off the side of the bed. Thank God for her private stash. Or rather, thank Tony. Not much he could do about stopping her now. She'd just have to finish up before the bills found their way to him, wherever he was.

Feeling a little better, Paula resigned herself to a productive week of hard work and trudged over to the desk.

"Listen ta me, ya bum. I got a trace on this here line! You botha me again and I'm cawlin' the cops, ya got that?"

"Ma?"

"Oh. It's you."

"Yeah, Ma, it's me. Whatsa matter? You're not gettin' nuisance calls, are ya?"

"Hell, yeah. I'm gettin' nuisance calls! Every night durin' my supper, someone cawls and tries ta sell me somethin': Magazines, insurance, them damned carpet cleanahs . . ."

"I keep tellin' ya, Ma." *Patience* "Lemme make a few calls. I'll get you an unlisted number."

"And what if someone wants ta cawl? What if your Uncle Al wants ta come home? How is he gonna reach me, if he don't have my numbah?"

"Ma, the man's been gone for fifty years! He probably died a happy man with that bimbo he ran off with."

"Such a mouth, you got, and to your mother, no less!"

Sigh. "Sorry, Ma. I just wanna know—"

"If I heard from the kid. Not to see if your ol' mother is stiff on the floor wit rats crawlin' awl over her?"

Glances at watch. "Listen, Ma, I'm takin' a little vacation. I just wanna let you know where I am, in case Paolina calls."

"Like I dunno where ya are. Don't worry, if I want ya, I'll find ya. Trade in that cheap pocket watch they gave ya for a bus ticket?"

"Flight 442 to Cannes now boarding at Gate Eleven. Flight--"

"Listen, Ma. I gotta go. I'll call ya when I get to where I'm goin'."

Giordano hung up the phone and grabbed his attaché from the booth's narrow shelf. Automatically, he checked the contents and joined the crowds rushing through the starkly lit terminal.

CHAPTER VI

Shiny gold elevator doors slid soundlessly open. Sporting flannel, jeans and a down vest, the American twirled the bulky hotel key on one finger as she sauntered toward the desk.

The desk clerk glanced up briefly from his work, looking up a second time, his jaw dropping at the red felt Stetson. "Are we off to le Rodeo, Madame?" he sniffed.

"Non, Madame is off to photograph and sketch Haut-Koenigsbourg for her *very* famous client." Paula slid the key to him and shifted her backpack. "Some of us actually do work for a living, you know."

"Better to enjoy the sights this week. Next week, most shall be closed for . . ." His voice trailed off; he stared after the American disappearing through the spinning doors. Standing outside on the landing, Paula tipped her face to the warm, bright sun. After a week of hibernation, intense research, room service and some self-reflection, she was bursting at the seams ready for Strasbourg as her mind raced with new artistic possibilities.

A spirited breeze rippled through Place de la Cathédrale, as the artist turned up her collar against the morning chill. *Let's see. I should be able to catch the number six bus on the Rue de—*

Paula stopped mid-stride; her attention captured by the square's latest side show. Two mimes captivated a gathering crowd, performing the soft-shoe, Chaplin style. The American grinned with pleasure and then joined in the laughter as the slapstick progressed.

Terrific! I've got to get closer. She sidled through the circle of onlookers and contrived to find a spot in front.

Their faces whitened above lustrous, black tuxedos; the mimes cavorted at the steps of the towering cathedral. One of the performers spotted the hiker in red and leapt toward her, falling to his knees folding his hands in a praying gesture. Paula giggled, unaware that the other made a show of strutting mischievously behind her. Suddenly, he snatched the cowboy hat from her head. Dark, unruly curls streamed over her face. The crowd roared with laughter as the mimes fought, switching hats, then parading around like tough guys from the American Old West. Finally, it came to a "shoot-out". The show ended as they both toppled, clutching their hearts.

Still chuckling, Paula removed the actor's hat from where it had somehow ended atop her head. She tossed a ten-franc piece into the crown and returned it to the first mime. He lifted a white glove to his lips and blew a kiss, before he propped the felt hat on its proper owner's head with a pat.

What a lovely square. I'll take a few shots for my watercolors maybe tomorrow if the area is clearer.

Charming half-timbered facades of white, pink, orange and green huddled the square in a cluttered arrangement of posh haberdasheries and souvenir shops, antique and pottery boutiques, plus tiny restaurants and galleries.

The faint aroma of fresh baked bread filled the streets and teased the American's appetite. *Whoa, that smells awesome!*

Paula spotted the minuscule bakery wedged between a fabric store and a ceramic shop, half a block down the pedestrian zone. *Alright!* Hunger raging, she hurried down the cobblestones, pausing at every other window to glance at the offered wares. Alsatian dolls sporting great black bows posed among the usual shot glasses and Soufflenheim pottery, glaring in gaudy glory.

Once over the bakery's threshold, the American's senses were overwhelmed by the heaping trays of pastries, bread and marmalade with creamy, fresh butter and coffee. *Ah-heaven!* Tempted, she glanced at her watch. *No, not enough time to sit and eat before the bus.*

"Five croissants, please," Paula called over the whine of the coffee machines frothing cream for cappuccinos. The young waitress unsuccessfully tried to hide a smile. "Five?" She repeated incredulously.

"Yes, five. To go," she repeated in perfect French…. Eying the steaming cups of cappuccinos, cinnamon sprinkled like tiny skiers atop the mountains of fluffy, fresh cream. "I don't suppose you have styrofoam cups, do you?"

Arriving at the bus stop, bag of croissants and coffee in hand, she plopped onto a bench: Place Gutenberg, grabbing a crescent roll, she surveyed the pie- shaped square. The famous printer watched the traffic merge onto Rue des Arcades from his granite perch. Old men passed the time on benches at his sculptured feet; mothers knitting, indulgently watching their children on the antique carousel.

Gosh, this place is like a fairy tale, Paula thought. *I could fall in love with Strasbourg. Too bad, I have to make a living.* She gave a great sigh and took another bite.

"Ahhh, the 'Sigh, the lack of many a thing.' Do not worry, lovely lady." The man's voice changed to heavily accented English. "This dreary fog usually burns away by noon."

The American looked up; her mouth stuffed with buttery pastry. Agog, she eyed the distinguished Gentlemen's Quarterly mirage quoting Shakespeare. *Oh, Lord, it's—*

"Henri De Bourchegrave," the dark Frenchman introduced himself with a slight bow and still seemed to say, "of course you remember."

"Permit me?" He gestured to the bench, smiling widely as his eyes unfastened the buttons on her flannel shirt.

"Well, to the bench and that's about it." Dragging her breakfast with her, the impatient artist slid to the far end and looked down at her watch.

"Please forgive me for following, Mademoiselle. But, when I saw you again at the patisserie, I became overwhelmed with, with—" He gestured to his heart.

"Lust?"

"Mon Dieu! Perceptive as well as beautiful."

"As well as uninterested." Paula retorted. "But, I bet that doesn't matter to you, n'est-ce pas?"

The daydream only smiled a blinding flash of light.

"Ah, Mademoiselle," he bowed deeply, sitting down.

"Moi, I am a Frenchman, after all. When it comes to love, I recognize no obstacles. In France, love is our passion, our raison d'être, our—"

"Fixation?" She glanced at her watch again. "Listen, this is all very educational, but I—"

Lifting an arm over the back of the bench, De Bourchegrave closed the distance between them. This close, she could see his latest dye job hadn't taken well.

"When I first beheld you at my little restaurant, I thought to me, myself: What a waste for such beauty to be wasted on that old fool."

She choked on the fourth croissant. "I beg your pardon?"

"Please, do not misunderstand me!" The Frenchman lifted a hand in condescending supplication.

"Myself, I do not criticize you, non, Mademoiselle, not at all! You are young and innocent to the passions that sleep within you."

"And you want to wake them up, is that it?" She edged just little closer to the far end of the bus stop bench, nearly toppling off onto the curb. *Damn it, where is that bus?*

"I find American women very refreshing," the Frenchman slurred and closed in on his quarry. Paula could feel his breath on her neck and . . . a trace of wine? "So open to new experiences. So, very willing to try different things. Moi, I find that irresistible."

I don't believe this jerk could resist anything, willing or especially, unwilling. The American stared blandly into his eyes, noisily chewing (rather difficult to do with a croissant) and slurping her coffee. *Thank God, it's cold.* Her strategy did not work.

"Might I tempt you with an aperitif, this afternoon?"

"You couldn't tempt me with the crown jewels, mon ami." *Ah, and thank God— the bus.* She bent to pick up the backpack and spied the last of the melting butter in its tiny plastic bowl. *Ohhhh-ho-ho— this is too good to resist!*

As Paula tilted her chin and batted her eyelashes in what she hoped was alluring acceptance, her fingers snatched up the butter undetected. "I guess," she wavered, raising her voice over the roar of the approaching bus. "Maybe, some time . . ."

"A votre service," murmured Henri, reaching for her hand.

"Oooh!" She squealed naively.

Encouraged, the Frenchman clutched her hand as the butter oozed out between his fingers, the oily mess sliding down his sleeve, landing in his lap.

Disgust cracked his otherwise smiling expression. Curses hissed between perfect teeth as the American jumped onto the bus, swiftly wiping her fingers. Pausing next to the driver, she slapped her cowboy hat just over her brow and shouted down to the shocked Frenchman, "No fool, like an *old* fool, n'est-ce pas?"

The doors slammed shut. Teetering down the aisle, Paula threw herself into an empty seat. Craning her neck to look back down the busy street, she spotted De Bourchegrave standing alone at the empty stop. Even from here, she could see the rage in those bedroom eyes.

"Uh-oh," Paula breathed and hurriedly faced front. *Maybe you shouldn't-a done that, Giordano.*

But still . . . She giggled out loud as she recalled the buttery glop on the expensive tailor-made suit. *It had to be done, if only to avenge the integrity of American women everywhere.* "Willing to try new things," she whispered disdainfully. "Sheez!" Happily, she swallowed the last of the fifth croissant.

Towers topped with green slate roofs jutted up from walls of rose-tinted grey, like great stone sentinels, dominating the flat Rhine Valley below the Vosges Mountains with a regal presence. Modern glass covered the windows, a reminder of Chateau Haut-Koenigsbourg's twentieth century rise from the ashes.

Adding a whimsical touch to the majestic guardian, a windmill spun laconically in the mountain breezes.

Paula shifted her backpack and ambled up the sloping walk that disappeared through a massive granite archway. A metaphorical portal beckoning to the eerie epiphany beyond. *Now, I know how Dante felt when Virgil reached out his hand,* she thought and stopped to snap several pictures of the coat-of-arms entablature.

A few late season tourists milled about, plus a family in line at the ticket office. Paula followed them up the narrow staircase into the castle proper. Secretly, she grinned as the father corrected his small daughter's misuse of the past tense. *Brother, the French.*

Looming stone walls opened into a courtyard, where a large well stood in the one ray of sunlight from the open roof. *Hm, must be where the servants drew water in times of siege,* Paula guessed. A faint dripping sound indicated the well still functioned, but now with an iron grate secured its black depths.

The family peered into the abyss, two little girls on tiptoe, made wishes and threw coins, giggling as they heard the centimes hit the water. They then moved on to climb the stairs beyond the well. Winding steeply upward, stone walls surrounded the stairwell, a lover's turret halfway up affording a keyhole view of the secluded courtyard.

Maybe, I'll just wait here a while, she decided, *and let the family get ahead of me.* She leaned against the wall, snapping a few pictures, then made several rapid sketches of the well. The sound of shoes on stone and children's happy giggles faded; only the dripping well broke the oppressive silence.

"It's like a church," she whispered aloud. *Kind of hard to find a quiet place to think in Europe. Always people around, always tourists crowding into the churches, museums and galleries. But, not here. Here in this castle courtyard, all is perfectly peaceful.*

The artist's thoughts drifted back to the Hudson Valley to the sleepy village of Croton. An image of her fiery grandmother came to mind, shaking her spatula as she fried those marvelous meatballs of hers, imparting her New York style Italian wisdom. Special times over the formica yellow table top, sipping coffee or swilling chianti with that earthy, little woman. *Wonder what she's doing right now,* she thought with a sudden rush of homesickness. *Wonder if she's heard from Tony . . .*

Movement on the stairs pulled her sharply back into the moment. Looking up and just for a second, she spotted a flash of brown hair through the lover's turret.

"HEY!" Paula shouted and gave pursuit. Feet clattering on the stone slabs, she rushed up the stairs, her backpack bumping the twisting walls. *Damn, has Tony found me already?* Her mind scrambled for possibilities. *Maybe, I can slip the guy a few francs . . .*

The American burst into the armaments chamber, cheeks flushed and panting from the climb. "Okay, you—" Words died on her lips, as the astonished family of four, the only occupants of the room, spun around, staring in unison.

CHAPTER VII

"Uh . . ." Paula coughed and donned an air of nonchalance. *Where'd he go?*
Whistling, she circled the room once, pretending interest in the spears and swords that lined the walls, then darted out the nearest door. Nothing. She looked up and down the hall. *I'm onto you now,* she silently promised her mysterious stalker. *Next time, you'll be sorry you ever took a dime from Tony Giordano.*

    The American wandered on through the stony labyrinth, with one eye out for the brown haired man. Stopping here and there to snap more photos and making rapid sketches. She sauntered through the great hall with its massive tiled fireplace, around the cannon room with leaden balls still stacked in neat piles on the dusty floor, then up onto the upper walks, where the panorama dizzied her.

    "WOW!" She breathed and leaned against the wall, forgetting the elusive stranger and everything else, in rapt absorption. Below her, far below, the Route du Vin (The Wine Route) gleamed in the bright afternoon, encircling tiny red-roofed villages in its coiling embrace. Sweeping vineyards spread westward toward the Rhine in the distance and beyond to West Germany, its legendary Black Forest, a dark line on the horizon. To the east, the Vosges rose sharply upward, its pines softening the slopes at the castle's base.

Now I know why feudal lords had such a god-complex, with this to look at every day. She watched, breathless, as a hawk swooped over the valley, intent on some invisible prey. Like the spirits of the builders still haunting the mountain, she imagined.

Just then, a velvety, x-rated voice from somewhere behind her on the walkway tickled the artist's imagination, coaxing Paula away from aerie fancies and back to the far more interesting present.

"Ah, mon Cher," the sultry voice purred in French. "You are far too devious! I am only thankful I am not the wife in this little intrigue."

Oh-ho-HO! A rooftop rendez-vous. Paolina Giordano, this is your lucky day! I've GOT to check out this Lauren Bacall number. Well, after all, it's the duty of an artist to study human nature.

Casually, with her eyes still on the horizon, Paula shifted a shoulder letting her backpack slide to the ground. *Whoops!* Yawning delicately, she knelt down to pick it up... *Just doing a little research . . .. darn—they're behind me.*

The voice laughed seductively. "Would that I had your finesse. My exploits could rival the De Medicis themselves!"

Whoa! I gotta SEE this! Fumbling though her pack, the curious American slipped her compact discreetly into a palm as she straightened up and ruffled her errant meshes with one hand. Then, like a veteran stage actress, she kneaded her lips together.

Yes, I do seem to need a dash of lipstick. Wand in one hand, compact in the other, Paula wagged the mirror back and forth with ease from habit, praying for a glimpse of the guilty pair. The other hand mechanically traced the outline of her mouth, or so she thought.

AHA! Smirking triumphantly, she peered closer into the glass. But she certainly wasn't prepared for the reflection. No one could be prepared for what she saw. Exotic, ebony waves coiled from an endless nape, wispy highlights of deep auburn weaved through the shining black, glittering like the Nile.

She stared, dismayed. "Life," she muttered, "just ain't fair."

"Ooh, Uncle!" The object of her sudden envy cooed.

Yeah, right. Paula snickered. *Venus at some secluded rendezvous with her . . . . UNCLE? Wonder what he's like. Some sugar daddy with a lot of moola?* Vying for a clandestine look at "Uncle," the artist maneuvered the mirror back and forth, but no luck. *Hm. Damn, all I can see is a great head of hair.*

Unwilling to accept defeat, she tried a few more acrobatics to catch Uncle Whoever. First, she spilled the contents of her sack, pencils and charcoals rolling about with the alacrity of a pinball machine. Then, she tried brushing off imagined lint, ever so casually.

Oh, give it up. Probably, just another Henry de Backyard, anyway. Pushing the Stetson back atop the ever-grateful mess, she bent down to retrieve her pack. *One step forward for adultery, one step back for peeping Paula. Anywho, you've got a bus to catch.* The American straightened up and stared directly into a familiar pair of twinkling eyes.

"I thought to save you further anguish and come reintroduce myself."

"Uh-uh-uh . . ." Paula's jaw dropped.

"You do remember me, yes?"

Oh boy, do I ever! Grey-green eyes watched her with an amused gleam as she stared in surprise at the man from the dining car.

"It *is* you!" The Jewel Thief exclaimed triumphantly. "I had hoped to see you again. Maurice Larsonnier, a votre service." He clicked his heels . . . *or did she imagine that?* Paula just looked at his outstretched hand.

"We had never been properly introduced," he explained, still holding out his hand.

"Paula Gi- Martino," she stammered with a red face. *Boy, this is so embarrassing. What'm I supposed to say— so what are you doin' way up here?* "Uh . . .well, this is certainly a surprise."

"But a delightful one, yes?" Obviously at ease with the situation, Maurice Larsonnier kissed her hand, his lips lingering for just a split second over her fingers. "Are you visiting friends here in Alsace?"

"Yes— I mean, no. I'm here on business. I'm an artist," she added lamely.

"Ah, so you are not, er— on the run, after all. I wondered, the way you disappeared so quickly." His smile widened to that delightful, boyish grin that made her instantly forgive him . . . . for everything . . . well, almost everything. She turned pointedly and eyed the other woman, who seemed more interested in the view than the unexpected reunion.

"Listen, if I'm keeping you from your date . . ."

Maurice followed Paula's eyes and winked. "Not to worry, she is only my niece."

"Your *niece*?" Paula repeated skeptically.

" 'I will maintain it before the whole world' — to quote Molière. You see, my wife has me constantly followed. So, my niece, kind, understanding soul that she is, comes out once or twice a week in various wigs to, well, keep the hounds on the scent."

Well, this certainly is a new twist. "Wouldn't it be easier to just tell your wife you're onto her?"

"And if I did such a thing, then, where would be the sport? I find the challenge stimulating. . . My Estelle is an extremely exciting woman," Larsonnier confided with a certain glint in his eyes.

For the first time, she noticed fine lines just around his lashes; they crisscrossed in a pleasing fashion, deepening when he smiled. Otherwise, his face was smooth as if he'd had a face lift. *Well, he wouldn't be the first Frenchman to do that. . . .*

More than a little impressed by his ingenuity, Paula glanced around the walkway. The family of four clustered around the wall and a few feet from them, a group of German college students seemed interested in the windmill.

"And there's a detective here right now?" She asked, scanning the crowd again.

"The brown haired man on the train," Maurice prodded. "You remember?"

"A detective?" Paula gave a sheepish grin. "Ohhh."

"Not a very good one, I fear," Maurice mourned. "We keep losing him." Then he changed the subject. "So, is eight-ish convenient?"

She blinked. "Pardon?"

"Tonight, around eight. My son gives the best wine-tasting in town." Once again, the mischievous small boy, Maurice tore away another piece of paper from the leather pad in his pocket. "Here is the address of his shop, *La Poésie des Vignes*. Not to worry, it is simple enough to find."

"But—"

"Till then?"

Paula stared at the piece of paper in her hand. "Well, I guess. . ."

"Splendid." Once again, he snatched up her hand, this time squeezing it lightly before he turned away. "Till tonight, then."

Helpless, she watched him stroll back to his *date*, wrapping an affectionate arm around the patient "niece" and escorted her down the walkway. Paula looked at the address again:

La Poésie des Vignes
Christian Larsonnier, Propriétaire
499 Rue Ste. Barbe

Hm . . . Well, I wouldn't mind a look at this son. And Maurice invited me, after all. I mean, it wouldn't be like just showing up, pressing my face to the shop window to get a glimpse of — what did he call him? — 'Strasbourg's most coveted playboy'!

Paula walked to the far stairs, dreamlike, trying to imagine what that title might imply. *Okay, I could do without looks, but unless there's something wrong with the Larsonnier gene pool, surely this guy can't be TOO much of a lemon. And let's face it, Paula, old girl, it's not like you've got the entire market to choose from.*

In the middle of the narrow staircase, Paula suddenly remembered the bruise on her cheek and came to a halt. *Oh, Lord! I hope it' not too . . .* Worried, she fumbled in her backpack for the mirror again. *Oh-NO!*

Her reflection stared back, aghast, the open mouth now sporting a pink cream mustache and equally adorable pink stripes on her teeth. Wiping away the misplaced pink, Paula muffled a whimper. *Well, at least, the bruise has faded . . . and Maurice never said a thing . . .even kept a straight face! That tears it, he must be desperate to fix his son up with someone— ANYONE.*

The group of German students barked guttural protests at her lack of movement. *Just act natural, girl, that's the ticket.* Regally, nose in the air, she complied.

"Endlisch! Danke-Danke, gnädige Frau," *(Finally! Thank you-thank you, honorable Lady),* they chorused sarcastically.

"Get a splatter screen you *haricot verts*! She shot back, smiling at the old French nickname of "String Beans" for the Germans, she suddenly remembered as she fled down the castle stairs.

"Come on, Marella. I know you're home. Pick up . . ."

"I don't have ta tell ya who I am, so I won't. I'm either not home or I don't wanna talk to ya. But leave your name and a short message, anyway."

"Marella? It's Paoli—Paolina. I know you're right there."

"Paoli?" The familiar, scratchy voice replied anxiously. "My God, how the hell are ya?"

Relieved, Paula flopped back on her bed. It felt good just to hear that reassuring voice. A long, long way from home, indeed. Kicking off her boots, she propped her feet up on the pillows. " 'Course, it's me. Who else?"

"So, how's France? You meet that kraut, writer yet? You know, now that I think of it, betta see he pays ya up front. You know them huns are cheap bastards."

Paula smiled. Somethings never change.

"Don't worry, he's a sweet, harmless, OLD man."

"Watch yourself, honey: They're nevah too old. They awl got one thing on their brains. Well, not on their brains, it's below the—"

"Yes, yes," Paula interrupted with a thought for listening operators. "They're all bums. Believe me, I've learned! But you worry too much. Everything's grea—"

"You met someone, have ya?"

"Not exactly . . ."

"Just don't fawl in love. I don't trust anything French. Well, maybe as far as I can fly. They hate Italians, ya know."

Silence mingled with static.

"Uhhh— how's everything on the Hudson?"

"Uh-oh, he must be a real looker—hah?"

"I really can't say, Marella," Paula answered patiently. "I haven't met him yet. For all I know, he might look like Cousin Lenny, except that he shaves." *I hope.* "Anyway, I really don't care what he looks like; I just hope he has—"

"Personality. Yeah, sure. So, when are ya gonna meet Mr. Personality?"

"I was going to say— money."

"Now, that's my girl. Thinking about the future. Other than that— don't you forget what the nuns taught ya."

"Grandmaaa…. I'm not sure there is any such thing as a Catholic Frenchman these days. Well, at least not, a practicing one, anyway."

"You don't know that!" Besides, I've been sayin' tons of Novenas for ya and I keep my Rosary rings spinning around my fingers most of the day."

"Really?"

"No— but, I try—sometimes. Anywho— I know my Paoli ain't stupid. You know your old bitch grandmother loves ya? Capiche?"

"Capiche."

Footsteps echoed through the cobblestone streets of Strasbourg's old city. Everyone going home. The doors to grocery stores and butcher shops burst open, then shut as Strasbourg sought the evening's repast.

Should've eaten. I knew it. My thirty second guilt trip diets never work. Paula paused before a window and eyed the regional creamy white cheeses, arranged with the panache only the French seem to master, next to delectable serving trays heaped with exquisitely prepared meats and vegetables. Strasbourg at its finest.

She peered one more time at the well-worn notepaper and glanced up at the street sign on the shop's wall. Rue Ste. Barbe. *Yeah, must be getting close.* Carefully, she folded the paper and returned it to her jacket pocket.

Maybe, I should have dressed. Nahh. Don't want to seem too eager. I really don't know if I can do this . . .What if he IS a flabby, bald pervert with meaty purse lips and small round glasses? How do I not hurt Maurice's feelings? Not that he has exactly been concerned with mine.

Let's see, forty-nine eleven, forty nine nine—-Ooh—that must be it. Wow, it's adorable! The American stared from the opposite side of the narrow cobblestone street.

Elegantly nestled between a bakery and a parfumerie, two rustic oak wine barrels with shadowy scarlet geraniums poured over the rims on either side of a study oak pot. A roughly cut slab of pine dangled from iron links, a single light propped in a basket, flared its hand-scrolling:

La Poésie des Vignes

Loosely woven wicker baskets showed off emerald and amber bottles sparkling through the shop's front window with brightly painted duck decoys perched between antique washtubs brimming with shiny red tins of foie gras and truffles.

Irresistibly drawn to the cozy little shop, Paula crossed the alleyway. Wet tires sizzled from the moist night air as she discerned cymbals tapping and bouncing blithely against the shop's glass. *American Jazz. Definitely, American.* As she palmed the brass door handle, her senses, immediately inundated with the sweet aroma of baking bread, old wood and the musky night air.

No cars waited in the street before the store. *That doesn't mean anything; it's a pedestrian zone after all.* Yet, no one on the sidewalks either. No one at all. *Am I that early?* She consulted her watch. *Yeah. Well, Marella always says the mark of a true lady is in being on time . . . ha! A real pair of ladies, aren't we?*

A ribbon of bells tinkled merrily as she closed the door behind her. *Tormé, that's what it is. And* **Lullaby of Birdland**.

"Bonsoir," a familiar voice greeted her in velvet French. "May I help you?"

"Uh-um . . .ah," Paula managed. *I really did not expect this,* she thought in bewilderment. *Surely, it's not . . .with the wig.*

A woman of exotic beauty looked back at the American with impeccably perfect helpfulness. Jet black hair, shortened and now moussed into tiny spikes, rose away from a creamy, mocha complexion. Smoothly chiseled features framed enormous black eyes with no trace of make-up.

It IS she!

"I am sorry, are you German?" The vision offered in English. "I do not speak German."

Feeling so very plain and inconsequential in the presence of perfection, Paula squeaked "No, I'm American. Uh . . . where is everyone?"

The impeccably perfect helpfulness blended into impeccably perfect confusion. "Everyone?"

"Yeah. For the wine-tasting." Even as Paula was saying it, she knew. *It's a joke. There is no party. This is all just some lonely, old man's way of diverting "babes" to his chip-off-the-old-block son.* "I must have the wrong address," she muttered and started to turn away toward the door. *Maybe I can just slip out before—*

"Perhaps you should speak with Uncle Christian," the goddess suggested. Perfectly slim legs stepped out from behind the antique oaken counter and made their way to what appeared to be a back room. Paula stared after her. *Venus in the flesh.*

"Oh, that's okay, I—" Too late.

Okay, Paoli, you got two choices. You can scuttle outta here like a frightened little mouse, or you can give 'em a show father and son'll never forget. She took a deep breath, anger mingling with a touch of curiosity. *Okay, I stay. Babe, he wants, BABE, he gets.*

The music tapped on and on, as Paula spun around glancing at the myriad of emerald bottles. *I hear 'em whispering back there.*

The back door opened slightly.

I'm being checked out. Okay, wanna show? Paula slid her hand under her jacket, then jerked out her Cami strap, pulling the stretchy elastic to its limits. "Cryin' out loud, stupid FROGS can't even make decent camisoles." She made a few adjustments, sliding the plastic adjustor to its highest position.

Out of the corner of her eye, she noticed the door whish open wider; she caught a glimpse of sandy colored hair. Outwardly admiring the alteration. She swiveled around, looking down and examined her right profile. Not quite happy with the results, she reached brazenly beneath the wool and readjusted. "There!" Smirking at her fait accompli, she slowly smoothed out her sweater and zipped her jacket.

"I'm not at all sure we sell here WHOM it is you're looking for." The man's voice cut through the smoky music with icy precision.

Paula turned around to face Maurice's son, her face innocent. "Sorry?" *Wow. This apple didn't fall too far from the tree!*

The apple extended his hand, eyes dark and narrow. "I'm Christian Larsonnier, at your service", he said, in clipped English, "you asked for me?" He was studying her with that famous French butcher-hook finesse.

"Yeah." Paula nodded, her "New-Yorkese" clinging and thick. "Ya see, got dis smart-ass hotel clerk at that fancy pantsy place across from the big church. I axed for help in orderin' up some, ya know, well, vino to my room. I was piggin' out on some egg pie and was wonderin' what might go best wit it."

The aggressor visibly softened, a smile prying the corners of his well-formed mouth.

"Imagine dat twerp tellin' me he had no experteeze in da area of egg pie!" She rolled her eyes and stamped her boot indignantly. "I tawt egg pie was SO French, like ya know, like FRENCH fries and awl. So anyways, he says, I oughtta 'venture out to the *conoYsseur* himself, **'MonsEEnior LarsonnEEr.'** "

Now, the smile widened. "So, I says showah, and poof, I'm heah in da flesh." Arms folded, she leaned against the antique counter. "So whaddya say, MonsEEEnior LarsonnEER, can ya Help?"

Silence. Then, "Certainly, Madame and by the way, my name is pronounced: Lar-son-y-ay." So challenged, the smile quickly disappeared, his jaw set in determined concentration, yet his eyes glittered with amusement.

"Egg pie . . ." Tapping the tip of his index finger against his lips, Christian Larsonnier paced back and forth before the various vintages. He picked up one here, then there, shaking his head as he seemed to consider her request with all the gravity of a duelist choosing his weapon. Finally, he walked toward the back corner, extracted two bottles and returned to his customer.

"Now, Madame — that is, I assume, it IS Madame. A woman of such obvious distinction and, well, beauty . . ." He bowed somewhat, his lips pursed in a near-grin, puffing tiny pouches around his cheeks.

"Married?" Paula shrugged. "Well, not any mowah. Tree of 'em dropped dead on me. In dah sack, can ya believe it?" She was shaking her head with rueful disappointment. "So, says I, I says betta lay awf men for a while, heh-heh-heh." *Aha, he's turning red just above his collar.*

"Get it? Lay AWF? Heh-heh-heh." She kept the croaking laughter up, till the blush rose to his cheeks.

Larsonnier nervously began clinking the bottles together; she took the cue. "So-o-o, dis is your match ta my egg pie? Pretty label. I'll take both."

"Yes." His normal color returning. "Whenever I dine on egg pie, either of these are the only 'match', as you put it, for egg pie. However," his voice adopted a teasing tone, "if the fancy for chocolate egg pie should seize you, I have something splendid." He was on a roll now. "Or even for cabbage pie or my personal preference, gelatin egg pie--"

"Whoaa- you French showah know stuff." Paula couldn't suppress a wayward smile as he busied himself at the counter, she nodded a secret approval. *Smart, yes, very smart. Yeah, this one could make me work. . . .*

"So, will this be cash?"

"Nah, credit." Opening her purse, she found the gaudy wallet Marella had given her last Christmas and handed him the platinum card. *Gracias, Pop: this'll keep my toes toasty for tonight.*

Tearing away the customer copy, the Frenchman studied briefly her sprawling signature. "Ah, so your *latest*—" he emphasized the last word, "—husband was Italian, Madame Martino?" His brows raised; eyes wide. "But, the card here says *Giordano.*"

Paula noticed that they weren't dark at all, rather green and amber, and pure, rich lavender circled the irises.

"OOh, him." She snatched back the card, hoping to hide her fascination by looking down, returning the card to its place in her wallet. "You'll never know how late-- The last two were of EYE-Talian persuasions."

The music stopped. Customer and patron stood for a few seconds, wordless, awkward: The Frenchman, with a question on his lips, rationale forcing his silence.

Paula backed away toward the door. "By the way," she dropped the accent. "Do you like Tormé?"

The eyes narrowed. "Very much," Larsonnier answered warily. "Why?"

"Just wondering," she mimicked his accent perfectly. "Rather fascinating, I think, how the unsophisticated popular form pleases the masses, whereas the culmination of genius of Beethoven or Mozart is generally ignored. None-the-less, jazz can be a delightful change of pace, don't you agree?" Hiding her laughter at the dropping jaw, she shifted the bottles in her arms. "Well, thank you for your help — MonSEENior." Now, she grinned openly.

"A votre service," he replied, his face a study in bafflement.

The door chimes tinkled. Christian wandered to the window and watched the tossed curls as she walked briskly down the street without a backward glance.

HERDS of women Maurice Larsonnier had sent to Christian's shop, always with the same pretext: a wine-tasting party. And always, they were the same kind of woman. Prostitutes or literally plain and cheap types. A standing sick sort of joke between father and son.

But, this, this . . . . .

Wait.. . What's this? Out of the corner of his eye, Larsonnier spotted her wallet still on the counter and picked it up He turned the cheap blue vinyl over in his hands, grinning at the embossed balloons, a bouquet of multicolored American tastelessness.

She had mentioned her hotel . . . "the fancy pantsy place across from the big church," she'd said. Most likely the Hotel de la Place. Perhaps, he could just drop it off at the desk or maybe send it via messenger in the morning . . . A little penury would do the brat a world of good. Chuckling out loud, Christian remembered her marvelous "egg pie" monologue. And then he thought about the way her deep violet blue eyes sparkled with fun as she spun the tale of her ill-fated husbands. *Surely, even bluer than the color of this dime store wallet. . . .*

"I am a fool." Christian uttered under his breath, as he dashed out of the little shop.

CHAPTER VIII

Frantic heels slapping the moist pavement assaulted Paula's ears as she leisurely strolled the quaint Rue Ste. Barbe.

"Madame! Madame Giordano!" Out of breath and looking as unkempt as an adolescent schoolboy, Christian Larsonnier, "Strasbourg's most coveted playboy", caught up with his quarry.

One-two-three— she turned around, eyebrows delicately raised in a naive question.

"Oui?"

"Your—" he choked, then inhaled impatiently, catching his breath. His hand absently combed his hair once; it fell back into place.

How'd he do that?

"Your wallet seems to have fallen from your purse in my shop."

"Thank you," Paula said with great dignity (she hoped). "I would've been up a creek." He handed her the wallet which she promptly zippered into her handbag.

"Well, goodb—"

"May I ask you something?" Larsonnier blurted, a hand on her arm. "About your, ah, husbands. Were you really married three times?"

Paula eyed the tall Frenchman. "Why do you want to know?"

"I should hate to be arrested as an accomplice to credit fraud," Christian replied. Suddenly smiling as Paula's heart skipped a beat, returning the smile irrepressibly cracking her reserve.

"Then I stand by every word." They just stood there a moment smiling at each other. Gathering her wits, Paula held out her hand in introduction. "Maybe, you should call me Paula. Then you won't have to admit to anything."

"Paula, then." Christian shook it slowly, his eyes clean sweeping the tiny antagonist.

"Given your recent widowhood, I presume you are somewhat unattached this evening?"

She nodded. "Inconsiderate of him, dropping dead just before our honeymoon, but what are you gonna do? What do you have in mind?"

"Here, let me," Christian offered and took her sack. The couple began to walk again.

"I must point out, first of all, that I am not a Monseigneur — or even a priest. But, I AM a Catholic," he added hurriedly at her cynical glance. "And like any good Samaritan, I can't stand to see a stranger at odds."

Paula automatically scanned his collar area for any signs of a telltale chain….. gratified, she could just make out the outline of something like a medal protruding from inside his elegant silk shirt.

Hmmmm. I wonder . . . "At odds, or just plain, odd?"

"Both, I suppose. I thought we might find something interesting to do with the evening."

Returning her "examination", the Frenchman also perused her collar area for the same thing.

"Why Monseigneur! I hardly know you." She slid her hand around his elbow.

"No fear." He was looking at her sideways (and enjoying the view). "I'm a gentleman as well as a Frenchman."

"Yin and Yang," she chided.

"Touché."

They entered the cathedral square, the moon billowing beyond the single spire as veils of clouds drifted by.

Paula ventured, "Maurice does this sort of thing often, I take it?"

He shrugged broad shoulders. "Sometimes once a week, sometimes twice."

"Oh, Lord." She visualized the elegant Maurice staked out on an ant hill.

"I'm rather used to it, actually," the Frenchman confided in that disturbing accent as he leaned against the cathedral's south wall. His right hand searched a jacket pocket, extracting a pack of cigarettes. He held out the pack, then, at her refusal, lit one for himself.

"I suppose it's his way of expressing paternal disapproval. Anyone over thirty, you see, should be settled — or saddled, rather."

"So, he's helping you find your way down the aisle, is that it?"

"The island?" He looked perplexed.

Paula pointed to the sleeping giant just behind him, amending, "The *Church* aisle."

Christian turned, then, understanding her meaning, let out a hearty laugh.

"And your parents? Do they impose the same expectations?"

She shoved cold hands into her jacket pockets. "My mother's dead, and my father, well, he's got some real strange ideas on the whole subject." Paula tried a lighter tone.
"So, I've been spared the agony. Truly, I think he'd be happier, if I joined a convent. Actually, I think my grandmother says Rosaries and Novenas for just that!"

Sensing, that the conversation was lingering on forbidden territory, he mused,

"So, you've married three times instead!"

"And watch out, I might just be on the lookout for number four! Here," grabbing the wine bags, "let me run these up to my room. Be back in a flash."

Christian watched her as she dashed across the plaza, then turned his sights on the magnificent Cathedral, silently contemplating each of the sculptures.

Moments later, breaking his reverie, Paula lightly tapped his shoulder, as she joined his contemplation of the great church.

"So, tell me, Madame Giordano, what then — or— who— brings you to Strasbourg, if it isn't for a honeymoon?"

"I'm collaborating on a book with Karl Junger— furnishing pictures and artwork for his latest textbook." Paula rocked back and forth on her heels, savoring the look of surprise on the young Frenchman's face. "Thought, maybe, I was a hooker, like the rest of the parade, didn't you?" She grinned, enjoying his embarrassed flush, suddenly coloring his face.

"Ah . . . well, perhaps, at first," Christian reluctantly admitted. "Before I saw you, that is. And then, I thought you were an actress my father hired for one of his little jokes. You know, you're very good with an accent —" to her astonishment, he mimicked her New Yorkerese perfectly — "if ya know whad-I mean?"

They both laughed this time. "You're not so bad yourself," Paula complimented him laughingly. "Just like a native. Where'd you learn English, anyway, the BBC?"

"Well," he tossed the cigarette to the cobblestones, where he smashed it underfoot. "Cambridge, actually. But we were discussing our plans for this evening."

"Were we?"

"Oui, Madame. We were." Christian looked directly at her. A smile playing around the corners of his mouth. "You cannot simply walk away, you know."

"My father would never forgive me." The eyes twinkling, the smile widened. Automatically, he straightened her wayward bangs. "And I'd never forgive myself for unleashing you upon an unsuspecting Strasbourg."

"I dunno," she wavered. "It's getting kind of late."

"Nonsense." With an arm encircling her shoulders, the Frenchman hustled her along.

Live Jazz drifted through the deserted back street of Place Broglie. Cymbals brushed an inviting beat and snares rapped to the lilting accompaniment of a piano. The mellow notes blended with the night's shadows in a kind of smoky nocturne.

Two beams spotlighted the polished gold letters "Le Trou Noir" over the café's dark mahogany door. Warm yellow glowed from the etched glass facade, obscuring the interior.

Paula took Christian's arm as he parted the thick velour drapery beyond the tiny foyer. Hazy silhouettes clustered around minute tables. Absorbed in conversation, they tapped countless cigarettes into brimming ashtrays.

Strasbourg natives huddled in clusters, greeted Larsonnier with a wave, a chide or a quick kiss on both cheeks.

Sophisticated women in chic evening apparel appraised the attractive Alsatian with obvious relish, their dissecting eyes flickering over the American in jeans. The men, equally elegant, traded banters, all the while studying Paula with curious speculation and raised eyebrows.

Christian scanned the room, then headed for a table toward the back of the café, gently guiding Paula through the labyrinth of people. She spotted a man waving frantically with boyish enthusiasm, and gesturing to two vacant seats at his table.

The Frenchmen shook hands and exchanged a few rapid words in French. Paula studied the stranger and pronounced him: *Cute*. Deep brown eyes that reminded her of a soulful beagle, could not seem to focus on the older Frenchman. Instead, he kept glancing at the American with disarming curiosity.

"Paula Giordano, I'd like you to meet a great chap, my friend, Marc Rouget, with the Strasbourg police. Rouget, he added in French, this is Paula Giordano, an illustrator here on business. Good God, man, don't stare like that!" He slapped his friend lightly on the cheek.

The younger man shook his head in mock disbelief and uttered in French, "Your Latin Beauty overwhelms me, you are a sorceress from the creamy white beaches of Sicily, come to bewitch all of Strasbourg." He grasped the astonished American's hands and kissed each one with reverence. "My immortal soul shall forever be your slave." His sable eyes tragically beheld hers.

Paula blinked. Then, with a mischievous naiveté, she appealed to Christian. "What did he say? My French goes as far as restaurants in Berlitz."

Christian flashed his friend an impatient glance and blandly reported, "He says he is quite impressed to have the pleasure of your company this evening. And that, he regrets that work has him so tied up, that he cannot stay long."

"Well, glad to know ya, Marc," she drawled, and withheld her laughter as Larsonnier 'interpreted'.

After dark, French cafés fill up with people of all ages and walks of life, anxious for conversation, one of their fervent passions. Steaming coffee in tiny after dinner cups, as well as cappuccinos, espressos and the Irish sort are served alongside more typical liqueurs or aperitifs.

European cafés are the crossroads of the classes. In a café, one might see a college coed in trendy spandex biker's wear, a banker in a tuxedo or a punker sporting starched purple hair, brushing elbows with the casual air of acceptance that is fitting theses children of the Revolution.

Voice levels clamored several decibels, deafening Paula's ears. Not unaware, Marc Rouget considered it his duty to repair her comfort, ordering drinks for her at an alarming rate. Very soon, she felt quite at ease, no longer out of her element.

"You tell me you're a socialist and I can't help but notice— the Italian suit, the cashmere overcoat, silk tie . . . and shoes from 'Bally'?"

"How very blunt . . .May I?" Christian fumbled in his coat pocket for his cigarettes, intent upon making his point. He raised his voice to be heard over the surrounding noise. "So, tell me, who does not or, rather, who would not appreciate the finer things? The scrubwoman, street sweeper, trash collector, grocery clerk . . .we all want the good things in life. And we all have the right to expect them."

"The right to *earn* them, yes. *Expect* them, *no*," Paula protested. "If everybody just expects a hand out check, where is the incentive to work for anything?"

Rouget leaned across the table, struggling desperately to make sense of the rapid-fire English. Christian took mercy on the confused gendarme and patiently translated.

Paula, only half listened, the teasing champagne tingling her thoughts. She liked the way his eyes changed color in the smoky light. The way the French just seemed to flow in a truly delicious way from those lips. *Sure, his views are a little cockeyed . . .*

Once Christian finished explaining, the gendarme joined in the argument, gesturing like a Spaniard, Rouget articulated in heated French and on his final point, slapped the table with his hand.

"What on earth did he say?" Paula feigning wonder, amazed at his vehemence.

"Rouget agrees with you, little capitalist," Christian grinned.

"Well, of course he does!" Feeling absolutely no qualms about it, she dimpled and batted her eyes at the diminutive Frenchman. Rouget clasped her hand again and simply held it, staring into her eyes with blissful devotion.

"And somehow," Larsonnier added drily, "it does not surprise me."

"Aha!" She crowed. "You're just saying that so you don't have to concede my point."

"And that is? I rather forgot."

"NOW, who has the convenient memory loss? My point is that since France has started all of this ridiculous communist . . . cr - -ah, these socialist reforms," she amended, flushing at her faux pas, "it's been strike, strike, strike—nurses, doctors, postman, metro, garbage, uh, rubbish . . . explain to me where all your bleeding hear— uh-um—the system improved things."

"Ah, and these things don't happen in your perfect America?" He retorted. "Everything is simply smashing, n'est-ce pas? Happy workers rush to their jobs every day, wanting nothing more than to produce so their employers might purchase that fifth motorcar."

"Well, I didn't say it was perfect. Oh, no, Marc, my head is spinning as it is. Oh, okay," Paula relented, seeing his crushed expression. She sipped the champagne tinged with strawberry liqueur, and wondered if she's remembered her aspirin.

Christian leaned across the table to interpret again. Paula's eyes moved beyond the ogling Rouget, as her interest wandered from the conversation.

Couples danced to the dreamy, sensuous notes of Duke Ellington under the universe of pinpoint stars projected from the ceiling. . . The musicians at one with their audience. Paula marveled at their artistic interpretation of the tune….

Continuing to ignore the conversation at the table, the young American watched the dancers with a glimmer of envy. Her shoulders swayed with every nuance of the percussionist. Fingers snapped beneath the tabletop. *Great, two men at the table and they'd rather talk politics than dance. I shoulda dressed in something a little less . . .moi.*

It was Rouget who offered. Noticing her lack of attention, he clambered out of his chair and gave slight bow. "Hon-air moi avec one dance, Mademoiselle?"

"Absolument!!" She clapped enthusiastically and added, "Ciao," with a salute to the bewildered Larsonnier.

Paula barely followed, engulfed by the lulling ambience, snapping her fingers as she sauntered past him. Marc fell in naturally with his own unique style.

Rouget made his slow approach to his partner, his eyes gloating with innuendo to his oblivious partner, who seemed lost in the music. Their dancing attracting interested stares, much to the young man's obvious pleasure. "Vous êtes incroyable!"

Paula twirled on his arm and fleetingly glimpsed the deserted Larsonnier. His face carefully nonchalant, his narrowed eyes were nonetheless fixed upon the pair. Cigarette in one hand, his other drummed the table top with impatient fingers.

Marc jerked the smiling woman to his chest, the role of matador for a moment then slid his hands to her waist. Their stares locked as they slowed with the sultry tempo of the famous Latin Jazz tune: *Jalousie.* All at once, Paula fell back on his right arm. Dramatically, her arms glided over her head, accentuating the sensuous dip.

*"Ah-hum--Marc, **DARLING**, you must introduce me."*

Slowly, the American opened her eyes to snake skinned stilettos poised only a few inches from her head, tapping irritably. Long slender legs gleaming delicately from silken hosiery, bent to stare straight into her eyes.

"Uhhh-- Marc, let me up, **s'il vous plait**?"

Too late, for the young gendarme sent his partner crashing to the floor.

CHAPTER IX

The entire café now held captive by the scene. Patrons swiveled to observe the frozen tableau. A sudden break in the melody, the turning of heads—

"Ouch! Damn it, Marc — Marc—Where are you going? Marc?" Paula swallowed hard, at the waft of leather, the tiny reptile clad feet . . . and the black leather mini dress.

"Simone, cherie! Positively a thrill to see you!" A strong hand reached under Paula's left arm, hauling her upward with a single swoop. Finding herself behind Christian Larsonnier, with curious eyes, she peered around his broad shoulder to get a glimpse of the unwelcome newcomer.

"And what do we have here?" Ice green eyes calculated the disheveled woman in jeans, as the blonde pushed past the elegant Frenchman. "I must compliment you on your, well, 'choreography', Ma-Dame. Your dancing rather resembles a — " She frowned unconvincingly, as if searching for the right word. "—Professional. Or do you offer special lessons for free? Give the public an appetizer, a bite, a taste of what they might sample, oui?" Her eyes, exquisitely lined, widened naively.

"Simone—"Christian warned.

Paula looked her up and down and then past her, as if she didn't exist and whispered into Christian's ear a bit too loudly, "So who's the *MADAME* in the plastic body bag?"

"Uh-um— Paula, this is Simone De Bourchegrave," Larsonnier reluctantly introduced them. "Simone, Paula Giordano."

"Charmed," both women said without enthusiasm.

"I say—" Christian coughed delicately. "We have a table just over there in the corner. Simone, have a drink, won't you. . . .before you leave?"

With a triumphant glance for the dismayed American, the Frenchwoman slid a hand into his jacket pocket and leaned against him. "Well, I suppose, one drink . . ." Simone purred and then looking at Paula in what might loosely pass as sympathy, "Such a pity, though, Ma-dame." She asked. "You seem to have lost your date."

"It's Mademoiselle," the American corrected in a frigid tone. "A MADAM, as you would know, is actually a *working girl* and that reminds me—"

"Actually," Christian intervened, flushing as he removed the be-ringed hands from his hair. "Mademoiselle Giordano is *my* date, Simone."

"Oh? But, how amusing!" The blonde entangled Larsonnier's arm in her own, so that he had to escort her to the table. Paula was left to follow, counting in her mind methods of inflicting excruciating pain. *The guillotine . . .nah, too quick. A stab to the heart? Too messy, though in her case, there probably wouldn't be much spillage. Matches under the feet? Yes, I like that . . .*

Simone De Bourchegrave insinuated herself into a chair next to Christian. *Goodness, she's practically sharing it with him!* "Tell me," the Frenchwoman cooed at the uncomfortable Larsonnier, "Since when have you begun taking little lost Americans under your, ah, wing? You never seemed interested in philanthropy in the past."

"De Bourchegrave . . . De Bourchegrave . . ." Paula repeated. The name finally registering. "Oh! Your husband Henry's a cook, isn't he?"

The smile seemed to dim just a trifle as Christian struggled to hide his grin. "Er, he is a restaurateur and *chef*." Now it was Simone's voice containing icicles. "And his name is Henri, pronounced: "AH-REE."

"Oh, so sorry," Paula waved an airy hand. "My French isn't very good."

"Yes, well, Americans . . ." The Frenchwoman shrugged it off. "Anyway, we do a lot of business with our darling Christian here." Simone's eyes were all for the Frenchman next to her, as her fingers lingered on the collar of his jacket, tracing widening patterns with a long, manicured nail.

"Oh?" Paula cooed in a sugary-sweet voice. "And what sort of business *is* that, Christian?"

"Wine," Larsonnier explained, not looking very comfortable at all. "My shop supplies a great *many* restaurants in Strasbourg."

"Ah, yes?"

"Henri constantly amazes me with the unusual circle of, ah, acquaintances he manages." Now the eyes moved across the table to dissect the younger woman. *Cat's eyes, that's what they look like. How very appropriate.* "He's a collector, you know."

"A collector? You mean he likes stamps?" Paula frowned. "Books? Insects? Butterflies?"

"Mm. Not exactly." The Frenchwoman sighed, as if the subject bored her. "He has quite a few trophies, though. A dancer would be such an addition . . ."

"Sorry to disappoint you, MADAM," the American said through stiff lips. "But I don't dance for a living." *Boy, I'd like to rip that rotten dye job right off that shriveled head.*

"I thought not." Simone's gaze raked over the scuffed leather boots, the worn jeans and the unruly hair falling out of the barrette. "You do not seem the type to ask for money."

"Now, look, you—"

The Frenchwoman ignored the angry American and returned her attention to Larsonnier. "I have friends at a corner table. But it was such a pleasure to meet Mademoiselle Whatever your name is." Simone waved a dismissing hand in the air. "My Eng-leash, like your French, is not so good."

Slowly, slowly Simone got up, managing to brush against the Frenchman at the same time. She leaned over very close and kissed him on both cheeks. Her arms draping his neck in what Paula termed a full-nelson, lingering at each ear.

"Simone, I don't think this is the time, nor place for —" His rapid, irritated French rose above the cafe's clamor.

All too aware of the woman's coy endearments, Paula resolutely gritted her teeth. The churning sensation in her stomach appalled her. *Good Heavens, do you really care all that much?*

Her eyes narrowed as she opened her mouth to speak.... And suddenly, Paula was aware of an instant change in the music. The piano began a rhythmic vamp as the young woman spotted Rouget across the Café, signaling a thumbs up to his friend.

Abruptly, the music stopped, followed by calls and chants of : **"Christian, Christian, Christian..."** The piano player stood beside his instrument as he waved in Larsonnier's direction, indicating he should take his place on the bench.

An amazed Paula gawked at the scene as the reluctant pianist rose from his seat to cheers from all corners of the café. As he approached the piano, he grabbed a mic and motioned to Paula.

Oh, no-no-no-NO! Rouget taking the cue, went to the piano and extended his hand as if to escort the lady to the diva's place of honor in front of the seven-foot grand.

Hundreds of pairs of eyes, smiling in blind anticipation of what this blue jeaned American would produce.

Then the familiar intro to a beloved song chimed crystal clear into Paula's ears....

Another of Mel's all-time greats....

The intro stopped as Paula faced her hopefully adoring audience. Christian's eyes sparkled in mischief, his smile and demeanor urging her to begin...

"We'll take Manhattan.... The Bronx and Staten Island too... It's funny going through... the Zoo."

Cheers and applause from all around the room boomed at the young singer, filling her with confidence and joy she hadn't felt in a very long time... Turning to look at her accompanist, she went on:

"The great big city's a wonderous toy, just made for a girl and boy...."

As if the previous scene never occurred, Paula's voice now ignited the music, electrifying the now hushed café with a sassy version of: *Come Fly With Me. . .* Sneaking a peak over to her accompanist, she glanced just in time to catch his eyes flickering a definite approval. . . .Song after song, Christian's fingers flowed and wove a beautiful, intoxicating tapestry, which Paula effortlessly floated her warm velvety soprano throughout a captivated café.

As the applause and Bravos faded, an arm encircled her waist and led her toward the exit of the café and Paula noticed the jaded cat eyes staring in disbelief in her direction. *What sort of look was that?*

"Come along, Paula. Time to shove off."

"Oh, and we were having so much fun!"

"Timing is essential. Knowing when to quit on a high note is key."

"I tell you what." Paula murmured as she returned the cryptic stare, "I'd love to tell that cook's wife a thing or two!"

"Perhaps another time," Christian suggested as he hustled the American through the crowd and into the bracing night air.

"A trophy— *really*. I'd like to improve on that bad nose job of hers..."

The Frenchman increased his arm's grasp on her waist and got her safely away from the café. "No doubt, you would." Larsonnier cheerfully agreed. "But, why injure those lovely artist's hands?"

Steaming with resentment, Paula disengaged herself from his arm. "So, just what kind of business do you do with their restaurant, the Fox?"

"Le Renard," he drily corrected. "Simone and I have very little business. . . . anymore." Paula only stared, very coolly. Christian found himself, to his astonishment, explaining, possibly for the first time in his life. "We're old acquaintants. And that's all."

"I think 'old' about sums it up," Paula replied.

"He lifted an eyebrow. "Pardon?"

"I said, it's sure nice to have old friends, isn't it?" She lied in dulcet tones. "Someone you can reminisce with about the good OLD days. Someone with whom you've shared COMMON experiences. Someone whose facelift doesn't fool you in the least, because you both know exactly how OLD. — Oops, there's that darned word again!"

Christian rolled his eyes. "We've all made mistakes in our lives we regret, haven't we? Let's not speak of her anymore," he coaxed and slid an arm around her shoulders. "It's such a lovely evening, we shouldn't let her bad manners spoil it. Let's remember only the evening with all the beautiful Jazz we performed together. Sorry, if you felt, what is the word, bamboozled into singing.... But I knew there was a voice in you the moment you began your egg pie speech. He chanced a side long view at the little brunette. "Say, where did you learn to sing like that anyway?"

"Hey, I'm Italian— we *all* sing. Whether good or bad, we belt out our best in the shower and anywhere else, our public can stand us." Paula smiled. "Aside from my gene pool, I actually once dreamed of becoming a Jazz Singer...... but that was eons ago..... So, that's good advice. Let's remember the music tonight....It was wonderful. Magical. And thank you," she finished looking into serious eyes. "You are quite talented yourself."

"*De rien*.... The pleasure was all mine."

"Maybe we could do an encore sometime?"

The couple crossed Place Broglie, their direction, the shining cathedral steeple over the darkened medieval city. Only a few clouds marred an otherwise perfect sky. The waxing moon cast a silver glow over Strasbourg's red-tiled rooftops reflecting upon the smooth, shining cobblestones. The stars reminded her of the twinkle in his hazel eyes.

The cashmere of his coat felt soft, so warm to her skin. She caught the faint scent of cologne. *Hmmm. Smells like a warm afternoon, a secluded meadow in the summertime...*

Their footsteps echoed against the cathedral walls, as they entered the empty square. Christian paused and withdrew his arm. "May I?" He pulled a pack of cigarettes from his coat pocket. "T'is a deadly habit, but one I cannot seem to stop."

She nodded. "You mean one you won't stop."

"Why, yes. I suppose that is what I am saying."

Spotlights at the base of the looming cathedral interpreted the brooding monument in a dramatic chiaroscuro. The play of light and dark emphasized the countless saints and sinners. They seemed to be watching the couple in the square from their sandstone pedestal perches.

Paula, lost in her champagne fog, dreamily watched the moon cross the square. Such a romantic setting. Such a romantic evening. Such a romantic guy . . .

Christian began laughing. His mellow timbre startling her from her reverie as she stared, uncomprehending. "What? — *What?"*

"Oh," he shook his head, his grin irrepressible. "I was just picturing what would have happened had you made your way back to Simone."

"Oh, just like a man!" She sniffed. The romantic moment lost. " 'Let's not talk about her.' Oh, su-u-re. Whatever happened to French chivalry, anyway? You manage to mention probably the single most embarrassing thing I've ever come close to doing and believe me, I could name plenty!"

"Surely, not," Christian protested with humor. "What I don't understand is, exactly whose honor were you defending, yours or mine?"

"Well. . . .well, I . . ." Paula felt herself turning beet red, then pink, then red again. Confident that the night sky hid her pigmented embarrassment, she continued, "Her paws were all over you and..." she blurted. "Oh, dear. I mean, I didn't mean, I . . ."

Christian bent over quite suddenly and muffled her rattled explanations with a kiss. His lips gently touched her own, softly sweet, for only the briefest hint of a moment and still it left her breathless. Then, he rested his forehead on her own, gazing very closely into her astonished eyes. "You," he vowed, "are irresistible."

"I am?" Paula blinked to un-tilt the world.

"Hmm-mm. Here I've sworn not to let Papa manipulate me any longer, and there you come breezing into my life with the force of a hurricane. Playing the perfect gentleman, or, at least, trying to but, every time you move those marvelously expressive lips . . ." He outlined them with a finger. "I am overwhelmed by this irresistible urge to kiss them."

"Oh, I see." A nervous kind of excitement fluttered inside her, like a roller coaster when it suddenly swoops. "I can see this is my fault. I'll just stop talking."

"No, too late." His arms pulled her closer. "Now I carry their image in my heart." This time, she was ready and somehow, her arms found their way around his neck. This kiss lasted longer and when they pulled away, a shiny disk slid out from Christian's collar. They were both a little breathless. "Ah, Mademoiselle," Christian sighed. "You promise to wreak all manner of havoc on my well-ordered life. I predicted it, the moment you threw yourself against me at the train station."

Paula grabbed the shiny disk, flipping it over in her hand and stared.

"Uh—That was you? So, what's this?" She said as she held the trinket.

Caught off guard, Christian quickly snatched the golden orb from her hands, slipping it quickly back beneath his collar.

"Yes, that was me and to answer the latter, don't you know?" He stared at her challenging.

"A Miraculous Medal?"

"Many people wear these. It's all about a Marian Apparition which happened in Paris."

Marella isn't going to believe this! . . . "Uh-I know." Paula felt inside her collar and extracted a similar object and held it out for his inspection. The romantic moment squelched. "I know why I'm wearing one, but what about you?"

"I thought you Americans were big on not discussing religion or politics. Something about etiquette."

"That's totally passé. So, answer the question."

"Simply a gift from my mother." You?"

"Pretty much the same. Only a gift from my *grandmother*."

The moonlight drifted across the Frenchman's face. Paula, sensing his discomfort decided to change the course of the awkward moment.

"So maybe, more like a good luck charm against your father's mismatched matchmaking?"

Christian couldn't resist a chuckle. "Mm-hmm." Flipping an errant curl from her forehead, attempting to recapture the previous mood:

"Didn't realize it till tonight when you landed rather unceremoniously on your— on the dance floor. So, you see, my father had really little to do with our meeting. It was inevitable. Perhaps the *charm* as you put it, worked."

"Fate."

"Destiny."

"Kismet."

"So, let's not tell him."

Their laughter died, the echoes fading away on the night breezes, yet still they regarded one another with a faint smile. Then Paula realized they stood before the hotel's front door. The clerk practically leaning across the desk, endeavoring to watch the. . . . affectionate couple.

"Well . . .um . . . thank you, Christian for a wonderful— no, a magical evening.... Well almost . . ." Then, thinking about her near cat fight, amended, "It really was the best evening I've had in a very long time." She leaned over and kissed him on the cheek. Looking above at the looming, glowing cathedral, feeling as though all the saints held her gaze, warning her . . . .

Taking her hand in his, Christian, following her upward gaze at the Apostles' stern reproach, then, gently kissed her right hand, looking back up to face her, "You are an unusual woman, Paula. You're intelligent, sweet, and very, very amusing. I like being with you. You make me laugh. You seem to always be yourself, even when you're telling ridiculous stories about three dead husbands and egg pie. If you could only know what a breath of fresh air you are."

Paula stared back, looking up again at the edifice behind the Frenchman, she squeezed his hand and whispered, "call me soon."

He watched her through the glass of the revolving door, as she stopped at the desk for her room key. The waves of her hair finally escaping their bondage and bounced about her shoulders in a glorious, tangled mess. Her designer jeans, dusty from the dance floor, her boot impatiently tapping the floor as the smirking clerk reached for her room key.

Slipping into the elevator, she caught a last glimpse of him, a teasing quirk on her lips and a mischievous wink, as the elevator doors closed.

Christian lingered there a moment longer, the smile still on his face. *How bloody marvelous it was!* He felt his heart beating erratically, perhaps for the first time in years.

Whistling a tune from the café, with one final glance at the brightly lit apostles, Christian Larsonnier retraced his steps back towards the hushed cathedral square and beyond.

"I don't have ta tell ya who I am, so I won't. I'm either not home or—"

"Marella! It's Paoli!"

"For crying' out loud, Paoli—" The New Yorker cleared her throat. "It's too late for tawkin'. Besides, what are ya goin' to tell me? You're in love, right?"

"Maybe, yeah, I'm in love, Marella." She giggled.

"You're drunk — go ta bed — or have you already?"

"All we did was talk and talk and talk." Paula sighed, feeling absolutely rapturous "We sipped champagne and danced— and I got to sing— just like when I was in College!"

"In a club, I hope — 'cause you mark my words you dance anywhere else, you'll nevah see dah bum again."

"He's not a bum, Grandma."

"He's French, ain't he?"

"Yeah."

"Well? They're awl bums— some bums dress well, some tawk nice, some wit good mannahs, you know— But, they awl wear velcro pants."

"But, he seems so . . . sweet."

"Sure, he's sweet. He wants to show ya his velcro."

"Yes, Grandma." Paula rolled sideways to gaze at the moon through her opened drapes. It seemed to shine for her alone. *It's smiling at me*, she thought. "You're probably right."

"I'm always right. I've lived it awl. But, ya ain't gonna take it from this wrinkled up SOB, are ya?"

"Nope."

"I love ya, kid— and I'm glad you got a chance to sing. You know, I always tole you that you had a special gift of voice . . . . But, hey, this is startin' to caust — and — don't forget to say a few prayers—."

"Oh— I almost forgot. He wears a miraculous medal! Can you *believe* that?"

"No— and so what. He's probably just wearing it for jewelry or for his mother's sake. You know, pretendin' to be the good son he most likely ain't— Now, this is really startin' to caust ya. So, I'm sayin' good night. And don't forget your prayers, Capiche?"

"Capiche . . ."

CHAPTER X

"Hold the damned elevator!" The early risers gaped at the barefoot, terry-toga'd American thundering down the carpeted hallway toward the packed lift.

"What the hell you lookin' at?" He growled as he stepped inside. The elevator bounced and he pointedly turned his back to the passengers to adjust the draping "robe". *Stupid foreigners can't mind their own business! Makes me sick.*

A small framed, elegant man pursed his thin lips and struggled for a blank expression as did every other person in the crowded elevator.

With a rush of air, the door sprang open on the ground floor; the crowd inside relaxed. The big man straightened his terrycloth toga and, as if hailing his eager public, stepped casually out into the posh grand lobby of Canne's most famous Hotel. A pattering of murmurs ricocheted throughout the elegant surroundings; a hushed chorus of laughter followed the man.

"Mon Dieu!"

"Mein Gott! Was ist—?"

"Dios mío . . .Julios Caesar?"

"Jolly good show. American: Small wonder."

Tony Giordano extended a hairy, blanched arm from beneath his drapery and flung his room key at the hotel clerk. "Can't a guy even go for a swim around here without stirring up a ruckus?"

More snickers.

Japanese tourists crowded into the lobby, immediately star struck by the toga'd American. Cameras clicked in a static chain reaction and strobe lights flared.

MORONS! I'm surrounded by morons. "Betchya wouldn't bat an eye if I went out stark naked, like the rest of you perverts on the beach . . ."

Some vacation. A guy works his butt off all his rotten life, never even takes one lousy day off. And I end up in Sodom and Gomorrah in this Marc Antony get up. Hell . . .I've dreamed about this vacation for years! So, here I am and I'm gonna ENJOY every moment of it!

He breathed in the soothing sea air as he sauntered to the edge of the wide boulevard bordering the beach. Cars, limos and mopeds screeched or at the very least, rolled down windows to get a close-up of Julius Caesar heading for the "baths."

What am I supposed to do? Close my eyes and make a run for it? No lousy crosswalk. The most expensive hotel in town and they expect ya to swing from the trees to get to the beach?

Humming an old Sinatra tune, the American took all the time in the world to cross the busiest of streets in Cannes.

"You heard me! Two, I said two umbrellas." Tony barked in French. "At the price you charge for them, I should be given a private beach!" The bronzed beach attendant scrambled for the extra umbrella. "No, not that one! It has rust awl over it. I want a clean one!"

After debating twenty minutes of so over which direction to precisely position each umbrella, the burly gentleman settled into a lush chaise, only a few feet from the clear faceted emerald Mediterranean. Lips parting into a huge smile, Tony inhaled deeply, still smiling. He watched the gently rippling waves splash over the pebbly shore, a soothing fragile sound, as if the waves themselves were made from delicate jaded glass, sweeping back and forth to the melody of the sea. *Sea chimes*, he thought and then chuckled at his unusually poetic frame of mind.

Oblivious to the topless bodies sprawled on the sand around him, Tony leafed through his briefcase and pulled out a stack of letters. An oversized forefinger lingered on a familiar scented stationary.

DEAREST Tony,
I'm tired of playing the game your way. Next move is mine. Rook to Timbuktu.
Paolina

Giordano looked away to the sea, squinting eyes to the tearing glare from the slick pebbles. He puffed his lips in regret. With deliberate neatness, he folded the note and slipped it back into its envelope, placing it with meticulous care against the pages of his precious Washington Post.

No worries, Paoli. We'll catch up soon and make up for lost time. That is . . . after, I get you home.

Extracting a red leather calendar from the stack, the American pulled the top off his pen with his teeth. He shuffled back and forth between two pages before he finally wrote: **Retreat at the Monastery des Antonitians** and circled FIVE OCTOBER. And now...

But, give her time to cool down. The woman has the temper of an Italian Fishwife. Anyhow, I'm stickin' to the schedule. I've earned this vacation.

Tony unfolded the September 15th edition of the Washington Post with consummate relish. Disdainfully, he tossed aside the front page, national news and the society page. *All crap.* No, he knew exactly where they were, neatly lined in alphabetical order, with names, dates and life stories encapsulated in one, brief paragraph:

The Obituaries

He settled back with a satisfied sigh and began with the letter "A". *Here's one: Not much older than me . . . and this one here, kept an alligator for a watchdog, forgot to feed it. Well, that's all a part of natural selection, weedin' out the stupid ones.*

The M's:

MORROW, JOHN —September 4th in his Georgetown home. Formerly of USAFE and member of the 103 Military Intelligence Division, Heidelberg, West Germany. Decorated with Distinguished Service Cross, October 1, 1961. Survived by no one.

He reread it three times, his breath coming in shorter and shorter gasps. Had to be a mistake. Had to be . . .

Twilight crept in slowly, as the last of the golden sun sank below the valley's horizon. What was once warm and golden, traded its sheen for a peaceful shadow of grey. From Heidelberg's castle terrace, he could see the lights twinkle on, one by one in the Altstadt and along the castle route beyond. Twisting and coiling along the foothills of the Odenwald, the sparkling panorama opened up where there were villages, narrowing to a vague pinpoint where the road ran alone.

He felt her first — though maybe "smelled her" was the more accurate, if not, poetic term. Carried by the mountain breezes, her perfume travelled ahead of her, weaving a spicy promise through the evening air. He was in love with her even before he ever saw her.

She came to join him at the wall. He could see what had happened to the colors of the brilliant sunset, for strands of it were escaping the dark scarf she wore around her head. Dark glasses covered her eyes, but he knew those eyes as he knew his own soul.

Guidebook open and clasped in properly gloved hands, she seemed intent upon finding a landmark down below, hiding somewhere among the clutter of roofs and chimneys of the Altstadt. "Verzeihen Sie Mir," she said in cultured German. "Could you point out the Church of Our Lady?"

A small shock, but then, of course it was inevitable she would come into his life in this way. A pause, then in English, he answered slowly, "The Frauenkirche is in Munich. No doubt. You mean the Heilig-Geist-Kirche, which was built in the same style."

"Silly of me." She smiled behind the obscurity of her glasses and offered a hand. "Julienne DeBrouillard. These passwords really are a fright, aren't they? And you're the Captain, of course."

For the first time in his life, he found himself speechless. "Of course," he managed. "You're with Interpol?"

She began to laugh, and if it was possible to fall in love twice over, he did it then. It sounded like rain. "You needn't sound so astonished," she chided him. "Mata Hari was a woman, wasn't she?" She slid her arm through his. They started to stroll along together quite naturally, as if a lifetime had already been agreed upon in one tacit minute.

"Now, there's more than one school of thought about that." Tony observed with a grin. "There are those who think-"

"Why, Monsieur!" She exclaimed in accented English. "You destroy my illusions . . ."

Tony took one, deep, controlling breath, holding it in for a second before exhaling, very slowly. Eyes narrowed; he re-examined the article more closely. *Wait a minute. This has got to be a joke. Yeah.* The relief soothed him, the breeze cooling the sudden flood of sweat on his neck. *Those jerks. Always givin' me a hard time about having the paper forwarded to the Amazon or Tibet. Yeah, they knew what'd get to me.*

Sick. Really, really sick. Disgusted at himself for working with such people, he meticulously returned the newspaper, front page and all, to its original format. Then he put it aside and resumed his contemplation of the sea.

For a second, and only a second, he saw her. She waved to him, and even from here he could see her laughing. Tony rubbed his eyes against the blinding sun. He looked again and she was gone.

⚜

CHAPTER XI

Gentle morning light filtered through the half-closed drapes and brightened the disheveled hotel room. With relentless purpose, its golden fingers crept across the beige carpet and wound its way up the side of the bed until it found the unconscious woman.

BANG-BANG-BANG!

What the — Reddened eyes opened and instantly shut. "Ouch!" Paula buried her pounding head in her arms, praying for an eclipse or the end of the world.

No luck. Carefully, with tender consideration for her raging temples, she rolled away from the ruthless sunbeams, cringing at her head-shattering report from the open window.

BANG-BANG-BANG!

I'm going to die. But not quickly enough. No, I'll linger on and suffer for a while.

Paula stretched, her fingers searching, then finding the phone, somehow stuffed between the bed and the nightstand. She waited for the three annoying, loud bleeps. The same clerk from the night before answered. "Oui?" He asked knowingly.

"One — no, two coffees please. Very, very strong. And . . .have you any aspirin?"

"I'm certain we could find some powders about, Madame," he answered imperturbably. *Or, did he?* Maybe, she imagined it, but he sounded so polite and yet so . . .insulting.

"I trust the noise outside did not wake you?"

"Noise?" Paula asked sarcastically. "What noise?"

"The scaffolding, Madame, around the cathedral. It must be built before the stone is cleaned." *That was it; he kept emphasizing the word, "Madame," more like MADAM. Like, did you have an interesting evening, MADAM?*

"My aspirin, please," she begged in a strangled voice.

The desk clerk took the hint. "I'll send it up directly, Madame."

She hung up without acknowledgement and covered her aching eyes with a pillow. Curses on Christian Larsonnier and his smooth words and . . .

Did she *have* to make a complete fool of herself by hysterically laughing at ANY joke: German jokes, army jokes . . .hmm. *Christian in uniform.* The buzz in her head relented with the image. *Funny, too. Just like Maurice. I wonder if they've compared notes by now.*

"Maurice, you old. . . .RASCAL!" With a vengeance, she swung a boot at the window; it swung shut.

A real pair, those two. And next time she caught that ridiculous bird-dog following her around, she'd give him a sample of real Yankee ingenuity — ha!

TAP-TAP-TAP

The same lobby clerk waited in the hall with a breakfast tray.

"Don't you ever go home?"

"This is my home," he courteously countered and placed the tray on the desk, just inside the door. "My father is the hotel's proprietor."

"Oh. How nice for you." She waited for him to leave, but he only stood there.

"You have two letters, Madame."

"Letters?" Paula frowned and glanced at the tray. Sure enough, there they were propped up against the two coffee carafes. And still, the clerk wasn't moving.

Oh. The American hastened to find some change and handed it over. Anything, to be alone.

"Thank you, Madame," the clerk said, reluctantly leaving.

Paula firmly locked the door behind him. "Whatever happened to the discreet doorman?" She muttered and reached for the first envelope.

"Paula," was all it said— *I must be the only Paula in the hotel*, she mused and tore open the flap. One sheet of paper within, and not even proper stationary at that, but something torn from a book and written on. . . .

She read aloud. "Captain, my cap—" *What on earth?* Frowning, she read the three stanzas.

What a strange thing to — Wait a minute. Like a rolodex file, her thoughts flipped back to the night before, and brown eyes beseeching her as the little gendarme promised eternal servitude. *Fancy yourself a poet, do you, Marc?* Smiling, she crumpled the paper up and tossed the wad toward the approximate area of the waste can. *Poor little guy, probably the only English poetry he knows. Well, I'll try to pretend I was properly impressed.*

Paula picked up the next envelope. "Hm, from Karl." So hard to remember she hadn't come to France to indulge herself. He wrote in careful, box-like printing on expensive looking cream hued stationary.

My Dearest Paula:

I look forward to seeing your initial sketches,
assured as I am they will prove excellent.
May we meet sometime soon?
      Sincerely,
       Karl Junger

Paula smiled to herself. *So, maybe I'm not the chic-est thing to hit France. Karl thinks I have talent; I gotta remember that.* She replaced the notepaper to the tray and considered the coffee.

Nah, a shower first . . . Dropping last night's attire as she walked, Paula shut the bathroom door behind her and turned on the spigot. Water sprayed against the flowered tiles, steaming the air with immediate heat. The woman stepped into the lulling sprays and reached for the tiny bar of hotel soap. Closing her eyes, she breathed in its delicate scent; its absolute femininity revived her . . .

Letting the water spill over her lifted face, she lazily planned the day's work. *Finish up Haut-Koenigsberg, start on the cathedral . . . And tonight? Maybe, I could —*

No. Resolutely, dismissing the attractive Larsonnier from her mind, Paula turned off the steaming water and opened the shower curtain. Cool air brushed her skin and she shivered again, but for a more practical reason. *Is there a window open in here?*

The refreshed woman reached for her worn green bathrobe, her favorite, hanging on the hook behind the bathroom door and padded to the window. *Hm, must've blown open again.*

Workmen scurried around the cathedral's base, lifting long wooden planks and metal piping. Already, they'd erected a third level in the skeletal grid work. Pretty impressive, she had to admit.

Now, where's my comb . . . ? When you make it big, Paula, she told herself as she sorted through the dresser's jumbled piles, *the first thing you spend your money on, is a housekeeper.*

Her hand paused over an open drawer; the blue passport lay open, the forged seal obscuring her features, which was probably the kindest thing . . . *Real smart; you want to get robbed again?* Closing the drawer, Paula got to the business of taming the frizzy, voluminous mess.

The two-tone pitch of an ambulance siren blared, then gradually faded into an oblivion of people and tiny streets. Crowds of Saturday shoppers flooded the avenues.

With barely room to walk, the American, several loaves of crusty, fresh bread hanging out of a bright pink net shopping bag, weaved her way through the riotous milieu. She dodged and hurdled through Strasbourg's obstacle course of "café potatoes," protesters with placards, strollers, street vendors and children freed from school, ricocheting from corner to corner.

The parade seemed to come to an abrupt halt at a busy intersection. Paula looked up at the street sign: Rue de Bonnes Gens: *Hah! What stupid name. Ahhh. But that sure isn't one!* She spotted **Le Printemps** department store and waited impatiently for the pedestrian light to change — along with the rest of Strasbourg.

Tinny horns beeped as a few daring natives darted across the avenue. The sounds of the city all of a sudden— severed — by a bloodcurdling scream.

A confusion of trumpets and horns blared, an organ thundered.

Shivers ran through Paula as she immediately recognized the music coursing through her: ***Phantom of the Opera!***

But, here in Strasbourg?

The next audible words confirmed as the actor pleaded with the audience to stay in their seats that the crash was merely an *accident.* Cymbals clashed; organ music shook the very streets, then faded.

A symphony burst the trembling aura. The melodious cry of a French horn floated high above the uneven rooftops and peaks of the medieval city. Paula's eyes followed the wave of traffic to the next block. Place Kleber. Bleachers filled with people stood to one side of the square, a makeshift stage with full orchestra at its base. Violin bows gracefully glided up and down in unison.

A green pedestrian light flashed; Paula found herself drawn toward the outdoor concert.

The strangely dulcet voice SOARED! Her voice pleading, racked with despair describing eyes with a eerie combination of threat and adoring love . . .

Paula could just barely make out a vision of a woman dressed in misty white chiffon, below endless black waves falling and sweeping with every turn and gesture.

As she drew closer: *Love me . . .*, the siren held her hands out in the universal gesture of futility. Tears streaming down an enchantress' face, the singer stood trembling with poignant pain atop what seemed a Gothic rooftop. An eerie statue of Apollo watched over the tragic scene.

Pleading, she turned to her love, the cloudy chiffon blowing in the autumn gusts.

Paula eyed a spot on a bottom bleacher and muscled her way in. Mesmerized, she let her bag slide to the pavement as she watched someone she vaguely knew, affecting ecstasy and despair with the clarity and lightness of her voice. Spellbound, tears streaming down Paula's face. . .

Larsonnier's niece poured herself into her singing. Every trace of her enraptured in mellifluent perfection.

Two silhouettes betrothed eternal love high atop the gabled roofs of Paris. As "Christine" ended her solo, her lover touched a finger to a teary cheek.

A euphoric reply to the woman in white, the dashing count stepped to the edge of the stage, his voice mellow and solacing, richly fluid as the Tenor sang along to *All I Ask of You.*

The words, the music, the touch of the sun against her cheeks, Paula dreamily closed her eyes.

With a crash of percussion, the violin bows froze in place. The stormy thunder of an organ bellowed through Place Kleber. Trumpets howled. Out from behind Apollo, a shattered, broken spirit, cloaked in black from head to toe, stepped out and whispered a cappella as The Phantom, heartbroken, ends his tormented song . . .

The lovers walked off stage . . . .

The Phantom's insane laughter. Angry thrashes of the organist.

"BRAVO!! BRAVO!! Spectators from all quarters of the city square burst in applause and cheers.

Paula jumped to her feet with the rest, the haunting music, the echo of voices in her head . . .

Her eyes misted again at the simple beauty of the words. From her world of secret dreams, she watched as the troop of performers filed out, each taking their bow. The woman in white broke away from the line. The crowd went crazy.

"BRAVA!! BRAVA!! BRAVA!!"

Gracefully, "Christine" bowed her swanlike neck, then looked out at the masses. Her eyes floated unemotionally about the square, hovering ever so briefly over Paula.

She spotted me! I'm gettin' the hell outta here; no need in feeling any smaller. The American looked around as people bustled about, picking up their things, gathering children and folding blankets.

Something wet slapped her ankle.

"AAAH!" Paula shrieked, but no one took notice. Big brown eyes stared up guiltily, the crusty evidence clenched in grizzled jowls.

"Stupid dog!" she hissed. "Get outta here! Beat it!" The dismayed American stared down at the wire-haired terrier, who stood his ground with her lunch between his teeth. Determined to retrieve the remaining baguette, Paula slowly bent down. Carefully, she reached a hand to her bag.

Paula stares.

Rover glares.

"Nice doggy."

Two sets of unblinking eyes.

Her opponent stiffened, its filmy eyes narrowing as its upper lip parted into a snarl.

"Grrr."

Stalemate.

"Look, you mutt," the famished human whined. "You already got your fangs into two of 'em! How about it, huh? Just leave me one. One, that's all I ask." Cautiously, Paula fingered the drawstring on the bag. In a snap, she snatched the loaf, but not quickly enough, for the dog anticipated just this. In the middle of Place Kleber, the animal and the human tugged the last loaf back and forth.

"Give it to me! Give it to me, damn it!" She growled, shaking her end.

Paula fumbled in her top jacket pocket. She slid out a black plastic box, her finger prone on the switch. "Let go, mutt, or I'll blast ya."

A threatening growl curled the dog's lip, unnerving her, and the victor pulled away the last loaf with a feisty tug.

His benefactress dropped awkwardly on her hind quarters. "Oh, hell!" Through hungry tears, she watched the dog scuttle away with the spoils.

"My, such an odd camera. Does it take good pictures?" Squatting like a toad in the middle of a concrete pond, Paula gawked up from her sitting position into the Athena-like face of Larsonnier's niece.

CHAPTER XII

Scrambling to her feet, Paula swiftly tucked her high-voltage stun gun into a pocket. Dusting herself off, she offered a smudged hand.

"Mademoiselle Larsonnier! I-I-I wasn't sure you spotted me. Wow, what a great show."

"Merci. I think it was a successful performance, but, please, call me Yasmine." Her tone distantly arrogant, the Frenchwoman's exotic black eyes coolly perused her. "And you, Mademoiselle? Is it Paula Giordano or— Paula Martino?"

"Er . . .ah . . .er," Paula stammered, "well, you see, I'm kind of traveling incognito."

"Oh?" The eyebrows lifted with all the grace of a bird taking flight. "You are a celebrity in your America, then?"

"Not exactly . . ." Paula searched for a reason. Inspired, she explained, "You might say that it's an affair of the heart." *Okay, so maybe that's not the empirical truth, but semantically, if one were to take it word-for-word . . .*

"An affair of the heart," Athena repeated. "Ah, I see. And you do not want your, ahem . . ."

"Lover," Paula imagined, throwing herself into the spirit of the thing.

A faint flush tinged the mocha cheeks. "—Lover, then, to find you?"

"He just can't get it into his head, it's all over," the American confided in a lowered tone. She pictured Yasmine repeating the sordid details to her uncle — *Ha!*

"Roses, gifts — got to be too much, you know? It was interfering with my work."

That touched a chord in Yasmine. "Ah," she nodded, spirited sister-ship sparkling in her eyes. "Ça, je comprends. I understand." The wind whipped up around them and Paula quickly grabbed her Stetson and held it firmly to her head, Yasmine simply brushed a disobedient strand to one side.

Figures: Even the wind is kind to her.

"Well, listen, Yasmine, this has been lovely, and I'd love to —" *humiliate myself before all of Strasbourg; why I'd love to be the human gauge for you. Just how beautiful is she? Ba-DA-dum. Check it out on the scale of schoolmarm frumpy walking next to her . . .* "— but, actually, I've got to catch a bus in about fifteen minutes."

The other woman stared intently. "See, here's lunch." Paula held up her filoche as proof.

"Then, I shall accompany you to your bus," the Frenchwoman proposed. "I . . .I would like to talk with you."

"Yeah, sure, but don't you have to change?"

"I am permitted to change clothes at Uncle Christian's," Yasmine explained, unperturbed. "I care for my own costumes." She firmly took the American's elbow.

"*Allez-y*--Lead the way."

Paula glanced down at the hand imprisoning her, surprisingly strong — probably from long hours at the piano— or the polo field, or wherever one played the game. "Great," she said.

The strange pair headed down the Rue des Grandes Arcades, so named, Paula guessed, for the arched passageway sheltering the storefronts from inclement weather.

"So," Yasmine's tone implied guarded curiosity, "tell me where you come from, Pah-o-la. Always, I am interested in Americans who come all this way."

Great. Now comes the inquisition. Maybe not so much interested in Americans coming, as in Americans GOING, and quickly. "There's not much to tell, really. Raised in New York by my grandmother and a part time Father, went to art school in the city and that's about it." *My entire life fits into one sentence.*

The Frenchwoman's cheeks puffed demurely below her arched cheekbones. "The Beeg-a-Pell, ahh, oui." She sighed "I have so often wished to see it. Is it really quite so fabulous?"

"Well, it's not Paris . . .it's not London . . ." She tried describing it as they crossed the bridge over the river. Tour boats cruised up and down the length of the silver ribbon and swans searched for food along its banks. "It's well, you know— New York— a beautiful, busy concrete jungle."

"I am determined to see it and quite soon." In Yasmine's eyes, a sudden, faint glimmer of rebellion. *Ha, so the perfect niece isn't quite so perfect, after all. Maybe Uncle Christian doesn't want to lose his free help at the sweat-shop.*

Ever one to sow seeds of discontent among the oppressed masses, Paula urged, "You should just get on a plane and go." *Please. Take the next one out.*

The glimmer vanished. "Ah, well, it is not so easy for me." Just as deftly as a matador swinging the cape, Yasmine immediately veered the conversation in another direction. "So, your boyfriend, will you marry him?"

"My— oh, my boyfriend, uh, Lance. Well, Lance just keeps begging, but I'm not sure . . ." She was beginning to enjoy herself. "I mean the proposals are flattering, don't get me wrong — the carriage rides through Central Park, the violinists at dawn . . .but, I'm not ready to settle on one man just yet, you know?"

"Oui, I think so." Yasmine seemed relieved. "Then you understand, my uncle feels the same way."

Ah-HA. Now, we get to the heart of it. Uncle Christian sends his niece to let the naive, little American down gently. "I couldn't care less," she smirked, "he's not even my type."

The eyebrows rose again. "Non?"

"I go more for the cerebral type: A man with brains. Lance has a Ph.D. — in nuclear physics."

Forgetting her mission, Christian's niece hotly took up the defense. "My uncle is very intelligent. He has a first from Cambridge and the Sorbonne."

"He does? I mean, I'm sure that's very nice, but he and I just don't have very much in common. Oh, look, here's my stop," the American exclaimed, "thanks for the escort, Yasmine, and . . .uh, let's do lunch, okay?"

She glanced at her watch in dismissal, but the Frenchwoman showed no inclination of moving on. She simply stood there in her flowing gown, oblivious to the stares from the gathering sightseers, her hands clasped tightly in front of her as if she planned to serenade them with an aria. "Uncle Christian is fluent in several languages and quite well-read," she continued in defense of her beloved uncle. "He is one of the most intelligent men I have ever met."

"I'm sure he is." *What is it about the buses in this city?* "But, like I said, Yasmine, he just not my type."

Athena was drawing a crowd. "Sounds pretty great to me," an American woman from someplace un-placeable snickered. "What does he look like? Does he have a brother?"

A German grandmother-type argued in broken English, "Looks. Vas its? You find a man vit a good job, is goot."

A boot tapped the curb. "I wonder where that bus is."

"And he is very kind and brave, and —"

I think I'm going to be sick. Father Flannigan himself. Christian Larsonnier: France's last boy scout. "Oh look, here it is!"

The green mammoth pulled over to the curb, and the crowd began to push forward. Paula let the surge take her away; she shouted back to Minerva-on-the-curb, "It's been nice talkin' to you, Yasmine. Let's do this again some time, okay?"

Ahh. There's a window seat toward the back. Shuffling her belongings, Paula glanced up and glimpsed a frizzy brunette in the last row. Swallowed by an enormous white felt beret, the woman casually turned away toward the window.

Why, that looks like . . . Paula shuddered. *Naahh, couldn't be.* She took her place as the bus lurched into first and spun into the busy avenue.

The nasal voiced tour guide was beginning her spiel again with obvious borderline numbness. Paula lagged behind, pocket sketchbook open, pencil poised behind an ear, camera slung over her shoulder.

A dusty corridor that stretched the length of the old fortification, the lower level of the Terrasse Panoramique held little attraction for the rest of the group. Its nooks and crannies held chipped and broken statuary behind locked gates; damaged perhaps in the world wars, or simply, by time. Dirty windows built high into the walls provided only a glimpse of the tiny villages far below; definitely the greater view of the valley was above in the open air.

The tour guide's voice faded away as the rest of the group started the climb to the terrace roof. Paula wandered deeper into the shadowy hallway. Her boots scuffing against the packed dirt, occasionally kicking up a small puff of dust.

She steeled herself to peek through metal mesh fencing into darkened crypts. Not that these were crypts in any human sense of the word. No rotting flesh, no disintegrating bone, but the remembrance of souls lingered unspeakably close in the crumbling faces staring back at her through the gloom.

With an artist's training, she felt no repugnance toward the mutilated plaster, rather, she appreciated the skill in turning an exquisitely sculptured limb here or there. No, the disgust she felt was, rather, more general toward the destruction levied against the sum total of a man's life. *Or a woman's . . .* Pausing, she stopped and studied the only statue resting within the next crypt, a lone Madonna with a lovely, gentle smile, disregarding her injuries. A filmy granite veil fell upon delicate shoulders that bore no arms, severed for all time from the child she'd held in loving arms.

"Been though some bad times, huh?" Paula wondered softly.

Cradled by the tranquility of the sleeping crypts, she took several reference photos, then, lifting her tablet, she began to sketch. She scribbled, erased, sketched and in what seemed like moments, then closed the tablet, satisfied.

Deciding against rejoining the chattering crowd on the top level, Paula elected to stay in the cool darkness where she could think about the myriad of fresh memories, the new faces . . .Maurice, for example. *What a card. And Karl, a sweet, old man. . . . Yasmine. The surprisingly unmarried would-be pin-up and her "uncle-adoration" that Freud could probably do something with. So how long a trail of broken hearts has that woman left behind? And why both Maurice and Christian are her "Uncles? Wonder what the story is with that? Strange bird. Literally. Too gorgeous, too talented, too prim . . . too gorgeous. . .*

Paula glanced at her watch. Better join the others, she decided and headed back up the dark hallway. *Gee, actually, I could walk back if I was in the mood for some serious hiking— would help shed those extra pounds, then take a shortcut through La Petite France and get a cold drink . . . Na-a-ah, and miss the next chapter of spellbinding local trivia?*

Before the Madonna's resting place, her boot froze mid-stride. She stiffened, staying very still, her ears straining for any movement around her. Not that she heard anything. No, it was more an awareness of something unnatural and very, very near. It concealed itself, somehow within these crypts, vigilant, waiting . . .

Prickles of ice-cold terror paralyzed her, the hair rising on the back of her neck, her arms and legs crippled beneath her. When had she last felt this way? On the Franz-Kunstlerstrasse, the thought flew unbidden, not far from the highway leading toward Checkpoint Charlie, the guarded border between West Germany and communist, East Germany.

She listened a moment more. The cold silence broken suddenly by the hustling of her tour group returning. The eerie foreboding abated and her nerves relented.

"Come, come everyone! We will just round out our tour by wandering one last time through the crypts. You have ten minutes before we board the bus. That is ten minutes," the nasal monotone enunciated clearly as the group, once again, invaded the tunnel.

It's this place, Paula scoffed at herself, *It's just too creepy for somebody with your history.* She closed her pad, then removed the two pencils from her ears and headed for the bus.

Reclining in her seat, Paula decided to do a little people gazing as the rest of the group relocated themselves. Most of the people, she guessed, looked like just plain tourists: Camera and video equipment slung hastily over shoulders and necks, white sneakers stained with dirt, fishing hats and comfortable clothes. Americans of one kind or another, servicemen and their families from the NATO nations, Canadians . . .

All seated, the bus cranked up with its noisy clatter when a man's voice accused vehemently, "I tell you, that's *my* 'World Herald'! Hand it over."

"Hey! You're not the only one on board who can read, you know! I bought this one myself." The woman in the white beret spit fire with each word. "And just because you're too damned cheap to buy your own, you have to pick on a woman traveling alone!"

Smirking like an old woman at juicy gossip, Paula swiveled, taking in the scene through the cracks between the seats.

"Look, lady, forget it." The man sat back down and folding his arms, sighed all too audibly.

The accused sat fuming behind him; Paula could hear the handbag's zipper as the woman tore through her belongings until she found a five-franc piece. Like a seasoned pitcher, the brunette flung the coin over the seat, hitting the man hard on his balding crown.

In a flash, he jumped up, his arm drawn back with the franc piece in his palm. "BITCH!! I oughtta—"

The bus lurched, then stopped. The driver hurried to the back and grabbed the man's pitching arm. "I must ask you to leave, Monsieur," the Frenchman stated apologetically, "we cannot allow—"

"Yeah, I'll go," the man interrupted, "but what about that MANGY BITCH!!" He was pointing a meaty arm at the frizzy brunette in question.

"MANGY BITCH??" The brunette leapt to her feet and grabbed at the man's collar. The bus driver squeezed between them. "YOU . . .you slimy worm, picking on a woman! I'll bet you got one at home you kick around just for the fun of it, huh?"

Tell him, bitch, thought Paula.

"Sir, I am going to have to insist you step off the bus here, or I shall alert the gendarmerie from my radio." The driver pointed sternly to the front of the bus and did not relent until the man stepped, grumbling, off the bus. Then his attention switched to the woman.

"Mademoiselle, I shall let you off as well, at the next corner," he said politely and started for the front.

"Sorry, you can't do that," the brunette crowed, as she smoothed her jacket and straightened her beret. "I paid for this trip and I'm staying right where I am." She zipped shut her vinyl purse and adjusted the dark sunglasses.

She DID take his paper. Cheap bitch! Paula felt embarrassment for every American on the bus. *I'd like to personally chuck her out on her butt at 100KPH.*

The bus driver cleared his throat, jetting a glance at the tour guide who was slumped feebly out of sight in the front.

The brunette softened. "Okay, okay. Please. Alright, I'm sorry, but if you throw me out, you'll have to throw my sister out as well, and . . .well, she's here on official government business." She lowered her voice. "Special envoy from the U.N."

Paula caught that. *I don't believe it! That stupid bus driver's falling for it. Sister, my foot! Who's the guinea pig?* She craned her head.

"Very well, let me speak with this sister of yours, then," he stared with questioning eyes.

Not so dumb, after all. Paula was enjoying herself.

"There she is!" The brunette pointed down the row of seats, over heads of interested tourists, directly at Paula.

All heads turned.

Riveted to her seat, Paula opened her mouth, then remembered the two priests in front of her. Helplessly, her mouth rounded into a silent "O".

"Hi, sis!" The brunette fluted and waved a cheerful hand as she lifted her sunglasses.

Oh LORD— it IS her! Paula stared, unable to speak. *I was right the first time.....* Suzie Carter. The wanna-be bimbo from the neighboring cubicle at Big Apple Greetings. I thought I left that baggage behind on 47th and Madison.

Smiling with joy at her long-*lost* "sister", Suzie plopped herself onto the aisle seat next to the *stunned* Artist. The driver surrendered, muttering in French under his breath as he retreated to the front of the bus.

"But . . .," Paula protested helplessly.

The frizzy brunette winked at his back, all smiles and wheezed insults between her teeth. "May the fleas of a thousand camels infest your hairy armpits."

"Just how in the HELL did you find me, Carter?" Searing blue eyes scorched the intruder. Wasted, however, as Suzie's own brown pair widened innocently. "Marella?" She imitated Paula's voice almost perfectly. "It's Paw-li. Help me out, would ya, Grandma? I can't remember which hotel I'm stayin' at, and I just know I left my confirmation number next to the phone . . . Actually, Paolina, it was much too simple." She popped off her beret, which did a nice job molding her frizzy hair to its shape. "You should tell her to be more careful; you never know what kind of crazies will call up a lonely, old woman."

Crazies. Oh, yeah, crazies. Paula still stared, speechless and dismayed.

Suzie Carter, fired from Big Apple Greetings--with probably the nicest bunch of supervisors anywhere--for her emotional outbursts and humiliating scenes.

Suzie Carter, who left pleading messages on Paula's machine for her father, no matter how many times she changed her number.

"Everyone knew you took off for SOME where. But FRANCE?" Suzie leaned close. "Who'd ya sleep with for this one, honey?"

The bus pulled into the enormous parking lot on the Rue de la Première Armée. Everyone already standing, the tour guide mumbling phony farewells with an outstretched palm as the entire tour began exiting the bus.

Coming to herself, Paula shoved Ms. Carter into the aisle. "Get outta here, BITCH!" She shouted. "If you think for one crummy minute, I'd ever," she paused and breathed hard, "I'd EVER help YOU into my father's life . . ." The tour guide noticed the angry American shaking her fists and vanished altogether.

"Oh, come on, Paula!" Suzie backed down the aisle. "Really, I thought you grew up."

Paula pushed her down the stairs, a move that should have sent her reeling to the pavement. Instead, it only hastened Suzie's graceful flight neatly to her feet. "I thought we could talk," she suggested as the furious artist pushed by.

"BITCH!!"

"Look, Paula, it's not like you think. Honestly!" She had to run to keep up with the red Stetson. "I just wanna see him, um, apologize for . . . .things."

"Beat it! Go away!" Paula stopped and faced her opponent. "When are you goin' to just get it into your thick scull—THERE WAS NEVER a HOPE of you bein' in Tony's life-- You are a stalker, plain and simple!!!! Just GO — NOW! I'm telling' you, I'll call the cops." Something in the hot little Italian's eyes frightened Suzie.

Her lips quivered, her eyes glistened with tears and for an instant, Paula felt as if the woman really were a lost little girl. *Oh, no, you don't,* she ordered herself. *Don't you dare feel sorry for her; you did that once too often!*

The other woman backed away, visibly crushed. "I-I don't have many friends," she sobbed, shaking her head. "None, really."

Guilt stung Paula. "So, why don't you go home and make some?"

"Listen, Paula, I know you're mad. We'll talk later. Maybe I can make you see—"

Suzie slid the beret back over her forehead and turned away.

"Forget it. There's nothin—" Paula was left with the protest on her lips, for the woman disappeared, fluttering around a corner.

Tiny pink, fuzzy slippers pointed, then flexed over a recliner's foot prop. Duke Ellington played *Honeysuckle Rose* and a gleaming pitcher of ice water sat waiting, as droplets trickled slowly down its side. A frail arm raised to grab the handle in anticipation.

The phone shrilled.

Laying perfectly still, she stretched and continued tapping her toes to the music.

"Why da hell haven't I gone deaf yet? Everything else has gone to pot."

Marella snatched the receiver, her lips tightly clenched together as she flung her glasses on the end table, rubbing her eyes with wrinkled fingers.

"Tawk ta me."

"MA?"

"Anthony." Marella chewed her dentures. "I'm still breathin' and no one ya care about has dropped dead — *LATELY*, so ya must need money? *FA-GET IT!*"

"No! Wait, Ma. All I wanna know is if Paoli is okay. Don't even tell me where she went, but *please*, Ma, is she *okay?*" Tony's voice audibly quivered.

"She's alive, she's well and havin' a tawdry affair, I hear."

"WHAT!!"

"She's shackin' up with some old pervert in a place YOU'LL never find," she lied.

"Damn it, Ma— that's a whopper and you know it!"

"Hey, don't shout at me, Anthony. Just remember who raised WHO after that precious slut-wife of yours died awf. I did the best I knew how wit that turd money ya sent once a year. Oh, wait! That's every year or *so* . . . and many more so's as I recall."

"I came when I could," said quietly.

"Yeah, every third year or so. Fahgive me, I'm seventy-six and I'm still takin' care of myself AND my thirty year old granddaughter, who's got more sense than the both a us put together. You wanna play Daddy now? So, go rent Barbie. I hear Ken has thrown her off for some young, blonder broad. . . CLICK.

Ring - Ring - Ring . . .
    11 rings.
    12 rings.

Hope nothing's wrong.

    13 rings.

It's not like her to leave her answering machine off.

    14 rings— "This had betta be good. Shoot, it's your lousy nickel." Heavy, rapid breathing.

"Grandma, why wasn't your machine on!"

"Sheez— everybody wants ta take care of me! Brings a *tear* to my eye just thinkin' about it! I'm OLD, not incapacitated! I've just had it!"

"The neighbors been coming by again, huh?"

"Like the Macy's parade. But, don't worry about me. Everything's fine, Paoli."

"You're up to something, Grandma. I can tell."

No answer.

"Marella, what's going on? Let's have it."

Okay, not that it's anybody's business. . . . I gotta job."

"WHAT??"

"Yeah, old Salvatore dropped dead las' week. No one even showed for the funeral."

"You're driving a cab! Grandma, that's it; I'm comin' home."

"Pipe down, Paolina. Trust me, everything's kosha. I get to wear a yellow cap, got my own cab and three or four times a day, I drive old bags aroun' town. It was Salvatore's time to croak, and my turn to have a career. But, enough about this old son-of-a-bitch, how are ya?"

"Feelin' pretty dumpy."

"So?"

Pause.

"There's this Frenchwoman here. She's an opera singer. She's tall, she's exotic, extremely gorgeous, Grandma."

"And you're uncomfortable around her. . . So, forget she's so beautiful—"

"I can't, I just can't! I feel like I should genuflect every time I look at her. . . or at least walk behind her, carrying her train."

Static.

"Why does my hair have to be sooo curly and frizzy? And my nose. Why did I have to get Tony's Italian Peninsula— And—"

"Fer cryin' out loud, you're complaining? Shit-I mean sugah— I can't believe I'm hearin' this! You wanna complain??" PAUSE. "Howdya like it if ever time ya washed ya face, ya felt like ya just read a best seller in braille? I got so many wrinkles and *beauty marks*; I can't tell the growths from my actual face... Or how about cellulite? A body so blessed wit it, when I move, it looks like moving lava beneath glowing white, crumpled skin! Complain: Go a-head, damn it! JUST make surah, you're qualified first. The day you get cellulite under ya finger nails is the day I sit down ta listen."

So right . . .

"Paoli— you're not exactly left-ovahs, ya know. You are what you are. I thought I taught ya that."

"Well, I feel like leftovers," Paula said miserably.

"Got dumped, too?"

"Yeah, Grandma, I got dumped."

"Bums," was her grandmother's sympathetic reply. A beep over the line.

"Oops, that's probably old Mrs. Goldstein. Goes ta Julio's Fish Emporium every mawnin', tells him his fish is rotten, that his finger nails are dirty and that his shop is filthy. Then, walks out. Lousy tipper, too. But enough already, these little cawls are caustin' ya. So, Marella advises: First, don't worry about me, I've been around too many times, second, as far as ya looks . . . wanna trade? And third— make a friend-a this woman. If she's that gorgeous, trust me, she hasn't a friend in the world. I know my Paoli, she looks behind awl that crap. SO--ADIOS! Vaya con Dios, CAPICHE?"

"Capiche . . ."

At night the sounds of Strasbourg aren't so different from any other city she'd ever visited. Cars roared in the distance at impossible speeds, ambulance sirens wailed and merrymaker's voices filtered through her open window as they wandered along the pedestrian zone.

Not so different from any other night for Paula Giordano. All alone and bored stiff.

Feeling very sorry for herself, she poured a generous helping of Tokay into a paper cup and, sitting cross-legged on the bed, opened her sketch book. *At least there's time to finish up before my meeting with Karl tomorrow. I don't know, maybe I should do this one over again . . .* She eyed it critically. *No, no.* Closing the portfolio with a firm decision, she tossed it on the nightstand and stretched out on the bed.

There comes a point when you just have to put it away, or you'll never finish. . . and I do think I did some pretty fine work. . .Instead, she studied the ceiling, a smile threatening to break through the cloud cover.

How about that Marella? Guess, I don't have to worry about her so much. . . Still, Tony, though. The smile disappeared.

And Christian never called. Downing the wine, and crumpling up the cup in her fist, she tossed it in the general direction of the wastebasket. *Ah, who needs it?* She buried her head in her arms. . . .

⚜

"Listen, it's gettin' late. Why don't you just stay over and drive back in the morning?"

Paula found a place for her wallet in her shoulder bag. Automatically searching for her keys, she reminded herself that Tony drove them both to the restaurant — for once.

"Can't. I don't like to think of Marella all alone like this. I wish I could have talked her into coming along."

Tony snorted at that. "Your Grandmother thinks the world is flat and stops dead at the Croton city limits." He slapped her shoulder: Tony's version of affection. "Ya shouldn't worry about her, kid. She's a tough, old lady. And, besides, the street watches out for her, anyway."

"Pop, I'm almost thirty years old and I pay my own rent. You think you could stop callin' me 'kid'?" She paused on the sidewalk. "Wait a minute. Here's another buck. I'll be right back."

"Ya gave her a big enough tip," her father said. "Come on! If you're gonna be so stubborn about headin' back tonight, I want ya on the road before dark."

"Oh— hold your horses. I'll only be a minute. Anyway, what the poor woman earns in that dive probably doesn't cover the soap it takes to wash the grease stains out of her uniform."

"Hey," Tony protested. "This place serves the best sausages and peppers in town!"

"Just get the car, will ya?" Paula shouted and kept walking back toward the restaurant. *Honestly, this is the last time I pay for a meal and let him pick the place. The man thinks haute cuisine is putting the ketchup in a paper cup.* Promising her stomach, a stop at the drug store later, Paula hurried through the diner toward their table, nearly slipping on a pickle.

Maybe I should worry less about Marella and more about Pop. His diet's gonna kill him. Discreetly, she slipped the folded dollar under the salt shaker. *I don't get it. How can a man be so cheap and never eat at home? A few vegetables wouldn't hurt. And a good breakfast. . .*

It happened all at once. The thundering crash, the flash of light through the diner's windows. Screams and—

"Tony!" Paula sat up in the darkness, the scream dying on her lips, eyes wide in horror. Her breath came sharply, in trembling gasps.

Where was she? She peered around the room, at first not remembering, and then breathing relief . . . *It really was only a dream. Only the same damned one.*

The woman rolled out of bed and felt her way to the window on trembling legs, just to be sure. No, the cathedral loomed in the night sky just across the deserted square: no cars, no people, no fires. . .

"Damn him," Paula whispered, as tears stung her weeping eyes. She stood in the open window, cooling her face in the gathering winds, catching the scent of rain. . .

Go back to bed, girl. All is well. Slipping out of her clothes, she crawled back into bed, closed her eyes and drifted away into sleep.

The curtains fluttered with the approaching storm. Only random lights shone from the apartments far across the square; few people were awake at this hour to watch the rain fall.

At the first flash of lightning, the gentle rainfall became a deluge. The next lightning flash illuminated the empty streets and the cathedral square. Water already accumulated between the cobblestones and in ancient impressions in the mortar.

The lightning flash was brilliant and the watchful eyes across the square had to blink. They opened again and continued their vigil.

CHAPTER XIII

The next several days found Paula hard at work as she combed the city on foot, camera and art materials strapped casually over her shoulders, methodically studying every point of interest her contract bound her to illustrate. Snapping shots from various angles with her polaroid camera and setting up her makeshift plein air easel and stool, when possible, to capture more detail with her pencils. Each night, spreading out her rough sketches on the spacious hotel desk with her water colors and pencils poised for finalizing alongside her instant camera shots.

On her last designated day for "research", looking up at a brilliantly sunny day, stepping into Place de la Cathédrale, the artist opted for a treat: *Perfect day for a boat ride around the Old City!*

Like a seasoned crowd negotiator, the New Yorker maneuvered and weaved in, under and around every possible style of tourist till she secured a window seat at boat's edge. The sun parted white puffy clouds, creating multiple flare effects in her camera lens. Great effect, she thought as she planned in her mind how she'd capture that in her illustrations. Smiling during the entire journey as the magnificent sites of Strasbourg floated by: The Ancient Duane, Palais Rohan, the Palais du Rhin and all of course, dwarfed by Notre Dame de Strasbourg.

Feeling quite accomplished by the end of her nautical "research", she opted for another reward. Shopping: Heading straight for the Avenue des Arcades, with the plan to hit every boutique en route to the illustrious Printemps. Pausing at a colorfully painted shop, Paula's smile ripped open wide as she reached for the door handle.

The tiny boutique hummed with the voices of women browsing the circular racks discussing possible trends with one of the petite sales clerks. Light rock filled the background, supplied by an invisible sound system.

The American turned this way and that before the triple mirrors. Brow lowered in critical concentration, she finally sighed and gave it up.

The conversation of other shoppers interrupted her inner debate. Her native curiosity revived; she pricked her ears to catch a slice of gossip.

"I think this will be positively lovely on you, Madame," the shop clerk gushed. "What with your coloring and strong bone structure."

She means your ruddy complexion and you could stand to lose a few pounds. Paula's eyes never left the mirror as she turned to her right. Then, she frowned at a little tightness around the jean's waistband. *Like I should talk!*

"I don't know . . ." the other voice wavered. "I'm not sure that red is my color . . ."

Atta girl. Don't let her con you. Go after that little blue number instead.

"What about this blue dress?" The customer wondered.

Yes, that's the one. That settles it; I'm goin' on a diet TODAY. No more croissants, no more booze, no more five-course meals. From now on, it's bread and Perrier— I'd better buy a larger size.

"Ah, Madame, you betray exquisite taste!" The clerk marveled. "This is so chic!"

Yeah, and it's SO expensive too. Sale racks are along the back walls, honey. Paula glanced down at the customer's shoes on her way to the counter. *Never mind. You definitely do not live on an artist's salary.*

If Place de la Cathédrale enshrines Medieval France, Place Kleber embraces the modern world with whole hearted fervor.

Connecting antiquated cobblestoned alleyways with a fashionably chic shopping district, the oblong square borders four of the busiest avenues in Strasbourg.

Tour buses and cars from every European Nation vie for the same narrow lanes as delivery vans and commuters. The only traffic law, indeed, seems to be none at all.

La Place itself buzzes with activity, occupied in daylight hours by independent flower vendors presenting foil wrapped bouquets, shoppers laden with netted filoches and shiny plastic bags, students toting angry picket signs protesting the latest outrage.

He leaned against the marble pedestal and lit a cigarette, his eyes never leaving the American across the street.

"Help the cause in Nicaragua!" The young student thrust a crudely written brochure in his face, blocking his view. "Stop the American Imperialists who—"

The student's spiel died on his lips.

No flicker of a blink, not a change in expression wavered in those eyes; they barely acknowledged his presence.

The boy backed away from the statue of General Kleber and the man standing beneath it, and found another target. "Help the cause in--"

Hm . . . Yes, roses. Might as well buy 'em myself; no one else will. Awash in a suffocating wave of self-pity, Paula handed over the shining coins.

"Voila!" With a bright blue ribbon, the petite Frenchwoman secured the crinkly plastic around the stems, careful not to prick a finger.

"Merci." Paula gathered up the parcels scattered around her feet and shuffled away toward the Rue du Dome. *Well, shopping didn't do it. I'm still depressed as hell. What's left . . .*

With a shriek, the American jumped back onto the sidewalk. The Citroën's driver honked again and accelerated.

"Yeah?" Paula shouted, balefully waving her sacks at the speeding auto. "Same to you, PAL!" *These people drive like it's the Grand Prix. The jerk's probably rushing to a café to sit around all afternoon.*

Just then, the light changed and she found herself carried along by the crowds surrounding her. *Maybe I outta try Printemps. That always cheers me up. Aunt Marella would die a happy woman if she had unlimited credit and a half an hour in their housewares department. And a great clearance rack—*

Paula stopped dead, mesmerized by the rich squares of buttercreams in Olivier's window. Her mouth watered at the creamy texture sprinkled with walnuts, not unlike Pavlov's dog and his dinner bell. And the way they manage to curl up the chocolate, right in the center. *How do they do that?* She sighed with passionate longing. *NOTHING like French chocolates, ESPECIALLY when you're depressed. Tony used to bring them home; when he bothered to come home, that is . . .*

No. The resolute American took hold of herself. *You can't eat and drink whatever you want and not expect it to catch up, sooner or later. And you did just buy that amazing blue dress in a SIZE LARGER . . .* She sighed audibly.

Personally, I don't think these Frenchwomen eat. Don't they ever get fat? Then again . . .

She eyed the tempting display. *Maybe there's something in French food that FIGHTS calories. Yeah right, Paoli.* She snickered.: *The more you eat, the skinnier you get . . .* "Uh-huh."

Regretfully, Paula turned away from the tempting display and fell into the willing arms of Marc Rouget.

His youthful face beamed with radiant delight. "Cherie!"

"Well," she managed. "*Marc*: What a surprise! Where did you come from?"

Marc Rouget frowned in concentration. Very slowly, he enunciated, "Ronald Reagan is the thirty-ninth president of the United States." He beamed with proud accomplishment.

Paula gawked at the little policeman. *Whaaat?*

Oh, no, he's trying again! "Alaska is the fiftieth—"

Ah, of course! "Non, non, non," she interrupted waving her hands. "Ce nest plus necessaries, mon ami."

"You speak French!" His pleasure practically bubbled over and couldn't help but affect her mood. She suddenly felt more herself, like a cloud passing away from the sun.

"And so beautifully!" He went on in French. "But I don't understand. I'm quite sure Larsonnier said—"

"Yes, well. . ." The American willingly handed over the cumbersome packages to the gallant Frenchman. "It's a little joke that has gotten out of hand . . ."

"But, how amusing! Trust me, petite Americaine," Rouget soothed her while juggling her purchases, patting her hand. With a gloating thought for his older friend, he promised, "This will be our little secret, yes? A little joke between friends, oui?"

He gazed down into the little face, her eyes veiled by those mysterious sunglasses, her smiling lips, enchanting. He remembered the sensation of her dancing so close to him.

"Er-ah, I have some time left on my luncheon break," he stammered. "Would you care to join me . . ."

"For a pizza?" Paula wrapped her arm around his elbow and dragged him down the sidewalk, ravenous after the battle of wills with the demon pastry shop. "I'm dying for one!"

Paula glanced around the intimate first floor of Maxim's with satisfaction. The shining wood, the green leather upholstery . . .*This should be one of those hangouts for reporters you see on TV*, she decided and speared her salami pizza with ravenous impatience.

Why is it Europeans eat EVERYTHING with a knife and fork? Even French fries and fried chicken, for heaven's sake! Pizza should be eaten one slice at a time— by hand, with the cheese slopping over the sides. Not that this isn't good! It's just . . . too neat.

"Is American pizza very different?" Rouget wanted to know.

"No," Paula lied. *Why shock him?*

Love-stricken eyes gazed with devoted fervor into hers, except when he ate, of course. Once his attention diverted to a passing miniskirt, Paula had to smother her grin with her napkin.

Okay, so he's not the most loyal swain. But he makes up in passion what he's lacking in fidelity. "Tell me," she mused in an off-handed fashion. "If something were to happen in Strasbourg . . . Let us say, a mugging, what would happen?"

"Nothing so different from your country. A report would be filed, and—"

"Oh, a report." *So much for that idea.*

"Pardon?"

"I said, whatever happened to you at the café?" The American twirled her straw in the bubbling brown beverage. The few chunks of ice clinked in the glass.

"Uhhh — well—uhhh," he stammered.

"Never mind. Five minutes of Simone De Bourchegrave and I can understand why anyone might want to make tracks." *Ha, wonder how much snakeskin goes for these days.* "She really is creepy."

"Yes, I agree," Rouget shuddered. "Simone and I have never been the best of friends. Particularly after I arrested her husband last year in rather dubious circumstances."

"No surprise there," Paula said drily.

Servers in the restaurant buzzed around with trays of coffees and large silvery tureens of chocolate mousse: the establishment's claim to local fame.

Boy, that mousse looks AMAZING! Maybe. . . just a spoonful or two—maybe three?

The policeman interrupted her reverie by suddenly clutching her free hand in a tender clasp; her other, as it were, occupied with the cola. "That night was a dream. A delight. A—"

"Marc, we danced," Paula reminded him. "You make it sound like we . . .uh, well, we were just dancing."

"To you, perhaps," was his sad reply. "Your heart is already lost to another. There is no place in it for a poor gendarme?"

I don't believe this. I'm getting propositioned over pizza! Disengaging her hand from his, patting his arm," sure there's a place in my heart for you, Marc," she assured him. "Right between the torch I hold for Robert Redford and my undying love for the Lone Ranger."

"You mock me," he sighed, his face tragic. "You doubt the depth of my passion."

"Mmph." Swallowing her beverage, the object of his passion took his hands in a firm grip. "Listen, Marc . . .Uh, how can I phrase this? . . . This approach probably works great on every other woman you'll ever meet, okay? I mean, you say some lovely things, and I'm sure it just sweeps them off their feet."

"But—"

"But, I'm not in the market for a man just now, okay? . . . Say, how about ordering dessert?"

"But, of course!" Rouget lifted a finger and a black vested waiter hastened over.

How does he DO that? She listened as he ordered two helpings of the chocolate mousse and coffee.

So, I'll diet tomorrow. Who am I being skinny for, anyway? Maybe I'll just blimp out and become one of those recluse artists that paint fruit and abstract indiscernibles.

"What about Larsonnier?" The discontented Frenchman blurted. "Forgive me for mentioning it, but you two seem so--"

"Friendly? That's *all* that we are. Friends."

"Oh." Her answer excited him. "If that is the case, would you honor me by accompanying me to the Haut-Koenigsburg masquerade next weekend?"

"A masquerade?" It tempted her. If she worked really hard . . . "Well . . ."

Rouget hastened to reassure her. "I swear, we go only as friends."

Yes, well, you certainly know all about that, don't you, Paoli? Paula lifted her glass and clinked it against the gendarme's wine glass.

"To friends, then. . . . *say,* think we could get some caramel with the mousse?"

CHAPTER XIV

Christian Larsonnier cocked his head and considered the *Eau-De-Vie* display from a distance. A flourished script, denoted each bottle's contents on a cream-colored label: Peach, apple, apricot . . . *Hm*. The Frenchman frowned. Carefully, he moved the apple liqueur . . . just a fraction of a millimeter and "Voila!" He nodded approval. "So much the better."

"So, Christian," a familiar voice complained in rounded French. "You choose not to greet your poor Maman properly anymore?"

"Maman!" Larsonnier spun around to face his regal mother. "I did not hear you come in. That bell isn't working again."

"It's working." Estelle automatically straightened a wayward curl over his ear with a dissatisfied air. "If you didn't have that ridiculous music blaring so loudly . . . So, will you kiss your poor Maman?"

Dutifully, the Frenchman kissed both porcelain cheeks, his eyes traveling to the luxury Citroën parked directly outside the little wine shop. "Maman," he explained patiently once again, "this is a pedestrian zone. You are not permitted—"

"Bah!" Madame Maurice Larsonnier dismissed her son's entreaties with a wave of a gloved hand. "I won't embarrass my only child, my little son for very much longer." She sighed theatrically. Christian inwardly winced; he recognized the usual signs. True to form, the Frenchwoman continued in a plaintive voice.

"I cannot guess how much longer the good Lord will grant me, my darling. My time so limited at my fragile age, and I only wanted to see my precious boy once more before—"

"Maman," Christian interrupted humorously, a twinkle in his eyes. "Your time is only limited because you choose to fill it up traveling between Monte Carlo, Paris and Metz. Now, come," he coaxed, taking her hand and kissing it. "Tell me why you've chosen to grace my little shop today."

Estelle's green eyes scanned the small shop disapprovingly. She pursed her lips, "Hummph. I had little choice, didn't I? Just like your father, always finding toys to play with. Well . . ." She softened, patting his cheek. "At least you have the decency to keep them to yourself."

"Thank you, Maman." Larsonnier tried to hide a smile. "Never would I dream of embarrassing you with my proletarian tendencies."

His mother fixed him with a scathing stare. "You are entirely too cruel to your poor Maman," she pronounced. "Perhaps I should just leave and—"

"Non, non, non." Christian gently took her arm and led her away from the door.

"I'm sorry, Maman; truly, I am. Please, tell me why you're here."

She studied her son and seemed satisfied with his practiced expression of remorse.

"Oh, very well. I only wanted to remind you about the dinner this evening. Your father has changed our plans again, as usual. We're now dining at The Bald Soprano." The ghost of a smile flirted with the corners of her lips. "Fitting place for you father, don't you think?"

"Dinner?" Christian said blankly and recovered. "Ah. Ah, yes. Dinner. No, Maman, I haven't forgotten."

Estelle tossed him a cynical glance, but said no more about it. "And an hour earlier. Your father has yet another meeting with his insufferable friends." Fondly, she straightened his tie.

"So very handsome," she approved and then innocently, as if she'd just thought of it, "You should invite the little Marie-Madeleine to join us tonight, darling."

"Marie-Madeleine?" He echoed confused. "I don't know a Marie-Madeleine, Maman."

"Why, of course you do, silly child. Marie-Madeleine St. Jacques."

At his continued confusion, she tapped his arm with her gloved hand.

"Albert's daughter."

"Ah. Well, actually, Maman," he lied. "I've another date later this evening."

"I see." She shrugged it off. "Well, bring your date, that is, if you really have one. Otherwise, I shall look forward to our dinner this evening."

Christian started as the phone shrilled in the back room.

"That's Paris calling back, Maman. I must answer." He quickly pecked both cheeks.

"Until tonight."

"Mais oui. Bien sur." Estelle complained to the thin air.

"Certainly, I may find my own way out."

Sheaves of golden sun washed against the gold speckled crown of the antique carousel. Streams of colorful horses, flashed brilliant clenched teeth, kicking their hooves, in perpetual frozen silence.

The old man carefully unfolded the crisp linen and draped it over the park bench. Gusty breezes cascading from the east lifted its starched corners before he could anchor the fabric with a jade wine bottle.

Touching a finger to the side of the glass, he tested its temperature and nodded in approval. *Yes, just right. Riesling must never be served warm. And now, for the paté...*

Slowly, Junger bent over the checker topped picnic basket at his feet, his right hand supporting the small of his back as he shuffled its contents side to side until he found the container of Strasbourg Foie Gras. Little girls in native dress herding flocks of geese on a white background. He decided to present her with the jar, a small token of their picnic on Place Gutenberg.

There. All was perfect. Karl Junger sat back and waited for his guest.

Henri's dark curls brushed against the cool cement wall. He shifted so as to not smudge his suit. The dark eyes ignited, as the American scurried down the hotel steps, her blue dress shimmering and floating in the wind. He tossed down the cigarette and left it there to burn.

Paula hurried across the Rue des Arcades. A Mercedes honked impatiently. "Yeah? Up yours!!" She shouted back and sprinted across the last three lanes. Two hours of getting ready and still late.

The old man recognized that gait: Hurried, almost impatient. One could say, brash, reminding him of a thoroughbred out on its first canter after a winter in the stables. The old man chuckled. "Dear me, how very fanciful," he murmured and squinted up as she rounded the bench.

"Guten tag, Karl." Paula offered her hand. He enclosed it in his own wrinkled pair.

"Sorry, I'm late."

The old man slowly got to his feet, waiting until she'd seated herself on the bench.

"Trust me, you are well worth the wait."

"Thank you." Self-consciously, Paula pushed her blowing hair from her face.

"Do you want to get straight to business, or—"

"Oh, please. Let us enjoy the day," the German pointed to the periwinkle sky,

"Over a glass of wine and a taste of some local delicacies." He fumbled through the basket, grimacing as he poured the clear golden wine into disposable cups.

"Plastic is not very stylish," he apologized, "but, I never know when I might take another embarrassing spill, like the one at Le Renard."

"I'm American," she answered quickly. "It's all the same to me. What shall we drink to?"

Karl lifted his glass in a shaking hand.

"To the successful completion of a long-awaited project."

They both sipped the tart Riesling and as an afterthought, he added, "and to a continuing association between this doddering old man and a beautiful young artist from New York."

"I'll drink to that!" Absolutely charmed by his innate gentility, she found herself wondering what sort of man he would have been back when he was, well . . . her age. *Really, I bet he was kind of cute, in an academic kind of way. Maybe he wore one of those darling tweed jackets, with the suede patches on the elbows.*

"You are sehr schön today, my dear. You should wear that color often; it suits you."

Paula glanced down at the blue silk dress and primly twisted it so the wind wouldn't billow it.

"Thanks. I'm afraid I have to confess; I've been spending my commission on frivolous things."

"There is nothing so frivolous as shutting one's eyes to the beauty of this world. A spring flower, a golden sunrise," he patted her arm. "A lovely woman."

"Oh, come now, you're embarrassing me," she blushed. "Not to mention, blatantly fibbing."

His blue eyes twinkled with mischievous merriment. "My dear, old men never lie; has no one ever told you?"

"No, they simply grow more charming with the years. I don't know what it is," she mused absently, fingering the rim of the makeshift wine glass. "Ever since I got here, I've just felt this need to change myself a bit. To experience new things: The food, the wine, just about everything."

"This is not so uncommon," the German assured her. "France seems to hold a kind of magic. Once people cross its borders, it is as if they enter another reality, where anything can happen. . . .Fantasia . . ." His voice faded.

"I can certainly believe that." The American gestured with her wine glass.

"Look at that merry-go-round. It looks like something out of a dream."

The old man looked across the tiny square to the elegant wooden horses, painted a creamy white with touches of glittering gold and silver.

"Ah yes, and it plays such beautiful music. It is much too chilly for the little ones today. Perhaps you will see it run next summer, when it is warmer."

Paula's glance lingered wistfully on the antique carrousel.

"I doubt that."

"Oh, dear me! I have grown so fond of you, my dear, that I forget your marvelous country has only lent you to me for a short time. I must see if I can convince you to stay."

"Well . . . who knows? Maybe someday, I'll be back."

The German spread the creamy paté on the fresh baked bread. He added some Brie and two slices of Gruyere to the colorful, plastic plates and garnished the light luncheon with a small bunch of green grapes.

"I shall pray that you never leave. But, old men are often lonely and inclined to selfishness. I am sure your father misses you, yes?"

"My father is quite the world traveler," Paula answered matter-of-factly.

"I'm pretty much on my own these days."

"Ah." The German offered no response and only nodded. Paula liked him all the better for it.

They sat in the sun for a time, enjoying the bright sunshine as they picnicked in the square. Though she could never be accused of being nostalgic for anything that happened prior to the previous minute, still Paula listened with interest as the old historian told her more about Strasbourg's past. In his wavering voice, he told her of how the Gutenberg press had been perfected here, probably on this spot and that the Marseillaise had first been written for the city's volunteer battalion— and had been 'borrowed'— in true Marseillaise fashion.

"You make it all sound so real." Paula said. "I can even imagine it. Just think: Napoleon probably passed right by this very spot with his drinking buddies from the university! And not one of them had an inkling of the future he dreamed of for France."

Junger patted her hand. "Who can tell? Perhaps your future, as well, will be determined, here, ja?"

"So, tell me, Karl. I've been invited to a masquerade at Haut-Koenigsburg this weekend. What's it all about?" Paula covered her lap with a brightly colored napkin and accepted the plate.

"How very delightful for you!" Karl paused before he explained, his old faded eyes on the statue of Gutenberg. "It marks a celebration of the best Nouveau Beaujolais in decades. Quite the social affair of the season; it should prove to be most interesting."

"Mmmm." She licked her lips to catch every soft crumb. "Delicious. So, does this happen every year?"

"Oh, dear me, no… Not everyone has been invited to attend. I was not aware you knew anyone in Strasbourg."

"One or two people. Will you be going? To the masquerade, I mean?"

The old man shook his grey head. "No, I have declined my invitation. These parties, they are for the young, not for old men who doze off after their dessert and coffee. Although, coincidentally, I will not be so very far away as I have plans to visit a friend up in the Vosges Saturday evening. Perhaps, you have heard of him: Herr Friedrich Kepler? He has written several books on the influence of the German occupation upon Alsatian architecture in the eighteenth century."

"No, can't say as I have," Paula vaguely replied. "But, I hear you're a celebrity yourself."

"At times," he sighed. "I regret not using a nom-de-plume, such as these modern day romance writers might employ. How disconcerting it is, to be introduced to somebody at a restaurant, or a soirée such as this one, and be given a list of inaccuracies in your latest work!"

"I doubt any of your books contain so much as a typo, or a comma out of place, much less, an inaccuracy."

"Ah, for your kindness, I insist you have another glass of wine." Karl proceeded to fill her cup.

"And that reminds me." She placed the half empty cup on the top of the closed basket and fished her portfolio out from under the bench. "I have some finished sketches here and I want to know if I'm on the right track."

Nervously, Paula handed over the stack of prints, protected by a makeshift cover. She looked away toward the carrousel, not wanting to see his expression change. *What if he doesn't like them? What if he thinks they're terrible? What if—*

"Why, these are splendid!" Junger cried out excitedly. "Absolutely perfect!" His eyes alight with pleasure, he thumbed through them again.

"You . . .you really think so?" Relief lifted the weight she'd been carrying around with her. Fear, that she would fall on her face and once again Tony would be there to say: *What the hell did you think you were doing, anyway?*

"Like them! Why, look here." He pointed an enthusiastic finger at the chateau's front arch. "See how you have captured the impressive arch, and yet you manage not to overburden the detail. These are wonderful drawings, my dear! Exactly what I asked for. I must write my friend Jorgi at once to thank him for his inspired choice."

Paula felt like crying happy, joyful, ecstatic tears. *At last! At last, I'm on my way!*

"Wel-l-l," she enunciated in a carefully professional voice. "If you think I'm heading in the right direction, I'll continue with that approach as I start on the Cathedral in the next few days."

Junger beamed with delighted pride. "This will be my best book yet!" He made a mock-embarrassed face. "If I do say so myself. And largely due to your skill, Liebchen. May I keep these? I would very much like to show them off to Friedrich." He lowered his voice in confidence. "He has been absolutely insufferable since his last work. And between us, I thought his illustrations were somewhat staid."

"Bonjour, ma petite Americaine." The honey voiced Frenchman plummeted her high spirits back to earth, smashing them hard against the cobblestones. "I see you have found your own amusement here in Strasbourg."

Oh, Lord. Paula squinted up into the sun to see Henri De Bourchegrave smiling down at her with that insulting leer on that perfect, botoxed face.

"Mr. De Bourchegrave," the American uttered without enthusiasm. "How nice to see you. You can see, I am in the middle of a meeting and I—"

"Ah, yes, I can see," he sneered. "As is usual, the great Larsonnier has moved on to fresher pastures and you . . ." His black eyes rested on the old man who watched the exchange with a curious frown.

"Bonjour, Docteur Junger."

"Ah, good afternoon," the old man said.

The Frenchman ignored the greeting. Turning to Paula, he offered," Perhaps you would like that drink this evening? My apartment, it is over the restaurant, and—"

"No, thanks."

Henri insisted. "Ah, but Mademoiselle, it is not good to be alone. Myself, I am certain Larsonnier feels the same way. Just last night I saw him at the Kammerzell. Interesting ambience, but the food, perhaps, is not to Larsonnier's liking. That is, he left with his beautiful companion quite early."

"Listen, amigo," her lips tight, "don't you have some onions to chop, garlic to mince, perhaps a soufflé to flop? Or do you get that stuff from a gag shop, along with the rest of your waxed food. Next time, I'll bring some rubber vomit along." Her eyes challenged. "But, wait, there's probably plenty of the real deal around after one of your lunches."

"Liebchen," Karl's calm voice interrupted the heated exchange. "Is there a problem with this gentleman?"

"You can call Henry many, many things," Paula told her employer. "But, *Gentleman* isn't on the list. I guess I'm the one domino in Strasbourg that hasn't fallen to his charms, so he's made it his life's work to follow me around."

"Ah, I see." The old man struggled to his feet and faced the handsome Frenchman with a serene demeanor. "Monsieur De Bourchegrave," he said quite formally. "This young woman is a colleague of mine, a gifted artist who deserves every respect. I must ask you to apologize to her now and leave us to enjoy our picnic."

The Frenchman clenched his jaw and raised his chin. "It is a public park and I am merely out enjoying this exquisite day. Only a lucky coincidence," his voice deepened, "that I should run into the lovely Mademoiselle." Henri snorted. "And why, may I ask, should I do such a thing? This woman is obviously in need of a better escort than you, *old man*."

"Then let me explain exactly why it is not such a lucky coincidence," the old German explained quite pleasantly. "You see, one of my oldest acquaintances in this fair city regulates certain health standards in our dining establishments. A little word over our evening sherry and your only clientele will be the rats in your wine cellar."

With narrowing eyes, De Bourchegrave scanned him up and down. But, Karl only endured the hostile scrutiny with the same good grace. Finally, the dark restaurateur turned to Paula.

"Très bien. Mademoiselle, my apologies. I regret to admit that I have misunderstood the situation. I shall never forgive myself for angering such a beautiful woman. Alas, I was utterly shameless."

Unable to bring herself to speak, Paula's face burned with humiliation.

"Sehr gut," Junger nodded. "And now for the second part off my request—*au revoir.*"

The Frenchman whirled away, his eyes sending a veiled warning. Paula, stared after his retreating back. *Its war.* The American's eyes glowed innocently. *That's okay, I like war. Choose your weapon, De Backyard.*

Karl exhaled. "Dear me," he murmured, and sat down rather quickly. "How very bellicose."

"Karl," Paula dropped down next to him. "I'm so sorry. This is *so* embarrassing!"

"Bitte." The old gentleman waved it away. "You are not to blame for that man's atrocious manners, my dear."

"Do you really have a friend on the board of health?"

Karl was fanning his face with his napkin. "Oh, heavens no. I have absolutely no idea about such things. But it worked out never-the-less."

His companion stared at him, totally nonplussed, and then suddenly burst into pleasurable laughter. Junger joined in, their laughing continuing for several minutes over their shared joke.

Finally, Junger gathered up the last of the picnic. "I must go back to my apartment and begin research on yet another dry textbook. And you," he directed with a twinkle in his eye. "You must return to your work and see that our book becomes a bestseller.

Helping him clear up their empties from their picnic, Paula thought, *Our Book.* How wonderful that sounded. "Will do! Promise!" Impulsively, she pecked his cheek.

"Thank you, Karl. For *everything.* You don't know what you've done for me."

The old German watched the young American hurry across the square with her portfolio beneath her arm. That sparkling vitality radiating in every direction from her small form. The silk dress blew about her legs and the tumble of dark curls blowing wildly in the playful gusts.

Karl smiled a gentle, old man's smile. "Ah, Liebchen," he softly said. "You do not know what you have done for *me*."

Turning, then hobbling away in the opposite direction, his mind already moving onto his next project.

The American breezed into the hotel lobby with the force of the Mistral, fluttering papers on the reception desk and humming some ridiculous Broadway show tune. The lobby clerk glanced up from his eternal book work in annoyance, but she only smiled sweetly and waved as she passed.

A good day's work. Things are definitely looking up. That's the secret, Paoli, old girl. You've got to focus on your work and forget all about these late-night-movie dreams of yours.... Let's see. Tomorrow morning, I'll catch the cathedral in the early light and then I'll only have a few more sketches to do. Who knows? If I do really well, maybe Karl will pass my name around. Paula, girl, you're on your way!....

"Mademoiselle!" The desk clerk accosted her midway to the elevator and handed her a familiar blue envelope. "You had a visitor," he stiffly informed her and just barely contained a wink before he returned to his tedious duties.

She stared at the vellum, blankly, not sure she wanted to open it. *Oh, come on, what's the worst it could be?*

Resolutely, Paula ripped open the envelope, scattering bits of paper here and there on the floor, to the displeasure of the desk clerk.

Paula,
Might we meet for dinner at La Cantatrice Chauvre - *The Bald Soprano-* **this evening? I want to try to explain my abominable behavior. At seven?**
            Christian Larsonnier

"Hmph," she thought out loud. Serve him right if I don't show up," Paula muttered. "Probably needs to earn another notch on his belt." She glanced at her watch and gasped at the time. Six o'clock!

The young lobby clerk paused in his book work and watched the crazy American stampede the elevator. With the back of her fist, she punched the button, her shoe making that detestable taping sound as she impatiently waited for the doors to close.

The elevator began its journey to the second floor as he returned to his work with a roll of his eyes. "Les Americans."

CHAPTER XV

An incendiary moon flickered from behind the shredded cloak of a thinly ashen sky. From its gauzy veil, sprinkling droplets poured from an opaque obscurity.

Faintly suspended in the night, singing voices transcending the storm, wandering peacefully without accompaniment. "Ma-ri-a-a-a . . . The souls of a chorus of men whispering in hymn. A solemn plea. A lullaby.

Brilliant headlights suddenly parted the downpour. Its piercing yellow flares followed a path of darkness, like a hunter from another time, lost in the dark, swinging his lantern about, tracing his steps to safety.

The car beamed its way through a thicket, flashing a huge crumbling wall. With an abrupt lurch, the auto stopped.

Sandled feet swung out and the car door slammed. From the shelter of a tree, eyes paused to ponder the familiar sight. Scythes of lightning cracked on the faraway horizon, the rain sowing its tinsel against a rifted sky. Further north on the Route du Vin, a raging storm, but here, only the tail of its echo.

An irresistible yen for a smoke gnawed at him and he fumbled for a pocket.

"Damn — whoops, gotta watch my mouth," Tony mumbled, impatiently hunting through the pleats of his robe to the slosh and clatter of rosary beads.

"Ahh." Cold fingers paused over the smooth touch of cellophane. He sheltered the lighter's flame from the misty wind, then jerked the heavy hood to the rim of his lashes, blowing smoke rings into thin air. His expressive eyes beheld the serene, stony facade. A lantern hung majestically at the entrance flickering softly through the sizzling patter of the rain.

The traveler, weary from a tedious journey lingered moments longer, in his mind somewhere, the musings of an unseen menace. He shook it off, lighting up again. This time he breathed uneasily. "Well . . . how does it go?" He flicked his cigarette into some bushes.

"Old soldiers never die; they just fade away . . . But what about their enemies?"

The heavy oak door swung open and the din of the chanting voices roused Tony Giordano from his thoughts.

A small bluntish figure of a man in a hooded white robe waved excitedly. "Brother Antonio!! Come in!! Hurry, Father Abbot is holding the evening meal in your honor! Hurry!!"

'Brother Antonio' reached into the backseat of his tiny car, slinging his duffle bag over his shoulder. Crossing the portal to the Antonitians Abbey, an anxious line of monks on either side of the threshold broke into chain reactions of smiles, warm welcomes and friendly embraces. The huge bear of a man, who seemed like Gulliver by comparison, was all smiles himself. The reunion might have been mistaken for the aftermath of a successful ball game in the dugout.

"How are ya, Brother Francis?" Giordano slapped the shoulder of a grinning monk, his French flawless and without accent. "And you, Brother Etienne? I see the Lord has been good to you . . . or to the dinner table."

Greetings made; he looked around for his oldest friend. But the bluntish man who called him in seemed nowhere about. Tony looked around and finally spotted him standing solemnly near a statue of St. Joseph. One of the monks retreating into the abbey's depths, called back, "Your usual quarters have been set aside for you. I'll bring your things along then."

"Thanks, Marty, uh, sorry, Brother Martin."

The other merely nodded and disappeared with the others.

"Vinny? How the he—, uh-hum, how have ya been?" Anthony Giordano's face alit with heart felt delight at the sight of his old friend. His heavy footsteps echoed against the sand-colored marble.

The plump, little man held his arms out as well. They looked briefly into each other's face, then embraced.

"So good to have you back, Tony," Vinny grinned, offsetting the severity of his attire. His English bore the unmistakable twang of Boston. "But I couldn't help noticing. Where's your briefcase?"

"In the car. I'll run out there later when everybody files down there for Vespers." He pointed to a grand balustrade leading to a chapel below.

"So, how's everything going? Have you settled into retirement? And how is your family?" The little man's eyes shone with caring. "Your mother called here yesterday."

Giordano raised both brows.

"Well, the woman who called didn't identify herself. But after the first few words, I began to recognize her voice. She's very good at accents, by the way. Sometimes, she's a British journalist, uh, doing research, or a Swedish photographer. This time, it was a Madre Arestia making a complaint about our last shipment of cheese." The men laughed whole heartedly and Tony Giordano wiped his eyes, still sighing.

Suddenly serious. "I guess, I'll do my reverence to the Abbot. He's waitin', right?"

The little man smothered a smile.

"Till supper, then?"

"Yep." Suddenly alone, Tony looked about. The grand entrance hall lined with ancient tapestries and a wood carving of a life size crucifix. Ever imposing and quite startling even after all these years. Slowly, he walked to the far wall. His eyes bound to Christs'. His tough guy veneer instantly evaporating before the tortured, serene face of Jesus on the Cross. Giordano looked from side to side, probably from habit, then fell to his knees, his lips moving silently. Then, standing again, "In the name of the Father," Giordano could not detach himself from Christ's humble lure. "And of the Son and of The Holy Spirit. Amen."

As he walked away, he made a small gesture of crossing his heart with his thumb as he put his hand to his lips, his thoughts changed to the present.

"Ughh," he grunted as he copiously walked up the creaking stairs to the Abbot's office. The hallway felt cold and desolate. The huge man's rosaries sloshing from side to side, the only sound in the narrow passageway.

He rounded a third corner, then at the end of the hallway, a door and Giordano stood, stalemating one another.

"Come on, Tone. He's not so bad." He straightened his hood and paused. An expression of futility fluttered across his face. "Oh, well." His hand gripped the door handle as he politely knocked.

No response.

He tapped again.

Nothing.

This time, he waited, deciding he'd count to twenty, then give up the game. We gotta think of a better game than this —one—two—three——twent—

"Entré!"

With the pleasantest expression he could fake, Brother Antonio's face beamed with a waxy, forced smile. *I feel like a game show host.*

An elderly man sat behind an impressive, antique desk. His hands serenely folded beneath the cuffs of his crisp, white robe. His clear blue eyes held an innocent air of mischief and his plush red lips parted to an impressive set of—

Wow. Looks like he got a new set of choppers. Looks good too. Not like those others. Sounded like the chariot race in Ben Hur when he ate . . .

"Antonio." He calmly rose as he held out a sturdy hand to the visitor. "You're back with us, yet, uh, again. How wonderful." He gripped Giordano's hand brusquely. "Still in discernment, I take it?"

Let go of my hand, Padre. The other squeezed with a stifling strength. *Must practice a lot of hand grips under that robe.* Tony returned the 'ardor' as best he could.

Finally relinquishing, the American retreated a throbbing hand into his cuffs. *One of these days I'll get up the nerve to hold an arm-wrestling match with this guy.*

Tony looked at the Abbot, his plaster grin in check. The Abbot smiled naively; his left brow raised.

Now, don't get paranoid Giordano. You know he can't read your mind. "Uh-yes. As you know, these things take time."

"Please, sit down." The Abbot smoothed his robe to his right elbow, as he sat, pausing briefly, then cupped his chin. "So. All is well with you, Antonio? You look as vital as ever, I'm glad to see." The priest began drumming his fingers.

"I'm retired for good as of last month."

Brother Antonio stared at the Abbot's hands, still smiling.

"What will you do with yourself? You know, it is most difficult to give up an enormously active life. And frankly . . ." He stopped and seriously considered the man across his desk. "I've never mentioned this, but you've always reminded me of General MacArthur—In spirit, that is," the Abbot amended.

He's playing with my mind. I won't let him get to me.

"How does that famous line from his last speech before Congress go?" He wrinkled his vast forehead, outlining his chin with his forefinger. "Something about old soldiers and fading away, I believe. Oh well." His face changed to the picture of serenity.

"Welcome, Antonio." He stood again and came around his imposing desk, looking straight into Tony Giordano's fixed expression as he grasped his shoulders.

"And please stay with us as long as you need to. And I agree, these things do take time." Then pointing to the corner of the room to a massive chess set, he continued. "And I am so looking forward to our next game."

Tony followed his gaze and stifled a smirk.

"Thank you, Father Abbot. You can't know how touched I am by your kindness. And I too look forward to our next chess match."

"Shall we then?" His draping sleeve gestured to the door, reminding Giordano a bit of the ghost-of-Christmas-future.

They walked in silence down the two flights of stairs and endless hallways, through the silent labyrinth of the old Monastery. The distinct aroma of roasted lamb becoming more and more pronounced. Dishes chiming and silverware clanged as they came to a large, warmly lit dining hall. Sconces offered a peaceful lighting to the echoing chamber. The table seemed endless, plate after plate, dotted with wine jug after jug. All life instantly ceased as the Abbot entered with the reverence and majesty befitting his role.

One by one, the brothers took their places before the table. Eagerly looking on as their friend of years gone by took his place of honor to the right of the Abbot.

Two large roasts were set strategically at the table, steaming flagrantly as did the bowls of boiled potatoes and fresh platters of vegetables. The Abbot raised his arms as all heads bowed for the meal's blessing. Tony followed suit. But, first, out of habit, scanning the group before closing his eyes.

Prayer said, the Abbot raised his glass.

"I should like to propose a toast." The Abbot's eyes seeming to challenge their guests'.

"To doors then." He paused, relishing Giordano's quizzical countenance.

"New ones to open and to closing of the old."

The meal passed pleasantly. There were many grateful toasts to their guest, witty conversation and tears shed from laugher. So, when the natural course of lull crept in, Father Abbot rose to signal the retreat before Vespers.

Tony waited only moments longer, then slipped out to his rental car for his briefcase.

Once back in his "cell", he silently waited for the chanting to begin, signaling the onset of evening prayers. Two sharp clicks of his brief case hinges echoed in the warmly lit, baron room.

A variety of hi-tech gadgetry lay positioned like minute pieces of a puzzle.

He whipped out a small metal sensor, turned the switch, then crept about the room cautiously.

After a span of seconds, he stood. *Okay, so maybe I am paranoid. But I'll sleep better knowing the room is really clean.* He slid the box carefully into its padded slot, removed a round silver object and what resembled a Swiss army knife, shut the briefcase, then gently slid it under the tiny bed.

His face tightened. His stare deadpan as he pulled up his robe, refastening his rope-belt, then slid along the wall toward his door.

A faint light glowed from beneath the frame. His grip caressed the door handle as he peered through the slivered opening. Eyes slitted as he crept out into the hallway, his back firmly against the damp plaster.

Deftly, he slid down the long passage. Coming to a stairway foyer, he looked up. Waited. Listened. Only the patter of rain laced with murmurs of prayer from deep below the abbey reached his ears.

Once safely up the steps, again he felt his way along the shadowy corridors of the monastery, stopping now and then to listen. Gregorian chanting with the percussion of raging bursts of rain clapped against the slated rooftop.

Tony Giordano stood penitently before the Abbot's door then produced his Swiss like knife collection. He stirred with several picks into the door which instantly opened with a delicate pop.

Swiftly closing, then locking the door, he seated himself before the great desk. At the sight of the portrait of Jesus clutching his flame spiked heart, Giordano laid a massive hand over his brow and picked up the heavy receiver. Adjusting his voice scrambler over the mouthpiece as he dialed—

0 0 1 1 . . . .

The phone rang in a darkened room as a hand fumbled for the invisible chain and tugged. Heavy footsteps sliding across yellowed linoleum shuffled their way towards the pealing ring.

"Yeah-what . . ." the gravelly voice chewed noisily.

"Ma? That you?"

A stagnant lull. Chewing and static.

"No," came the sarcasm. "She ain't here at the moment. She's out with the Duke of Danbury this evening."

"Come on, Ma, let's stop this already. Isn't this "Madre Arestia—"

"Hey. It's a mother's Divine right to know what her good for nothing kids are up to." She coughed deeply away from the phone. "And what's with the voice scrambler—it's not like I know your voice no matter how you try to hide it."

"It's not for you, Ma, it's for anyone who might be listening in—anyhow--you okay— MA?"

"Like they don't know already who's calling me??— Can sure tell you grew up watchin' **GET SMART!** --Yeah, sure. I'm fine— my sinuses are leakin' like an old urinal. I can hardly hear, my head feels like I'm under water even when I'm feelin' good . . . .for cryin' out loud, I'm seventy six years old— what the hell do you want anyway?"

"Ma—listen up. ARE . . .YOU. . . OKAY?"

"Look, last I checked, I didn't flush my brains down the toilet. I heard ya already. And, yeah, I got gook like melted mozzarella oozin' down my troat. I got a good for nothing bum for a son. Hey, life's lookin' up, I tell ya."

Static.

"Say, who da hell is this anyway?"

"Your good for nothin' son." Tony grinned and ruffled his hand in his thick greying hair.

Then he dared another glance at the PORTRAIT, when at the corner of his eyes, he notices the edges of a newspaper peeking out from a drawer.

"Enjoyin' your vacation, Tone? Not that I know what a vacation is."

Irresistibly, he pulled it out. A section of the Washington Post. Mechanically, Giordano flipped through it.

"Yeah, sure, Ma. I'd enjoy it better if I knew where my kid was. "Are you going to let me know if Paoli is okay and where the hell she is?"

"My lips are sealed like your poor, dead father's. "

"Hey—I showed up for the wake."

"Such a look of surprise on his face, too."

Tony's eyes slammed onto the newspaper's heading:

IN MEMORIUM

Giordano, Julienne
In loving memory of Julienne, on her anniversary, 6 October 1987. Only my burning memory left of the cherished times we knew.
But the passion that ignited memory's torch will linger my whole life through.

Eternally, Johann

"Anthony? Ya still there?"

Unhearing, he replaced the receiver in its cradle. The name shattered his thoughts now falling away like fragmented shards of glass. An infinite barrage of memories shrouded him as he dropped the paper and stared out into the raging night.

"Damn!" Giordano violently bunched up the paper and threw it against the door, where it bounced and landed on the scrubbed pine floor. With another oath, he flung himself into the Abbot's oversized chair and rested his grey head in trembling hands.

CHAPTER XVI

Unfortunately for Paula Giordano, she arrived at La Cantatrice Chauvre ten minutes late. If she'd had the good sense to be early, she told herself later, the impending scene might never have played out. She could have gracefully slipped out of the restaurant and saved herself the embarrassment. Maybe, she could have sent a note, a gracious refusal, possibly a vague reference to another engagement.

And then, switch hotels in the morning.

But, no. Such a chain of fortuitous circumstances are not in the stars for one such as Paula Regina Giordano.

The evening began with an audible *ri-i-i-ip,* as her broken nail punctured the weave of her only pair of stockings. Consequently, she ended up having to run to the nearest hosiery shop and beg for any replacement she could get.

And that is why she found herself standing alone in the restaurant's doorway, uncomfortably awkward in her brown skirt because, of course, she's discovered a mud splotch on the back of her new blue dress. And what would follow, would forever brand itself in her mind as a close shave with disaster. A well-played scenario, if she did say so herself.

Hopefully, Paula searched the crowd of diners for a familiar face; an unforgettable set of brown amber green whatever eyes. It was Maurice Larsonnier, seated strategically with his eyes on the door, who spotted her first. With a broad smile, the older Larsonnier jumped up from the table and came running.

Paula stared, confused "Maurice? But I thought . . ."

"What a wonderful surprise," Maurice exclaimed and bent over her hand to kiss it. Face glowing, with seraphic innocence, he added, "Will you not join us this evening, Madame de KGB?"

It was the confident overdone naiveté in his tone, arousing immediate suspicion, but too late, for the happy Frenchman clasped her hand in his and practically dragged her to a table of astonished faces.

One glimpse told her the whole story. Christian's well shaped jaw dropped at the sight of her. His eyes widened in horrified astonishment. And his lips rounded in a silent, French, "What the—" Then, she thought about the note, really thought about the note and how little it sounded like the younger Larsonnier.

*That . . .that, **old** rascal*! Her eyes sliding sideways to fix a scathing stare on the cheerful Frenchman beside her.

Coming to the same, instant conclusion, Christian inwardly lurched. Oh, his father knew him well; well enough, in fact, that his most carefully worded denials hadn't fooled the older Larsonnier. Christian Larsonnier wore the unmistakable signs of smitten.

And now, here she was, standing so close, he could detect her perfume, a light citrus and spice blend that made him think of Moroccan nights. So near, he could reach up and tangle his fingers in the rich, brunette cloud . . .

Do something, you idiot. Christian blinked. *Well, she's been far too good a soldier this far. I won't give her the slightest reason to even blush. But, Maman . . .* His eyes flashed across the table, to the face of his observant mother.

What sort of vulgar creature is attached to my Maurice? The detectives never photographed this one. How dare one of his trollops track him in MY presence. Estelle Larsonnier adopted a casual pose, matching her husband's, as if she were viewing an insect discovered in the main course. *She looks Latin. A common whore, no doubt.*

Scalpel please, Paula flushed.

"Paula, love." Christian instinctively jumped to his feet. "I see by your expression; I might have neglected mentioning my parents were also dining with *us* this evening." He pulled out a plush chair, into which she dropped without a word. As he brushed by his father, he whispered, "I applaud your taste, Papa, but did we have to include Maman in this?"

Paula nailed her eyes on Maurice, who seemed oblivious to everything.

Christian cleared his throat. "Maman, I knew you'd never forgive me if I didn't introduce you to Paula."

"Et bien, oui? Estelle arched a perfect brow in mock interest.

"Maman, Miss Giordano is American and knows no French."

"Oh, but--" Paula and Maurice said at once. Their eyes meeting over the table, one green pair, curious, one violet pair, horrified. An eyebrow lifted—she could read her silent question. Giordano? But you told me your name was Martino. *I'm done for, she glumly thought.*

But Maurice surprised her once again. That roguish twinkle reappeared; the ghost of a wink.

"Then, we shall all practice our English tonight, oui? Myself, I am quite proud of my ability in the language. As Poguelin says, 'Always show your front to the world.'"

Estelle's other brow joined the raised one.

"Maurice, what are you talking about? Forever quoting Molière, n'est-ce pas, mon amour?"

Paula's lips twitched.

The younger Larsonnier snapped his fingers to a waiter, who hurried over with an already opened bottle of Pinot Blanc. "Do forgive us for starting without you, Cherie," Christian apologized charmingly. "I, ah, needed a drink."

Yeah, I just bet you did. My God, he's going to see this through. "I was late, after all."

Paula answered his smile with one of her own.

"Rough day?" She resisted adding "dear."

"Er-well," he shrugged. "Quite busy, what with the new Beaujolais, the tourists . . ."

"The Nouveau Beaujolais is quite an occasion in France, my dear," Maurice volunteered. "The cafés and restaurants fill with people eager to sample the latest harvest. Then they argue whether or not it is better than previous years. It is all very exciting."

"Et vous, Mademoiselle," Estelle wondered. "Air you ere to, ah. . . .sample zee harVEST?"

"Miss Giordano is an artist, Maman," Christian quickly informed her. "She is collaborating on a book with Karl Junger."

"Karl Junger, zee historian?" Madame Larsonnier inspected the American more closely. "You air Docteur Jungair's azzosiaht?"

"Actually," Paula took over, more confident now. "We've become very close. Karl was just telling me today that I'm like a daughter to him." *Sorry, Karl, but I'm sure you'd understand.* "I simply *adore* the man."

Suddenly, Estelle's English improved, her tone genuinely inquisitive. "Are you a student at the University, Mademoiselle?"

Paula let out a pleased chuckle. "How very *kind* of you, Madame Larsonnier! No, I'm afraid, I'm not so young."

Then, how did Docteur Junger hear of you? Have you published before?"

With a touching pride in his wife, Maurice put in, "Estelle is a great patroness of the arts, Mademoiselle. She belongs to several organizations in the city supporting the galleries, the opera . . ."

"Why, that must be *fascinating*!" Paula took the cue. "To be involved with the arts in a place where they are truly appreciated." She leaned toward the Frenchwoman and confided, "I wonder if art and music will ever be supported properly in America. You know, I have some friends at the Met. I just *know* they'd love some ideas from someone like yourself. That is, if you would be so kind. . ."

Christian relaxed as his mother showered the young artist with a barrage of questions and advice. *This evening might turn out to be pleasant, after all.* Not that he'd ever doubt Paula's ability to charm the fur off a fox. Certainly, she'd charmed his mother, for there they were, enrapt in a discussion about the use of perspective or something else just as unintelligible.

"Ehh, my son?" He felt a nudge. "Did I do good by you, or what?" Maurice's eyes beamed with pride in his find. "I know, I know," he raised hands in mock defeat. "I over extend myself from time to time. But surely, the results were worth the momentary discomfort." His voice broke above a whisper; his son grimacing.

"But, when I saw her on the train. . ."he continued, lowering his voice at his son's signal.

"It was Kismet." Christian smiled.

"Exactement!" Maurice slapped the table.

The two women were instantly roused from their tete-à-tete. "Vraiment, Maurice," Estelle admonished. "Always you revert to your childhood before one of these foolish club meetings."

"Club meetings?" Paula questioned.

"You see, Mademoiselle," Estelle explained with pride, "My Maurice is one of the famous and last of the very prestigious Voyageurs. Ce soir, they meet to become little boys again, to look at filthy movies and naked whores who come to dance for them." She raised a victorious eyebrow at her husband, as if she knew that such a revelation would ward off any *fond* inclinations this young American might have harbored toward her irresistible mate, or vice-versa.

Oh, I can resist him. "So, what are these voyous, or whatever they're called?"

Both Larsonnier men laughed.

"What's so funny?"

Christian intervened. "Cherie", the term slipping off his tongue almost of itself, "I believe you refer to Les Voy-a-geurs. 'Voyous' means, 'thug' in your language."

"Apropos, none the less." Paula smiled sweetly. "So, what are they, anyway?"

His chin in the air, Maurice proclaimed with hauteur, "We are a very ancient, fur trading associaSHUN, TRUE adventurers." The irresistible grin appeared again and Paula couldn't help herself; she grinned back.

And with that, followed an elegant and savory dinner, courtesy of the Larsonnier sublime palate. Everyone relaxed somewhat, assisted, naturally by the assembly line of wine bottles with each delectable course.

Conveying a sense of coziness, despite its booming business, La Cantatrice Chauvre possess a definite medieval soul. The waitresses, seemingly so rare in French restaurants, masquerading in traditional Alsatian costume; grand silk bows of green, pink or black tied about their heads. Delicate, white chemises, flattering intricately embroidered bodices, with smooth aprons of stiff white cotton over ankle length skirts.

Obscure proverbs advised the clientele from stained glass windows of blue and red, while candlelight gleamed and streamed on wooden walls and polished brass fixtures. Devoid of that ever-present elevator music, the restaurant buzzed with whispered conversations, interrupted only by the occasional clatter of silverware.

Eternally grateful, Christian saw to Paula's every whim, persuading her to sample every dish. Laughing, his smile indulgent, he instructed her in the proper use of the alien pliers and tiny fork, as she gamely plucked the tender snails from their butter laden shells. He scolded her for "baptizing" her wine by also drinking water and coaxed her into, at least, tasting the hot raspberries over vanilla ice cream.

For Paula, the wines mixing a pleasant kind of tingle, basked happily in the attractive Frenchman's indebted attentions. On her absolute best behavior, she praised everything, from the crudités to the cheeses and even restrained herself from asking for more than one dessert from the tempting dessert cart. But, she could not resist a glare from time to time, at the elder, more elegant Larsonnier, who only winked paternally, an on-call tear, welling up in his eye.

Glancing away, she mused, I *wonder if he wears contacts… surely, no one has eyes that color.*

Only once, did Paula's foot inch near her mouth. Somewhere in between the third and fourth dish, she mentioned Yasmine's Place Kleber performance.

"She was grand," Paula enthused. "And the way she sang, well, it made me cry. She gave such feeling to the part. I've seen Christine played before, but . . ."
Suddenly, she realized the table had become oddly quiet.

Estelle stiffened; her expression suddenly withdrawn. Maurice shook his head in warning and she felt Christian's hand touch her, as if telling her something was wrong. *She doesn't approve. She doesn't like Yasmine being on stage.* "Er . . .ah, that is--" she stammered.

"Maurice, stop rattling your head; something will come loose!" Estelle turned to her husband. "Naturellement, I know that Yasmine is singing. And what kind of a guardian, well, "mother" or Aunt, would I be, if I did not? Someday, when you have children, Mademoiselle, you will understand. You watch over them, you think only of them. Jamais, never, never do they listen. Always, they think they know--"

"Ah, but Maman, we've had the finest teacher life could offer," Christian smoothly interposed. "Surely, we should be excused for our over confidence."

Good save, Larsonnier. Paula hid her grin as the Frenchwoman melted in the warmth of her son's adept regard. "It is not dear, little Yasmine that I blame." She flashed a glare at her husband. "Not with such an example to follow."

Christian turned to Paula. "Papa is the family thespian," he explained with a hidden twinkle. "When Maman met him, he was performing a very bad Tartuffe in Paris."

"Ah, so that explains the Molière," Paula laughed. "Monsieur Larsonnier, I had no idea!"

"Neither had the critics," Maurice impishly confessed. "But, every so often, the lure of the stage . . .I find it almost irresistible!" He sighed dramatically. Then his eyes met hers in a secret joke. Paula laughed inwardly, remembering his performance at Haut-Koenigsburg.

Dinner dispersed soon after with an extraction of a promised luncheon. Estelle asked that Paula bring samples of her work; as Maurice pulled out her chair, he whispered his congratulations.

"I haven't forgiven you yet," Paula hissed back, but he only chuckled.

The married couple boarded their Grand Citroën amid another round of good-nights and motored away. Just barely, Paula could hear Estelle scolding her errant husband for some misdemeanor. *Ain't love grand, she smiled wickedly.*

Christian locked elbows with his American "interest," a thousand versions of "I'm sorry" spinning his head. Yet, all he could manage, en route back to the Hotel de la Place, was a meek: "Forgive me."

"For what?" Paula asked. "I had a great time. Though, I gotta admit, your mother was nothing like I expected."

"Expected?" He decided to play along. Maybe she didn't realize. (And maybe he was as smooth as his reputation claimed).

"Well, let me first confess," she said impishly. "I did kind-a fall in love with your old man on the train."

Christian was not at all moved.

"But not the kinda love you'd expect." They walked briskly past the cathedral. The scaffolding now embracing its south and west walls. The rose-colored monument seemed a great spider trapped in a glistening, metallic web. Christian was largely ignoring her. He inwardly rehearsed a thousand ways to coerce her into another date.

"And GOODNESS— he is SO handsome," she sighed. "I guess I saw him with a woman sans brain, no offense. You know, the kind of girl who'd fall for smooth lines, a pretty face. I'm sure YOU'VE met the type. But, not your mother. Nope, she's sharp as a--"

"Paula, will you see me again tomorrow night?" Christian blurted out. His eyes uncertain, he squeezed her arm to make her stop and face him.

"What's with you, Mr. Suave Larsonnier? I thought you playboy types preferred to ride bare back." *(You jerk, to what are you inferring? Too much wine, I can't get my metaphors straight).*

"Please, Paula, just answer."

Paula sighed again, as if struggling internally which way to go. She eyed him carefully. "OH, why not."

His eyes widened; he even swayed a bit. He gripped her shoulders, kissed her on one cheek, then lingered over the other "I'll be in the lobby at five tomorrow evening, then."

"Your eyes are always laughing," Christian said as he fussed with her bangs. "That is what I cannot forget about you: Those laughing violet blue eyes." Smiling now, he kissed her bewildered forehead and gave her a tiny shove in the direction of her hotel.

"I'd say the same about you, if I could just figure out what color yours are." She ignored his rough prompt, taunting his manhood with her smile.

"Flatterer. Now, off you go." He grabbed her arm and lightly pushed her into the revolving door. Then, with a grin, he spun the door round, which quickly popped her indoors and finished through the glass, "Or I shall soon forget I'm a gentleman."

CHAPTER XVII

Planning to take full advantage of the last warm days, Paula wedged her breakfast into her knapsack and made her way to the Church of St. Paul, a somber Romanesque facade on the banks of the gentle Il.

Okay, so it's not part of Karl's list, she told herself as she found a spare bench on the river bank. *But, all work and no play...* Digging into her bag, she found her cache of raspberry preserves (filched from the hotel's breakfast room) and dabbled a hearty portion onto a brioche. *And now, for the coffee...* She unearthed her new thermos and poured a full, long-awaited cup. *Ahh...* Crossing jeaned legs so they stretched out in front of her, the American sat back and let herself dream.

Easy to do in such a setting. The lazy Il twined itself around the Centre Ville in a spiral fashion, so it was nearly impossible to walk very far without seeing a bridge. And here she could see several, for at St. Paul's spire, the river forked not once, but twice, on both sides of the church. And what a view, with the old brick bridges gracefully spanning the river and the stately buildings of the university on either bank.

For an hour or so, she sketched, or rather, she tried to. Her pencil seemed to have its own plans. Yes, and then a smile, one lovely, strong nose... *Give it up, Paoli. You aren't getting anything done today.*

Say, isn't Karl's apartment supposed to be somewhere around the university? Paula considered dropping in. *Nah... One just doesn't drop in on Europeans, no matter how friendly.*

Her mail! Anticipation bubbling, she rummaged through her backpack and withdrew the stack of letters from the States. A postcard from Marella — she smiled — where did she manage to come up with a postcard of a garbage scow floating on the Hudson River?

> Paoli,
> Just to remind you what you're passing up.
> Emiliano's splitting up. — again.
> Roberta engaged — again. O.B.

She turned the card over again and studied the glossy photograph. Croton's Senasqua Park, the glittering Hudson River and in the background, she could see the New York City skyline, the twin towers, the Empire State . . . Something misted her eyes.

Let's see . . . bills, overdue library books . . . — Someone's watching me. She stiffened, the nape of her neck bristling, her heart beating faster. Sitting quite still as if she were still reading her mail, Paula slipped one hand under the flap of her backpack. *Where's the . . . there.* Her hand gripped tight the small black box. She swiveled around.

Yasmine hovered on the sidewalk, passing behind the bench as if unsure she should approach or not. She jumped too, at Paula's sudden movement.

"Oh! I am so sorry; did I —Pah-ola, are you alright?" She stammered, for Paula was doubled over, clasping her chest.

Thump-thump-thump-thump. Breath in, breath out, breath in — "Just catching my breath," Paula gasped. "You startled me!"

"Oh, I am SO sorry," Yasmine said again as she gracefully sank down on the bench next to Paula, who was still shaking. "I never thought . . ."

"This sounds nuts, but lately, I've had this— I mean, since I was mugged."

Paula suddenly realized she was babbling and incomprehensibly babbling at that, for once again the perfect face frowned in perfect confusion. "Oh, never mind. Were you looking for me?"

Yasmine shook her head. She had her hair back in a ponytail, so it bobbed back and forth as she spoke. Yes, a real, fifties style ponytail, only a cheerleader would dare wear in public and she looked like a million, sultry bucks. "The theater is over that way." The black head nodded to the right, and the ponytail brushed a pore less (Paula could swear) cheek. "I had an early dance class."

Paula eyed her with a twinge of envy. *What is it with French women? In an old pair of pink stretch pants, baggy cotton sweater and a scarf carelessly draped around her neck, Yasmine looked like the cover of a fashion magazine. In the same outfit, the only fashion statement she could possibly make, would be "slob." And how do they sit so . . . straight all the time? I need another brioche,* she decided miserably. "You don't look like you've been sweating," Paula criticized as she pulled out the jelly jar. "Would you like a roll?"

Yasmine's exotic eyes rested on the gooey offering. "N-n-non, merci."

Oh, ho! So, you've got a sweet tooth, do you? "Suit yourself," Paula cooed and slowly, temptingly, she began spreading a thick coating of the tangy jam onto the softly powdered rolls. Yasmine watched intently as the American bit into the first. "Mmmmm," Paula sighed rapturously.

The Frenchwoman blinked rapidly. "Err, I did want to apologize, Pah-ola. For what I said at the bus stop."

"Oh, really?" Paula wiped away a crumb from her chin. "All you did was defend your uncle. I can't fault you for loyalty." She took another deep bite and added, with her mouth full, "As a matter of fact, I'm seein' him tonight."

Lips licked. "Vraiment? But, what about your, ah, Lance?"

"Lance? Who's — oh, Lance and I have an agreement to see other people. Sure, you don't want a roll?"

"No, merci." Curious, Yasmine picked up the postcard from where it lay face-up on the bench. "New York?" She said incredulously.

"It's a joke. Go ahead and read the back. Only, don't ask what O.B. stands for, because it isn't repeatable." So she did, while Paula began to open the next envelope.

"Who is Roberta?"

Paula was busy unfolding the piece of paper she'd pried from the plain white envelope. One side of the lined paper was torn, as if it had been ripped from a notebook, no, more like one of those old composition books. "A cousin," she answered. "Well, wait, a second cousin really. She makes a habit of getting engaged, loaning the guy every penny she's got and then getting dumped — oh, no, not again!" Paula stared in stupefaction at the scrawled verse.

Yasmine peeked over her shoulder and read aloud. "Captain, my Captain — I don't understand. Is this another American joke?"

She turned the paper over. Nothing. "No. I mean, I don't know. I don't understand it, either. At first, I thought it was Marc, but now . . ."

The Frenchwoman actually giggled. "When Marc is in love, he writes his own poetry. It rhymes and is very bad, but rather sweet, really." She pretended to find a speck of lint on an impeccable white tennis shoe, hiding the slight flush as she bent over to flick it away.

So, so, so! A hopeless love affair, maybe, between the servant's son and the princess of the dynasty? What would Uncle Christian say if he knew Marc Rouget had an eye on his precious niece? Paula barely contained the cynical snicker. *So much for liberty, equality and fraternity.* Interest piqued, she promised herself a further, more in depth inquiry over a bottle of chianti (the time-honored truth serum of Italians everywhere).

Must be tough for her to get a date, or be asked anywhere with a face like that and an uncle like that. Musing upon the back of the woman's head, Paula recalled Marella's words: "If she's that gorgeous, she hasn't got a friend in the world . . ." *Okay, okay, Marella, I'll try and look past it.* She cleared her throat.

"Uh, Yasmine, I have absolutely nothing to wear tonight, except one brown skirt that the female lead wore in *Planet of the Librarians.* Maybe, we could go shopping . . . that is, if you don't have to work?"

Pleasure lit Yasmine's face. "I would like that very much," the Frenchwoman at once assented. "Uncle is at the shop today, so I am quite free."

"Good, then let's do the works — all the boutiques, a manicure, hair . . . You can let me in on the secret."

Yasmine looked puzzled. "Secret?"

"Yeah." Paula waved a hand toward her apparel. "How do you French women do it? Like you just got up outta bed, threw on your lover's clothes and said, 'let's go for coffee.' You know . . . sexy!"

For the first time, she heard Yasmine laugh. "Then you must teach me how to appear so relaxed in your blue jeans. I am so envious of you American women."

"A day of cultural exchanges." Paula was beginning to enjoy the idea. "Then we'll split a pizza at a little place I've been eyeing across from Le Printemps."

Yasmine made a mournful face. "I adore pizza," she sighed. "But, I gain weight very easily."

Paula grinned like the Cheshire Cat. "Yasmine," she said as she pushed the last of the jellied brioches toward the Frenchwoman's end of the bench. "This looks like the beginning of a fattening friendship."

CHAPTER XVIII

Warm amber light tunneled onto a shiny stone wall like search lights through the smokey ancient chamber as smoke rings from multiple sources spiraled in every direction over a massive oak table.

Multiple sets of eyes, peered through the nicotine fog.

"I'll meet that bet and raise you two truffles."

Eyes ping ponging to the opposite side of the table.

"I'm calling your bluff and I'll raise you three tins of foie gras to your two truffles."

"Four Truffles."

"Honestly, Tony who's your supplier?"

"Hey, I never plan a trip here without stocking up."

"Okay, I'm done. I mighta stayed in the game if you were willing to throw in the pig with those four truffles."

"Show your hand, Tone."

"Gladly, Marty."

With a confident grin, Tony Giordano slapped his cards on the table.

"Straight House." His eyes gloating at the five cards in hearts.

Brother Marty responding in kind, slid his hand onto the table.

"Check it out Tone— the best possible lineup: A Royal Flush. Whaddya say to that?" Marty's sparkling eyes betraying his triumph.

"Okay, you got me this time, Marty. How about another hand? Gimme a chance to win back some of my truffles."

"Not a chance, Tone. I can't remember when I last had truffles."

"Handy that you work in the kitchen so that you can spice up your— or should I say— *our* meals. I know you know all about that "spirit of charity" that we all must abide by."

"Won't that certain *aroma* rouse Father Abbot's sensibilities?"

Marty's smile turned serious. "I doubt he has any sense of smell left at his age."

Laughter around the old table broke the tense mood as the brothers counted up their winnings.

"How about a brew or two?" Brother Vinny interjected.

"Well, the Abbot is gonna have our hides if he ever found out how we repurposed the old crypt side chapel here. Besides, it's not like there are any more stiffs in here. They moved every*body* to the renovated part of the crypt."

"Besides, at least tonight, I know he's packing for another one of his trips—some ecumenical conference or other."

The quietest of the "gamblers" spoke up.

"You guys really think he has no clue?" Brother Jerome pointed out.

"I got the brews chillin' just outside the old entrance here," said another gambler, his tins of foie gras clinking as he rose from the crime scene to bring in the liquid gold.

"Thanks, Vinny. I'll get the beer steins," said the tall, older monk, Brother Albert.

Clinking, and clanging— toasts raised, brews enjoyed: Glazed chestnuts, figs, walnuts all passed around to accompany the brothers' midnight rendezvous. The mood shifting to a more serious tone.

"So, Brother Anthony," began one of the monks, "how are things going in your search for your daughter?"

Tony's relaxed posture stiffened. "Well, between my old contacts in Alsace, I've narrowed the search down to eastern France and then lately, Strasbourg. Seems she must have gotten short on cash and started using my credit card."

"You're not worried that maybe her funds and credit cards were stolen?"

"Anything is possible. I'm not ruling anything out."

"We're here to help. What are old comrades in arms— old birds of a feather good for anyhow, once they retire?"

"This sure does seem to have been the hide out— I mean landing place for many of us in the business."

"What is the saying? Old spies never die, they just —- fade away?"

"Nahhh. Not fade away. PRAY away."

Laughter.

"Good one, Tone."

Wiping the beer foam on his sleeve, Tony responded, "Well, where else would us old Catholic single guys end up, but a great place like this. A *real* brotherhood, close community of like-minded chaps—- we're really lucky, don't ya think?"

"Here-here, Tone!"

"Here-here," one after another chimed in.

Brother Marty was the first to break the spell, rising abruptly from his seat, pockets bulging with his well-earned, precious truffles.

"That's a wrap, guys, uh, I mean, bros."

"Yep, let's get ourselves to our cells where we shoulda been for the last . . ." Brother Albert glanced at his watch, "oh... three or four hours."

"Who's got goat duty tomorrow—I mean today?" Brother Vinny asked.

"Dunno," Tony yawned. "I'm doin' the bees this week."

Laughter all around. "Be careful, Tone. Remember what happened last time."

"Yep."

"Has Father Abbot challenged you to your usual game of chess?"

"No, not yet. I think, maybe he won't since I managed to checkmate him the last time."

Chuckles all around.

"Well, I'm in the cheese building this week." Brother Jerome boasted. "And I'm so glad I never learned to play chess!"

As the brothers exited their makeshift casino, they all quietly replaced their hoods on their heads and noiselessly returned to the upper monastery without so much as a squeak.

The next day, proved to be a sparkling sunny day. Tony, emerged from a shed, in what he called his "astronaut-or HAZMAT getup" and headed for the bees.

Smiling to himself as he headed for the apiary, he thought, *wish I got a little more sleep seein' as I have to deal with the bees today . . .*

Down the steep hillside, the crisp Autumn sun bleaching eternal rows of carved stone . . . Under the dappled shade of a dying pine, Brother Anthony decided he would take a few moments before he executed his duties and dusted the brown, dry needles from a bench and sat down. Way down the steep slope in the distance, two men in caps were raking fallen leaves into loose piles. A lone plane reflected the sunlight as it passed overhead. He could just make out the sound of its engine as it disappeared from sight. The two men clambered into their truck and jostled away.

Alone with his thoughts and the stones, he closed his eyes and remembered . . .

"How very shameless you are, Monsieur! And in broad daylight!" She gently pushed her lover away. "And your Maman, she is right to hold fast to her rosary."

"She knows that every priest in Europe knows her writing on the offering envelopes." He pulled her hair away from her face. "And every variation of my name."

"Let us see . . ." Playfully, she screwed up that delicate nose in concentration. "And that would be "Anton, Tony, Tone, Antoine, Antonio . . ." She giggled helplessly. "Bon Dieu, but I forget! I shall simply call you--"

Tony pulled her to him and kissed her fervently.

"Antoine, please! I must insist!" She managed to wrestle away.

"Okay, okay," he relented and the two slid down the side of a tall palm, sitting close to watch the sunset over an emerald sea.

"Mmmmm . . . smell the jasmine on the wind. Oh, watch now, it is almost time." She squeezed his fingers.

Head-to-head, the two sat motionless, rapt in awe as the pink sun touched the water and instantly kindled the sea into an eternity of brilliantly burning ripples.

"Ahhh," she sighed rapturously. "C'est Magnifique."

He smiled at her enthusiasm. The flaming balloon sank deeper and deeper into the horizon as the light film of twilight floated over Cannes.

"Time to get back," he finally said and helped her to her feet. "My plane leaves at midnight."

In silent reverie, they walked along the boardwalk, his mind already away on another continent.

SQUEAK-SQUEAK-SQUEAK

"Damn." Tony glared at the quarrelsome buggy wheel. "I meant to fix that before I left."

"Oui, Well, still it will be here when you return." Her light tone dispelled any complaint; she never complained about his absences, and that made him feel even worse.

Giordano shrugged it off, after all, he had a living to earn. His eyes fell on the toddler's face all scrunched up in a concentrated slumber. He couldn't help laughing. "I think that damned squeak sends in the sandman."

She laughed too. "Ah, oui," she breathed and fussed over the flannel blanket. "It is the only way she will nap every day. She is not meant for the quiet life, this one."

Every evening passed the same. Together, they strolled along the length of the U-shaped walkway, always finding a nuance, a trifling bit of awe at every turn. From the sound of the sails clapping to the temper of the Mistral-like snatching gusts, to the rows of tiny blue lights that dotted the shore, refracting bluish streams along the cozy harbor . . .

Tony opened his eyes, the honey bees buzzing. Jarring him from his past. "Damned bugs" he muttered and rubbed his tearing eyes.

Waiters raced up and down the winding stairs of the two-story restaurant, some shouting orders through the window to the kitchen, others balancing clinking arrays of bottles and citrus slices clinging to glasses.

One pm - the height of lunch hour. The buzz of murmuring voices rising from the leather booths lining the narrow aisle. Stuck, as usual, in a corner under abandoned coats and hats, Paula pushed away a sleeve and poured them both another glass. "Then, you and Marc aren't serious."

"Bah." Yasmine waved her glass in the air. "Who has time for men? It is all that I can do, to work and sing."

Yet another waiter approached the table — Paula had long ago lost count — and soulfully asked Yasmine if she needed anything else. She lifted a hopeful eyebrow to Paula.

"Dessert?"

"Do you have any chocolate mousse?" Paula asked the waiter, but, of course, he didn't hear her, so Yasmine had to repeat the question in French.

"Bien sûr," the ogling waiter managed. Hurrying off to do her bidding, he tripped over a loosened fragment of carpet, then juggled the emptied bottles to safety.

"Do you always have that effect on waiters?" Paula wondered.

Yasmine shrugged uncaringly. "Waiters, clerks, doormen, butlers, tailors, accountants, policemen--"

"Okay, okay, I get the picture. Just don't make me feel any worse —PLEASE."

"It is sometimes messy, yes?"

A clatter of plates, and the busboy fumbled to catch the pile of dirty dishes as they slid off his tray. The women looked at one another and tried to stifle a shared giggle.

"We should all have such problems," Paula sighed. "Do you sing again soon?"

"Thursday evening, I . . . oh, what is the word . . . I stand in for the troupe's diva. I will be Gilda in Rigoletto." A frown actually marred the perfect forehead. "Aunt Estelle, she does not approve."

"Yes, I, ah, gathered that."

"This is very . . . traditional, vous comprenez? She is only trying to do the best thing." A fond smile touched her lips. "Uncle Christian, he talks her into it, and I sing anyway. But, I do not like to upset my Aunt. She has been very good to me."

"Say, not to pry", Paula interrupted, "but how is it that it's both 'Uncle Christian' and 'Uncle Maurice'?"

"Ah, yes, exactly. You see, both of my parents died many years ago, leaving me an orphan with no other family. And since Uncle Christian and my father were very close, like brothers, I ended up here with the Larsonniers."

The waiter brought their desserts in record time providing a perfect detour to the awkward conversation. Paula noted with resignation that Yasmine had been given twice as much, while she — "he forgot to give me a spoon."

Yasmine craned her already lengthy neck in search of a waiter. "I'll just -Pah-ola-- She lowered her voice. "Do you know Henri De Bourchegrave?"

"What, that creep? Is he here?"

Gasping, the French woman grabbed Paula's arm and yanked before she could look. "No," she hissed. "Do not encourage him. He has been watching you for several minutes."

Paula found her trusty compact in her backpack and opened it. Sure enough, all too familiar black eyes glittered from the far end of the restaurant — their burning intensity made her shiver. "Ooooh, he sure gives me the willies."

"If by that you mean, *les horreurs*, I agree." As if to demonstrate, Yasmine shuddered.

She closed her compact with a snap. "I wonder if he's the one sending me the poetry. Though, I really can't see old Henry as a fan of Walt Whitman. I think I'm going to go have a little chat with him."

Yasmine stopped her as she began to stand. Her face going pale, she pleaded, "No, Pah-o-la, do not! What if he--"

"What's he going to do in a crowded restaurant? Really, Yasmine, if you want to go to New York, you'll have to learn to handle bums like him." Paula sat back down. "Anyhow, he's gone." The door was still swinging over the café curtain, as she caught a glimpse of shiny black hair. "Coward." Then, she realized Yasmine was still shaking. "Has he bothered you before?"

The French woman shook her head. "No, he would not dare. Not when Uncle" ---She bit her lower lip. "Stay away from him, Pah-ola- *Please!*"

Paula stared back at her in surprise. "Of course, Yasmine".

She didn't look reassured. Her black eyes darkened even more as she dipped into the rich chocolate mousse.

Whoa, just a minute, Paolina Regina Giordano. How can you be such a perfect dunce? Even to someone as dense as you, it's pretty obvious her uncle had some kind of a thing going with Henri's wife. There's bound to be some bad blood there. Not to mention, Yasmine's probably embarrassed that her idol's got faults, just like the rest of us mere mortals. Paula stabbed at the frothy chocolate. Suddenly everything seemed . . .flat.

"Oh, there you are!"

That whiny, breathless voice, all too familiar from a hundred telephone messages. "I've been looking all over for you, and --"

Suzie, Paula winced.

Hair frizzing out in all directions from under a brown felt fedora with an orange feather, an overly tight orange jumpsuit betraying every bulge, Suzie stood expectantly.

Paula glanced at Yasmine, who was staring up at the distraught American with a fascinated gleam in her eyes. "How many times do I have to tell you? Go away! Go find yourself a real boyfriend and stop this fantasy—this obsession you have with my father—he's an OLD man and NOT interested really in ANY woman! AND JUST STAY away from me!"

"Come on, Paoli!" Suzie wheedled. "I just want to know where he is, that's all."

"Forget it! Listen, Suzie," Paula lowered her voice. "There was never anything between you. It's all in your mind--- you definitely misunderstood somehow...I'm tellin' ya--Hell, I don't even know where he is. Now, please, just go home."

Tears were threatening; *Oh, Lord. Not another scene!*

"You don't understand, Paolina. You don't know what it's like to love somebody, not really. Please, Paoli!" The whine increased in pitch, like a factory whistle as Suzie fumbled with her shredded tissue. "Tell him, I miss him--"

It was Yasmine who intervened. "Pardon me, Mademoiselle." The Frenchwoman's voice carried through the restaurant, resounding with such strength and authority, that for several moments, complete hush reigned throughout the establishment.

Stunned-captivated, Paula gawked in awe.

Yasmine's dark eyes fixed upon Suzie's widened pair. She stood mesmerized, motionless, like a helpless mouse staring into the eyes of a famished feline. In the same calm voice, as she dropped a pile of francs onto the table, Yasmine said, "We are leaving now. You will not follow us. Come, Pahola."

"Er, yes." Paula shook off her own amazement, quickly gathering her bags and followed the French woman out of the restaurant. Suzie stood frozen, unmoving.

The door closed behind them. Paula looked at Yasmine with new respect. "Yasmine, that was . . . that was *incredible*! How did you do that?"

Yasmine, perched a pair of sunglasses on her nose. "Voice lessons," she explained. "One must learn to hold the attention of an audience." Shivering, she added, "Such an appalling woman. There is such an orange aura surrounding her."

"Her outfit," Paula cracked.

A faint smile touched the unglossed lips. The French woman shook her head ruefully, the bobbing ponytail, an exclamation point. "Certainment, but, you have definitely stirred things up in our little city, my friend."

CHAPTER XIX

"What a complete jerk! I can't go out looking like this!" Disgusted, Paula tore off the lime green jumpsuit in question.

Flinging the garment across the room, it landed in a crumple atop a pile of discarded clothing now blocking the bathroom door. Well, so much for jeans, jumpsuits, pantsuits, long skirts and just about any other outfit she had in the closet.

Shoes and jewelry were sent tumbling from the bed with an outstretched, impatient arm. Sitting down, thoroughly depressed, she thought, *well, this is just great! I have absolutely nothing —NOTHING to wear.*

"What would Marella make of this guy?" *He's nuts! He's gotta be; just look at his letters! Or, he's even smoother than most of 'em! He's gonna drive ya crazy till ya just get too tired to fight him off!* "Yeah, that's what she'd say."

The shrill of the phone interrupted her thoughts as she dashed to the nightstand.

"Yes?"

"Whisper to your gigolo lover that you're quite bored of him and his replacement waits very patiently in the lobby."

Paula nearly dropped the receiver as she turned to look at the time. "Christian! Is it seven o'clock already?" *Where's that damned travel clock? Ah—under the bed where I threw it this morning.*

"I'm probably early. My wristwatch doesn't seem to be working properly."

Next, he'll say they don't make those Swiss jobs like they used to.

"Give me five minutes, okay? I . . .um, just have to wash the pastels off my hands; I was in the middle of a sketch."

Paula replaced the receiver and once again considered the heap of rejected finery. *Hm. One last bag . . .* The elegant woman on the side of the silver-grey plastic sack seemed to be waiting, as if she'd known all along, this was *the* dress for the evening.

Hesitating a minute more, Paula slowly reached into the bag, her fingers meeting with such a soft sensation, she closed her eyes, relishing the tickling feeling. *Angora . . .This shouldn't be wasted on sheep.*

Nervously, she unwrapped the delicate tissue, gently unfolding the arms, then held the dress to her bare skin. Completely different from anything she'd ever owned: A cream colored fluff of Angora perfection, with large dramatic shoulders, puffed sleeves and a neckline that flirted with her delicate collarbone. Even the hemline exposing the knee seemed risqué . . .

Paula studied her reflection with merciless candor for a moment more as a slight, satisfied smile curved at her lips "Not bad. Not *bad* at all." Humming to herself, she slipped the dress over her head. *Tony's orbs are gonna pop out when he gets the credit card bill for all this. . . . . . . But, Yasmine was right to insist on getting this— plus the new do—* "Yes, indeed, not bad at all," Paula mused out loud with one final turn in the mirror.

Ring-ring-ring— Ring-ring-ring!

The transformed young woman, froze, staring at the telephone— contemplated for a moment whether or not to answer it. *Never know— it could be Marella or something important....*

"Hello, yes?"

"Paulina?"

"Uh."

"Uh—what--It's Melanie!! Remember me? — your *oldest* college partner in crime, best friend from those bygone days of Jazz Lounge gigs?"

"Oh— MELANIE— HOW ARE YOU!! *Crap! I totally forgot about Melanie— Sheez, Paula, doesn't take much to wipe your brain cells out!*

"Wow, Melanie— I was just thinking about you!" Paula lied. "How's the concert tour going?"

"It's going really WELL! But, I'm not calling, fishing for compliments or to just chat about me— I wanted to give you my address here in the area. *REMEMBER??* Oh, Paoli, you haven't changed, ever the absent minded one.... Anywho....
Bill took a month's leave, so we rented a *gorgeous* gite here in the area. In Mundolsheim. It's about 10 or so minutes outside of Strasbourg. It's even got an indoor pool— which CJ is just thrilled about...... makes him happy being homeschooled when you get to have such perks!"
Paula glanced at her watch— *Christian, must be thinking I'm pulling a Diva's late entrance schtick.* She smiled. *I kinda like that . . .*

"Yes, give me your number there and the address. I can't wait to see it— and of course all you guys too!"

The Diva jotted down all the info as another thought crossed her mind.

"But, does this dream gite have a *piano*?"

"I'll wait for you to come and see for yourself tomorrow. We're still on for you moving in with us for the duration, right?"

Paula glanced around her simple, but nice accommodation, then began tallying in her head the cost against her modest stipend.

"Are you *kidding?* Thanks so much for the invite, but that would have to be the day after tomorrow. I've been invited to a Masquerade at Koenigsburg Castle…. And after that— we'll *really* have TONS of catching up to do! Can't wait! I wouldn't miss staying with you guys for the world! Listen— believe it or not, I got a date waiting for me in the lobby. He's bound to start thinking that I've stood him up. I'll touch base day after tomorrow about my ETA to your place."

"Fabulous! We're at 1111 rue de Mundolsheim and our number is….

Okay— got it! SO, glad to hear from you, Melanie— till then!"

"Bye- doll— till then!"

Christian opened his hands, palms up. "Where did it go?" He exclaimed to his rapt audience.

Three small children stared wide-eyed at his empty hands.

"Ah, wait a moment!" The Frenchman pretended to examine the head of the youngest, a little girl in a demure smock dress who shook with shy giggles. His hand snatched out and suddenly, he clutched a coin between two fingers.

"Voila!"

The children clapped with excitement as Christian offered the coin to the little girl before she scampered off to show her parents. His eyes followed her, with a strange kind of sadness mixed with satisfaction.

"Bonjour Christian." Paula startled him with her sudden appearance. "So, you're a magician too."

Christian just stared in reply with a stunned expression on his face.

"So . . .Are you going to say anything?"

"If I were Houdini himself," he murmured, "I could not summon a more lovely vision than you, here and now. And if I truly were a jewel thief, like my father, I would reform, for even the brightest gems are mere trinkets after a glimpse of your eyes." Bowing, then taking her hand, he softly kissed it as their eyes met as if making a secret pact.

Hoping not to blush, "I take it, you like the dress."

With difficulty, his eyes left hers.

"Er— why, yes! I like the dress. No, I love the dress!" Touching her check with tender fingers, he went on, "this week has been so tediously long."

Paula darted a glance toward the desk through lowered lashes; the clerk dropped his gaze a fraction of a second too late and noisily shuffled papers on the counter.

"I think we have an audience."

"Yes, of course." Larsonnier grinned rakishly. "Emile's son. Quite the gossip. Let's indulge him, shall we?" Before she could — or would— protest, the Frenchman swept her up and swung her out the door.

Paula waved an airy goodbye to the nosy desk clerk, as they sailed past the front door.

"*Really*, some people need a life."

Their carefree laughter mingled with the festive mood of Place de la Cathédrale. Vendors accosted the pedestrians with their beads, necklaces, leather hats and various unusual toys. Late season tourists snapped pictures of their families before the horse drawn carriages. The mimes were gone, but a Caribbean ensemble played loud and lively music in the crisp autumn air.

"Come on! Let's listen!" Paula begged, grabbing his arm. The Frenchman good naturedly letting her drag him along.

They weaved their way through the circle of listeners and found a spot just a few meters from the band. Dressed in costumes of bright island colors, the musicians smiled at their audience as they performed a lively calypso on their various instruments.

Larsonnier leaned closer. "Makes me wish for warmer weather."

"Sand and palm trees," Paula sighed. Her toe tapped the irresistible beat. "A beach party, with lots of seafood and a sunset . . . And dancing, lots of dancing!"

Suddenly grabbing her arm, Christian led her into the open spot before the musicians. He flung a few Francs into one of the hats on the cobblestones, snatched her other arm and began dancing.

Embarrassed and a little shocked, Paula tried to make an escape. But, Christian only held on tighter as they calypso'd amidst the lively beat and the Strasbourgeois.

"Bravo! Bravo!"

The surrounding crowds cheered and several others joined in on this impromptu scene with coins brimming in the musicians' hats. The music changed rhythm, never taking the couple off guard, as if they'd danced all of their lives together. They danced for an hour, or maybe two, holding each other, laughing, giggling, totally captivated with one another.

The last rays of the golden sun touched the steeple's top, when the musicians abruptly ended the concert. Time to go. The crowd in the square thinned, the tourists moving on to their next destinations, the natives back to their homes.

Paula and Christian still embraced, lightly dancing, rocking back and forth. Everything in the world seemed to stop. No tourists, no traffic, no music. Unaware of everything but one another, the man and woman danced on. Only the pigeons went about their business as usual.

The cathedral's doors swung open to thundering organ music, shattering the silence of the cobblestoned streets of old Strasbourg.

Christian slowly released Paula from his embrace, reluctantly breaking the spell. He said almost inaudibly. "So beautiful. As if we're intruding . . ."

"Hmmm . . . yeah . . ." Paula closed her eyes, taken away with the music.

He wrapped an arm around her. "What do you say? Shall we go in and enjoy the concert — another concert for a bit? Looking at her with twinkling eyes, "not exactly island music, no dancing here."

Crossing the great gothic threshold, nothing quite prepared Paula for what she was now seeing and most of all, feeling. Not all the tour guides, photographs, brochures, nothing came close to the reality of this ancient, holy place. Her eyes rose upward, as if drawn toward the lofty arches and tremendous pillars. First, a small tingle, then a sudden rush of chills ran through her as she stood motionless, taking in the profound beauty and the hushed atmosphere of this medieval, sacred space as the organist pounded with furious exuberance consuming the sanctuary with a Bach Toccata and Fugue. Paula felt as if she too were consumed, cradled in a strange and quiet peace.

Christian lingered at the entrance as if he appreciated what Paula felt. She left him there and wandered down the aisle toward the main altar. Her heels tapping against the giant blocks of sandstone, blending with the sounds of other tourists moving throughout the great gothic edifice.

The organist ending his song, leaving only lingering echoes. The hush that befell the church only enhanced the beauty of Bach's masterpiece. Murmuring voices rose to a crescendo against echoing walls.

Having traveled throughout Europe with her various "careers", Paula was no stranger to these amazing cathedrals, yet it always seemed to affect her the same way with each visit. It never got old.

Wow, that was incredible, she thought as she made her final inspection of the outlying chapels. *Christian! Gosh, I hope he hasn't given up on me.* Spotting him back at the entrance, she sighed, *there he is, waiting patiently.*

They didn't say anything at all as they left the church, still overcome by the brooding tranquility. Outside the south door, Paula whispered, as if still inside, "It's so beautiful, so magnificent. . . . I just can't express how much I appreciate — no wrong word— how much it affected me."

"I know exactly what you mean," he squeezed her arm as they started descending the sandstone steps.

Paula lingered behind to gawk at the sculptures encircling the three wooden doors. The foolish virgins, the wise, the tempter . . . each could stand alone on its own artistic merit. "Gosh, I'll have to come back here first thing, take some pictures for the book for reference and maybe sketch a few reliefs. You know, I read that all these sculptures, I think they number about two thousand— when cleaning the exterior, it was discovered that originally, all these statues were painted in vivid colors. Can you imagine what an amazing sight all the villagers here would have had? Not to mention how long and tedious the work to paint all of these would have been! It just takes your breath away! Karl wants me to try and capture all that— I hope I'm up to the task!"

Suddenly losing her balance, narrowly missing a tumble down the few steps, Paula awkwardly slid to the brick landing. Christian barely realizing what was happening before she sat hard on the cobblestones, clutching a shoe.

"Zut, alors!" He gasped and knelt at her side. "Are you alright? Are you hurt?"

"Never mind *me*! Look at my shoe!" Paula held out the beige leather pump, now heelless, for his inspection. Three thousand Francs," she pronounced with hearty disgust. "That's what this is, three thousand Francs. Never—*never*—NEVER in my entire life had I ever dreamed about wearing shoes that expensive."

She shook her head sadly. "But, they really were exquisite, you know. So, I get carried away and dream a little and where does it get me?"

Christian was trying very hard to suppress his laughter, but without success. Eyes dancing with charm and warmth, he promised "I will tell you where it gets you . . ." Briskly, he whisked her off the cold stone surface and cradled her easily into his arms.

Slowly, Paula put her arms around his neck, eyes never leaving his, heart beating in six-eight time. A charge shivered through her, very like static electricity.

Upon reaching the bottom step, Paula squirmed and broke the stalemate. "Are you crazy, Christian? What are you thinking of? Everyone's staring!"

"Do you really think so?" Christian only shrugged. "This is France, remember, where a little public affection shocks no one. At any rate, tell me the truth, can you move that left foot?"

"Yes!" Paula answered automatically.

"Well, go ahead then, if you must. Try to move it." Larsonnier waited knowingly as she flexed her toes.

"OUCH! I guess you are right."

"So, let me indulge myself," he suggested and proceeded toward his parking spot beside the Chateau de Rohan. "It isn't every day that I can play the gallant to a lovely American. At any rate," he continued, "there is one thing that puzzles me, and perhaps, you can solve it."

"Hmm . . .What's that?" Paula tried to listen, but couldn't, engrossed as she was in surveying all the smiling, chuckling passersby.

"Well, why is it you Americans have this rather nasty habit of putting price tags on everything? It seems to me, that with you people, beauty is rated by its cost in dollars."

Paula released her hold on his neck and raised a hand, hitting him squarely on his left cheek. "Honestly— what a lousy thing to say! Put me down right *now*!"

A smile playing at his lips, Christian relinquished his hold and the American slid down. "Just where do you get off saying something like that? Price tag on beauty . . . That's such a pompous thing to say . . .really, Christian, sometimes I think you just try to find the most appalling things to say to me in order to get a reaction! — Stop smiling at me! I'm serious!"

Hopping away, Paula tried to limp on her injured foot. This time, The Frenchman anticipated her fall, rushing just in time, to her rescue.

"Here, let me--"

"Forget it!" Paula shoved him causing them both to lose their balance. Ending up in a laughing heap on the cobblestone street, Christian pointed a well-manicured finger at his target.

"For your information," Larsonnier informed her, grinning widely, "I never buy anything on sale."

The American struggled to her feet and began hobbling on one foot. She held out a hand to her companion. He grabbed it and held it tightly as he rose to his feet. Catching her completely off guard, Christian drew her to him and planted a stern stare directly into her mischievous violet eyes, caressing her face lightly with his fingertips, enchanted with that curious purple light in them. Brushing her dark bangs from her forehead and kissing her very gently there.

"Let's get you off that foot." Christian picked her up again, but this time, Paula did not protest, perfectly pleased just where she was.

"So . . .The Frenchman began. "Believe it or not, I know just the cure for that foot." Once installed in the front seat, he knelt beside her to examine her foot.

"You know, I think that this is nothing so serious. It looks as though you probably only twisted it a bit. I would say most of the agony was suffered by this." He pointed to the disfigured shoe in his hand.

Paula wanted to say something, but Christian put his finger to her lips, stopping her.

"Please, let me apologize for what I said back there." His carefully phrased words were sincere. "You must understand that when speaking a foreign language, so much becomes muddled in the translation. Up here," he pointed to his forehead, "the slightest, most innocent of comments, become insults without warning. Yes, I have mastered the words, but trust me, the subtleties are quite foreign to me. I was only curious to learn if there were any truth to the . . .er . . .the stereotip?"

"Stereotip? I think you mean stereo-*type*," she laughed spontaneously. *Being so close to him should make me uncomfortable*, she thought. But oddly enough, the fact that she was so easy made her uneasy.

Christian shut her door and got in the other side.

"Yes, well stereotypes are interesting, do you not agree? For example, what might an American imagine a Frenchman to resemble? Let us see. . . He would have a dark beret . . ."

"So, where is yours?"

Christian looked amused, but continued. "Do not forget we are all so short, wear thick mustaches . . ."

"And you are all great cooks," Paula finished.

"Chefs," he corrected her proudly. "Anyone can cook."

Larsonnier went on to monopolize the conversation and Paula contentedly listened, pondering their destination.

The streets whizzing by held more beautiful churches, half-timbered buildings and a conglomerate of Renaissance structures Christian identified as the University of Strasbourg.

"So, that's where Napoleon went to school," she mused. "I wonder what the campus was like back then. Maybe for homecoming, they played the Prussians?"

"Home what?"

"Never mind."

The scenery began to change: Autumn yellows and rich greenery of varying sizes became more plentiful as they passed residential areas. They turned onto a smaller street now. Strasbourg seemed another place, far away from this rural setting.

Then suddenly, a dreadful thought occurred to her. "But, what about our date?"

Larsonnier squeezed the American in a gentle rebuke. "You forget, I am French! It takes more than a mere sprain to discourage me. I know just the remedy to save our evening."

CHAPTER XX

Twilight fell into dusk and the lake in the Orangerie shimmered with lights from a restaurant across the water.

"Wait here." Christian carefully bundled her onto a bench and left her there. Without explanation, he strode down the pier toward a little shack perched precariously on the edge of the dock.

Paula amused herself by contemplating the lush park's scenery; a hazy world cooled by sudden autumn gusts, graceful plane trees glistening silver in the last gleam of sunlight. She let her mind drift away, lulled by the falling light and the constant splash of water against the dock.

In minutes, her date returned, accompanied by a little old man in a black beret. They spoke together out of earshot, as the little man pointed to one of the rowboats tied to the pier.

With a nod and a wave, he hurried back inside and Christian joined her at the bench. She began to get just the least bit suspicious.

"What?"

Larsonnier bowed and gestured with a sweeping wave toward the rowboat tied just below. "Your *gondola* awaits, Mademoiselle."

"You *can't* be serious." Paula dubiously inspected the boat. It didn't seem very big for such a *large* lake. "Its nearly dark! And with my luck, I'll probably end up swimming back to shore."

"Come, come, it's just the perfect time of day," he coaxed. "I thought you were game for anything. A little 'joie de vivre'. That's all you need."

"You know, she observed, "I could take that the wrong way."

Her companion's expression changed to embarrassment, then just as quickly, he showed surprise as she burst into a grin.

"This time, it is you who misunderstood. One has nothing to do with the other."

"Touché, mon Frenchman."

"Watch how you say that. I might just take you literally." Despite his bantering tone, the sincerity in his eyes told Paula there might be more behind his words.

All at once the breeze swirled, crooning melodiously.

"Well . . ." *I'm not sure I could say no to this man,* she realized. *I outta be frightened, but I like the feeling. Kind of like falling head first into a river, in the purest figurative sense, that is.* "Okay. If you promise there will be no moonlight swims."

"Not unless you feel the need." Christian helped her into the swaying boat, careful not letting her stand on her ankle.

"So, where's the bottle of wine and the gypsy with the violin?" Paula demanded. Just as she uttered the words, the little man with the black beret rushed out of the cabin, balancing a bottle of champagne and two glasses.

Larsonnier chuckled as her jaw dropped in astonishment. "Touché, petite Americaine. But, we cannot fit the gypsy in the boat, I'm afraid."

"Oh, that's alright. You can hum, instead."

The little man untied the boat and waved the obviously lunatic couple away from the pier. Shaking his greying head, he returned to the warmth of his cabin and his interrupted dinner.

Christian removed his jacket and offered it to Paula. "So, you won't be chilled," he explained and easily rowed away from the dock.

Wrapping herself in his suit jacket, the young woman settled in for the adventure.

Paula felt suddenly lifeless for a fleeting moment as her past flooded her reverie.

"A nickel for your thoughts?" The gentle Frenchman took her hand in his.

Paula chuckled, but could not reply, stunned that once again, this uncanny man read her thoughts.

"I think you mean a *penny* for your thoughts," and laughed out loud, relieved that the uncomfortable moment dissipated, resolving to let the night, the moon and the twinkling sky, cloak and comfort her. She leaned back in the boat, offering no reply.

"Ah, got another one wrong—well, give me credit, I at least got the American Currency correct, did I not?" Smiling wide, Christian, realizing he tread on forbidden ground, fell into silence himself. They were perfectly at peace here, the cool and serene reflections, distant laughter and lights.

"Is this how you and your father escaped the Tower of London when you made off with the crown jewels?"

"Exactly." They reached the tranquil waters in the lake's center. Fastening the oars, he continued, "We lowered the rope from a window and rappelled into the Thames. Would have made it, too, but for a garbage scow."

He expertly uncorked the champagne with a soft pop. The wooden cork coming away in his hand without a drop spilled.

"Bravo," Paula applauded. "Whenever I pop a top like that, I end up drinking some cork with my champagne."

Tipping each tulip shaped glass slightly to one side, he expertly poured the bubbling froth with a flourish.

Twilight suddenly fled into an ebony night; the milky moon seemed to pour over the park's rippling lake as they sipped champagne . . .

"Have you ever tasted Champagne Rosé?"

"Well, I've had the tacky pink version in the States," she answered with a sparkle.

"Makes me want to drop a scoop of ice cream in it."

Cringing at the thought. "Ice cream! Really, but, why?"

"Have you never had an ice cream float?"

Larsonnier shook his head in bewilderment.

"Well, it's not really something one can explain. You just have to experience it. But, it's basically soda, with a scoop of ice cream in it."

"Perhaps, then, you'll make me a float one day," he suggested. "That is, if you decide to stay around."

The miracle elixir tickled her throat with its gentle effervescence. "You're the second person to say that to me recently."

"Oh?" He lifted an eyebrow. "Is there a rival I have to concern myself with?"

"Just Marc," she sighed, ever so delicately. "We had lunch together earlier this week."

"A nice sort of chap."

"Oh, *yes*. He's *adorable*."

"I didn't say adorable. I said nice." Christian corrected. "If you like a fellow who can't seem to keep his mind on one thing at a time. More champagne?"

"Mm. Please." She took the opportunity to just watch him, as he busied himself with the bottle. His light hair blew in the sudden breezes, and his profile pleased her, with its strong, decisive lines. The crisp shirt betrayed the broad shoulders beneath the fabric. *I wonder what it'd be like . . .* Paula quickly averted her gaze, as he replaced the bottle and straightened.

"Here you are."

"Thanks. So, that was quite a show you put on at the hotel. Do you like kids?"

Larsonnier pensively smiled, then sipped his drink before responding. "They're usually a good audience."

Stars began to fill the night sky, one by one, shining down upon the couple on the lake with an approving twinkle. The quarter moon might very well be full for all its brightness, for the lake glistened with a white opalescence as the incoming clouds from the south glowed with a silvery sheen. A melancholy feeling stole over both of them as they sat in silence, listening to the lapping water against the boat.

"Once when I was small," Paula said suddenly, "I lay out in the yard and tried to count the stars. I got to a hundred."

"And then?"

"I lost count." She smiled a little sadly. "I was only seven, after all." Then, my Grandma told me. You could get lost counting all those stars. Your soul would just sort of leave your body and float away into space. Scared the hell out of me. I think she was just trying to get me to come back inside.

The pensive woman looked over at her new companion. She could only just make out the faintest outline of his face. He seemed somber, strangely distant, alone. He opened his mouth and spoke in a voice void of the usual lilt, mellow and filled with sadness . . . soft and flowing, the Frenchman quoted:

> *"Let me not to the marriage of true minds*
> *Admit impediments. Love is not love*
> *Which alters when it alteration finds,*
> *Or bends with the remover to remove.*
> *O no! it is an ever-fixed mark*
> *That looks on tempests and is never shaken;*
> *It is the star to every wand' ring bark . . ."*

Shocked at himself, Christian straightened and glanced at Paula.

"Frightfully sorry," he stammered. "I suppose must have gotten carried away with . . ." He gestured to the luminous sky. "Well, with the moment."

"Oh, please don't apologize." Paula reached over and squeezed his hand on the oar. "Shakespeare, Sonnet 116, one of my all-time favs. You know, you recite it from the heart. It was lovely. Funny . . . . in the stone age, when I was a Freshman in College— by the way— my father sent me to one of those Vassar, girly schools— but, my first semester, I had an English teacher whose only requirement for his students was to memorize poems. The final was all the poems we learned all semester. . . ."

Picking up where her date left off, awkwardly at first, then gaining in confidence in her memory:

*"Whose worth's unknown, although his height be taken.
Love's not Time's fool, though rosy lips and cheeks...."*

The American's voice drifted away across the lake . . . .

"Uh hum— or something to that effect."

"But bears it out even to the edge of doom . . ."

"And speaking of tempests and doom," Paula abruptly added, breaking the poetic moment, pointing to the flashes of lightening and the quickly moving black clouds.
"I think we'd best head for the hills—or rather the shore!"
Christian turning to look at the same impeding scene, grabbed the oars. "So how did you do on your final?"
"I actually cannot remember." She laughed uncomfortably, still staring at the approaching clouds, crossing her fingers. "But, I still remember a lot of the poems."

Few patrons occupied the tables along the shore. The night air was growing quite chilly and the breeze promised rain.
He sat alone in the shadows, the smoke from his cigarette curling above his head and then scattering in the sudden gusts of air from the Vosges. His glass of wine waited on the table, untouched, but extinguished cigarette butts filled the ashtray before him. He lifted the burning cigarette to his lips and inhaled, his eyes never leaving the lone boat on the water.

Laughing aloud and dripping wet, Christian swung her through the apartment's door and paused to let her shove it closed with a foot. Lightning crackled and illuminated the dark room for a split second, then darkness again till he found the light switch.

"Voila!" He pronounced, and flooded the room with light. "My humble abode."

Paula felt her jaw drop and closed it quickly. The warm, golden glow from the sparkling chandeliers above refracted prisms of lights from one end of the room to the other. The room bespoke a man comfortable in life.

Sliding her onto the nearby sofa, Christian observed, "Good thing we got out of the lake just before the worst of the storm hit. Though, your hair seems to have taken in most of the damage."

A stunned Paula, touched a hand to her curly locks, taking in the bachelor pad.

Rich, dark paneling on either side of the room was complemented by textured walls of earth tones. Two enormous arched bookcases displayed old leather volumes from wall to wall. The heavy, plush sofa she now found herself in, completed the effect of old world charm and prosperity, for its richly brocaded tapestry upholstery was a fashion long forgotten most everywhere.

"There is more. Would you care to see it, or shall we dine first?" He looked directly into her eyes, smiling that boyish grin.

"What's for dinner?" I'm famished," she confessed, her face earnest as she met his dancing, hazel stare.

"Very well. Please make yourself at home. There is a stereo behind the sofa. Plenty of good music: Mozart, Beethoven . . ."

"Tormé? She asked into thin air…. As Christian disappeared, Paula assumed into the kitchen.

Spying an elegant onyx chess set tucked into the corner of the room, Paula smiled.

"So, you play chess?"

"Oh, that," came the reply. "Not really, but my father is quite the local chess celebrity. He and his local Voyageurs—or Voyous, as you put it, are enthusiasts."

"Yeah, right," Paula muttered, smirking. *I can just picture it, a group of old men sitting around playing . . . well, not chess, that's for sure.*

The tired woman tossed her shoes as she sank into the deep cool cushions of the sofa. She contentedly put her feet up, then looked around again. Not just any man could do all this. Her artistic eye appreciated the deep, dark woods of the strictly provincial peasant style complementing to perfection the contrasting Moroccan carpet. The dewdrop design of the three overhead chandeliers definitely created a distinct mood of fantasy and indeed Paula felt as if she just stepped into one.

"So, what do you think?" Christian called from the next room.

Paula smiled knowingly as she listened to the hurried footsteps clanging glasses and fumbling silverware.

"But, then," he continued, "maybe you should reserve judgement till we have had our supper."

"Can I help with anything?" Paula reluctantly asked, unwilling to leave her resting place.

"No—no."

She studied appreciatively the dark woods of the various furnishings. A shining white grand piano dominated a corner of the spacious living room and sitting at the far end, a massive fireplace invited lighting. Even the leopard skin rug beneath the coffee table added a tasteful accent to the surroundings. Struck by a sudden impulse, Paula stretched out her uninjured foot and ran her toes through the plush fur with a blissful sigh.

"So!" Christian came out of the back. "I've managed to find a robe. No, no, no, don't try to stand." He swept her up as easily as if she were a doll. Paula felt content right where she was.

"I don't know." She brushed his damp bangs from his eyes. "I might have to be carried around for the rest of my life."

The Frenchman laughed as he dropped her before a dressing table in what she supposed to be a guest bedroom. "Now, be a good girl and dry yourself off, while I finish getting dinner."

"I'm really only a bit damp. Most of the damage hit my hair, waving the offer of the towel away. "Thank goodness, we got to shore before the worst of the storm erupted."

"Never the less, you will feel better with something dry and warm."

Unceremoniously, he tossed her a towel, then closed the door.

Paula hummed as she vigorously dried her rapidly curling hair. "Gonna be a frizz by morning," she murmured and scouted the top of the dressing table for a brush, any brush. *Hmmm. . . hairpins, powder, perfume . . . . Wait a minute. Hairpins? Powder? Perfume?*

Carefully, slowly, so as not to make a noise, she opened a drawer. Eyeliner, lipstick . . . *Hm*. She looked up to survey the bedroom through the mirror's reflection.

The room bespoke a classic elegance . . . a feminine elegance, that is. Muted grays and browns still managed to convey a sense of the woman who lived there, in flowered prints that nonetheless managed to avoid the frivolous. A pot of fresh flowers on the nightstand betrayed recent occupation, as did the blotted tissues carelessly scattered atop the vanity in front of her . . .

Well, I'm not exactly dripping wet, just damp, but I hope Angora doesn't shrink too badly. The robe draped across the bed, a bit big, perhaps, but covering her nicely, slid onto her shoulders with an intoxicating coral silkiness. *Wow, does this ever feel wonderful.* She studied herself as she tightened the sash and nodded approval.

Paula hopped back into the living room, where Christian had managed to build a crackling fire and changed the lighting to a quieter mood. The pouring rain outside added a staccato rhythm to a piano nocturne emanating from the stereo.

"Everything alright?" Christian called from what she assumed to be the kitchen, for she could hear clinking glasses and rattling silverware.

"Mmm, yeah," she answered and fell back into the sofa. *Hmm...Well, you just can't worry about it all night and not ask. Come to think of it, you haven't even asked if he's married, after all.*

"Errr...Christian?" Paula raised her voice as he popped his head around the corner from the kitchen. He'd found the time to slip into a fisherman's sweater and jeans.

"Yes?" His eyes took in the flattering attire, but he made no comment; then again, with those eyes, he didn't need to.

"Ummm. Whose bedroom is that?" With a casual hand, she gestured back to the hallway.

Christian grinned, as if he knew exactly what was on her mind and was amused by it. "Yasmine's. She stays here when she is performing as I'm much closer to the theater district."

"Ohhhhh." It came out with a rush of relief. *Yasmine.* She had forgotten all about her. *Yes, Good, old Yasmine. Good old, the lovely **niece**,* Yasmine.

The Frenchman returned to whatever he was doing in the kitchen; Paula dropped her head back onto the sofa's arm. With reassuring contentment, she watched the flickering shadows dance on the ceiling.

Christian hurried about, frantically grabbing up the silverware, wine goblets, linens and plates. He stepped away to admire the arrangement and frowned. *Something. Missing...Ah! A single red rose...*

Humming along to the sultry music, he carried the tray into the living room and paused at the doorway to admire the picture before him.

Paula lay comfortably stretched out, like a cat in its lair. Her toes moved to the music's rhythm, as if they never could stay still. Her arms, crossed, propped up, her froth of dark curls and her deep violet eyes seemed to focus somewhere beyond the ceiling.

The essential counterpoint to the room, he thought out-of-hand. *Exactly what was needed.* Then, he cleared his throat. "Dinner is served, Mademoiselle."

And what a dinner it was: A perfect meal of foie gras, smoked ham, salad niçoise, a baguette, goat cheese and a small scoop of sorbet, the understated finale. Christian watched approvingly as she savored every bite. All accompanied with a Chateau Margaux whose woody bouquet blended perfectly with the rainy night.

Sitting on the throw, they fell into easy conversation about life in general, interesting people they'd met and even a little more poetry. The storm outside lent a coziness to the magical, midnight hours.

Drowsy from the lulling warmth of the fire, Paula nodded to the piano. "Does Yasmine also play?

"Yes, she plays a bit. I am mentoring her. Would you like to hear something?"

"Oh yes!" She accepted the hand up; their fingertips touching lightly, that current running between them, not for the first time. "Something to suit the rain."

The Frenchman, rose, then seated himself at his piano, fingers over the keys and with a curious smile, he began playing a Sinatra tune, singing in a mellow tenor: *The Way You Look Tonight . . .*

Somewhere between wakefulness and sleep, Paula's head dropped to the sofa's pillow . . . The last verse drifted away on a crack of thunder. "Wha—?"

His tone was lightly teasing. "You fell asleep. It must have been the night air."

"No, I didn't," Paula argued, afraid he'd call it a night and the dream would end. "I was just . . .thinking."

"Oh, I see. Would you like to hear something else?"

"Play something pretty."

Without a pause, he began Chopin's Prelude Number 2 in A. Lulled by the melting notes and the crackling fire, the rain pattering against the terrace windows, Paula felt her eyes grow heavy with sleep.

Unable to keep her eyes open, she felt herself slipping into irresistible slumber . . .

He was talking . . . something about how her eyes sparkled like sawdust, no, stardust, that was it. He has a wonderful voice. So soothing, just like his music.

Soothing music. He said I smelled like flowers. That's nice . . . .

Paula yawned again, and this time she couldn't hide it. She sighed, head dropping back against the soft sofa's pillow and murmured so lowly that Christian had to lean in close . . . *Coqulicos . . .*

As Paula fell into a deep sleep, even her light snuffling made Christian smile, and almost paternally, he slid the fuzzy throw over her shoulders.

"Sleep well, ma petite American." . . . .

***

Paula cuddled fluffy pink slippers beneath the fluffy down quilt. Wide violet-blue eyes skimmed the top of the leather-bound book and stared beyond the slippered horizon; a wad of curly brunette hair held captive by a bright pink bow toppled the arm of the old wing back chair.

The fire before her crackled and sizzled, igniting the svelte amber blades into a hypnotic dance as the antique grandfather clock began its tolled march into midnight, the liquid flames an unsettling sea, rising and falling as if conducted by the chimes.

Slender fingers reached lightly to the brimming bowl of popcorn. Delicately, she drew a few kernels into her palm. The book sliding down her lap as she rolled a kernel absently with her free hand.

"On the first day of Christmas, Uncle Sam said to me . . .Come to Europe and serve your country."

She flicked a morsel of popcorn into the fire and smirked sarcastically as the piece popped, then fizzled.

"On the second day of Christmas, Uncle Sam said to me . . . Be a CUT a-bove—come to Europe and serve your country."

"On the third day of Christmas, Uncle Sam said to me . . . Teach the rotten beggars, BE a CUT a-bove — come to Europe and serve your country."

Flinging three more kernels into the minute inferno, she leaned forward from her ample chaired sanctuary, elbows akimbo as she admired the five-kernel salute.

Parting lips in muted appreciation, she sank back onto her adored chaise, the slight bounce, liberating several spirals of her hair. Automatically, she brushed them away, then returned her attention to the stereo system meekly playing a twinkling glockenspiel.

Boredly, she looked about her cozy apartment, warmly lit by the hearth as threads of sadness knit at her brow.

"AHHH . . . who cares anyway." And she grabbed the bowl of popcorn and sang between fistfuls . . .

"Five days of DETENTION!
Four spit balls
Three hecklers
Two class clowns
Then hop a flight and go back home to New York."

The thought irresistibly chased any lingering doubts and she lightly clapped the salt off her finger tips. Then, with renewed gusto, she amassed another handful of edible grenades and proceeded to launch them.

A piercing sound of what always reminded her of a household fire alarm, lurched her from her aim. The marble sized weapon prone for the flames, she froze. "NO . . . can't be," she thought, "he's never found my phone number this fast." She snuggled her face against the corner of the wing chair and burrowed the quilt to her nose.

BLEE-EEE-EEE-EEE-P!

It'll take him months to catch up to me. Peering over the side of the chair like a precipitous child, she looked around fearfully at the darkened threshold to her bedroom.

Thirty years old and I'm still afraid of Daddy Dearest. Like a parachute from the sky, the quilt popped off her lap and in a languid thrust, she was up trampling toward the mechanical intrusion.

With a determined index, she popped it off the cradle.

"Ja-bitte?" She inquired automatically.

"Helluva night for solitaire, don't ya think?"

The hollow clopping of poorly fitting dentures, instantly reassured her.

"Marella," her voice sweetened. "Merry Christmas."

"And what's a beautiful brunette, Italian-French, Irish or whatever da hell ya mother claimed, kid like you doin' sit-in' home alone at Christmas?"

She was clutching her elbows. "Enjoying," she lingered over the last syllable, "the rest. I really earned the peace, Marella," she chuckled.

"You're a rotten liar, Paoli . . .but, I'll buy it—that you need the rest."

Street Sirens blared in the young American's head. Quick— run— they're coming! Paula began to run— THUD! HUH? Where am I? She looked around the strange room . . . the heavy mahogany furniture, a gleaming white piano. . . . Ohhhh . . . Thank God— another dream . . .
Struggling to stand in the darkness, a dull pain suddenly reminded her about her twisted ankle.

All at once, the evening's events came back to her. Slapping herself a sobering chastisement— *Paoli— what the hell have you done?? A little champagne and red wine and you turn into Mata Hari— Oh MY GOD! Okay, well a LOT of Champagne, and wine and music and dancing— I gotta get outta here! What will Marella think?? Sister Dolores Marie! Stop it, Paula, the sun'll be up before you name all your audiences. . . .*

Testing her ankle, she determined, it "safe" enough. She quickly ran into the bathroom praying her Angora dress would be dry enough— popped it over her head as she raced back into the living room— spotted a desk, opened a cupboard door, several video cassettes, no pen, then opening another, grabbed a pen and the back of an envelope and jotted down a quick note.

Thank you for a great evening!
Have a ton of work to finish for
the book. Will call soon! P.

CHAPTER XXI

Masquerade

The Great Hall flamed with the light of a thousand candles, lending a fairy tale glow to the closing night's Nouveau Beaujolais Celebration soirée at Haut-Koenigsburg Castle.

Waiters in red livery rushing everywhere, serving sparkling champagne in crystal flutes, alongside red goblets of the best vintages, while masked guests in opulent costumes whirled about the floor in three four time. Laughingly, they tried to deduce their partners' identities, or rather, they pretended to. That they recognized their neighbor, or their patient or client, didn't really matter. For this one magical evening, everyone played a part, a role, a romance. For tonight, everyone could waltz. Well, almost.

Eyes lingered on the handsome Frenchman, who seemed so strangely natural as the Villain du Rochefort. Glances invited him and smiles coaxed him, but he didn't see any of it. No, he saw only the woman in his arms. The candlelight paled to the sparkle in her eyes as the music blurred to the sound of her laughter. Her sparkling, white dress rustled whenever she moved, which was all the time, of course. And she'd restrained that glorious hair in a proper chignon, but it didn't plan to stay that way. Even now, tendrils escaped from the hairpins and flew about her glowing face.

With a sudden swoop, Larsonnier swung Paula on the crowded dance floor, spinning her round and round with dizzying exuberance, through the open French doors and onto the starlit balcony.

Once around the low wall, they then slowed and stopped. The music's last notes drifted away into the night and the murmur of voices rose and fell from the ballroom.

The orchestra began a beautiful ballad, a fox trot, a dreaming interlude between waltzes. With one hand lightly touching her back, Christian led her to the low wall surrounding terrace and gestured to the Route du Vin. It's twinkling lights twisted and coiled along the foothills, aglow where there were villages, a vague pinpoint where the road ran alone. The soft starlight above answered the highway's glitter with a light of its own.

"When I was very small, my father brought me up here, to this very spot. It was a night very much like this one, except it was in summertime. So, the stones on this wall," he patted it with his free hand, "were still warm from the sun. We sat here together, on this wall and my father gave me the lights."

"What a wonderful gift!" Paula leaned back against him as Christian wrapped his arms around her.

"Mmm." The Frenchman kissed her hair, his gaze still on the lights so very far away, but his mind on the softness of the curly, dark strands.

"I can come up here, whenever I choose and still see those lights." His gentle hand smoothed the hair coming loose and curling over her ear. "I'm glad you approve, for I give them to you. I would give you the starlight too, but you've already captured it in your eyes."

"Mmm, I do approve. Thank you."

Christian bent down to the curve of her ear, with the lightest of kisses. "Then why don't we slip out," he whispered.

Somewhere in the back of her mind, Marella's scratchy voice preached cold reality "What will it mean? He dumps ya, the minute it's over . . . the nuns taught you better!"

"I . . . I just . . ." racking her brain for a viable excuse— "What about Marc?" She sighed and tilted her head just the smallest fraction of an inch.

"Heartbreak is good for a young man. I'm certain he'll enjoy it."

She wavered. "I don't know . . ."

"Your skin is warm and sweet— and fragrant," Christian breathed. "I can feel you here." He kissed the wildly racing pulse, just beneath her ear . . .

"Ohhhh . . .you're not playing at all fair, you know."

"Non." He lifted her hair and nuzzled the nape of her neck. "I'm a hopeless scoundrel when it comes to matters of love."

She shivered at his words. "Alright, alright!" She spun to face him. "Let's go."

His eyes intent on hers, smoldering with kindling . . . "Très bien, then. Let us--"

"Why, Christian, pet!" The heavy French accent caused them both to stiffen.

"Simone, cherie," Larsonnier greeted the gloating woman in white without enthusiasm. "How . . . . ah, how, very nice to see you."

"Simone," Paula cooed from behind the Frenchman. "What a LOVELY surprise. Is your darling little Henry here, too?" *Those flashy clothes, that yellow blond hair, all too vivid on the virginal white veil. Honestly, Simone—ESMERALDA? And, what's that under her dress? Sequined spandex?* "Love the costume!" The American finally said, gesturing a thumbs up.

Simone pointedly ignored her and surveyed the Frenchman with predatory eyes.

"You look absolument *adorable* tonight," she told him in a throaty, inviting voice.

"But, then, you always played the *bad boy* with such panache, did you not?"

From where Paula stood, she could see the red creeping up from Christian's collar.

"Now, see here, Simone," he began in a strangled voice. "I'm not interested in stirring up old ghosts. We were just about to leave, and--"

"Mais, non!" Her sultry voice managed to convey just the right amount of shock and amusement.

"How could you even think of it, when so many of your, ah, past *acquaintances* have waited all evening to dance with you? Why," she added with calculated naiveté, "all night long, I have heard nothing but speculation: Who is that divine Duke de Rochefort? So handsome, so tall, so dashing in his costume. I am afraid you will disappoint half the women of Strasbourg, pet."

"Then they shall have to be disappointed," Christian firmly replied and took Paula's elbow. "As I said before, Paula and I are leaving."

Simone smiled with sudden comprehension. "Naturellement! How silly of me! Perhaps your little friend would not like you to dance with the other guests." Her eyes behind the mask slid away to look the woman in the white chiffon gown up and down.

"You must forgive me, Christian darling. It must be so easy to feel a bit . . . insignificant."

Larsonnier stopped himself from saying something. "Come along, Paula," he said, but the American hung back. Her eyes locked with those of the older woman.

"No, Christian," Paula disentangled her arm and patted him on the shoulder. In a voice deceptively sweet, she suggested, "Why don't you dance with your OLD friend? I have to find Marc, anyway. Give him my excuses. You know."

"But, I don't want to dance," he protested impatiently. His eyes pleaded with her. "What about our, ah, plans?"

"Later," the American promised. "But, Simone is absolutely right. I'd HATE to be the cause of her disappointment." Lifting her skirts, she paused at the door to smile fondly at the Frenchwoman. "So hard to get a dance, isn't?"

Torches lit her way and cast dancing shadows on the great stone walls. Upward she climbed through the inner courtyard and around the winding staircase. No other guests dared this lonely route tonight.

Except for two. Paula quickly drew back out of the torchlight. Looking right and then left, she slipped into the armaments room and risked another peek. There, at the top of the next staircase, Rouget had engaged a costumed guest in a rather heated embrace. *Gee, I wonder who . . .* Paula narrowed her eyes against the gloom. *Someone in a nun's costume . . .*

Well, she stifled a giggle. *Guess he won't notice my disappearance. Now what? I don't want to get caught sneaking around. Oh, hi, I was just snooping again. . . .* Paula surveyed the great chamber behind her.

The flaming torches reflected against the suits of armor along the walls, causing their shadows to rise to ghoulish heights. *Gosh, in this light, they look like they're alive.* Paula swallowed hard.

Faint music drifted through the far doors. *The party must be through there. Sounds like a ghost orchestra. I wonder who the audience is . . .*

"Creepy," she muttered.

Come on, chicken. Just walk right through to the other door. Don't look right or left or one of the ghosts'll get ya! Paula let out a nervous giggle and prodded herself forward. Her fingers lifted the door's latch, but—locked. *So much for a short cut. I'll just have to risk the embarrassment.*

"You'll have to walk around."

At first, she imagined the man who stood in the doorway might be a castle inhabitant. Masked eyes watched her from beneath a plumed hat and in the flickering light of torches, they seemed to glitter. He leaned on a sword and she noticed he wore one of those outfits she'd seen in an old Three Musketeers movie.

Stupid, he's just another guest. The American cleared her throat. "Uh, yeah. I just realized that. Thanks."

The man in the musketeer's costume smiled. "This castle has so many twists and turns it's lucky you didn't wind up in the dungeon."

All she could really see behind the mask were the eyes. They studied her with a strangely intense light.

"Uhhh . . ." Paula sidled around the man, her goal, the open door. He stayed where he was, smiling mildly beneath the mask.

"I have to go. My friends are going to be worried about me." Her voice echoed in the room. "They are just up the stairs, there. Not too far away at all. In fact, they can probably hear me . . ."

Brilliant, Paula. Let's just get him riled by asking him if he's the ghost of an axe murderer.

But the stranger didn't seem at all insulted. He bowed with a sweeping gesture to the hallway. "Then you shouldn't keep them waiting."

With a last look at the phantom musketeer, Paula scurried out of the room. Glancing up, she saw Rouget was gone, so she veered right and hurried down the shadowy stairwell.

Now, where the hell is he? Paula's eyes swept through the dancers in the ballroom, crowding the floor, but while there was an abundance of musketeers and Richelieu's, she could see no Duke de Rochefort.

But, another couple had replaced them on the terrace. *Hmm.*

"Alone this evening, petite Americaine?" Henri De Bourchegrave approached her from behind.

No mistaking that voice.

Paula's jaw dropped as she squarely faced De Bourchegrave, scanning him up and down.

"The Marquis de Sade? Gee, Henry, did you think this was a come-as-you-are?"

His black eyes behind the mask sparked in the ballroom's candlelight. "Maybe we all did, **Madame Bovary**." Henry replied with a suggestive smile.

"Would you like to accompany me away from here and give me a sampling of your wares?"

She stared at the dark Frenchman with cold eyes and wished with all her heart she could smack him right in front of everyone.

"You're a real jerk, Henry, you know that?" Paula added sarcastically and turned away to watch the dancers.

"And I'm dressed as Christine Daaé from Phantom. But obviously you wouldn't recognize class if it hit you in the face."

She felt his hand touch her shoulder, lightly, tracing the line of her back zipper which Paula instantly shrugged it away.

"Does that mean your answer is- *no*?" Henri chuckled. "You seem to have lost your date this evening?"

"If it's any of your business I'm here with Christian Larsonnier. In fact," she added as a warning, "I'm looking for him right now."

"Ah, Larsonnier." De Bourchegrave nodded in a bored kind of way.

"I just saw him, actuellement."

"Really? I don't believe you."

"Go see for yourself." He waved casually toward the door. "Up above, on the upper terrace. But, I would not go up there if I were you. He seemed . . . quite occupied."

"Yeah, right." Paula picked up her chiffon skirts and walked away from him with an instinctive shudder. *Creep. Reminds me of the slimy stuff on the bottom of a rock.*

She hesitated a moment before climbing the steps to the upper terrace. *Christian probably wouldn't be too pleased at having been left with that female French snake.*

Or, was he? She stopped dead on the top step, widened eyes intent upon the steamy tableau. Her heart seemed to stop and freeze as she watched the couple in the shadow. The kiss was interminable and it wrenched an involuntary sob from her throat.

With a hot face, Paula whirled around and flew down the staircase, nearly tripping over her costume on her descent.

"Paula— Paula," came the voice. But the furious woman fled, raging self-admonishments as she escaped the scene.

CHAPTER XXII

The hunchback of Notre Dame limped from the ballroom out onto the terrace. *Damn, I could sure use a smoke.* Assuring himself of his solitude, he straightened up with a groan. "This is the last time I crash one of these whoop-de-doo parties," Tony Giordano growled. "The booze stinks and the food, though tasty. with such small portions— never enough of it anyway!"

I feel like a stupid chaperone. Oughtta just pick her up and carry her outta here before she gets herself in real trouble. Like I don't have enough problems already.

The lighter flickered and illuminated the grotesque mask. He took a grateful puff of the cheap cigar. Ahhh . . . *Hard to get a smoke with all those padres sneaking' around and sniffin' everything. Gotta do somethin' with the kid, before I plan my next move. That ain't gonna be easy. Doubt she'll even talk to me, much less take any advice. I really don't know what's happened to her.* He shook his grey head in bemusement. She never used to be so damned sensitive.

What about the people in DC? He dismissed that idea as soon as the thought occurred. *Nah, they like her better than me.*

"Pardonnez-moi?"

Giordano swiveled and barely managed to contain his surprise. "Oui?"

The Duke du Rochefort hovered in the doorway, one hand on the latch.

"I do apologize for intruding," he said, "but have you by any chance seen a woman in a white fluffy dress? She's dressed as Christine Daaé from Phantom.

The hunchback puffed a couple of times and scrutinized the Frenchman. After a moment, he withdrew the cigar. "A woman in a white flowing dress?" He repeated, as if trying to remember. "No, I'm afraid not."

"Oh. Well, thank you anyway." The Duke replied turning away.

"Not a smart thing to do," the hunchback's voice stopped him. "Leaving a woman in a white flowing dress to her own devices."

Christian turned back. "No," he agreed with a smile. "Especially that woman."

"Hm," he grunted and flicked the ashes onto the flagstones. "Dangerous, eh?"

"What an apt description." The smile widened into a grin. "Yes, dangerous. That describes her perfectly."

The American stared after the Frenchman as he disappeared through the half-opened door. *THAT does it.* "Well, I'll be damned." Thoughtfully, he puffed on his glowing cigar and meditated the Route du Vin.

Paula grabbed at her flimsy chiffon sleeves, the cold night air piercing through to the bone. The moon, luminous and nearly full, guided her with its subtle light. Her goal, the sleeping village below.

Why the hell didn't I go back and get Marc? He got me into this — damn it! What kind of man dumps a date for a costumed nun? And his playboy amigo! Ha! They both belong in a stye somewhere!

"No doubt whatsoever!" She raised her fist and shook it angrily at the tranquil heavens. "PIGS EXTRAORDINAIRE!"

She paused mid step. The road gleaming in the bright moonlight, forked in two directions, both equally shadowed by the heavy pine overgrowth. *Right or left? Oh, hell, when in doubt . . .eeny, meeny, miney . . .*She chose mo.

"I hope I die out here. I hope they find my frozen body after the snow melts and everyone will blame Mr. Left-Wing-Communist-Last-Of-The-Believers-in-Free-Love-Larsonnier!"

On the last syllable, her foot caught the hem of her dress. R-r-r-i-p! *Hell! Ohhhh, hell!* Paula bent over and examined the damage as best she could in the starlight. *Oh, crap, and now I've THIS to pay for!*

She couldn't get rid of the thought. Every time she thought about it, she dug her fingers into her palms, but even that old trick didn't work. Tears filmed her eyes and dropped, plop-plop on the ruined white flowing fabric.

The sight of Christian in the arms of that . . .that dried up, old Ophelia. Paula sniffed and wiped her nose on her sleeve. "I wouldn't mind shoving her into a river right about now."

The worst of it is, you nearly fell for it, you naive jerk! Oh sure, you talk big and you pretend you know something about it, when the truth is, you're probably even more sheltered than nuns in a convent! You bought every cornball line that Frenchman dished out, didn't you? Hell, if it hadn't been for his ex-bimbo, you would be joining his cast of thousands. You should even thank her for it!

Marella is right. As usual. They're all pigs! One track minded Schweine, Cochons. Pork in any language.

Okay. Paula took a deep, cleansing breath. *You've had your cry. I hope you feel better now, because it's time to think about your present situation.*

She contemplated the panorama before her, the sleeping Vosges, unlit farmhouses, the million stars overhead, her eyes still sparkling with unshed tears. The cool air fanned her shoulders, warmed from the long walk. She could smell the pine and the frost in the air.

"Now you've gone and done it," she said aloud as the sound of her own voice comforted her. "You've made a fool of yourself over a French cad and you got yourself lost to boot. Tony's gonna have a field day with this one."

A grinding, choking clatter broke the tranquil silence of the mountains. *An engine!* Maybe she could hitch a ride down to the nearest—

Wait a minute. What's that other sound?

"Chevalier de la table ronde, goutons-bois si le vin est bon . . . goutons-bois (*let us taste*) . . . oui, oui, oui, goutons-bois (*yes, yes, yes, let us taste*) . . . . non, non, non, *let us taste, if the wine is good!*"

Oh, perfect, perfect, PERFECT! A truckload of singing drunks! Paula gathered up her skits and darted back and forth, looking for cover. But, stone walls, lined both sides of the mountain road.

"Let us taste, if the wine is good. . . .let us taste . . .oui, oui, oui! Let us taste . . . . non, non, non—-eh— regards la bas! Look over there— A vision in the darkness! Stop the truck, Marcel!"

"A vision, where? You're so drunk, you imagine women at every turn. Old fool, you are even dumber than you are hideous!" A chorus of drunken laughter followed the slurred pronouncement.

"Wait! Back up this heap, Marcel! Bernard is not so crazy. I see her too!"

No bushes, no walls, no trees whatsoever offered shelter for her. Paula sprinted, limping, stumbling and tripping as fast as the tight, laced boots would permit, taking her down the deserted country road.

"Bonsoir, Cherie! What are you running from? Mais, stop, you beautiful vision! Are you real or are you an angel?"

"A dark angel! Look at that hair! OOOH LA LAAAA!!!!" They all groaned in unison.

The ancient truck, dilapidated as it was, clanked and choked down the incline, till it managed to cut her off, shining its seamy yellow headlights in her face. Five men jumped out the back, then two more from the cabin, all bleary-eyed, staggering in her direction. The stench of cheap wine reaching her before they did.

The crackling radio blared a tinny waltz, which most of the men had already begun dancing to, clinging and turning each other or their imaginary partners to and fro.

"Allez! Dansez!" A short, meaty man in dirty overalls weaved forward, his arms outstretched. Instinctively, she dodged him with a quick step to the left and the drunk fell to the ground, laughing, his left hand still holding a near empty wine bottle. Concerned over the loss of precious liquid, then seeing no damage done, he regained his balance. "Allez — let's dance, you little whore."

This time, Paula's leg kicked from under billowing skirts with lightning precision and the drunk fell, stunned against the truck. "Say, the little whore knows some steps of her own!" Another drunk shouted. "Let's get her!"

"Come on, come on!" She taunted. "I've about had enough of all you pigs! Anyone who wants to— Oh, *damn!*"

They rushed her all at once. No match for so many, they whirled her around to the music like a marionette. Laughing uproariously, the drunks passed her back and forth, her arms flailing in the air as she tried to land a punch somewhere—anywhere!

No one heard the engine's angry roar until the car was upon them. Bright yellow beams surrounded the ugly crowd, the horn deafening. The car halted just before the drunken, dazed men and the driver's door opened. The hairy arm around Paula's throat dropped as a menacing shadow unwound from behind the wheel and stood over the frozen group.

The rickety engine coughed to a start and the truck began to roll down the hill, half the men chasing after it, frantically scratching at its side and tumbling in.

The shadow waited a moment more, not speaking at all. Just standing there.

Oh, GOD- now WHAT! Paula looked right and left, desperately searching for a possible escape.

The figure moved, stepping out of from the headlights and her jaw dropped at the costumed musketeer standing there.

"Maurice?" She shrieked, not believing the vision before her.

"Why, it IS you." The familiar, silky voice exclaimed as the "musketeer" stepped away from the Citroën. "I was not certain, what with . . . I thought I saw you having a fine time."

"Wait a minute," Paula held her hand up, her torn sleeve hanging down as she spoke. "So, you are ALSO dressed as Rochefort?"

The steamy scene reigniting back into her thoughts. . . . . . .

"You were with Simone?"

"And our friend with the brown hair was very busy with his camera! Now, let's get you back to your hotel."

Paula felt the tears well up, as misery and relief blended together into a confusing, exhausting mess. "Oh, Maurice, I'm so glad to see you," she sobbed. "Yes, PLEASE just take me back to my hotel!"

The Citroën slowly accelerated on the gravel road and mercifully, Maurice said no more. She leaned her head against the seat and closed her eyes to shut out the pictures of the preceding nightmare, the lonely road, the drunks and— Christian and Simone. . . .no, Maurice and Simone.

The phone. Memories, dreams falling away like delicate flower petals in one swift burst of reality, Paula reached an arm to find it, her gaze pinned to the ceiling. "Oui?" She croaked.

"Uh-hum. I pray your pardon, I must have the wrong room," said a faltering voice.

"Karl?" No, no, this is Paula." Shaking off her fatigue, she sat straight up in her bed as if Sister Dolores Marie were glaring at her from the blackboard.

"Oh, my dear. You are not sounding at all like yourself. Are you ill?" His wavering voice filled with concern. "I've been ringing you since yesterday. I was frankly worried. I thought perhaps you might have — how do you Americans say it — dumped me."

"Oh, Karl, never! I, well, I've been a little hung over since the Masquerade. All is well, I promise. I'm taking a bit of extra time to get all the illustrations just right. After all, I want my work to be worthy of yours."

"Ah, my child, you need not fear. What you have sent me is perfection. Do you know, your capacity for intricate detail is utter genius."

"Thank you, Karl," she said a little awkwardly. "I wouldn't exactly call it that."

"I did not call to play the taskmaster, at any rate. You have only the details of the Renaissance porticoes and the one Gothic left. Take your time. Afford yourself some luxury to play with your muse, your inspiration."

"Yes, I will do that. I want those finishing touches to be just *perfect*."

A short gasp. "My dear, you are a pearl. I cannot praise you enough. Because of your diligence, I shall be able to send off our work to the publisher before I leave Strasbourg."

Paula tingled with excitement. Everything was perf — leave Strasbourg?

"Leave Strasbourg?"

"Only for a short time, a little holiday. I am going to visit friends who own a vineyard in the Bordeaux region. Shall I look for the drawings then, by the week after next?"

"Yes, once completed, I shall have them delivered special delivery," she promised.

"And . . . might I impose myself one final time?" His voice uncertain.

"Only if you promise to have dinner with me soon."

He chuckled. "I see you have anticipated the foolishness of an old man. I shall be more clandestine in the future."

So, genius, was she? Paula rolled off the bed onto her feet and looked around the tidy premises.

Hate to disturb all this "neat", but I'm outta here! Off to Mundolsheim to stay with Melanie!!

Her valise, waiting inside the ornate armoire; Paula caught her reflection in the mirror. *Ugh! A candidate for Madame Trousseaux's horror chamber! A steaming hot shower is definitely in order!*

Humming, then singing in relief with the pelting massage effects of the shower head, once finished, she pulled away the curtain.

Glaring fuchsia letters scrolled harshly on the tile staggered her balance; she grappled for the shower's wall to steady herself.

NOW WHO'S THE SLUT??!!!

Paula slapped a hand to her mouth, muffling a cry. Reeling, her eyes raced back and forth over the words. Then, she dropped her hand to her side: No terror rising, no instruct to bolt, no fear at all.

"Suzie Carter!" She spat and raced through her room, flinging open her panty drawer. Frantically, searching for the bra with the passport pocket; scratching at the bottom, she tore away an envelope addressed:

La Pauvre Paolina "Martino?"

With trembling fingers, she opened the envelope:

What are "sisters" for if they can't
borrow from time to time? Wouldn't
you know, I forgot to pack a few things.

Thanx, Pal

That does it! Ripping the note into teeny-tiny bits, Paula let them go, fluttering to the carpet.

A break from all the drama, Paula mused. It's all been overwhelming: Leaving the Company, Big Apple Greetings, fleeing New York, Tony— memories…. the book deal, meeting the Larsonniers…… yes, especially the young, playboy son . . .
Yes, definitely time for a much deserved petite sabbatical from the current chaos.

The hotel clerk helped her organize a car rental and Paula smiled as an involuntary chuckle escaped her lips…. *always wanted to drive one of these classic Citroëns……*Wait till Melanie gets a load of me in this!

Having carefully planned her route from Strasbourg, Paula enjoyed the independence of getting on the road, cruising past the now familiar monuments, and onto the Route du Vin……

Once in Mundolsheim, Paula pulled over to re-examine her map, locating **Rue des Petites Oiseaux**, she lunged back onto the village's main drag, carefully checking the names of each street as she passed:
Rue des Anciens Vignobles, Rue Sainte Odile. . . . . AH! Here we are . . . Nearly clipping the side of a small vehicle, Paula quickly turned onto the street where her oldest and best friend, Melanie Rogers, née Melanie Martinelli rented a home for her Alsatian Concert Tour……
Lace curtains parted, an adolescent boy, cradling a small white poodle in his arms, stared at the approaching blue Citroën…….
"MOM! I think your friend is pulling into the driveway!"
"Ruf-Ruf-Ruf" barked little Rascal, the family pooch who leapt towards the front door, spinning around in circles, his tail in mini helicopter motion . . .
"Okay, CJ, I'm comin'— don't open the door, Rascal will probably run away *again*!"

Too late, Christopher Joseph, CJ, had already opened the door, Rascal shot like a dart out toward the Roger's visitor who was popping two large duffle bags out of the back seat.

Cool! Camera equipment, thought CJ as he rushed to Paula's aid, ignoring his little furry buddy's happy yips and yapping......

"You must be Christopher. I haven't seen you in ages— you're quite the big guy now," huffed Paula as she deposited one of her bags into CJ's curiously helpful arms, his eyes pinned to the open pockets where different lenses stuck out....

"Uh, yes. That's me. Mom'll be right out. She was doing something upstairs as you pulled in."

"PAOLI!!!" Leaping over the front landing, fussing with her stray hairs. "I didn't expect you till a bit later! NO BIGGIE! My goodness, you look . . . ." Paula's friend stopped before embracing her old chum, then stood back and looked at her school pal with concern . . . "Tired . . . well, never mind", she softened as she hugged her friend of many years. "Let's get you settled in— you're gonna love this place that Bill found to rent!"

Meanwhile, Rascal kept up his cheerful yapping as he followed the group back into the house.... tail still spinning like a top.

Standing in the simple farmhouse foyer, CJ immediately took the luggage upstairs to the guest room, his little white puff trailing happily behind....

Feeling a rush of calm and relief, the artist took in her new surroundings . . .

"Not now, Paoli—follow Christopher upstairs to your digs, I'll give you a tour later. Right now, you must be all wound up.... Let's have a little swim in the indoor pool, maybe a little local heavenly pizza and a glass of wine— no, maybe a bottle of wine or two- to celebrate our reunion- then we can catch up.... how does that sound?"

Tired and overwhelmed by the last few days' excitement, the Roger's visitor wasn't sure what she was hearing: *Swim-Indoor Pool— Pizza— bottles of wine? Okay whatever. I'm in. I'm gonna go with the flow . . .* And she followed little Rascal and CJ up the stairs . . .

"Okay," Paula shifted in her friend's borrowed swimsuit as she descended the stairs. *Not exactly my color or style. But, it sure would make Marella happy. Nothing shows.*

Following the sound of splashes to a great open, but glassed in courtyard.... "Whoa. This is amazing! How on earth did Bill figure this one out?" An astonished Paula mused as she located her friend sitting poolside, with 2 trays of bubbling pizzas, two table top wine coolers artistically arranged on an ornate white iron table. Plates, silverware and champagne flutes standing at attention on either side.

"Bombs away!" CJ was amusing himself launching himself in a variety of canon ball dives. His little poodle swimming alongside.

Catching Paula's expression, "CJ will be completely oblivious to us and whatever we say. He has hardly left the pool since we've arrived. He may well turn into a little prune before we leave. Any HOW— I see the suit fits!"

An irrepressible grin burst onto Paula's face. "This is JUST what I needed." Then, turning her gaze to the Italian feast on the table, "Did you make these? I think I could probably eat both of them. Where's yours?"

Laughter. CJ and Rascal look up from the pool for a second, then resume their playing.

"Well, first question first: Bill and his amazing, diverse contacts at USAFE heard about this rental through the grapevine. You know the European Parliament is here— so there are all sorts of interesting people needing high end rentals for temporary stays- so puff— Voila, here we are! There's even a music room with a gorgeous Pleyel grand for rehearsals . . . And NO, I didn't make the pizzas. They are from a brick oven pizzeria around the corner and of course, the booze is everywhere here on the Route du Vin. We could go wine tasting for the next couple of days . . ."

Somehow, Paula stopped listening about midway through Melanie's lengthy explanations. Already barefoot, she stepped toward the pool and dove in.

Hours later with CJ and his pooch hopefully long asleep upstairs, the two friends huddled around the rustic, floor to ceiling fireplace with a roaring fire crackling. lulling the two women into intimate conversation.

"Okay, you first, Paoli. What gives? Last I heard from you, you were happily employed at Big Apple Greetings, doing your Maxwell Smart's, Agent 99 thing on the side. I know you always had that wild hair about you— I remember well our Saint Catherine's school days—you were always the ring leader getting us all into all kinds of trouble."
Paula remained quiet. She didn't quite know how to phrase what she'd been feeling and even dreaming about.

"How about the time you talked about a dozen of us to escape campus, through the horse stables, over the fence, cross the highway— to that diner where we'd OFTEN go and get some burgers and fries— or how about that time we both were in the bathroom making up gossip about Carla Melancamp getting into bed with— FLUSH—and then finding out she was—FLUSH! We sure thought we were really funny— laughing our brains out as we walked back out into the hallway, right into Sister Mary Edwin!"

Swallowing the last of her red wine, Paula, popped her glass down on the coffee table, leaned back on the plush sofa pillows, letting out a giggle, then the grin widened until she exploded with laughter. She hadn't thought about all that in years!

"Okay, Touché, Melanie! Well, we never did get caught for running over the highway to Benny's Diner . . . . And now that I think of it . . . talking about hair-brained ideas, I wasn't the one who wanted to start a new Religious Order for Music Liturgy! Just whose big idea was that one? — and we were planning to petition the Holy See for it!"

Melanie's lips clamped shut. "Well, I still think that's a great idea. Has the music gotten any better, in your opinion?"

"Not sure that I'd know right now."

"*What?* Are you saying that you aren't going to Mass anymore? You? Graduate of Saint Catherine's Convent School for Girls, Graduate of Saint Odile's School of the Performing Arts? PAOLI!"

Melanie's dark brown eyes assessed her friend, lips pursed into an awkward silence.

No reply.

"Sooo," Melanie began as she stroked her auburn waves to the back of her head, still looking intently at Paula. "Here you are thirty something years old, unmarried and unattached." She paused . . . Now, I do remember one of our visits to the convent when you blurted out all of a sudden that you thought you had a calling." She leaned in closer to her friend sitting next to her, patting her shoulder, she continued softly.

"Is that it?"

Paula began to gurgle. She wasn't sure whether she wanted to laugh, cry or run away. "Are you kidding me? . . . Well . . . maybe . . . I don't know . . ."

Slowly, a kind of dawning came over Paula Regina Giordano. She knew she had never spoken of all of this to anyone. Maybe, it was time to open up. If not to Melanie, then who? Tony? *Fagetaboutit.* Marella? Did she want to live past her thirty something years?

"That group you stumbled into all those years ago, what was their name . . . Petite something. . . . what was it. . . ?"

"The Petite Josephines. No, I shook them loose long ago. They do try and contact me now and then. But nothing lately . . . . Melanie." Paula returned the serious stare: "Look at you. We're the same age, went to the same schools, grew up together in New York. You are married, successful. You have a great kid, a wonderful and successful husband. Look at all this— and then— look at me? *Nothing* to show for all my years loose on the world?"

Melanie's lips pressed into a concerned motherly line.

"Are you kidding me? Look at *you*? Miss child prodigy artist who could draw, paint, charcoal, water color anything in her path in record speed, got all the guys from Stepinak to line up to ask you to dance at those dreadful mixers, **Miss-Got-Discovered** having a La Scala worthy voice during a stupid sight singing class by our voice department chair, Dr. Whateverhisnamewas, she joins the Foreign Service, is a sharp shooter, travels the world and now is commissioned to illustrate a book by a world famous historian— LOOK AT *YOU*! You, my friend are the enviable one."

"I never met a special someone like Bill."

"Oh, so that's what this poor me fest is all about?"

"Yes".

"Well. I'm still Melanie Martinelli and I still believe that whatever is meant to be, will happen. And if that's what's written in your stars, then it *will* happen. Now, enough of this talk. Both of us have had *way* too much wine and champagne, it's late, you're tired, I'm tired. We're both turning in and we'll have a lovely ride into the country side tomorrow and the next days and maybe we'll even go visit the shrine of Sainte Odile, patron saint of good sight. Seems appropriate, don't you think?"

Never was a sight more welcome to Paula, then the beautiful brass bed topped with a myriad of fluffy pillows and a huge billowing comforter. She didn't even bother to change— she flopped and that was that.

The next several days passed in a whirl. Bill came home from parts unknown, leaving Melanie and Paula free to play the American tourists, visiting all the best sights of the Alsatian country side: They hit wine tastings and bought boxes and boxes of wine, red, white, rosé and the sparkling variety. They lit candles at the various churches, took bottles of "miracle" waters from the Shrine of Ste. Odile and on the third day, they decided to rest, do some serious swimming to shave more than a few extra pounds they'd piled on during their hiatus.

It was late afternoon, the two were dripping off after a makeshift race in the pool. Melanie won. The boys, CJ, Bill and Rascal were out somewhere hiking.

Melanie turns to Paula, holds her breath, hesitating for a second. "Sooooo, how would you like to check out some amazing artwork by the artist, Bayré…."

"Ooohh. You're kidding, really?"

"Yes, he's designed stained glass windows here in the area. . . and . . .uh."

"Uh-oh. I sense a bribe."

"It's right here at our local church, Our Lady of Perpetual Help." Melanie theatrically slaps the side of her head, knowing the jig is up. "And, wouldn't ya know— Mass starts in about 20 minutes. Wanna go?"

How could I expect any less from my oldest, Catholic, Convent School friend?

"Sure. But we'd better get a move on, get dried off and get going."

And so they did. Both dressing in elegant dress slacks, turtlenecks and light jackets.

"Shall we take my rental?"

"Nah- we're walking. It won't take but a minute or two."

So, off the two friends went to Mass. Arriving several minutes early, the two went down the sides of each aisle examining the beautiful, modern stain glass works of art and the famous Icons above the Altar. Paula, brought along her Minolta and snapped several shots, promising herself that she'd commit several of these into water colors as soon as the opportunity availed.

As the organist began a prelude, both women looked at each other conspiratorially, knowing that their educated critique would have to wait until the service ended and they were far away from gossiping temptations.

A suit clad fellow appeared at the podium and announced the Entrance hymn. Something neither woman knew. No matter, they both read music and were able to almost follow the organist's chopping rendition of the score.

A golden Gospel was held high as the Celebrant and the required entourage slowly made their way to the Altar.

Paula's nose was deep in her hymnal as the hair at the back of her neck suddenly prickled, giving her the feeling of being watched.

Looking up, she turned to watch the approaching ensemble, the lectors, the priests and finally—

WHAT—who??? Calm down Giordano— it can't be.

As the group came close, Paula's eyes slammed onto the very familiar gaze of a charming— shall we say Strasbourg's most eligible "playboy" who was holding up the revered tome, staring right back at his "admirer".

Sensing her discomfort, Melanie turned to her friend. "You know him?"

"Know him— I'm nearly almost *knew* him till I sobered up and escaped him."

"Well, we just can't up and run outta here," whispered Melanie who put a calming arm around her old friend. "We'll talk later."

"I'm outta here as soon as it's over." Paula wheezed back.

The service went as expected. The music unnoticeable. Then, the moment for the sermon hit and Christian Larsonnier stepped up to the microphone.

"I think I'm gonna be sick."

In a voice of authority, Larsonnier began with, "Just what does it mean to love the Lord your God with your whole heart, mind and strength and your neighbor as yourself. . .?"

Paula's forced her mind to shut it all off. Her thoughts teemed with plans of revenge and of course, of self-admonishment. *How could she be so stupid? Marella's gonna have a field day with this one? What does she always say about trusting anyone?*
Well, here I am living another 'I told ya so moment'. Sheez.

"OH, no— qu'est-ce qui ce passe?"

"Oh-La-LA!"

"OO!"

"OOLA!"

Heads throughout the congregation turned in unison as something seemed to be rushing around beneath the pews. A faint cloud of white zipped with alarming speed in between feet, up and down each side of the church, then finally up to the priestly throned island of the sanctuary and behind the brocaded curtains......

A stark, long shadow appeared at the back vestibule and slid down the main aisle.

Melanie was the first of the two to look back at the larger-than-life ghostly image.

"Christopher!"

Just then, the congregation burst into laughter as a small white snout, with a tiny black nose emerged sniffing from under the priest's chair, unbeknownst to the clergyman.

Melanie felt herself ready to bolt. She wasn't sure whether she wanted to strangle her 12-year-old son, vault over the pews to catch the pup or make a running escape out of the church, when she suddenly spied her son's hands from behind the sanctuary curtain where the priests sat. The curtain barely moved as the hands snatched the little beast. A door, probably at the back of the sacristy, slammed.

Paula barely stifled her laughter, a few nasal snorts escaping as she covered her face with a tissue. Glancing sideways at her relieved friend. "That's some kid you've got."

Mass finally over, Paula, who barely waited for the priests to make their exit into the sacristy, went immediately airborne and out into the street, racing back……. It was only just after noon and she was going to head back into the city and give that priest-creep a piece of her mind.

Melanie unable to catch the angry woman, trailed behind, watching as she lunged back into the house, taking the steps two at a time. Bedroom door slamming.

Moments later, as her hostess crossed the threshold, a puzzled Bill sat at the dining room table. "Something went wrong, I take it?"

"You have no idea." She replied looking up the empty stairwell. "I think I'll let her simmer down and make a couple of cups of chamomile tea……"

Face down in her pillow, Paula let out a few well-placed screams. *I'm going straight to Hell— he's a PRIEST!* She lifted her head for a moment, then thought again. *NO—HE's going straight to HELL! This is something straight out of a stupid movie!*

Three light taps at the door.
No Answer.
The door creaks open a crack.
"Like it or not, I'm comin' in."
Paula sat bolt up.
Melanie slid a small tray with cups and a pot of steaming tea on a little antique table. She sat on the sofa and patted a spot next to her for her friend to join her.
"So," Melanie began, "That gorgeous man at church is your mystery new amour?"
Paula felt her face redden with humiliation, rage, embarrassment . . . .
"And he's a priest."
"Well, Paula. You should have known better. Maybe it has been a long time since you've been to Mass. He's a Deacon. Didn't you notice his stole was over only one shoulder?"
Feeling stupid, Paula replied with some relief.
"You sure, a Deacon?"
"Positive."
"Oh, Mel, just when I thought I was about to have some fun in my very over protected, closeted, former convent girl life— I meet and am completely *charmed* by a suave, highly educated, sophisticated, fun and funny French—uh-hum—Deacon!! How is this possible?"
Mel arched one eyebrow— "The self-proclaimed convent girl has to ask?"
"Just when I thought I'd finally broken outta that mold, starting a brand-new life as the new me," Paula whined as she plopped her head on her friend's shoulder.
"Well, have you considered that maybe he was looking for the same thing? Maybe, he was trying to break out of his mold and find a new, exciting, mysterious and beautiful American Artist— and maybe he's now thinking the same as you are right now. Of course, he knows the charade is up. . . . but, he might just be thinking the same about you."
"His father says that he's Strasbourg's most eligible 'playboy'."

"Yeah, right. And now you know why. His parents probably don't approve of his man of the cloth career path. I hope I'm jarring your memory— but you do remember that Deacons can be married and have their own separate careers. So, it's not like you have to cross him off your dance card."

Groan.

"Look, Mel. I'll think about all this." She took a big gulp of her tea. "This all just comes as *huge* shock. We'd been out on a few dates. He never mentioned anything."

"Did you?"

"NO! Why should I have?"

"What would Marella say?"

"You already know the answer to that one. Every time I talk to her, she always mentions how many Rosaries, Novenas and candles she's lighting for 'my cause' . . . ."

"See?"

"Oh stop. I thought we're supposed to have free will."

"Well, you are free. You can walk away. And so can he."

Paula tipped the teacup into her mouth, finishing the last of her chamomile and stood up.

"I'm going to Strasbourg to confront him. It's the last thing he'll expect. Since here in France, women are ever so much more compliant, than we American women."

"Will you be back tonight."

"I doubt it."

Melanie raised both eyebrows, looking directly at her friend.

"I don't mean *that*."

"Well, what then, new and improved Paoli?"

"I kept my room at the hotel. I want to put a few final touches on my sketches, have them delivered to Karl while I'm there….. and tie up a few other things."

"Okay, well, keep in touch. Let me know how things go."

"Fingers crossed."

"Really?"

"Honestly, Mel—stop being so sanctimonious."

Grabbing her bag, her hair a mess, Paula Giordano left in a flash. The guys downstairs only heard the slamming door, followed by a revving engine, gravel spraying, then silence.

The journey back to Strasbourg passed in a blur as Paula's mind flipped through various possible confrontations with Christian. The sights, the streets, seemed to mesh together out of focus, until she came to a familiar tiny square and spotted, **La Poésie des Vignes**, Christian Larsonnier's business, no that's, Deacon Larsonnier's second career . . ."

Stopping the car with a lurch, she pulled up the emergency brake with a vengeance. Ready for battle, she ejected herself from the vehicle, launching herself toward the elegant little shop.

Bells tingling as she opened the door, not able to stop herself, she bellowed:

"EH Larsonnier! Ou est VOUS? Or should I say, Monsieur le Diacre!!!"

Silence.

Rustling from the back.

Good. Got 'im.

"Come on out, or do you still have your vestments on- need a moment to change, do you?"

Silence.

A small rustle, then the little door to the back creaked open.

Paula's face fell.

"Oh, Yasmine. I'm sorry. I thought I was talking to your uncle."

"Yes, I thought so. He is not back yet."

"You mean from Mass in Mundolsheim." Tight lipped, Paula's stare challenged the elegant Yasmine.

"Uhhh— yes, that's right. How did you find out?"

"I was there."

Visibly uncomfortable, the Frenchwoman, reached into a counter drawer and slid out a white envelope.

"A message for you."

Snatching the envelope, the American tore open the envelope and read.

> **Paula,**
> **I know you are furious. I understand. But, so am I. We need to talk. Meet me at midnight at the South Entrance to the Cathedral where we both might be tempted to tell the truth.**
> **Christian**

Still seething, Paula tore up the letter, strips of it floating to the floor as she left. Beelining for the hotel, she quickly put her sketches together neatly as she planned to ask the desk clerk to have them delivered first thing the next morning.

Hours later, near the appointed rendez vous time, rummaging through the armoire, she noticed that her jacket and Stetson were missing. So, she opted for her new Inspector Clouseau raincoat and a very French cap. *Sure, don't want to sneeze through every minute of my take down of that MAN!* She double wrapped the belt around her, affecting a stylish trench coat effect and slid the small brown cap over her brow and smirked at her image in the mirror. *I look like I'm on a case. Gaslight-chic.*

Out in the street, a damp mist clung to her face with its sticky, yet oppressive weight. No souls mulled about the deserted square, only an occasional tinny horn from a distant street melded with the symphony of running and dripping water. But, the lights along the way encouraged her around to the far back South Entrance to the Cathedral, her feet splashing in the standing water.

The cathedral's great bell thundered its last of twelve midnight tolls. The deserted streets rumbled with the vibrations and fell silent to the sound of the rain resuming its plight. Eerie phosphorus torches, the street lamps glowed beneath their hovering blanket of mist and the wind moaned and whistled like soulful French horns.

Her hollow wooden heels echoed against the walls in the old quarter. Pausing just outside the square in the shadows of the alleyway, Paula faced the sleeping giant head on. South entrance around the other side.

Now, barely distinguishable beneath its intricate silver web of scaffolding, Notre Dame seemed to watch the intruder from its darkened windows. The shredded plastic protecting the planks from the elements, flapped in the wind. In her present state of mind, Paula felt the sharp sound, a kind of reproach at the intrusion.

I don't like this. I think I'll just go back to Melanie's— tell that Frenchman off another time. This is plain weird. I'm cold, I'm wet and I'm scared spitless, and—

Another sound, the scrape of a shoe on the stones. Paula opened her mouth to call. A hand covered her mouth, another clenched her shoulder, dragging her back into the shadows.

"Shh! He'll hear!" The warning, hissed in English, cut through her sudden panic. Suzie Carter.

Vehemently, she bit the other woman's hand. Her adversary gasped and jumped away. "Suzie," Paula spat. "What do you . . . What the hell are you wearing?" Anger colliding and mixing with her strangled nerves, she stared at the American in her own jeans and red Stetson with a dizzying sense of deja vu.

"Paula, please, don't run away from me." Suzie whispered, her eyes shining with tears. Coming close, she grabbed Paula's wrist and clung, sobbing a mournful, helpless cry. "Help me, Paula! Please!"

"Help you?" Paula repeated. "Listen, if it's about my police complaint, you asked for that. Why don't you just give back the passport?"

"I did!" She whimpered. "I gave it back this afternoon."

"Well, good then," Paula sighed, greatly relieved. Looking the distraught woman up and down, she softened. "Let's just forget this ever happened, okay? Look, if you want, I'll meet you for lunch tomorrow, and we can talk about--"

"You don't understand!" Suzie's screech shattered the silence. Her other hand reached up, involuntarily tearing at Paula's collar. "You don't understand at all! Someone's after me!"

Trying to disentangle herself, Paula demanded, "What do you mean? Who's after you?"

The woman shook her head. "I don't know. I don't know. A man. He--" Eyes glazed with fear darted away, around the square, down the dark alleyway behind them. "He's followed me here. I know it."

She's hysterical. She's finally gone off the deep end. "Suzie, think," Paula reasoned. "Nobody's following you. It's just the night. Hell, I was spooked myself." She tried to smile; it felt tight on her face. "Tell you what. I'll walk you over to the hotel, okay?"

Suzie backed away. "I know what it is," she whispered. "It's you. You and Tony. You want to get rid of me before I tell anyone, don't you?"

Paula stopped dead. "Tell anyone what?" She stammered.

"About you and Tony and --" Eyes slid back and forth. "Them," she added in a whisper.

Them. Melodramatic, yes, but still the word chilled her. A flash in her mind, and the sickening sound of explosion. "Stop talking like that," Paula snapped, nerves raw. "You've been watching too much television. Now, come with me out of the rain and--"

Suzie snatched her arm away. "Stay away from me," the distraught woman begged. "Please don't hurt me."

She's really one over the edge. What am I going to do? I've got to find her a doctor— but, if she talks to anyone the way she's talking now . . .But, I've got to do something. "I'm not going to hurt you," Paula lifted a hand in the air. "I swear it on . . .on my mother's soul."

Suzie's eyes narrowed. "You do?"

Neither woman saw the small red circle as they faced each other beneath the great church. It materialized on the American's back and hovered, dancing a midnight dance neither could see, finding the spot just over her heart, then up to touch the brim of the Stetson, and finally relenting, moving downward.

Paula didn't see it, her eyes steady on Suzie's as she slowly moved closer. "Yes, Suzie, I swear, I won't hurt you. Tony won't hurt you." She took another step. "We used to be friends, didn't we? We still are." Step. "I think I know what you've felt like, now. I mean, loving someone and them not loving you back. But it's no use, you see. You can't make someone love you. Hell, I could have told you that." Step.

"I tried for years, and I used to think it was me. But, it's not." Her hand was on Suzie's sleeve now. She squeezed her arm. "It's not you, either. He's just no good at it."

Suzie wavered. "Will you help me, Paula? Will you help me get home?"

Paula smiled, relieved. "Yeah, sure, Suzie. I'll--"

The first shot struck Suzie, the red dot exploding into flesh, bone and blood. Her eyes bolted wide with shock. She catapulted into Paula's arms from the force, sending them both crashing to the wet cobblestones as the second bullet ricocheted against the cathedral's sandstone, a puff of dust flying up with the impact.

The Frenchman froze at the corner of the church, horrified at the scene. Paula lay on the ground, her red Stetson covering her face, blood quickly mixing with the rain. A woman, her own face obscured by a brown hat, clutched the lifeless body, and piercing, horrible screams filled the square, as if the angels bolted from their perches above, enraged at the sacrilege.

And then, he saw that it was Paula in the brown hat, squatting on the ground in the water and the blood and screaming hysterically, shaking the woman's body as if she could wake her.

"Suzie! Suzie!"

"Paul--" The word stopped on his lips as he spotted the red circle traveling the ground. Slowly, almost playfully, it slithered away, then moved down the cobblestones toward the woman in the blood smeared trench coat.

The keening American felt a hand on her arm. She shoved it off, unwilling to leave the dead woman behind. "No! No!" It tightened its grip; another arm wrapped around her waist and pulled her away from Suzie's body. She struggled wildly to return to her friend lying face down on the street. Something whistled past her ear.

"Paula!" She dimly heard Christian's voice calling to her. "Paula, she's dead!"

He dragged the screaming woman around the side of the church into the shadows away from the macabre scene. Then he picked her up and carried her fighting frantically to the waiting Peugeot and locked her in. Tires squealing at the sudden acceleration, the car toppled over the curbs and into the pedestrian zone.

He held on tightly to the wheel, cursing over and over again as the car spun through the square and past the corpse in front of the cathedral. Paula's eyes fixed on his leather gloves, expensive ones, blood-soaked now and wrapped round the steering wheel as if it might fly off into space. "They're all bloody," she said in French and fainted.

CHAPTER XXIII

Day was breaking far to the east, a sliver of light burning over the Black Forest like a fire slowly spreading westward. On the Route du Vin, false dawn, that grayness of neither the dark nor the light, like the murky plane between life and death. Paula shuddered and darted a peek at the driver.

Christian's eyes watched the winding road ahead without expression. Driving dangerously fast, whizzing past village after village, he seemed intent on planning his next move, whatever that was— she really didn't want to guess. Once they'd stopped at a light and she grabbed at the handle, but the door was locked from the driver's side. *What a stupid idea,* she thought wildly. *If I live through this, I'm writing the manufacturer.*

The Peugeot lurched off the road, bouncing onto a grassy clearing and sped across a field. Paula held on for dear, precious, wonderful life as she was jostled up and down, trying to see where he might be going. There, up ahead, a dark form materialized, some kind of barn or something . . .

She guessed right. "Stay here," he ordered abruptly and slammed the door.

Shivering, Paula watched as the Frenchman ran to the barn and pulled the sliding doors wide open, revealing a waiting Cessna poised as if for flight. He disappeared inside.

She considered running for it. But where? Searching the dim light in all directions, the closest building, at least half a mile away. And he took the keys to the car. *If he can't catch me on foot, he could simply run me over.*

She sniffed — and on top of everything else, she was catching cold. The door on her side opened and Christian briskly pulled her out by the arm. "ALLEZ!"

Suddenly, Paula realized his intention. "NO!" She shrieked and swung with her free hand, followed quickly by a kick to the side of his knee. With an oath, the Frenchman let go. *Now!* She sprinted, running across the field toward the lights out across the valley, but within seconds, he'd jumped up and gave chase. Hurling himself at the fleeing woman, he tackled her legs and they both fell flat in the mud. Frightened, screaming, Paula kept swinging blindly, kicking her feet out and Christian did his best to dodge it all. "Stop it," he shouted. A fist slammed into his ear. Quickly, he grabbed it, grasping it to the other and sat on her stomach. "Stop it," he shouted again.

Paula realized she wasn't going anywhere. She stopped struggling. *He's going to kill me. He's going to kill me too and throw me out of the plane!* Clenching her jaw so she wouldn't snivel out loud, she stared defiantly up into his eyes. "Go ahead and get it over with."

Christian looked confused. "Get what over with?"

"Getting rid of a witness." She tensed and waited for the first blow.

"What are you talking about?" He demanded. His eyebrows lifted. "Surely, you don't think that I . . ."

"You won't get away with it, though. The police will find the note and --"

"Ah, so that's it." Christian sat back, the toes of his leather shoes — a thick cake of mud covering the polish — digging into the ground.

"You think I had something to do with murdering that poor girl."

Her jaw trembled. "You did, didn't you?"

"Of course, I didn't," he snapped.

Hope fluttered — suddenly remembering the scene at the Mundolsheim church.

"You didn't?"

"No, and I didn't write the note either. I found it where you left it shredded in a million little pieces all over the floor and counter."

That little Christian ism, so ridiculously normal in this setting and under these circumstances, made her want to weep with relief. She settled for a gasped, "Oh, thank God. — and *you*, a Deacon!"

"We'll discuss *all* this— *later!* Now, if you don't mind, I'd really like to get out of the mud. If you promise to be a good girl and not run off again, I'll let you up."

So thrilled to know she wasn't going to die and be thrown from the skies to her demise, Paula would gladly have promised him anything. "Yeah-okay."

He eyed her a second more, then apparently, satisfied, got to his feet and offered her a hand. She trailed him back to the barn, pulling away at the wet, wrinkled clinging raincoat with disgust. "Where are we going?"

"Somewhere safe." He clambered onto the wing and opened the cockpit door.

"Shouldn't we go to the police?"

Larsonnier gave her another hand up. "An excellent idea," he agreed as she climbed into her seat. "Then you can explain to them why you're in France on a false visa. Not to mention the fact that that poor dead woman was wearing your clothes. Did you think that perhaps, it was you, who was actually the target?"

The door slammed and echoed in her stomach. Paula sat quite still, swallowing as he made one last check around the plane. Then he boarded on his side. She watched his movements warily, waiting for him to say something. But, he didn't. He just busied himself with getting ready for the take-off. His hands moved expertly over the switches and dials as if he'd done it in the playpen. She couldn't stand the silence anymore.

"You're not using the radio."

"No," he answered calmly enough. "I'm flying under the radar today. That's why I drove in circles until sunrise: I didn't want to risk flying without instruments at night. And I needed to make sure that we were not followed."

The propellers began turning, their motors whining a protest and then rising to a well-tuned hum. The Cessna rolled out of the hangar — for in the dim light of an early, rainy dawn, she could see that's exactly what it was, and the field, a private airstrip.

With one gentle bump, the plane pulled away from the ground. Paula's heart lifted, too, as if she'd left everything down there in the world; which was rapidly shrinking under the airplane's wing. The wing tilted down as Christian swung the plane south. Dizzy, all of a sudden exhilarated, Paula looked face down onto the world, the clusters of rooftops, the little racetrack roads . . .

Then, the plane righted and to her right were the mysterious Vosges, their slopes still covered in shadows and to the left, a sunrise, a blinding, golden sphere of light vying to break free of its grey prison. Christian flipped a few more dials and buttons.

"Why don't you tell me how you come to speak French?" He suggested.

Paula plummeted back to earth. How did — the cathedral. "High school," she sulked. "I took French in high school. I can tell you where to stick your pen in three different tenses."

A brief, spontaneous smile quirked the corner of his mouth - or was it a nerve?

"And. Your passport. Or should I say, passports?"

An explanation rolled right off her tongue so quickly, so fluidly, it almost scared her.

"That was my husband's passport. My husband, uh, Tony."

The plane dipped. "Your husband?" He choked.

"Yeah, the husband on my credit card, remember? I did tell you about him. Okay, so he isn't quite, er, dead, but we've been having problems and — and — and I lifted his passport so he couldn't follow me. He's very possessive. In fact, that's been one of our problems all along. He--"

"I can see we aren't getting anywhere talking about this and quite frankly, I don't care to hear about your supposed marital problems," Christian interrupted through clenched teeth.

"You asked, and how about we chat about Monsieur Le Diacre/Deacon back there at Our Lady of Perpetual Help Church?"

Hands tightening on the steering, "Like I said we *will* get to *all* of that— *later*."

"You asked," Paula mildly pointed out and turned her attention to the view outside the window.

To her right and down, Haut-Koenigsburg crowned a peak, a sprawling guardian over the city of Selestat, on the Route du Vin. A little further down, she recognized, Mont Sainte Odile where only the week before she had visited with Melanie. They strolled the beautiful mountain top grounds, filled bottles with the holy waters from the shrine — it all seemed like ages ago, almost a dream. . . .

The lines of the grape vines spread out like soldiers standing at parade rest, spiraling down the mountain from the sacred sight, lining both sides of the winding road. After a time, she broke the silence again, pointing to a fortified village straddling a low hill.

"What's that?"

Christian leaned over to see. "Colmar." One of the few settlements that survived the last two wars relatively intact. You've heard of the Colmar Pocket, of course?"

"Of course," Paula lied.

"Some of the bloodiest fighting of the Second World War, and it happened here. Hard to believe now, n'est-ce pas? Since the time of Caesar, these vineyards have been cultivated, and they will be here long after we are gone."

"Considering the last six hours, that's not saying very much."

He grimaced. "Yes, I am afraid you have a point." Christian loosened his grey tie — now grey with brown splotches of wet clay and mud — and automatically Paula leaned over to help him take it off. He flinched from her touch.

"Merci, I can do this for myself. This woman in the square, who was she?"

"Suzie Carter," Paula promptly reported. "I worked with her in New York."

"Why was she in Strasbourg? Why was she wearing your clothes?"

"She was on vacation, of course. We ran into each other by accident, just the other day on a tour bus. She'd lost her luggage on the plane, so . . ."

"So, you lent her yours." His voice hard. "Unfortunately for her."

Paula stared. "You make it sound like I intentionally set her up!" She cried out. "For your information, the woman stole my clothes! She's always had this weird obsession for — for Tony, and she's followed me here to --" Suddenly, Paula had a vision of herself in the dirt with a shovel. *I'm diggin' my own grave,* she panicked.

"You see the difficulty," Larsonnier said.

"This anagram you're assembling from half-truths and these outrageous stories of yours are beginning to fit together a little too well."

He was right. The passport, the scenes Suzie caused on the bus and the restaurant. "I don't know what's happening. Really, I don't," she pleaded. "Please believe me."

Christian glanced at her. "I do," he answered shortly. "I was there last night, remember?"

Paula risked a glimpse from under her lashes. Poor man, his suit was a silken, sodden disaster. She was hell on his wardrobe. And there was a smudge of mud just under his right eye. This man who'd only known her a short time, had risked his life to save her and here she was dishing out more crap than a pig farm. She sighed.

"Almost there," the pilot warned her. She looked doubtfully at the range of mountains rising up beyond her window. "Where?"

The plane swooped like the wild ride on a roller coaster. "There," Christian said and Paula found herself looking down on a fairy tale.

Flanked by delicate firs on both rambling wings, the stone walls of an old vineyard house glowed golden tan like the sand on an empty beach. Its roof sloped low over the shuttered windows of the second floor; stone chimneys sprouted from the red tiles like a seedling forest. The vineyard house and its outlying buildings rode the swell of a gentle slope just under the rising peaks of the Vosges front range, with crumbling chateaux, its only neighbors. Rows of carefully tended vines marched down toward the sweeping expanse of valley where the Route du Vin spiraled and curled like a giant serpent.

"My gosh," she murmured reverently. "Who lives there?"

"I do," Christian answered with unmistakable pride. "Now buckle yourself back in."

The Cessna touched down on a straight strip of tarmac bisecting an open field, smooth as a knife spreading butter. Paula was quickly developing a new respect for the pilot. The propellers' sputtering died as they sat in silence for a moment, the noise of the engines still roaring in their ears. Then, Christian leaned under his seat and pulled something out.

"Stay here," he directed. He pressed a button, popping out the magazine of a 9-millimeter gun and checked the rounds; Paul stared at the gleaming weapon, reality of their predicament hitting her like a cold, wet cloth smack in the face.

"B-b-but what if --"

"Just a precaution," he reassured her, and then he was out the door and scrambling down the wing. Paula watched him go, fear catching in her throat so she couldn't even say what she wanted to say.

The rain had stopped, at least. The back of her head rested against the seat. She contemplated the line of the forest just up the slope from the field. The dusky green of pine just after a rain storm . . . Paula remembered her high school Frost. "The woods are lovely, dark and deep . . ." She drew the bloodied raincoat closer, suddenly chilled.

CHAPTER XXIV

Regional sausages, salamis and hams dangled over heavy earthenware trays of vegetables and pastas. Aromatic coriander, rosemary and thyme overpowered the pungency of aged cheeses and fresh patés. A customer lingered over her change, counting it carefully before closing her handbag. Then, she straightened and secured her purchases in her wicker shopping basket with one hand and shoo-ed her child toward the door with the other.

One last customer stood at the glass counter at the back of the *Chacuterie*-butcher shop. Unusually tall and rather inclined toward taking up a great deal of space, he was pensively scratching his well-manicured beard with fingers resplendent in costume jewelry. Heavily fringed lids blinked behind circular tortoise shell glasses as he assessed the display of meats en croute. A salt and pepper ponytail trailed over the collar of the black leather coat; a tiny diamond starred the braid's point, just above the big man's waist.

The butcher rolled his eyes. *Artist, probably.* Withholding a snort, he strode toward the back and greeted the customer with a jovial "Bonjour!"

The customer said nothing, only reaching into a coat pocket and tossing a white card on the counter. Curiously, the butcher picked it up and read:

Pierre de Montrachet
Photographier
18 Rue de la Tour, Paris
33 66 24

Twitching his profuse handlebar mustache and one long, glorious eyebrow, the butcher opted for a more serious expression as he considered dark brown eyes nearly obscured by the tiny lenses.

"Un moment," the butcher muttered and disappearing into the back, returned with a cumbersome manila envelope. He waited patiently, his eyes on the ceiling, till the artist pulled a letter sized envelope from his own black leather pocket and handed it over.

"Merci," the butcher smiled and gave the packet to the artist.

"I'll be back the day after tomorrow," the Frenchman told him shortly. Busily counting his francs, the butcher glanced up and his eyes fixed on the suede "elf boots" prancing to the door. Irritating the way that ridiculous braid swayed back and forth. He jammed the envelope into his bloody apron pocket and went about the business of closing up.

Eyes tearing from the contact lenses, Tony Giordano pushed the round wire frames up to the bridge of his nose with buffed nails. He resisted the urge to reach inside the leather coat and realign the enormous shoulder pads that, paradoxically thinned him out. And the black ankle boots promised painful blisters. The price of beauty, he thought sourly.

Pierre de Montrachet passed through Place de la Cathédrale without raising a brow at the monument's overwhelming beauty.

First order of business: Find a safe place to stay. Somewhere old Pierre can come and go. Some place . . .

His eyes narrowed behind the thick frames. "Pension", the faded blue lettering announced on the small white sign over the street. *Hm.* Pretending to adjust the camera bag's strap, he glanced up and down the street. Ten or fifteen university students clustered about paint chipped tables at a bistro three doors down to the right. To the left, three youths were either discussing Sartre or making a buy. All of them too self-absorbed to notice the comings and goings of a Parisian Artist.

Ask, and you shall receive.

Giordano took the small stone stairs two at a time and gave the heavy, rotting door a theatrical heave. It slammed shut behind him, as he strode down the unlit passageway toward an antiquated front desk in a clean, threadbare lobby. Automatically, his eye took inventory of the plump woman behind the polished desk, her dark puff of hair bent over "Le Figaro".

Another bad dye job. What is it, these people —can't stand to use a whole bottle of dye at once?

Well aware of her audience, the woman slowly turned the page. Flat, red marks pinched the bridge of her nose, betraying her vanity. Tony noted the indentation on her left hand. Probably a reluctant divorcée or a relieved widow.

The concierge cleared her throat as she folded her paper and set it to one side of the desk. Her hands clasped together on the counter. Brilliant pink lips broke into a surprisingly attractive smile. Black eyes snapped with challenging intelligence.

Tony found himself irresistibly smiling back.

"Monsieur." She held a slender hand up to stop his interruption. "Please. Permit me. It is a little game I play. Indulge me, if you will, one moment."

Tony grinned acceptance of the challenge.

She walked around the desk and hands on hips, looked him up and down. Finally, she slapped the desk. "You are obviously some sort of successful photographer." She stopped short, eyes narrowing, and continued. "I say successful, because from the obvious quality of the leather you confidently wear — not so much on your back — but those gloves: Divine quality." She pointed at his fist clutching the bag strap.

Giordano allowed himself a chuckle. "Madame is quite clever. You are exactly correct." He reached into his coat pocket for a business card.

"Mais, NON! Don't bother." She walked around him again. This time, Tony heard an audible sniff as she brushed by his shoulder. "You are beyond doubt . . . Parisian. You live in Passy, probably with a view of La Tour. But," she held up a knowing index finger and flashed him a daring smile. "AND, by the aroma of your exquisite cologne . . . Definitely *not* gay." She clapped her hands together, then walked back around the desk, flipped open her register book, spinning it around for Tony to sign as she offered a felt tipped pen.

"Welcome, Monsieur. Your room is One Hundred fifty francs per night. Breakfast is from six to seven. Lunch starts precisely at noon and dinner at eight on the dot. If you desire laundry service, it will be ten more francs per day and my nephew collects shoes from behind our guest's doors at eleven each night. Monsieur shall find them again at six the following morning.

"Très bien, Madame." Tony replied without accent in French and scratched the name Pierre de Montrachet illegibly across the allotted line.

"I'll need the room for several days. I'm on assignment, so my hours will be somewhat irregular." He picked up his bag and slung it over his shoulder and paused.
"In fact, you might be able to help . . ." He found the pocket photograph of his daughter.

"The concierge accepted the wallet sized black and white and pursed her lips. "What an interesting face," she mused. "A school girl, I think?"

"She's much older now, about ten years." He frowned: *or was it eleven?*

Eyes narrowed; the concierge closely inspected the picture. "She has interesting eyes. A creative should, I think, oui? And such a cute uniform— convent school?"

The "photographer" bowed with respectful surprise. "You've done it again, Madame. She's an artist. And yes, she attended a convent school . . . Have you seen her?"

"No. A face like that, you do not forget." She flipped it over and read the name. "Paolina. Is she your assignment, Monsieur? Or . . . is it something, perhaps, more personal?"

He squirmed under the scrutiny of those eyes that missed nothing. *Stand here any longer and I'll be babbling about everything —she's more lethal than a shot of truth serum.* He opted for a half truth. "A little of both, actually," Tony hedged.

The Frenchwoman held out the photograph. "Perhaps she has visited our galleries," she suggested. "There is the museum at the Chateau Rohan — it contains a fine collection of Alsatian art . . . and then, the Museum of Modern Art . . ."

"Yes, I'll do that," he reassured her and with a brisk "merci", stalked off to the elevator. *Art museums — why didn't I think of that? She's always draggin' me into one.*

"Paris Match, isn't it?" The psychic-concierge called after Giordano as he closed the archaic cage to the elevator.

Within the modest comfort of his room, Tony dropped his bag on the bed and repaired to the WC to check his "stage appearance", smoothing a crease of makeup around his eyelids, then checking the hair pieces for skin tightness. *My own mother wouldn't know me.*

Memories as he stared at his reflection, rising up from where he'd buried them like fragile autumn leaves caught by surprise in a brisk gust . . .

⚜

Pale pink in the setting sun, the Basilique du Sacré Coeur spiraled up over the city of a thousand sights like a dream from the Arabian Nights, or a shimmering mirage in the desert.

Already the steps teemed with tourists, Parisians and pickpockets alike; the Captain took his place among them, scratching the three day stubble on his chin as he lifted the brown paper bag to his lips.

An old man — at least, he looked like one — on the step above him, nudged Giordano's shoulder. "One drink?" The wino begged, eyes the color of his nation's flag. "Just one?"

Tony handed over the bottle. The vagrant took two drinks before giving it back, smacking his lips. "Merci. Is this your first illumination, my friend?"

The Captain carefully wiped his bottle's lip with his shirt. "Yes," he answered in the same language. "I've just come from Dijon to look for work. The lighting of the tower, I hear, is particularly impressive."

"Ah, the tower is indeed a sight to see," the old man agreed. "But my own favorite is Notre Dame." He glanced around once before leaning closer. "Captain?"

Giordano grunted. "No, I'm the ghost- a- Napoleon."

The "vagrant" chuckled. "If you are the Little General, my giant friend," he said in accented English, "then, I am the Sun King." He accepted the bottle again and took a drink.

"Pah," the agent grimaced. "You are in the greatest wine producing region in all the world, and you drink this pig-slop? What is it?"

"Cookin'sherry," The Captain replied. "Mother ain't exactly lavish with the expense account. And speaking of the old b—battle axe, what do you hear from her?"

The old man's face deepened with even more lines, so that he looked like a piece of dried fruit. "The news from home is not so good. Mother writes there has been a death."

"A death?" Any idea of the cause?"

"Cancer," the vagrant told him. "And it is malignant."

Their eyes met in grim understanding. Tony mused slowly, "Then, I'll be sure to watch for the symptoms."

"That would be wise," his companion agreed. "It often runs in families."

One by one, the great monuments in the city below the Basilica came to light and the spectators oo'd and ah'd their appreciation, but the Captain wasn't one of them.

Enough. Shaking it off, he strode back to his bed and opened the manila envelope.

Junk mail . . . back issues of the Post . . . He held up a business envelope and grimaced. More charge bills. He opened the flap and thumbed through the blue slips.
Mrs. Tony Giordano. Mrs. Tony Giordano . . . One by one, the blue slips fluttered to the bed. Magmod . . . a shoe store . . . some kind of wine shop . . . another shoe store . . . "How many feet does she have?" He grumbled.

But she is here. ***She IS here!***

CHAPTER XXV

"Hold still: This will sting a bit." With a cotton swab, Larsonnier daubed iodine on her scraped knuckles. He was right. It did sting. She sucked in her breath.

"Ouch."

"Just a moment longer . . . there." He let go of her fingers and capped the bottle.

Paula sat on the countertop and blew gently on her hands to dry the medication. It was staining orange, like the tint she'd used to paint geraniums in La Petite France. She glanced at him through lowered lashes.

The Frenchman pulled two snifters from a bleached pine cupboard and generously splashed them with cognac. He wasn't being terribly communicative about anything and his jaw was working back and forth.

"Here, drink this," he tightly ordered.

"T'will ward off a chill."

"Thanks." Paula upended the glass and gulped, which was, of course, impossible to do without choking. The fiery amber liquid burned going down and flamed in her throat, making her eyes tear. But, it felt good. She cleared her throat.

"You're angry with me, aren't you?"

Enough was enough. Christian's snifter crashed down onto the counter, spilling cognac everywhere, and splintering the glass' stem.

"Damn it," he shouted and grabbed the startled woman's arms.

"Of course, I'm angry! Last night a girl was murdered before my eyes and I thought it was you! Have you any idea how that made me feel?" Suddenly, he realized he was shaking her, and dropped his hands. They stared, each a mirror of the other's confusion. Somewhere in the house a clock chimed the hour of two. It broke the impasse.

Christian turned away to get another glass. "The two of you look very much alike," he finished, his back to her.

He'd sloshed cognac onto Paula's raincoat.

"Bite your tongue. I'm nothing like Suzie," Paula said half-heartedly as she reached for a paper towel. Avoiding his gaze, she dabbed at the stain and blurted, "OKAY, Christian— Cards on the table time! Admit it— we BOTH have some *confessing* to do. Nothing between us is as it seems. Yes, Suzie is dead and that overshadows EVERYTHING else that's been going on— but—I just can't get the image outta my head of YOU at Mass— YOU A DEACON— YOU giving— okay a pretty good sermon—- but—why did you hide that from me??"

Red exploding over Christian's face:

"Okay— what would you have me say when we met— when you came into my shop with that ridiculous talk about Egg Pie, smoothing your sweater for anyone to see— OH— excuse me, could you please not do that— I'm a Catholic Deacon here in the diocese of Strasbourg! Or did you expect a neon sign to the effect hanging over my shop's window?"

"Yeah, well— why NOT! Here I had been told by your father that you are Strasbourg's most coveted PLAYBOY!! Really!! And how about those kisses you landed on me- not exactly like kissing the Altar— HUH??"

Christian spun around abruptly at the accusations...... grabbed the bottle of cognac, refilling their glasses.

"Alright, let's take a breath— calm down. We have a very huge scene playing out with Suzie…" He reached for Paula's shoulder and squeezed.

"Yes, I am involved in the Church— but I am not yet ordained. I am sort of in the discerning phase. But, I am thinking very seriously about it. I have been for most of my life. But, then, all of a sudden you burst into my life and I admit it, I confess— you charmed me. It made me question my vocation."

"SO— I am a TEST— a question mark—is that it?? Did you pass the test?? After what happened at the Orangerie—and then at your place. I got myself out of there— just in the nick of time!!"

Slamming his snifter back onto the counter. "I am afraid that it is you who misunderstood. I never intended for *anything* to happen. I just wanted to see if . . . ."

With a nasty comeback on her lips, the realization of what he'd just said sunk in— *I am not yet ordained....* involuntary relief coursed through her or maybe that was just the effect of the cognac. But she refused to show it.

"Okay, SO, then, how about at the Masquerade? Just what then did you have in mind when you convinced me to leave with you? Maybe a midnight game of CHESS??"

"As I recall, you didn't exactly refuse....*and*, now that I think about it," Christian continued, "you and your friend were at the Mass— singing away at all the parts like a couple of old nuns yourselves. How, do YOU explain *that* one? Not every American, can show up at a French Mass for the first time and follow along as if they'd been there many times in the past? So, *what* gives— as you Americans say— what's the deal with *that* one? Yes, please explain that one to me— slowly, okay?"

Case and point, thought Paula. *Guilt* and Marella's stare firmly in her mind, she opened her mouth to begin. "Okay, so maybe, we are not so different. Long story short: I'm a cradle Catholic: I went to a Convent School, a Catholic Fine Arts College, I've been involved with various organizations, I toyed with a vocation myself . . .

My mother died when I was a baby. I was raised— somewhat— very part time by my spook father and full time by his mother, my Grandmother, Marella in a sleepy, tiny village, Croton-on-Hudson, just a few miles west of Manhattan. . . . Grandma attends Mass every day and never stops praying. Well, in her own way . . .
I spotted the medal around your neck almost at our first encounter……. I too, was testing myself. My father— whose credit cards and fake passport you saw— is a third order Antonitian, frequently goes away to stay at various monasteries worldwide with his other spy friends. I speak French, German and some Italian, have been in the Foreign Service and have contracted to a few other spook agencies. I am a sharp shooter and can handle any semi auto with ease as well as an AR-"

"Stop. That's enough. I don't need to hear any more." Christian interrupted, hands in the air cutting her abruptly off. His face deadly serious.

"Let's agree for now that we both can see the hand of God in our paths. But, right now and more importantly, we have a pressing fiasco to figure out."

"You can bail out any time."

The Frenchman flashed her an angry glance as he finished his cognac.

"Maybe you will finally realize that I'm not the sort of man to bail out."

Paula lifted her head and watched him open and close cupboard doors. He pulled out a skillet and placed it on the stove.

"So, we're in this together?" She asked, hardly daring to believe it.

"Yes," he said decisively. "But just now, I'm going to make some food. I can't think on an empty stomach." He dumped a jar of freshly canned tomatoes into the skillet.
"I was here just yesterday, but not for very long, so we shall have to make do with what is on hand."

A strong, illogical wave of relief washed over her like the warm water of a soothing bath or Melanie's pool. Truth. It all felt so good. The anger. The accusations. The misunderstanding. Gone. It was as if a cloud passed away from the sun. She settled herself on a stool near the stove, pulling her raincoat close around her and finished her cognac.

The farmhouse kitchen shone with the unmistakable gleam of elbow grease and the ceramic floor reflected back the bottoms her feet. Everything in its place, exuding the warmth of everyone's plump grandmother. Marella would definitely approve.

"What are you making?" She sniffed; already the mix of herbs and sauce spiced the air. "Spaghetti?"

"I haven't decided," he frowned. "I simply mix things together till something comes to mind." He found another wooden spoon and offered her a taste. It was heavenly, tomato sauce, garlic and peppers . . .

"Delicious," she pronounced. "Is there anything you can't do?"

Ignoring the question. "Why don't you go mill around in the upstairs bedrooms and find something of Yasmine's that will fit. You need to get out of all those clothes."

"So do you," Paula pointed out with a wicked smile.

"Point taken." Ignoring the innuendo, "I'll take care of that as soon as my sauce is finished."

This new take on things could definitely turn out to be a little bit of fun or, just maybe, a LOT of fun! Paula thought as she headed upstairs.

⚜

Clad in expensive pink velour oversized sweatshirt and barely fitting black leggings, plus thick furry shearling booties, Paula made her entrance back into the kitchen to find Christian also newly changed and in an Irish fisherman's kind of attire.

Not bad. Thought Paula.

"Dinner ready?"

"No, he grinned. "But, I was inspired. Now, be an angel and find the parmesan. The cheese grater is in the second drawer to the right of the refrigerator."

Paula headed for the refrigerator worthy of cooling a cow, she swung open the drawer to the meat compartment. Oh, here. She carried the block of fresh cheese back to the counter and per instruction, started grating.

The conversation lulled as they worked side by side. Paula with her cheese and Christian tossed ingredients into a modern pasta maker. He was mulling something over in his mind, for every so often he'd mutter aloud in French — Alsatian Dialect so she couldn't understand a word. Finally, he asked aloud, "Who else knew of your itinerary in Strasbourg? Surely, not only Suzie."

"I see." She dropped the grater with her nervous hands. "Whoever sent the note to your shop had to know I'd be bee-lining it back to arrange a new date with you. So, if we list the people who knew my movements, we can figure out who wanted me, uh, dead, right?"

"Well, no," the Frenchman said apologetically. "Perhaps such a plan would work if everyone were as closemouthed as you. I've always been skeptical of the modern detective novel for that very reason." He pointed the cleaver at his listener. "'Mademoiselle, it was YOU who knew the true identity of the deceased. Therefore'" --

"I get it, I get it," she interrupted impatiently. "Most people can't wait to spread around dirt about their own grandmother, much less another "jeune fille", recruit, joining the ranks, right?"

Christian threw her a cold look. "My home is not a barracks," he informed her. "And it certainly isn't a hotel, where women check in and out."

"Much to the greater public's disappointment." She started scooping up the snowy cheese. "Maybe one of your wanna be "girlfriends" was trying to eliminate the perceived competition," she reflected. "Or maybe, half of Strasbourg's wannabes dropped dead overnight and we don't know about it."

He was losing his temper. "Damn it, Paula. I told you-"

"Watch your language, Monsieur le Diacre-- Just look at your French literature. Everyone's involved in hopeless love affairs and no matter how it turns out, all the characters throw themselves off the roof in the end. That's bound to affect some minds out there."

"Are we going to discuss literature, then?" He asked pleasantly through gritted teeth. "I have a plan . . ."

"Simone would know, husband Henri de Backyard who has been following me all over Strasbourg would also know," she volunteered.

He looked confused. "I beg your pardon?"

"You asked who knew of my movements," Paula blandly explained. "So, I'm telling you. Simone knows by default. And Marc. And your father--"

"Papa?" Christian gasped, losing color.

"Probably having wedding invitations engraved as we speak," she added spitefully stung at his expression of horror.

"Something with cupids and hearts. I can just see the announcement on the society page: The parents of Christian Larsonnier announce the forthcoming bans to that American of questionable background — name withheld because we don't remember it."

A pregnant pause.

"Allow me to rephrase," the Frenchman suggested with his drop-dead smile.

"But, of course, I am positively thrilled Papa thinks he knows about the two of us— it will get him and my mother off my back about Holy Orders."

Paula snorted-- "If only they knew the truth about the TWO of us! What's your plan?"

Adopting a casual air, de Montrachet turned the lock with the heavy iron key. No one was about in the third-floor corridor. The only sound came from below: An old phonograph blaring a scratchy recording of Edith Piaf. Satisfied with his choice of hotels, he straightened the assorted cameras and lenses dangling on leather straps and peeking out of the various pockets, he trotted down the creaky staircase.

Camera in hand, he wandered the medieval city in an apparently aimless fashion. "Très belle," he murmured before the cathedral's west front and lifted his camera. Inwardly, he wished for the clean lines of the First Federal Bank on Avenue of the Americas, or just a pair of golden arches.

Great. Another mime show. Tony paused on the edge of the circle of onlookers and scanned the crowds through the camera's lens. Face after face, laughing, critical, talking . . . He lowered the camera, the feeling of detachment overwhelming.

Light applause as the mimes finished a routine, then they compassed the crowds with black top hats. Centimes clinked: the mimes bowed and blew flirting kisses. One mime, in a tuxedo offered his hat to the photographer. "Get a job," he snapped in French. The mime pretended to cry.

"Beads! Many beads, good prices!"

Tony recoiled as a handful of rattling necklaces were thrust into his face. One bumped against his nose. "Damn it! Get outta my face," he cursed in English, forgetting his cover.

But, the determined street vendor, clothed in a wildly colorful outfit, only smiled wider. "Very pretty, mister! You buy. You want to buy, yes?"

"No."

"For the pretty gentleman," the vendor coaxed. He pointed to the chains around Tony's neck. "Girlfriend buy you necklace, yes?"

Giordano glared. "Listen, pal, don't want any of your beads and trinkets, got that? Now, quit botherin' me!"

"You buy! Jewelry for the pretty mister," the vendor clamored as he followed the photographer in his hasty retreat down a side street. Tourists and shoppers alike glanced only once at the noisy spectacle and looked away, fearful they'd be the next victim of the persistent peddler.

"Meester, meester!" The man brayed.

"Get lost!" Tony darted under a small arch and found himself cornered. Rear walls of buildings blocked his escape, weeds grew in forgotten cracks of the bricks underfoot. An ancient Citroën, the color of its barracuda body, nearly obscured by rust, squatted in a corner. Some boards and bricks were piled against another wreck.

Tony's eyes skimmed the few windows over the tiny courtyard. Nobody seemed interested in the goings-on below. Shabby lace curtains half covered the glass, grime covered the rest.

The vendor entered the courtyard and stopped.

Tony faced him

The other man shifted the bright purple bag on his back and slowly approached the "photographer". His face impassive, he looked the American up and down. Then he spoke.

"Should have bought some beads, man," the "emigré" sadly fingered the black leather coat. "That's just not your color."

"Real funny," Giordano growled as he tore away the tortoise shell glasses. "Maybe you outta get in on the nightclub circuit with your act."

Two women laden with shopping bags and long loaves of bread passed the courtyard's entrance. Tony waited until their laments over the high prices faded away down the street.

"You here for a reason?"

The agent dropped the multi colored bags that looked like a balloon bouquet and rubbed his tennis elbow. "You've got some nerve asking that. What are *you* doing here, Captain? This is hands off; the French made that real clear. Didn't you retire?"

"What's hands off?" Giordano demanded. "I'm just lookin' for my daughter."

"Sure, sure, Cap'n," the other man nodded cynical agreement. "Just see you stay out of my life. I've got enough problems with the French asking 'what dead girl', without you sticking your nose in the whole thing and pissing them off." With that confusing announcement, the agent swung around and left him there.

Tony stared after him. "What dead girl?" He called out, but the protagonist had already cornered an unfortunate young couple.

Paranoids. He worked with paranoids. The Captain slid his wire rim glasses back on his nose and hurried out of the dilapidated courtyard.

Discouraged and feeling every second of his age, Giordano leapt up the pension's stairs two at a time, cursing under his breath at the tight fit of his boots. A door opened in the hallway as he passed.

"Monsieur de Montrachet?" The concierge's dark head popped out. "Have you had any luck with your search?"

The photographer closed the lift's door again and came back down the hallway. "No," he sighed. "Nothing. I think she might have left town."

Bright button eyes assessed him, missing nothing in their merciless scrutiny."You are tired," she finally said. "And very hungry. I am just about to sit down to supper. Please," she widened the door, "won't you join me?"

Tempted by the strong smells wafting out of the apartment, Tony knew, he must quickly make some calls, and find the city mortuary…. but, he didn't want to arouse the suspicions of this clever woman.

"It's simply a cassoulet," the concierge said. "But, there is too much for one and my nephew's family is out for the evening." She was smiling again, and gestured. "Please, do come in."

So, Tony Giordano in the guise of Pierre de Montrachet, Frenchman, was bustled into the crowded parlor of the concierge, who introduced herself as Jacqueline DeLis and suggested he sit on the worn red settee with the faded gold braid.

Dinner passed, that's just- *barely*. "Pierre" scarcely choked the dry wine past his newly whiskered lips and Jacqueline easily maintained a constant, yet melodious chirping for the duration.

He tried to shake off the sudden doldrums by concentrating on the present business. "I see you have a video player," de Montrachet said and nodded toward the black and white television on a cheap metal rack in the corner.

"Ah, yes," Jacqueline nodded, sipping her coffee. "It is a gift from my nephew, so that I can see films of the opera and what they call 'old movies' now."

"I wonder if I might impose upon your charming hospitality even more," Tony said, donning his most helpless look. "My editor sent a tape to help with my assignment, but I'm afraid I have no video mach--"

"Oh, but, please, feel free," Jacqueline invited. "I am afraid, I must go back to the desk and relieve little Odette for her supper, so . . . if you will simply close the door when you leave?"

Left alone, Giordano went directly over to his camera case, careful not to make eye contact with the feathered anarchist in the corner. Jacqueline hadn't mentioned whether or not his wings were clipped— Tony didn't plan on taking a chance.

The machine clicked and the screen flashed on. Tony sat quite still on the edge of the coffee table, face frozen as the scene played out. He lifted the remote control and played it again, and again, and again and in his mind, he played another scene. . .

Scene opening the same way as it does in a thousand paperback books and bad movie scripts, husband home unexpectedly, door left ajar, clothes strewn on the carpet. But somehow, the trite phrases, the threadbare scenarios, they never adequately describe the sound of the laughter. That, he'd remember always, and the walk down the hall toward his bedroom, knowing what he'd find, but having to see for himself.

It was the laughter in her soft, murmured endearments that turned his stomach, not the sight of his wife, naked and in bed with another man, some army officer she'd introduced him to at an embassy party she was always insisting on going to.

Oh, he knew his lines. "Well, well, well. Ain't this cozy," Tony remarked. "Lieutenant Morrow, isn't it?"

The officer actually stiffened into the closest thing to attention a man can be when he's sprawled out in someone else's bed. It made Giordano want to laugh, for some reason. Morrow knew his lines too.

"This is all a mistake," he stammered.

Julienne had gone white as per the part of the guilty adulteress caught in the act. "Anthony," she whispered.

Tony looked at his wife and suddenly he just felt very tired. "Get some clothes on," he gently suggested and left the room.

The baby slept soundly in her crib — too soundly. Tony checked her breathing, lifted an eyelid. *Drugged. She'd actually drugged her own kid so that they wouldn't be disturbed.* That's what finally made him angry.

He didn't have to turn around to know she was standing behind him. He could smell her perfume and *feel* her there, like he'd always been able to feel her. "I want you out."

A rustle, like she started forward and then she stopped herself. "What about Paolina?" Her voice quivered.

It was another line, he knew, but hell, it was a night for the Oscars. "You even come near her again, I'll kill you."

Tony realized his hand had tightened its grip on the remote control and the tape froze in place. On the screen, his daughter, left to lie on the dirty floor of a bathroom somewhere . . . He pressed the play button again; she dragged herself to her feet.

She's okay for now, Tony told himself. *Whoever made this tape, that's what they're trying to tell you. She's alive for now. But, Paoli* — his heart thumped painfully in his chest — "where are you?"

The sound of high heels clicking on the hallway floor roused Tony as he immediately pulled out the video and turned to face the opening door.

"Ah, Monsieur, I see you've seen your video. Well, I just came back from relieving Odette and the TV is all full of this business of a dead American girl on the Place de la Cathédrale! Have you heard about this then? She was American, wearing a red cowboy hat and jeans. She had a passport on her, but the police are not releasing her name as yet."

Tony felt as if his knees would buckle. He steadied himself against a wall as he stared back at the Frenchwoman.

"Yes. I heard."

The next few hours passed in a blur. Phone calls made, visits to the gendarmerie and then the city morgue. Tony Giordano found himself facing the cold, wet body of a plumpish, dark curly haired woman on a metal table.

"So, Monsieur, is this in fact your daughter, Paolina Giordano?" The young coroner gently asked.

The video still fresh in his mind, Giordano, aka Pierre realized that if he agreed, then the price on Paula's head was null and void. *She is dead— to the public and her attacker. But, very much alive. But. Where?*

"Yes," Paula's father replied as he quickly turned, wiping a tear from his eye.

CHAPTER XXVI

The wind from the Vosges brushed against the pines and they sighed a murmured discontent, their branches soaring up to embrace the clearing sky overhead. Paula's pencil wavered over the flapping paper. *Oh, what the heck.* She signed it "Paolina", and tossed the pad into the open cabin door.

Her hair blew wildly around her face and she pushed it away as she squatted down on the toes of her borrowed loafers. Stuffing cold fingers into the pockets of Christian's bomber jacket, she talked to the pilot who was working under the tail. "Please don't do this banzai thing," she begged.

Christian deliberately finished his task and emerged, wiping his hands on his handkerchief and stood just behind the wing, gazing up at her from the ground.

"Have you a better plan?"

She nodded emphatically. "Yes, as a matter of fact, I do. Don't go."

He shook his head. "You are forgetting my family. If we don't expose this madman, his next target could very well be one of them."

"Or you," Paula argued. "And what about Yasmine? Talk about a target! Call her. Tell her not to perform."

"The day has long since passed that I could tell Yasmine to do anything. She'd never agree. Performing is everything to her. I assure you; she'll be adequately protected."

She tipped forward onto her toes. "Let me come, too," she urged.

Christian looked mildly shocked. "I most certainly will not. You will stay where it's safe: At my apartment. The best place to hide is always the most obvious one. No one will think we came back there. You will be perfectly safe."

"Yeah, I bet."

"I beg your pardon?"

Paula raised her voice. "I said OKAY," she sulked.

Nimbly, the Frenchman pulled himself up onto the wing and sat next to her. He patted her shoulder. "Good girl," he said approvingly, awarding her his most charming smile.

With a satisfied sigh, he crossed his jeaned legs, displaying leather boots that must have cost him at least a case of his best wine. His hair curled around his ears, but even the wind wouldn't dare disarrange it. Paula eyed him suspiciously.

"I think you're enjoying this," she accused.

"I must confess," he winked without a twinge of guilt.

"I can't remember when I've been so challenged."

"Do you remember that day when you ran into me at the train terminal?" She asked.

"How could I forget? But it was you, as I recall, who ran into me."

"Oh, whatever. That's when I met your father, on the Heidelberg run." She laughed. "Remember, he told me he was a jewel thief."

The Frenchman rolled his eyes. "Yes, I recall. Actually, it wouldn't surprise me if he were; simply for the fun of it. I do hope you didn't accept any mysterious packages."

"No-o-o," she conceded. "Just a kiss."

"The man is positively incorrigible," he vowed with a laugh. "Vraiment, I don't know how Maman manages."

I do. Her lips twitched. She has a dog on him day and night. "It's like something out of the movies, isn't it; Estelle falling in love with a down and out actor?"

"I never said my father was a down and out actor, only a bad one. Both he and Maman come from solid bourgeois rich, textile families. At least, that's what they claim. For all I know, Papa could have very well been a jewel thief."

She looked at him. "Why the mystery? What happened?"

Christian didn't answer at first. His eyes were dark as he watched a truck faraway on the Route du Vine and when he replied, she sensed a restlessness she'd never sensed in him before.

"The war — the last one. The Germans executed his two brothers and his father for their work in the Resistance. And his mother died of a broken heart."

"How awful."

Christian shrugged. "It is common enough in Alsace."

Down the slope, the roof of the vineyard house shone like ice in the morning sun.

"What's that thing on the roof?" She asked, pointing to the metal pole springing from the tiles like a television antenna. Atop, where an antenna would fork out in a grid, a giant lump of something squatted, round and kind of ugly.

"It looks like a --"

"A nest," the Frenchman finished. "A stork nest. A stork is to Alsatians what a four-leaf clover is to you Americans. But, I suspect this to be an old wives tale contrived by women."

Paula cast him an arched glance. "Why do I get the idea you're going to make a crack about babies and storks?" She threw back her head and laughed heartily at his uncomfortable flush.

"You can rest easy, mon ami," she assured him. "Your singular Deacon-status is safe with me. Remember that night we met? Didn't we say that the suffering marriage seems to inflict, is only second to the bubonic plague?"

Christian grinned again. "Never been married then, or even close?"

Wide eyed, Paula responded with conviction. "Not even close. Besides, you're the one with the stork nest on your roof?" She replied with a wink.

"Merely deference to tradition, that is all. I assure you, one day, La Maison Blanche will be the most progressive vineyard in all of Alsace!" His eyes glowed with the pride of ownership as he looked out onto his land. Suddenly, struck by a notion, Larsonnier snapped his fingers. "Bon Dieu, why did I not think of this before? You are an artiste, n'est-ce pas?"

"I like to think so," she dryly replied.

He jumped up and without explanation climbed into the cabin. Paula waited, mystified and soon, he emerged, holding an empty green bottle. "This is a sample of the vineyard's label," he explained, crouching next to her, he handed the bottle over.

Paula inspected it. "It's ugly," she truthfully told him.

"That's one of things about you, I like most— you do not— I think the expression is- you don't mince words, do you?"

Paula stared.

"Of course, it's ugly. That is why I want a new label designed. Can you do it?"

At first, she wasn't sure what she'd heard. "Me?" She repeated stupidly.

"Why not?" He pointed out.

Yeah, why not? Excitement began to stir.

"How much?" She asked, half joking.

He pursed his lips and rolled back on his heels.

"We could marry," he countered. "And then you would have a lifetime supply of wine for your table."

Paula snickered derisively. "Yeah, right. Get serious. I need cash. Your credit's no good with me."

Larsonnier chuckled. "Très bien, then. We shall discuss the terms another time. I have a feeling they will prove quite costly."

"I'll throw in a watercolor," she offered. "All your guests will be impressed you have an original Giordano. And you can smile to yourself because they'd never guess what you paid for it."

"Dearly," he replied with a twinkle in his eyes.

Now taking flight, the plane circled once, then headed north, the sound of its engine dying away like the echo of a lone bird, leaving only the sound of the wind in the restless pines.

⚜

Shoes clopping the cobblestones with a metallic ring, the horses trotted along the Rue des Beaux and came to a halt on the Place du Chateau, between the sprawling Chateau Rohan and the great cathedral. The team danced back and forth, impatient to be off, causing the black coach to bounce on its spoked wheels. Glancing around first, the driver tapped the roof with his whip and the passenger door swung open.

Pierre de Montrachet stepped down into the street and tossed the driver a centime. The driver nimbly caught it, and sarcastically, made a great show of testing the metal between his teeth. Then, with a flick of the reins, the coach circled the square and clattered away down the street.

Three or four people wandered through the looming vaults and arches inside the cathedral, their voices muffled and distorted with the mind staggering height of the vaulted ceiling.

Before the statue of St. Anthony, the photographer lingered, gazing up at the serene countenance of the patron saint of lost things. Six francs clinked into the offering box. He lit two candles and knelt, covering his eyes with a hand as he prayed. Rows of red votives flickered and bobbed with the draughts eddying the massive marble pillars on either side of the shrine. In one collective glow, they shone upon the face of the saint and illuminated it, so that it seemed to be watching its supplicant with a faintly, smiling, compassionate expression.

"Captain."

It came as a whisper, a hoarse, choking sound that carried just above the shuffling of feet and the murmur of voices.

Tony stiffened; his head jerked up and he spun around on his knees, hands bracing the kneeler. Quickly, his eyes searched the gloom, ears keening for a betraying footstep, a stealthy shadow. He rose to his feet, still tensed and somewhere, a door closed.

Giordano crossed into the nave and closely inspected the occupants of the spartan "pew" chairs. Their heads bent close; two teenage girls giggled in one of the back rows. Toward the front, an elderly couple knelt on the hard wood. *Maybe, everyone's right: Maybe, you ARE gettin' too old for this.*

He entered the north transept and sat down on one of the pews in a minor chapel.

I could use a good night's sleep, in my own bed. Why the French can't make a decent mattress when they spend so much time on 'em . . . He closed his eyes, and smothered a yawn . . .

***

O-two-hundred. Any time soon. And then? The deck under the officer's feet heaved with turbulence of the Rhine's rushing waters. Just off the aft, he could see the Lorelei beckoning him with its siren song. How many seasoned captains had forgotten its deadly lure? And how many men had died on the rocks jutting from the middle of the great river, drowned or murdered by the pirates waiting on the river's banks?

The pirates were all gone now, as well as the noble lords in those castles on the cliffs, who preached order and drank the wine salvaged from the wrecks. Now prosperous vineyards blanketed the steep slopes on both banks. Modern highways wound through tiny German villages, meandering south toward France and the Route du Vin. Striped umbrellas shaded the terraces of the gasthauses and weingartens, where customers sampled the tart wines of the region.

But after the last of the boats have docked and the tourists have gone and the laughter is drowned by the river's thunder, one can still hear it. Still, the Lorelei calls.

Mueller killed the engine. He felt at peace as he always did after a job well done. One bullet, that was all, and from such a distance the fools would be chattering about it for months . . .

"Evenin', Morrow," the voice said just behind him.

Neck prickling, Mueller turned around. Those eyes. Even in his dreams, he saw eyes like those, watching him, never wavering. But they were real, and they reminded him of the Siberian winter when a man is left to die in the cold. He cleared his throat, trying unsuccessfully to hide the sickening shudder. "Captain," he croaked. "This is a small world."

"Not small enough," Giordano observed.

Mueller licked dry lips. "A cold night for a swim. We should both be at home sipping schnapps."

"Beer man, myself." In those wintry eyes, he could see no reprieve. "You should've retired, Mueller," the American complained. "It was too easy finding you. Morrow, Moreau, Mueller, you keep using such similar names."

"How very predictable of me," Mueller said. "I must be more circumspect in the future."

"Yeah, well, I wouldn't be countin' too much on one right now." He shifted his great feet on the deck. "So, where is she?"

"Do you really want to know?" Mueller reasoned. "Your daughter is . . . what? Eight? Nine? She thinks her mother is dead, doesn't she? Isn't that better for all concerned?"

"Damn it," the Captain stepped forward. "Tell me, where she is."

"So, you can have her?" Mueller hissed. "She isn't yours, Captain. She's mine. She always was. When you were with her, she was thinking of me — ME."

The American cocked his head and contemplated him with a disconcerting calm.

"Are you so sure?" He asked.

In Paris, when they would lie together in HIS bed, and she'd laugh, there was something, something . . . "No!" Mueller spat. "No, you'll never have her again. I'll see you in hell first."

"Hey," the Captain remarked. "Now, that's an idea."

Now! Mueller twisted and in one fluid movement, snatched the gleaming blade from the concealed sheath at his back. It glittered as it flew through the air, and at the same time, the American fired his gun, the bullet exploding the wet fabric in a black maw. Pain, agonizing searing pain! Staggering backward, Mueller swore, "I'll be back for you, you bastard!" Then he found himself propelled backward, somersaulting over the railing and into the embrace of the cold, unrelenting arms of the jealous Lorelei . . .

***

Someone softly coughed, and Giordano's eyes flew open. A hand in his pocket, he swiveled in the pew and saw who it was. "You," he pronounced exasperated. He let go of the Beretta. "What the hell do you think you're doing, sneaking up on a person?"

"You called me," the agent reminded him. "Did you find your daughter?"

"No. No, not yet. But word on the street is that she is dead, murdered."

"Yeah, I heard."

They were alone in the apse, so Tony got to the point. "I want to know what you were talkin' about yesterday. This dead girl thing— one and the same, right?"

"Yep," the agent responded annoyed. "Jeez, man, can't. you--"

"Hey! Watch your mouth!" Tony growled. "Remember where you are."

The agent lowered his voice to a whispering hiss. "I told you, Captain, its hands off. I nearly lost certain body parts I won't mention when I asked too many questions. I think they've got a man working on it."

"Working on what?" Tony insisted.

The man sighed and leaned closer. "Remember that nut job at Apple Greetings? The receptionist on fourth?"

"Vaguely." Tony blinked. "What about her?"

"She's the dead girl. Mistaken for your kid. She was shot just outside this church the other night." The agent frowned. "Say wasn't your kid also with Apple Greetings?"

But Tony Giordano was already out of his seat and stumbling down the aisle, heart pounding wildly, and his breath coming in short, shallow gasps. Blindly, he shoved open the door with his shoulder and escaped into the fresh air outside. He leaned against the sandstone and forced himself to breathe in and breathe out, breath in, breathe out . . .

His head cleared; his pulse rate slowed. He gulped for air. *God help me,* Tony prayed, and whether it was the prayer, or the extra candle to St. Anthony, he took what happened next, for the miracle it was.

There, across the square. Tony straightened and studied the hotel's facade with an intense expression. That's just the kind of place she'd hang out, especially on my credit card. His feet were already moving down the steps and over the cobblestones to the swinging door. He squeezed through, hands fumbling in the duffel bag on his shoulder.

The desk clerk knew her at once. That's Madame Martino," he affirmed.

"Are you sure?" De Montrachet asked, afraid to hope too much. "Look again; the photograph is very old."

The clerk gave him a reproachful look "I don't need to. Madame has an unforgettable face . . ." he sniffed. "And manner. Anyway, she left here days ago, two, I think. But, she has not checked out.

Two. Two days ago. Tony started being afraid again. "Did she leave any message or address to where she was going?"

"Well, no . . ." The desk clerk hesitated. "I don't like to gossip, but . . ."

Sure, I bet you don't. "But?" He prodded.

In for a centime, in for a franc. Glancing both ways, the clerk leaned over the desk and with a low voice, confided, "I believe Madame is having an affair," he informed the photographer in a scandalized voice.

Tony's mouth opened and closed like a tuna's. "How do you know that?" He managed. "Who is he?"

"Monsieur Christian Larsonnier — he owns *La Poésie des Vignes* a wine shop on the Rue Ste. Barbe. At least, that is the man she left with three days ago. She did not come back till quite late that night, or I should say, quite early the next morning." He winked and de Montrachet winked back, wanting to punch him. He was ready to punch anything.

"The Rue Ste. Barbe, you say?" De Montrachet nodded. "Thank you."

All at once remembering his Directives for Effective Hoteliers, the clerk called out, "Ah, Monsieur!"

"Pierre" stopped in his tracks. "Oui?"

"Ah, may I ask your name, sir?" The clerk hemmed. "In case Madame Martino asks after you, that is."

He didn't blink. "MONSIEUR Martino," the man in the ponytail snapped back and strode out of the hotel.

CHAPTER XXVII

The photographer wandered in a circular pattern around the old city, his destination, the Rue Ste. Barbe, and as he moved in that direction, he clicked the shutter on a hundred different scenes, maintaining his "character". He came upon the wine shop from the far side, facing the cathedral and congratulated himself on his instincts: The angles were rather more believable, more alive, with the immense pink sandstone rising up at the end of the street and filling up every possible part of the horizon.

The wooden sign, **La Poésie des Vignes**, welcomed him. He stopped briefly to admire the display in the window, tapping his cheek with one finger as he cocked his head to one side.

Sometimes, I get the artiste moves down so good, I scare myself, he thought sardonically and leaned closer to the glass for a better view inside.

No one moved about. *Good. I'll get a quick browse before someone spots me.* The door chimes moved delicately, not betraying a note as Pierre de Montrachet deftly entered. Instantly, he spied the door to the back room. It was closed. A woman's contralto shrilled from behind it. "You mean to tell me you have lost him again? You idiot: Dijon is a trifle of a town! No, I don't need to pay your ridiculous fees; I already know where he'll be this evening."

Great, sounds like I've got a minute. Swiftly, Tony perused the establishment. The desk with obvious business cards — he palmed one. The neat stack of client receipts under the counter. Like a seasoned card dealer, he leafed through them. Mrs. Tony Giordano, dated last week. He shoved the bill into his unzipped bag. *No point in paying for something I didn't drink.* As he was about to reach for the note pad, the back-room door swung open and like a gymnast, Tony leapt to the opposite side of the desk and busied himself studying the wine labels.

"Bonjour, Madame," Giordano whinnied in a falsetto that hurt his vocal cords. "I'm so glad to see someone is here — I almost left."

Estelle bit down on her retort and tightly smiled. "Forgive me. I was in the back room," she nodded, satisfied with that. "Yes, inventory. It is the season of the Nouveau Beaujolais, you know."

De Montrachet bowed slightly. "I marked the passing of last year's season with much regret." He offered in perfect Parisian French.

"And this year will be even better. That is, my son tells me so. He's considered an expert on such matters," she added proudly. "He's constantly traveling off to some region or another on an invitation. Is there something I might help you with?" Estelle's confidence evaporated as she glanced around the well-stocked premises. "Perhaps, a rosé?" She asked desperately.

"Cognac, please. This damp region is playing havoc with my sinuses." The photographer touched his throat and made a frog noise.

"Ah, yes. Nothing so graciously soothes the throat as a properly aged cognac." Smiling uncertainly, Estelle pondered the shelves. The sheer numbers were formidable. Playing for time, she cleared her throat. "Tell me, Monsieur, your accent gives you away. Where in Paris do you live? I have an apartment on the avenue Charles de Gaulle."

"Rue de la Tour, of course," the "Parisian" proudly proclaimed. "My job takes me to the splendors of the world and yet, my 16th Arrondissement, Passy calls me home every time. I'll never leave." *Nice legs. Waxed. Old money.*

"That's how I feel about Alsace." She smiled at his smirk and continued, "Oh, you don't have to tell me what Parisians think of Alsatians. Too German, too rural. But we're as French as any of you." She tried teasing him with a playful smile. "Just try saying we aren't."

Great cap job, too. Tony returned the smile, but with a hint of contrition. "Ah, Mademoiselle, I shouldn't attempt to claim any such thing. No, I only come to you humbly in search of a cold remedy. I'm at your mercy." He bowed again.

Estelle studied him a moment longer and her eyes began to glow with unexpected mischief. "Ah, well, then! If you are indeed at my mercy." Eloquently, she slid past him with a muffled "pardon" and turned the key to the shop.

Tony's heart jumped up to his throat.

The Frenchwoman turned to face him with a sparkling smile. "Monsieur," she confided. "I simply cannot stand playing shopkeeper any longer. You see, my son, the *Deacon*, has run off and left me here to run his business. Not that he even bothered to ask my help, but when his clientele begin complaining to ME, well, here I am, as any good mother would be!" She waved her hands in the air in a graceful gesture of angry futility. "I won't stand for anymore! I'm exhausted, simply exhausted. So! You must sit and share with me a taste of the new Beaujolais. And in exchange, tell me about the splendors you photograph."

Did she just say, her son, 'the Deacon'? Tony's jaw clenched bear trap tight and obeyed her directive, placing his cameras on the counter and offering a be-ringed hand. "You are too kind, Madame, ah. . . ."

"Madame Maurice Larsonnier."

Jackpot. "I'm surprised that. You even have a son old enough to own such a prestigious business. Surely, he's a stepson." *An old line, but it generally works.*

Estelle giggled as she poured them both a glass. "I married very young — and Christian was always precocious."

Yeah, I bet. "He's very fortunate to have such a devoted mother. You must be even more proud that he has a vocation."

Estelle's features sank, then recovering herself, "well, he's not been ordained as yet— I can only hope that he will soon come to his senses — but, does he appreciate his Maman? No!" Estelle vowed. "No, our children will do as they wish and never think about their parent's wishes. Even now, he is off with an American woman somewhere . . ."

Tony wanted to shout. But, he shook his head sadly. "I'll never understand this unnatural attraction theses Americans hold. So gauche and uncivilized."

Estelle confessed, "I feel I must defend this Paula and say she isn't quite as barbaric as most of them."

"Oh, yes? How so?" De Montrachet asked.

"Well, she's a gifted artist actually, here on assignment for *the* Karl Junger."

Who the hell is Karl Junger? "Really?" The photographer said, impressed.

Both hands draped Estelle's chest as if to support it. "I could hardly contain my shock! Imagine, an unknown American, chosen to illustrate for such a reputed scholar as Dr. Junger!"

"Imagine that," de Montrachet added, nodding.

"Of course, this will solve everything," Estelle decided, talking to herself now. "Her reputation will be established in France and throughout most of Europe and she'll have no time for my son."

"It would be for the best. Then, there would be no obstacle to his ordination." Tony agreed. *Might even push him faster to an ordination.*

Estelle's smile faded. "I hadn't thought of that."

The phone in the back room shrilled. She frowned. "Now, who is that?"

"Perhaps, your son," de Montrachet hoped.

The Frenchwoman went to the back room.

Very slowly, quietly, Tony slipped off the stool.

"Allo-oui?"

Pause.

"Ah, Inspecteur Rouget! You finally remember your friends. Marc, you must tell me where Christian is."

Pause.

"Do not take that tone with me, Monsieur Inspector! Wasn't it I, after all— my friend, Rouget, stable boy— who gave you your chance with the illustrious Sûreté? Illustrious, ha! They can't even help a mother find her son! Really, I'm quite anxious and --"

Pause.

"Because Yasmine is performing at the opera house tonight, that's why. It was at Christian's insistence that I permitted it, and — Rouget, are you listening? Marc! Marc!"

Furious, Estelle slammed the phone down on its receiver. "Ungrateful . . . je ne sais quoi." Taking three deep breaths, she turned the door's handle and her eyes widened in surprise. The shop was empty.

"Monsieur? Monsieur?" Heels clicking on the tile floor, Estelle went to the wine shop's front door and opened it. She peered down the alley and caught a glimpse of black leather fluttering around the corner.

"Zut," Christian cussed and let go of the ends of his black tie. "I just can't seem to --"

"Here, let me," Paula offered. Her fingers deftly worked the twists and ties and in seconds, she finished a perfect bow. "Voila, Monsieur, le Diacre. Shouldn't you be wearing your clerical collar?"

"Très Amusant. I told you, I am not yet ordained." Christian cocked his head and inspected the American with a quizzical gleam in his eyes. "You've had some practice at a man's tie," he observed.

"My father's, of course. With his line of work, he or we had a lot of black-tie events to attend. Then, there's the matter of all of his disguises. I think he secretly took a page out of Inspector Clouseau's playbook— he does a rather convincing outrageous Parisian Artist and of course, one of his favorites is Harold Blankenship, Mortician . . ."

The Frenchman let out a frustrated sigh. "After the opera tonight, and Yasmine is safely on a train somewhere, you and I are going to have that deep discussion about--"

"About what?" Paula challenged.

"About *everything*." Christian replied suddenly gravely serious.

"Promise?"

"Absolument! And now, I'm leaving before I do something I'll regret," he muttered.

"Like what?" Paula followed on his heels into the apartment's plush living room.

"Tie me to a chair and make me listen to Wagner?"

"Hmm." Christian pretended to consider the idea while he donned his dress coat, "No," he finally said. "More likely, Philip Glas . . ."

She tried wheedling again. "Let me go too," she begged. "I'll be good. I'll sit nice in my seat and I won't say a word, and --"

He was shaking his head. "No," Christian firmly stated. "It is simply too dangerous."

"And it's not, here?" Paula narrowed her eyes and looked him up and down, suddenly suspicious. "Oh, I get it, you've got a date, don't you?"

Sighing, Larsonnier confessed, as he opened the door and smiled, "Actually, yes. It's a priest friend of mine who is in town giving lectures. He's the famous motor cycle priest, Father Jean Gilbert. What do you say to that? Now lock this door!" He smiled and closed the door behind him.

"Have a good time." Paula whispered to the door, resigned to good behavior, she did as she was told.

So, what am I supposed to do, stand in front of the window with a red circle over my heart? Or maybe, I ought to take a shower and wait for Norman Bates. "Ohh, I wish I hadn't thought of that," she muttered with a shiver. *No doubt about it, Paoli. You've got to stop watching so many horror flicks.*

Just to make herself feel a little better, Paula dragged her backpack down from the foyer's shelf and opened the front flap. Stun gun . . . pencils . . . lipstick . . .

Wait a minute. Hold the fort, amigo . . .

Thoughtfully, she considered the bus pass, turning it over and over in her fingers as she remembered that morning last week and the picnic on Place Gutenberg. Henri's eyes when Karl forced him to apologize and the way he sneered as he walked away. "Maybe, it's you, Henry, old boy," she mused aloud.

I've got to warn Christian. Paula ran to the living room window and shoved aside the heavy drapes. No Peugeot of any color was parked on the Rue des Samaritains.

But . . .

A brown haired man sat behind the wheel of a dusty red Audi. *Ha! Estelle's watch dog! He must have lost Maurice.* Smiling, she waved. He dialed down, down in the seat till all she could see was a single brown cowlick.

Wait a minute. Who's that?

She quickly stepped back through the curtains and peered at the newcomer through a thumbnail slit. *Well, well, well, what do we have here? I don't believe it.* Paula couldn't help giggling at the ridiculous fedora down to his nose, the oversized raincoat, (clear skies) . . . *What is it with this family? Any more people watching this building and they're going to need crowd control.*

Damn that man, that overbearing, egotistical, arrogant, FRENCH man. Sure, while he's out having fun, I'm supposed to sit here and knit. Why else would Marc Rouget be standing out there like a flasher waiting for a bus? It really would serve him right if I slipped out the back.

Thoughtfully, chewing on her lip, Paula considered the idea. *Wait, isn't Henri's restaurant closed on Thursdays? I could slip in there and snoop around a little. Imagine Christian's face if I found somethin' useful. And wouldn't it prick that overinflated male ego of his?*

What I need is some kind of disguise . . . I'm not my father's daughter for nothin'!

Suddenly inspired, Paula began tearing through the apartment, trying to remember where she saw — *ah-HA!*

Wedged discretely between the stacks of video tapes, blonde hair spilled out onto the rug. *Yasmine's wig!* She triumphantly snatched it up.

***

The brown haired man jumped as the passenger door on the rental Audi flew open. Stunned, he gawked at the blonde who, already half sitting in his lap, threw her loaded filoche on the floor.

"Uh-Mademoiselle!" He stammered.

"S'il vous PLAIT, Monsieur!" The Frenchwoman squealed as she wriggled in the gauze film dress leaving little to the imagination. "You must help me! He is mad, quite mad!" The hysterical woman clung to his wide lapels.

"M-m-mad?" His eyes followed hers upward to. . . "But, that is--"

"He has seen you down here," the blonde confided sotto voce. "Watching us. He thinks you and I — oh, I blush to say it! He thinks you and I are lovers, Monsieur and he is quite insane with jealousy! He has a gun, Monsieur!"

The detective quickly disentangled himself from her embrace. "A GUN?"

"Please, Monsieur! Please take me away from here before--" Her high pitched voice was drowned out in the roar of the engine. The tires protested the sudden acceleration and the car made a perfect U-turn. The Audi sped away from Number Thirteen at an impossible speed.

The man on the corner craned his hatted head to see into the car.

"Sorry about this," Paula said in English and threw her arms around the driver's neck. One eye on the spectator, she planted a kiss squarely on the lips of the astonished detective.

Sweetly, beautiful in her gown of pristine white, Gilda pleaded with her father for his trust before the hushed audience:

> "Quanto affetto! Quali cure!
> Che temete, padre mio?"

Her voice, crystal clear and carrying to the highest rafters of the old opera house, conveyed a touching naiveté and all the stifling restlessness of a young girl craving a taste of the world outside her domestic prison.

She's magnificent, absolutely brilliant. From where he stood in the wings, Christian could see his parents up in the Larsonnier box. *If Maurice were to beam any brighter,* he chuckled to himself, *they could extinguish the stage lights.* He couldn't see his mother's face behind the opera glasses. He suspected she was masking her own pride from her gloating spouse.

Enter the Duke. Tossing a purse to Gilda's servant, he concealed himself behind a tree. Gilda barely heeding her father's uneasy goodbyes, promising the usual and maybe even meaning it at that particular moment.

Rigoletto left the stage via a door on the set; Christian watched as the singer mopped his face, careful not to smudge the stage makeup, and nodded to whispered direction by the stage manager.

He always knew she would be here one day. Perhaps, not in this particular place, but on a stage, mesmerizing her audience with her special gift . . .

"Truly, my friend," Michel laughingly assured him, "perhaps it would be for the best if you would take to the cloth. So many women at once, and so many names, this must be quite exhausting for you." He slapped the younger man on the back and laughed heartily at his friend's rueful grimace.

"It is a tempting idea," Christian had to admit. He grunted as a man hurrying by bumped against him. "Oomph! Et, Alors? Could we not meet in a quieter spot? A soccer event, maybe or a bull fight?" They passed a stall where a woman was selling scarves of bright paisleys and flowers. She eyed the younger Frenchman and called out something vulgar in Spanish. He retorted with a grin, to the delight of the woman and the vendors in the neighboring booths.

Michel was laughing, but then, he was always laughing. "I told her you are a priest . . . . Oh, never mind, old friend," he sighed, still chuckling. "I rather doubt you could ever keep to your vows. Yasmine! Not too far, my darling."

The ten year old had wandered several booths beyond them. There, a musician had seated himself on a stool, his hat on the ground before him as he strummed something classical on his guitar. She listened intently, her hands folded demurely before her, as the performer started to sing.

"She takes after her mother," Christian observed.

"Yes," Michel agreed. "She has Fatima's beauty, that is for sure and her passion for music as well. I wish she were here to see . . ." But, sadness was foreign to his nature and the smile reappeared on his face. "One day, my wayfaring friend," Michel warned, a hand on Christian's shoulder. "One day, you will find a woman like my Fatima, yes?"

"I very much doubt I ever will," Larsonnier shook his head. "There was only one Fatima."

Michel nodded. "Yes, only one Fatima. And now," he added as they joined his daughter. "We must be going. I have an appointment --"

His daughter looked up at her adored father with a pleading expression in her dark eyes. "Please, Papa," she begged. "Only a little while longer? There is so much more!"

He fondly smoothed his daughter's hair. "If there is so much more," he gently said, "then, it would be so much longer. I am sorry, darling, but this appointment is very important."

Other children would be pulling at their father's belts and demanding their way, but not Yasmine. She just nodded and tried to hide her disappointment as she obediently answered, "Yes, Papa."

"Why don't I stay with Yasmine?" Larsonnier proposed. "I don't have to be in Madrid until tonight, so I have plenty of time."

Michel smiled down at his daughter. "Would you like that, Yasmine? Would you like your Uncle Christian to be your chaperon for a time?"

Yasmine nodded demure agreement. "Yes, please, Papa."

"Very well, then. Christian, see that she doesn't talk you into buying any more trinkets, yes? I will see you at dinner, then." And he was off, striding through the throngs of the open-air market toward his car. Larsonnier and Yasmine watched him disappear and even then, he'd had a vague sense of something bad . . . flames exploding, screams, panic . . . tears . . .

"E fin l'ultimo mi sospiro,
Caro nome, tuo sara . . ."

The audience erupted into applause as Yasmine's Gilda turned and started up the stairs toward the "house". Christian applauded from his vantage point in the wings. If only Michel were here to see . . .

His gaze fell upon another pair of eyes. Or rather, a pair of holes in a mask, where the eyes would be. Instinctively, Larsonnier took a step forward, but the man in the mask vanished into the cluster of masks.

Winding his way through the ropes and stacked scenery, the Frenchman made his way around the back of the stage, careful not to interfere with the working help and tense performers (Yasmine would never forgive him).

Where did he go? Christian paused in the wings of stage left, dismayed. A draft — he spun— the exit door closing. He caught it just as the tongue caught the latch. He sped through and ran smack into a human wall.

"Hey!" A man shouted in a startled voice and pitched back down the stairs, cameras smashing, taking Larsonnier with him, so they rolled like a ball and bounced on the cobblestone.

With a muttered apology, the Frenchman was up and off. He could see the masked man, already down Quai Koch and over the bridge, running furiously down the street into the old city.

Around St. Etienne's, down the Rue des Veaux and past the chateau, the distance closing. . .The masked figure darted through the shadows of the great cathedral and disappeared around its corner.

A burst of speed, and Christian rounded it too. He stopped dead. There was no one in the square: All quiet.

Click.

The door to the spire! Feet slapped against the stairs a flight up. Christian followed, ten steps, fifty, one hundred, two hundred . . .The last step: by then his lungs heaved from the climb. Cautiously, he opened the door leading out onto the catwalk.

Crowded together like a jumbled stack of playing cards, the rooftops of slumbering Strasbourg were afire with the moonlight. He could see the twinkling lights of La Petite France over there and beyond, the barges on the Rhine.

He listened intently. No sound. Nothing. Surely, he hadn't jumped . . . Christian peered over the carved sandstone balcony, just to be sure.

The hair on the nape of his neck tingled; he whirled around, hands up, but too late. Bleached hands reached out and pushed with nightmarish strength and the Frenchman found himself toppling over the edge.

CHAPTER XXVIII

Larsonnier ventured a look down and truly, truly wished he hadn't. Down, down far below his swinging feet, the tiny square spun back and forth, back and forth, like a crazy kind of child's top. He averted his gaze toward the horizon and said a quick prayer.

The baluster, abrasive under his snatching fingers, the sandstone scraped and rasped against his skin. A foothold? Twisting this way and that, the Frenchman performed a feat of acrobatic finesse as he tried to assess his plight. Just beneath his black shoes, a recess and an arched window. Straining, pointing a toe . . . *No hope there.*

"Hang on," a gruff voice shouted advice from above. Several hundred startled pigeons, or so it seemed, flapped and fluttered out of their nests. Distraught wings brushed against him. Christian sneezed and sneezed again. "Lower your voice!" He complained between sneezes.

"You want me to come up or not?" Despite the threat, a huge hand groped the sandstone just centimeters from his own. "Damn." The hand receded. "Too far. I'll have to get a rope."

His arms ached from the strain. "There's no time," he gasped. "I can't hold on much longer."

"Okay-okay! Gimme a minute, will ya?"

Several silent, agonizing seconds.

Larsonnier began to swear.

"Shaddup! I can't think!"

Every joint of his fingers screamed in anguish. He risked another look down and found himself wondering what sort of impact he'd make.

"Wait a minute! I got it!" The man above cried out.

Another few seconds and something soft tickled his nose, he sneezed again. "What —"

The braid of hair jerked. "Shut your yap and grab it, will ya?"

With a prayer, he grabbed at the hair and let go of the baluster at the same time. Miraculously, Christian was being dragged up. The stone scraped against his chest and elbow, shredding his tuxedo into silk confetti; his knuckles bled. He bounced once at the rail; a large hand pulled him over the edge.

Christian fell flat, lungs heaving, onto the stone, blessing himself repeatedly, thanking God in French, He lay there for a moment, trying to catch his breath.

"Thank you," he gasped as he sat up.

"Me or God?"

"Both. I don't know what I should've done."

The stranger snickered. "Fallen, I guess. You're Larsonnier, aren't you?"

Christian looked up and took a second look at the long leather coat, the feminine boots. He blinked. "Do I know you?" And then he remembered. "Didn't I run into you at the theater?"

Smoothly, the stranger pulled a pistol from a pocket and leveled it at Larsonnier's nose.

"Where's Paoli?" He demanded in a gruff voice.

Christian sat quite still, his eyes on the Beretta. "Forgive me, I don't understand. What is a Paoli?"

"It's short for Paolina, moron," the American snapped.

He shrugged.

The man with the gun let out an exasperated breath and said, "She's short — about so big. She's got long, dark, curly hair that's always gettin' in her eyes. And she wears a stupid, red cowboy hat — Damn it, Larsonneer, you were with her!"

"It's possible," Larsonnier agreed. "I am with a great many women . . . as you probably know, if you know my name. And I know several women who wear red hats. Why, just the other day --"

He suddenly sprang, throwing himself onto the man's chest, and the giant fell back with a grunt. Scrambling over the thrashing feet, Christian rolled onto the stairs and grabbed at the railing, pulling himself to his feet before he plunged down the spiraling steps.

⚜

Nothin' like a good knife. Dropping the Swiss army knife into the backpack, Paula slipped out the door and closed it with her heel.

CREAK — CREAK — CREAK!

The Fox swung back and forth over the street with monotonous repetition. She flipped the torch's switch. Nothing. Impatiently, she slapped the lens. The bulb flickered and went out. For good.

"Oh, hell," she whispered. *Okay, now, Paoli, girl, get a hold of yourself. It's only the dark. Nothing there that isn't there in the — no, forget I said that.* She stood where she was and waited for her eyes to adjust. *See? It's not even really dark. There's the moon shining through the skylight. That's safer than using the flashlight anyway.* She pictured herself explaining things to a skeptical gendarme: *Really officer, I just wanted to borrow Henri's favorite dress.*

Shouldering her backpack, steeling her resolution, Paula bent down and crawled on all fours under the window and around the potted plants toward the door leading to the basement. Reluctantly, with hands stretched out in front of her, she descended into the inky blackness.

Now, which way, right or left? Right or left? She tried to remember her path that afternoon. There'd been a woman mopping in the — *oh, yes, that-o-way.* Her fingers skimmed the wall as she inched her way, touching on a plastic switch at shoulder level. *Well . . . really, there's no reason not to use the lights in the basement.* Quickly, gratefully, she flipped the switch.

Finding herself just outside the ladies' room, Paula started rummaging through cupboards and drawers along the hallway, under the sink. *If I can just find that dress . . .Oh, hell.*

She stood in front of the bathroom mirror and meditated on her next course of action. Her hair, pulled safely out of the way for the night's nefarious activities, was already coming loose, a strand spinning down and blending with the black pullover she'd filched, *ah,* appropriated from Larsonnier's closet. Her face, nearly matched the sweater, well, in some places, from the mud in a geranium pot.

Her eye caught something in the mirror's reflection. Unconsciously, she leaned over the sink, trying to get a closer look and then turned around. There. The intrigued woman crossed the tiny bathroom and peered up at the vent, high in the wall. The yellowing paint had chipped around the grate's edges. She squatted down, fingering the flaky dust, the janitress had missed in the corner. *Hm.* She straightened and looked up again. *Yes, it definitely looks as if someone removed that grate.*

Oh, well, so much for a decent manicure. Paula dropped the backpack to the floor and pried off her loafers. She jumped and shimmied up the side of the metal stall, one foot over and sat astride the wall. *There!*

And now, to get a look at that vent . . . Paula's left hand gripped the stall for balance, as the right reached and reached toward the vent. *Come on, now.* Stre-e-etch . . . Her fingers touched the metal mesh and then entwined the grid work and with a wrench, the vent popped open. *Ha!* She smirked, and then, *yech, it's really dirty!* Distaste wrinkling her nose, she let the vent clatter to the tile floor and wiped her fingers on her jeans before inspecting further.

Pressing her knees against the metal to maintain her position, Paula leaned forward, intently trying to see into the rectangular hole in the wall. Her jaw dropped, her eyes widened, her heart began to pound with adrenaline as she stared full face into the lens of a security camera.

Surprised, she lost her hold, teetering precariously sideways and falling. *Whoops!* One hand grabbed at the top of the stall, catching it just in time and a knee, so that she hung upside down, groping wildly for a hold with her other hand as her dangling foot tried to make contact with some level surface.

Well, this is just plain embarrassing. Paula bent her head back and up, or rather, down to gauge her distance to the floor. It seemed *awfully* far . . . .

"So, you have come for that drink, after all, yes?" The slurred voice, out of place in the feminine sanctuary, startled her; she lost her grip. Something ripped.

"Umph!" She hit hard.

Henri De Bourchegrave upended the bottle he held by its neck and finished the contents. Dark eyes ogled her as she pulled herself up to her knees. *"Oww!"* Drawing in a breath, Paula quickly took the weight off her right hand that had somehow landed beneath her in the fall.

De Bourchegrave was either too drunk to notice her discomfort or didn't care. In fact, he seemed distracted, his eyes on another part of her anatomy. Paula looked down and flushed — so much for returning Christian's sweater. With her good hand, she tried stuffing the two ragged edges into her waistband.

"Late, is it not, for your false modestly, ma petite burglar?" He sneered.

"Okay, so you caught me," she said very crossly. She got to her feet. "Go ahead and call the police. I'll just tell them all about your movie studio here, amigo."

His eyes flickered past her, up toward the vent. "I see! You have discovered my little hobby! Oui, the good gendarme would be most interested, yes!"

Paula crossed her arms in belligerent pretense. "I'll say! You're really a pervert, you know that, Henry?" Her eyes strayed to the backpack on the floor. Its flap had fallen open when she'd dropped it. A corner of one black plastic box protruded. One chance. Her voice carefully casual, she began to edge her toe sideways. "Why don't we call 'em up and invite them over for a private screening?"

"We will not disturb them at this hour," Henri suggested. "Perhaps, together, we can arrive at an agreement."

And she knew just what kind of an agreement the sleazy restaurateur had in mind: The leer precluded any doubts. For just a second, no, more of a fraction of a millisecond, Paula weighed the idea. With a repulsed shudder, she just as quickly rejected it. "Thanks, but I'll take my chances with the rack and whip."

Probably not the smartest thing to say to a pervert like Henri, but he got the message. His brow lowered, his eyes flashed, his lip curled. "Whore," he hissed. "American whore." He waved the bottle wildly in the air.

Her toe touched the strap; she started to drag the backpack toward her.

CRASH! The bottle smashed into the ceramic sink and showered them both with a thousand little shards.

Paula dove for the backpack.

Henri's body slammed against hers. *"Mmph!"* In a jarring crash of lights and sound, her head hit the metal stall. She lay stunned, vaguely aware of her attacker's hands fumbling with her sweater. "Will you scream?" He whispered. "I like them to scream. I like them to struggle and fight as I take them." Then his lips were on hers, cruel and bruising. Glass crunched under her back and she could feel his fingers on her skin.

Christian paused at the corner into Rue des Samaritans. *Where the devil is that idiot?* "Rouget?" He hissed, but the detective had vanished.

No lights burned in the windows of Number Thirteen. *She's asleep*, he thought with relief. Quickly punching the numbers of the security door, he slipped inside and opted for the elevator— *please, no more stairs*. He leaned his head against the wall and watched the numbers, planning his next move. He would take her to Paris. He could find help there, and —

The door opened; he stepped out into the foyer. A flash, a huge fist flew into his face, smashing against his jaw and sending him crashing into the elevator. He lay there, stunned.

"All right, Larsonneer," a familiar voice growled. "I'm just about outta patience. Where the hell's my daughter?"

Mon Dieu, but how did he get here so fast? Christian stared up through the spinning lights at the great bear. "You --" He stopped mid-shout, as he spotted the open door. "Paula!" He cried and leapt to his feet.

"Hey!" The bear roared, but Larsonnier ignored him, pushing by as if he were a potted plant. He pushed the door wider. His apartment was dark. "Paula?" He called, but he knew already. "Paula?"

The lights flashed on at his touch. The Frenchman's gaze passed over the shambles, uncaring. "Paula?" He checked the other rooms quickly, and then, as an afterthought, the foyer closet. The backpack had vanished. "She's run away," he said aloud, dismayed.

The giant was doing something very strange. He'd lifted his head and was sniffing the air in the living room. "I smell something," he announced.

He was right, there was something different in the air. "Perfume," he said automatically. He gave the intruder a scathing glance. "As you've probably deduced, your daughter was here."

Giordano shook his head, a strange expression on his face. "That's not my daughter's perfume."

He breathed in again. The rough American was right, surprisingly. Paula's perfume called to mind the fragrance of bazaars, the blends of teas and spices. Inexpensive, but it never failed intrigue him, while this . . .something elegant, subtle . . ." I know it," he exclaimed.

The American's face was white, and his voice shook with raw emotion. "Yeah," he grunted. "So, do I."

The fetid smell of alcohol roused her from her stupor, and something else too. Something edged and sharp cutting into the palm of her hand — a buckle from the backpack! Hope rose sharply.

Henri's lips were on her neck. The stench of wine brought up her lunch. *No,* she commanded. *No, don't move. Don't . . . move . . .* Slowly, slowly, her fingers crept toward the open pocket . . .

"Oui," he whispered, breathing hard on her skin. "This, you have wanted, yes? And this . . ."

There! Her fingers nudged the plastic, and in one quick move, she'd grasped the box and pulled it from the pack.

Henri screamed, his eyes bulged, as one thousand volts of electricity surged through his body. He jerked up and seemed to freeze there. Then he slumped over sideways back onto Paula. His head smacked the floor; his eyes rolling back into his head.

Paula lay still, braced, ready for the next attack. Nothing happened. She opened an eye. The Frenchman lay draped across her stomach, like a pig at a luau. Paula risked a furtive jab at his arm. It just rolled away and rolled back. *He's unconscious. Or maybe dead.* Hysteria surging up in a wild wave of panic, she frantically pushed at the crushing weight of his body, but he didn't budge. She shimmied sideways, wriggling out from underneath — *free!*

Paula leaned against the sink for support against wobbly legs. She caught her image in the mirror. The dirt was smeared and mixing with blood from her lip and her temple. Her head pounded and pounded, and. . . . .

Think. Paoli, think. You need help. A last wary glimpse at the prone Frenchman as she pulled on her loafers, staggering along the hallway and half crawling up the stairs. . . . Light peeped under the swinging door from the kitchen. *Henri must have scavenged the last bottle of cooking sherry,* she thought, and giggled hysterically as she made her way in that direction.

A phone. There's got to be a phone in the kitchen. There was, of course, a black one, on the wall just inside the door. She leaned against a counter and picked up the receiver. *But, who?* Only one name came to mind. Only one . . .

It rang once, twice: "Allo. C'est Christian --" *Damn! How long does an opera take, anyway? She's singing' Rigoletto, not the Ring.* Involuntary tears filled her eyes. She wiped them away with a dirty hand. *No time for that now. Henri needs a doctor — if he's not dead. But, I need a doctor. I need . . .*

Karl! Hope sped her fingers through their task. With a silent prayer, she put the receiver back to her ear. One ring, two, then:

"Abend. Junger?"

Oh, thank God, thank God! "Karl?"

"Paula?" The quivering voice, anxious, fearful "Paula, where are you?"

The precise, mathematical German was so very reassuring. "Oh, Karl, I've done something terrible! I broke into De Bourchegrave's restaurant and now he's unconscious on the floor and --"

"Shh, shhh, shhh, Liebchen," Karl cut short her confession. "Slowly, now. Slowly. You are at Le Renard?"

Something rustled; she spun around. A tiny brown mouse skittered across the kitchen floor. Paula inhaled a deep, shaky breath. "Yes, yes, Karl. I think he shot — oh, you don't know about that. Karl, I'd never dream of involving you in this, but--"

"You must leave at once," Junger insisted. "The police will never understand."

Another hiding place. She was so tired, and her head hurt. "Yes, Karl, but where?" She wailed in a tremulous voice. "Where can I go?"

Junger's breath rasped on the line as he deliberated. "Haut-Koenigsbourg," he finally said. "Ja, it is perfect. Can you find your way there?'

"The castle? Well, yeah. I think so. But isn't it locked up for winter?"

His voice was dry. "There is a private event of the Voyageurs this evening which should be finishing up about now. Yes, Haut-Koenigsbourg is best. It will be almost deserted. I shall join you as soon as possible."

"Okay." She touched a finger to the button, pressing it down and rested her head against the wall. *Come on, Paoli. You've got to get out of here.* Paula picked up the backpack and limped out of the restaurant.

CHAPTER XXIX

Tony Giordano cut the last corner and carefully, slowly, pulled away the rectangular glass. Sitting, he slid down the sloping roof to where the Frenchman was braced against a jutting chimney and stopped himself with a foot, as if he'd done it all his life. The American scowled, "I dunno," he whispered. "I got a pick. We outta try the front door."

Christian flashed him a glare as he tightened the rope around his waist; the other end he'd slung around the chimney. "Typically American," he hissed. "If we must go through with this plan of yours, we will do it my way. Breaking and entering is illegal: I don't want to be locked away before I have it out with that brat of a daughter of yours!" He turned sharply at the knot. Satisfied, he readjusted the black stocking hat on his head.

"Fair enough, but you're gonna have to stand in line." Leaning back against the sloping roof, Giordano peered up toward the open rectangle. "Mebbe I outta go first, eh?" He suggested in an uneasy voice.

The Frenchman arched an eyebrow. "Concern for my safety?" He murmured sarcastically. "Mais, Monsieur, how kind of you."

The blue eyes narrowed. "You can rot for all I care. I'm thinkin' about my kid. What if ya screw it up?"

"I won't." Larsonnier jerked the black leather gloves onto his fingers. "I have done this sort of thing before, if that will ease what passes for a mind in that Neolithic cranium of yours. I don't particularly enjoy it, but I'm quite good at it. Just hold tight to that rope and don't let it drop too quickly. I don't trust these old buildings."

Giordano considered the Frenchman with a cocked head. He looked like a giant raven, garbed as he was, and perched comfortably on the roof as if he'd nested there. "Mouthy bastard, aren't you?" He complained. "Look, I'll do what I have to do. Just get my kid outta there."

"Agreed," Christian snapped and started to climb. One glove grasped the broken frame; he used it to pull himself up and over, slipping head first through the open rectangle. Whatever his feelings for Anthony Giordano, he was obviously a professional. He lowered the rope with all the gentleness of a cat carrying kittens. Christian spun into the darkness, expertly turning against the spin, and as his eyes adjusted, he began to make out the forms of tables and chairs.

Three meters more . . .

A sixth sense or was it the scent of perfume? Christian precipitately lurched to the right, like a toddler on a swing, as the rope swung wide, the blade's sharp breath whispering just by his ear.

"HEY!" The American bellowed in pain on the roof.

The knife glittered again and this time he kicked at a table, spinning left so the blade missed its fatal stab at his heart. The Frenchman corrected his spin and kicked out as his assailant grunted in pain, falling back onto the floor. At the same time, the rope slackened. He dropped and jumped up, dodging the knife as his attacker jabbed and then kicked again. The knife flew across the room and clattered harmlessly against the counter.

The assailant fled. Christian leapt, tackling the shape around its waist and dragging it down to the ground. Furiously, it kicked and screamed and cursed him, but he knew who it was before he heard her voice.

Abruptly, light washed the room in anemic fluorescence. Christian turned his head away, but held onto the wrists arched to strike. Then he looked straight into those eyes spitting green fire. "Where is she?"

Simone stared back and slowly her lips curved up in a mocking smile as she relaxed under his hands. "So," she purred, "we are back to this. It is good; I have often thought of you, my Christian and how you --"

"Damn it!" He shouted. "Where is she?"

She smiled up at him, saying nothing.

A hand grasped his collar and lifted him easily onto his feet. Simone's eyes widened into two cat's eyes.

"*You*," she whispered.

"Geddup!" Giordano barked.

Silently, they faced one another, the emotion between them so palpable, Christian backed away a step. The American spoke first, in French, crystal-clear and fluent.

"What is it they say? Cobras travel in pairs, don't they? Where's your boyfriend, Julienne?"

Simone started to laugh. "Anthony, Antoine." She said almost fondly. "All these years and still you believe in the sunset. I am with him because I have nothing else. That is all."

Giordano's voice was quiet. "There could have been more. It was your choice." He stirred. "Is she here?"

"She was." The Frenchwoman shrugged. "She isn't anymore. Henri attacked her. He is dead."

Larsonnier interrupted. "You are saying she --"

"That one?" Her lip curled. "No, she doesn't have it in her. She is very much like you, Antoine. It was I who slit the pig's throat. I did not want him to touch me again."

Giordano made a noise of disgust in his throat. "And the Carter woman?"

"No, that was Johann. He did not know where you were. He sent you messages and the tape and still, you did not come. He thought of it, when he saw Paolina with that stupid woman. They looked very much alike."

Larsonnier broke. "I don't understand. Why? Why not Paula?"

The Frenchwoman arched a penciled eyebrow. "But Christian, darling, did you not know? Did Antoine not tell you?" She pursed her lips and shook her head.

"Tony, always you have been much too secretive," she scolded.

"Shaddup," Giordano ordered, his voice cracking.

But, already, he knew. He'd known since she'd laughed. But what his mind knew, his heart hadn't wanted to accept. Once, years ago, they had shared a date or two . . . Appalled, horrified, Larsonnier stared at the woman, not knowing her at all.

She smirked at his expression. "Please spare me your Gallic sentimentalities, cherie. Tony stole my daughter from me twenty-eight years ago. You cannot expect me to feel this overwhelming need to succor and nourish, can you?"

Tony cursed and suddenly his hands were around her throat, shaking her hard. She laughed. "Do it," she taunted breathlessly at him, her head rattling back and forth. Her hairpins flew as the blond hair fell around her shoulders. But she kept laughing at him as he squeezed . . .

It was Larsonnier who pulled him off, dragging him away as he still kept trying to strangle her.

"Do it, "Simone hoarsely tormented her husband. "You will always wish you had."

Giordano shoved at the Frenchman holding him back. "I do now," he growled. "Damn it, Larsonnier, let me go!"

"And Paula?" Christian demanded through gritted teeth. "What about Paula? What will you tell her after you have killed this monster and the truth comes out?"

The American stilled, his face haggard. "Okay," he muttered, releasing his grip.

"And you, Christian?" Simone wondered. "What will YOU say, when she learns the truth?" Her mocking laughter sent prickles up and down Larsonnier's spine. So very familiar and yet so distorted, like a voice underwater. "I want to know where she is," he said quietly. "Or I will strangle you myself."

Simone tilted her head and assessed him through slitted eyes. Like a cat, he thought out-of-hand, pretending to sleep as the mouse creeps across the floor. She reached up and traced a line on his lips with a fingernail. "I think you would," she mused. "For her."

"Simone," he warned.

She pouted red lips. "Oh, very well. Why not? Your passion amuses me. Not the holy man, now, are you? She telephoned that old fool."

Larsonnier frowned. "Doctor Junger?"

"Yes. I think so. They agreed they would meet at Haut-Koenigsbourg. It is there you will find your little dancer, mon Cher."

Giordano spoke just behind him. "Get out of Strasbourg, Julienne. I don't have to tell you not to come back."

Both men stayed where they were as she moved toward the door. As she passed Larsonnier, he could detect her perfume. It was unique, possibly a blend designed for her chemistry and hers alone. Simone, Julienne — whoever she really was, she paused at the entrance. "Au revoir, Antoine," she softly said.

Giordano's face bleak: "Like hell."

The door closed.

Christian stood still, staring after her, vaguely aware of Giordano as he went to retrieve the Beretta from where he'd dropped it on the floor. The Frenchman shook himself and turned to see him checking the weapon's magazine. "You let her go," he protested. "Surely, she'll warn him."

Tony snorted. "Who, her?" The mag snapped in place. "Nah, she'll be on the first train outta here." He reached around and shoved the Beretta into his holster. Then he let out a breath. "Well, Larsonneer," he said, "it's been interestin' "He started out the door. But the Frenchman was there first, blocking him.

"You're not going alone," he stated.

Blue eyes raked over him. "Go home, Frenchy," Tony said evenly. "This is none of your business."

Christian tilted his head and regarded the American skeptically. "No?" I think your daughter is very much my business. I made her a promise."

"Like your Deacon's pro— vow?"

Sigh. "I am not yet ordained as I keep telling your daughter and now again, *you.*"

"So, what does that mean— you can live it up all you want in the meantime— using my kid as a test for your well--"

Hands up in the air at Tony— "Look, you have a point. But, this is a conversation for another time--"

"Butt out, Frenchy," Paula's father said cheerfully, pushing past him, opening the door. But by then, of course, Larsonnier had slipped the Beretta from his belt. Gripping the barrel, he brought it smashing down on the American's head.

Night had long claimed the castle, its ungodly walls towering in monstrous isolation. Paula's worn brown loafers scraped the stone floor as she carefully shuffled along, her fingers clutching tight Christian's semi auto pistol.

Looks like the Voyageurs have long gone . . .

She tried to shrink, shrink into herself like Alice, burying her face in her arms so she could pretend she was anywhere but here. *Maybe Karl forgot about me,* she worried. *He's pretty old and forgets things all the time.* Something flapped by her ear. *Oh, God, a bat.* Hysterically, she slapped at her hair with both hands, nearly braining herself with the pistol. *Put the gun away, Paoli, before you shoot yourself.*

And get out of here. She pushed her back against the wall and straightened her trembling legs. Her clothes tearing against the stony wall as she peered through the darkness, not seeing much of anything at all. *No, wait. There, at the far end of the room, the door.* Steadying herself against the cold wall, she inched her way around the ancient chamber. The drumming of her heart's increasing tempo welling in her ears.

Rats — I'm sure there's gotta be a thousand of 'em — like the colosseum and cats. She shuddered, but made herself take another step. *Damn, how I hate the dark. Think about something else. Think about anything else. A poem. Yeah, that's it.*

Let's see . . . I saw eternity the other — Ouch! Damnit, who the hell put the chair there? Paula rubbed her shin and bit her lip against the threatening tears. *Oh, what's the use — they flooded her eyes. I'm never gonna find my way out of here.*

And nobody's gonna come, 'cause it's actually closed for the winter and there doesn't seem to be anyone left from the Voyageurs event. Karl must have had his dates all wrong. I'll probably freeze to death before I starve, anyway. Can you die from a concussion? Hell, yeah, you can die from a concussion. She leaned against the wall and let the pitiful tears flow. *And nobody, nobody's gonna show up for my funeral . . .*

"So, ya gonna sit there and sob awl night till ya drown in it or what?" Marella bawled at her in her mind. Paula steeled herself. "You're absolutely right, Grandma . . . as usual."

Taking a deep breath, she began to move again, one hand feeling her way along the wall. *You're gonna die,* she told herself. *Too bad, but you're just going to have to face the dark,*

She lifted her chin, squared her shoulders as if the gesture of outward bravado might hearten her step.

After what seemed like exhaustive hours, Paula found the doorway and stepped through, praying it wasn't a stairwell. Tame gusts swirling through the myriad halls ruffled her hair, softly moaning a soulless melody and with the overture, the percussions of the night joined in the nocturne. A door opened somewhere. She faced the air and felt her way.

Several steps; she stopped cold. *What's that sound?* If she'd been a cat, her ears would have swiveled.

. . . Drip-drip-drip . . .

That sound! That sound — I know I've heard that sound before. Desperately, she clenched her teeth, searching her memory, trying to remember the castle's layout the day she'd run into Maurice. Dripping water, drip — *The well room. I must be just above it. Must be . . .*

The wind's beleaguered chorus heightened her fear . . . *The stairs.* She stopped, a foot hovering in space and realized she'd nearly fallen down the winding stairwell.

Close one. She slapped her hand to her raging heart — *breathe — breathe — breathe — exhale.* As her breathing slowed somewhat, she groped for the modern metal railing and descended. The water's endless drip filled the darkness around her and intensified. She let the sound lead her down, down into the castle bowels and stepped out into a shaft of moonlight peeking through the open roof.

The shaft flooded the well room's center with an eerie white light and painted the corners in dark chiaroscuro, so that standing there at the well, Paula felt like an actress in a theater on the round, the dripping water, the introduction to a play not yet begun.

The light heartened her; she clung to it, reluctant to leave it. *I'm gonna make it now.* She smiled weakly. *I can make it now.*

So faint at first, the new sound nearly escaped her notice at all. It could very well be the echo of the water against the sides of the well, until it separated in pitch from the dripping water and became its own sound.

. . . tap — tap — Tap — TAP — TAP —

Rats? Bears? Don't be stupid, Giordano. Rats don't tap, they rustle. Birds, then?
The tapping came closer, strangely rhythmical, even. *Couldn't be birds. Couldn't be anything, really, but —*
Paula blinked at the familiar figure entering the well room from the hall, his cane tapping the floor for footing. He saw her and paused just inside the funnel of light, like an actor awaiting his cue.

"OH!" She shrieked, her knees threatening to buckle. "Thank GOD!" Paula, relieved, stopped thinking, forgot everything as she ran across the spotlight and threw herself into his arms. His cane flung to the floor as he embraced her. She hugged him tightly, the worn tweed jacket reassured her, scratching her face, but she didn't care. "Karl! Oh, Karl! Thank God you came!" With renewed childish awe, she burrowed her face in his overcoat.

He didn't speak. His posture rigid. Paula pulled away a little and peered into his face. "Karl?" She questioned reluctantly. "Henri, is he . . ?"

In the moonlight, his features seemed more aquiline, wooden. A strange embodiment of lifelessness carved in his eyes. His lips parted, displaying dark, yellow teeth parting as if in excited anticipation of a hard-won prey. "No need to think about him." His voice soft, yet cutting. "No need to think about anyone else, Paolina darling, now that you're with me."

He jerked her to his chest and for a long savoring moment, he glowered down at those frightened, unbelieving eyes. Streams of saliva trickled from the corners of his mouth, the smile cut wide open, the glare in his eyes, blinding. With his lips, he smothered hers as she started to scream.

CHAPTER XXX

The haunted rhythms of the night reveled in the obscurity, fearlessly playing beneath the mask of darkness. The stony fortress, an ebony phantom neatly carved into a marbled night sky, the nocturnal amphitheater. The halls and chambers of Haut-Koenigsburg resonated with a mortal silence, but within the realm of the surreal, each stone, each brick sighing, breathing, mourning the murderous secrets of centuries past.

The light from the chandelier glittered on the ghastly assortment of axes and swords that lined the walls and gleamed on the polished metal of the suits of armor. Like life-sized chess pieces, the knights stood at blank attention.

Paula uneasily watched her captor pace back and forth and around the hall like an animal, caged. He fondled his stiletto as one might a delicate jewel, and muttered the poem like a mantra " . . . the prize we sought is won . . ."

"Don't you know any other poems, Johann?" Paula complained from her chair. "Wait, I've got one! There was an old man from New Guinea --" *Keep trying, keep trying.* At her back, aching fingers desperately worked the knots. *Don't give up, keep trying, keep — Oh, it's no use. . .*

Tears stung her lashes. *NO! Don't cry in front of him! Don't you dare!* She bit her bleeding lower lip. *"So, Paoli,"* She could hear her father grunt, *"you really screwed it up this time. Some spook — HA!* And her head hurt, it hurt so bad . . .

One bright spot: Mueller was getting worse. Reciting that damned poem over and over, maybe he'd lose it and forget his plan.

"The port is near, the bells I hear --"

Help him along, Paoli. "They're ringing' for you, Johnny," she taunted maliciously. "They're ringing for you! I wonder what it's like in hell, heh, JoHANN? Probably WET!"

Mueller spun on his heels with a curse. Tearing the head off a suit of armor, he flung it violently, just missing her head as she cringed down in her chair.

"You bitch!" He hissed. "You think I'm something to laugh at, do you?" Out of his mind with rage, the killer stalked across the room and grabbed the arms of her chair.

"Where is he?" He screamed into her pale face and shook the chair as if it were a toy. "WHERE IS HE?"

Paula lifted her quivering chin and locked eyes with the colorless, hopeless depths. "I told you; I don't know! Probably running native at some nudist camp dripping in coconut oil."

Shaking with fury, Mueller lifted his palm and struck again, once — twice — Lights exploded in her head.

"You are a very foolish girl," Mueller spat. His voice dropping to a soft murmur. "You could live. You know that. You could tell me where the Captain is and --"

Paula spat in his face.

Mueller's pallid complexion blanched further and then it erupted, snarling veins leaping from his neck. "THAT was really STUPID!" He shouted. "Stupid! Is this the way you want it then?" His voice dropped to a whisper as the stiletto's tip touched the first button of her shirt. It fell onto her lap. "Did your father tell you about me, Paolina? Did he tell you your mother and I were lovers? Oh, yes, Paolina," he nodded as she stared up at him with widened eyes.

"Your mother was a slut; did you know that? Are you like your mother, Paolina? Maybe you are. You wasted no time climbing into that Frenchman's bed, did you?"

"You're lying," Paula hissed. "You killed my mother. You killed her and Pop killed you. Damn you, why didn't you stay dead?"

"Oh, is that what he told you?" Mueller started laughing. It creaked, like the grating noise of a coffin as it closes. Paula flinched reflexively. As his laughter died, he just stood there silently, regarding her with a thoughtful, bone-chilling smile.

"Oh, he thought I was dead. He really did. But I waited and watched. . . . watched YOU, Paolina. Yes, *you*."

The stiletto circled round and round the second button. Paula stared down at it, hypnotized.

"You are so much like her, Paolina," he sighed. "And him. I wanted to hurt him. That is all I have wanted all these years. And I knew there was only one way." The button bounced on her knee and onto the floor, where it rolled under a knight's foot.

"So, I watched you and after a time, I found myself wanting you as much as I wanted him."

Good Lord, DO something! She dragged herself out of her stupor. *It's the concussion. You can't think with the brass band in your brain.* His last words reverberated, like the relentless echoing crash of the cymbals. *Wanting you —*

Wanting you — wanting . . . She licked her lips, tasting blood and eyed him as he eyed the gap in her shirt. The smile that neither mocked, nor warmed, those eyes that held no light at all: An exquisite veneer of petrified features covering a human abyss of fathomless madness.

She shuddered. *I can't do this. I can't do this.*

Inwardly, Paula compared this ageless monster to her father, given to years of greasy diners and a disdain for exercise. *Pop's hamburgers,* she thought and then she was talking and quickly, so she wouldn't dissolve into a blubbering, quivering mass of yellow jello.

"Please, Johann, don't hurt me," she whimpered, eyes pleading. "Please don't hurt me. I'll do anything, anything." Voice artfully trailing away.

Lashes downcast, but she felt those eyes on her, watchful, assessing. She trembled, but that was okay. At first, she thought he wasn't buying it, because he didn't say anything. Then, his hand touched her cheek; it was cold, ice cold.

His voice caught. "You *are* like her, aren't you?" he murmured and started to pull her collar away from her neck. He bent toward her.

"I know where he is," Paula quickly spoke up, before those lips could hurt her again. "I know where you can find him."

His lips paused just over hers, working as he struggled between two obsessions. "Where?" He finally said.

"It's written down," she told him, trying not to shrink from the dank breath in her face. "In my backpack. But I left it in the well room. If you'll go down and get it for me —"

"Later," he whispered and leaned toward her.

Oh, God, she panicked. "B-b-but I might change my mind," Paula warned him. "I might not be so frightened . . . then." She did her best to smile and fought to arch an eyebrow. Probably she looked like she had a facial tic, but he got the idea.

"Very well," he breathed. "I'll be back."

He left the room. Paula sagged into her seat. Her skin crawled from his touch; her head pounded with the William Tell Overture.

No time now, Paoli. No TIME.

She started to rock in the chair. Back and forth, back and forth . . . teetering . . .

CRASH! Splintering apart as it impacted the hard stone floor, the chair shattered. She was free, lungs heaving, nose flat on the ground. *I can't get up, I can't,* she realized and planned to die right then and there.

Then, she heard him, she heard him dash across the room and then his hand was gripping her arm, dragging her up.

"NO!" Furiously, she swung and kicked, using words she didn't even know she knew.

"Merde!" Swore the voice and it wasn't Mueller's.

She peered up at him through the blinding, shifting lights in her eyes as he pulled her mercilessly to her feet.

"Christian?" She wondered, disbelieving.

"Let's be off," he briskly said and with an arm supporting her, helped her out of the great hall and up the steps. Up they climbed, toward the open walkway, trying not to make a sound on the stairs, not talking, hardly daring to breathe. And then, they were out in the air and as it cleared her head a little, the wind swept up from the Vosges slapping her face.

Far away, lights twinkled like a crystal necklace on the Route du Vin, unaware of the drama being played out on the mountain. The lights, Paula realized. Somehow, he'd extinguished the great spotlights illuminating the castle. That means . . . the horror of it possessed her. *That means he's killed the caretaker, too.*

Christian led her into the shadows of a turret as she clung to him, holding tight for her knees weren't working as she kept sagging to the ground. He lifted her face, cupping it his hands, her hair tangling in his fingers.

"Thank God," he was saying. "Thank God you are safe."

"He said, my mother —"

"Shhh."

Paula buried her face in his sweater, scraping her cheek against its rough weave to ease the feel of Mueller's hands on her skin. His arms reassuring her that she was not dreaming.

An unearthly howl rose up from somewhere below. "Mueller!" She cried out, but Christian stifled her, covering her mouth with his hands, so all that resulted was a whimper, born of hysteria. She trembled at the thought of that monster finding them here, of him putting his hands on her again . . .

Christian was talking to her in a low, reasonable tone that carried over the screams from below. "Where is my pistol?"

She blinked, hardly aware of what he was saying. "Your . . . oh. Oh, Lord. I left it down there. Oh, Christian!" The screams died; all was tense, listening silence. "He's coming," she sobbed.

"Shh, shh. Listen to me. Listen," he said dragging her tear-streaked face back to look into his. "I want you to leave. Take the back stairs. Here are my keys — Paula, stop shaking your head, you must listen to me. I'm afraid they've killed Rouget and he's the only one who knows. Listen! There's a restaurant halfway down the mountain, remember? Can you manage the door?"

"Yeah," Paula gulped her tears and let out a hysterical giggle at the same time. "I think I can handle it."

"Good. Very good. Use the telephone there and dial the operator. Ask to be connected directly with the Service de Documentation Exterieure et Contra-Espionage — can you remember that?"

"Oh, God." She took a step back. "You're with them?"

"Just do as I say," he said. "I don't have time to explain. Paula," his fingers tightened on her elbow, "he won't ever touch you again, I swear. But you must trust me. Please, *please* try to trust me."

Paula looked into his eyes. They were nothing like Mueller's, no fathomless depths, but clear as if she could read his heart in them.

Silently, she took his keys. He grasped her fingers and kissed the tips still splotched with scarlet medicine.

"Now, go," he commanded and spinning her around, pushed her gently from him.

Trust me, he said, and the words rang in her ears as she flew down the back stairs. *Trust me, trust me, trust me* . . . The silence ominous, the darkness waiting . . . Paula threw her weight desperately against the huge wooden gate and it swung open, just a crack. With a sob half-swallowed, she slipped through and escaped the castle into the night.

As if trapped in a nightmare, unable to waken, scarcely able to breathe . . . she reached the restaurant . . . then somehow ended up back in Mundolsheim, banging on the door of Melanie Rogers . . .

Every nerve, every hair on his body danced. The Frenchman pressed further into the turret, ears keening for any sound, any movement. Another part of his mind was with Paula. Had she gotten away? Would she have enough time?

No point in trying to reach the well room. Mueller had probably found the gun and would most likely use it against him.

A sound.

The faintest creak of a leather shoe. He was there, not three meters down the steps. He tensed and waited.

Creak! The sound came again: Mueller had a creak in his right shoe.

He forced himself to wait, not to spring too soon. One, two, and —

Larsonnier hurled himself against the surprised assassin; he turned but too late and the gun went clattering across the terrace flagstones as the combatants landed hard on the rock tiles. Rolling, rolling, teetering on the brink of the stairs and then back . . .

Christian kicked the pistol out of reach.

Then, abruptly, Mueller flipped sideways and laughing triumphantly, pressed a stiletto to the Larsonnier's throat. His knee thrust into his victim's chest, so he couldn't breathe. Smiling down on the Frenchman, his face, like death in the moonlight.

"So, you didn't die, Frenchman," the assassin gloated. "No matter you will now."

Desperately, he grabbed the blade and pushed back. His fingers bled; his arms trembled with the effort.

"Where is he?" The German hissed in French. "Where is the Captain?"

Larsonnier tried averting his gaze from those hellish orbs. "Dead" he answered through clenched teeth. "Julienne got to him first."

"NO!" Mueller screamed. "NO! He was MINE!" Enraged, the killer bore down on the knife and it tore into Larsonnier's hands. He held on for his life, barely breathing under the weight of the killer's knee.

" '**Rise up, for you the flag is *flung!*'**" A familiar voice quoted from the stairs.

"Maybe, you should give up playin' camera man and get a library card, maybe, eh, YO-HANN?"

Mueller's head shot up. Hollow eyes fixed, pupils narrowed, he stared raptly at the figure standing next to the stairs.

"The Captain, at *last*," He breathed.

Giordano jerked his head. "Seems like just yesterday I saw you go over the side of that boat, Johann. Damn, I was so sure you were fish fodder."

The killer licked pale, crusted lips. "I never forgot, Captain. I never forgot the cold, the dark coldness of the water. Wanting to breath and drinking in the water . . ." He shuddered at the memory. The knife twitched at Larsonnier's throat as if it had life of its own.

"I remembered, all those years. I watched and waited. You, and that bitch daughter of yours . . . taunting me, always laughing your laugh, no less." The German looked down at Larsonnier. "But she won't laugh any longer," he crooned.

" 'Oh the bleeding drops of red . . .' Drop your weapon now, Captain or the Frenchman dies."

Giordano actually chuckled. And then he laughed out loud. A great, booming blast of laughter bouncing back and forth off the castle walls, to the astonishment of both killer and intended victim. He leaned an elbow against the low wall to support himself.

Mueller's eyes narrowed. "You find something amusing?"

Christian silently cursed the man, and kept pushing against Mueller's arm.

The Italian-American wiped his eyes.

"Johann, you're gonna like this; it's what they call eye-runny. See, you're under this illusion that I want Frenchy to live."

He had Mueller's attention. "You don't?" Mueller warily asked.

"Hell, *no!* You'll be doin' me a personal favor." Tony's sardonic gaze dropped to the Frenchman as he shook his head mournfully.

"Think of it. Lookin' at that face over the dinin' room table the rest of my recliner years."

Mueller sat quite still, his focus on Giordano. "What do you suggest?" He asked almost humorously.

"Well, I got a solution," Tony confided.

"You slice Frenchy's throat, I wax you. No muss, no fuss and the kid'll never know the difference. And think how dramatic it'll look in the obits — though. You'll be dead and I won't, so it shoots the hell out of your credibility."

The silence pounded. Finally. "You're bluffing, Captain," the killer rasped.

Giordano shrugged. "Suit yourself. Most likely, I'll wax you anyways."

Mueller's pressure on his lungs relaxed. *NOW!* Christian kicked up with his knee, the killer fell back with a grunt and Larsonnier rolled away toward the wall.

"NO!" With a ghastly shriek, the German lifted his knife and rushed at the Frenchman. Christian braced for the blow and at the same time, heard the Beretta spit once, twice.

Mueller stopped; his eyes widened. As if in slow motion, his hand dropped and with a hiss of breath released from stagnant lungs, he slid dead to the ground.

"So much for a quiet retirement," Giordano complained and lowered the gun.

"Where's Paoli?"

"Safe." Christian slumped against the wall. He fumbled for his cigarettes and tried to light one, but he couldn't quite manage with a bloody hand. Sighing, the American did it for him, then lit one for himself. They sat in silence for a time, smoking, watching the stars in the sky overhead.

Giordano cursed. "All these years, I tried to keep it from her. And now this. What the hell am I going to do?"

Grudgingly, Larsonnier felt for the man. "Perhaps, the best thing would be to tell her the truth."

The American cast a cynical glance at Christian. "Yeah, right. She's mad enough as it is. So, you want me to screw up the rest of her life. And then," he added guilelessly, "there's this disgustin' business of you and her mother . . . Mind you, I'm the forgivin' type, even when you go and do something stupid like hitting me over the head. But, Paoli, now, she's more Italian than I am. Jealous as the sun of its orbit and burns ten times as hot."

Christian sat up straight. "Simone found out about her husband's, ah, eccentricities," he promptly began. "Jealously: She murdered him and disappeared, never to be seen again. Mueller, of course, was quite mad. Nothing he said could possibly be taken seriously."

Tony considered this. Finally, he nodded with reluctant admiration. "It could work. But, what about the police?"

Larsonnier found his handkerchief and blotted his hand. "I'm quite certain, they'll be satisfied with that," he assured Paula's father. "After I speak with my people in Paris."

Stunned blue eyes looked over the Frenchman. And then, Tony started to laugh. "Well, I'll be damned," he chortled, slapping his leg. "You're one of us."

All at once, everything began to make a crazy kind of sense. Christian stared at Paula's father, dismayed and in a strangled voice, repeated the operative word, "Us?"

BANG — BANG — BANG!!

Snores ceased with a snort, the figure jumped up out of bed, running his hand through his hair.

"Melanie— wake up— wake UP!"

"Huh?"

BANG — BANG -BANG-BANG!!!

"Someone's at the door, Superman, go and see who it is and I'll get the shotgun."

Melanie Rogers swiftly unfurled the thick comforter off the bed, sending it flying as she grabbed her robe and scurried down the stairs.

Nothing in the peep hole. *Maybe, it was just kids. They seem to be gone.*

Not leaving anything to chance, she undid several deadbolts, keeping the chain engaged, cracking open the door.

Slumped across the landing, unconscious . . . lay a woman in shredded, bloodied clothing . . .

Melanie instantly went into action.

"OH MY GOD— BILL— IT'S PAULA!!"

CHAPTER XXXI

Electric excitement charged the very air of the old city's streets: Strasbourg's first snowfall. Housewives hurried from the grocery to the bakery, their baskets brimming with meats, fresh fruits and the inevitable crusty baguette. Old men gauged the low hanging clouds from their park benches. With cheerful pessimism, they predicted a harsh winter and worse rheumatism, while the children darted through the crowds, their shouts louder than usual, if possible.

The American peered at the ominous skies from under the brim of her Stetson as she waited for the light on the Rue des Arcades. Her toe tapping an silent cadence, her artists' folio clasped in two red hands.

Snow. I'm ready for it: the latest mysteries stacked next to the worn wing chair, a box of chocolate truffles stashed in the top cupboard, just behind the rice cakes (never used) and, thank the stars, a radiator that finally works.

Green. She followed the flow of pedestrians across the thoroughfare, her thoughts on the telephone call of the night before:

Ring. Ring. Ring.

Click.

"You've reached the First Lady. Ronnie and me ain't here right now —"

"Grandma? It's Paoli."

Worried. "Paoli? Is everything okay? How's the head? Ya gotta watch those head injuries, ya know."

Reassuring. "My head's fine, Marella. It's my life." Paula pulled at the hem of her old blue bathrobe so it covered her chilled toes.

"So? What's wrong with ya life?"

She took a swig of cold Alsatian beer before she answered. "I'm going to end up like old lady Spinelli," Paula said miserable, a tear on her cheek. "I'll live with about a dozen cats named after famous dead artists, and I'll have to repaint my house after every Halloween from all the rotten eggs."

Snort. "Is that awl? Listen, with all this energy ya got to wallow in, ya must be awl right. So, here's advice from the old bitch, not that you'll follow it: stop moonin' over the French Deacon and get on with your life. Ya got talent, which is more than most people ever dream of, so use it. Now, put down that beer and go to bed— life stinks enough without gettin' fat and having' dark circles under your eyes."

"Okay, Grandma."

"I should be on the clock wit all this free advice."

Okay, Marella, so I'll get on with my life. I've got my own place, and a job with Yasmine's troupe and soon I'll be making a name for myself. A perfect life, she told herself. *What I've always wanted . . .*

Her artist's eye skimmed the half-timbered facade of the Maison Kammerzell, automatically planning how she'd paint the wood reliefs sandwiched between the five floors and the steep, sloping roof. Then, it dropped down, down to the cobblestoned street, where one American sat alone in the middle of a cluster of wrought iron tables and chairs.

He didn't see her — or at least, he pretended not to — his nose, firmly planted in his newspaper until she'd dropped her backpack into one chair and herself into another.

"Good Lord, Pop." Paula complained. "It's got to be thirty degrees out here. You want to catch your death or something? Where's your hat? Where's your scarf and gloves?"

The paper rustled. "Left 'em at Mass," Tony lied.

"Listen, it's awfully cold out here. Why don't we go back to my place? I'll fix you a hot meal." Coaxing. "Your favorite, sausage and sauerkraut."

Tony snorted. "Thanks, but the word's out you need your walls painted. I did my share haulin' up your crap those five flights."

Who talked? Paula wondered. A waiter armed with a tray, hesitantly approached the crazy pair sitting out in the cold. The behemoth curtly ordered two beers. The young woman in the very strange hat intervened and asked for a cappuccino.

"So." Her father settled back with an audible screech of the metal seat. "What's so important you couldn't tell me on the phone?"

"Oh, just a little unfinished business." She found the bulging envelope in her backpack and set it on the table with both hands as if it were a precious document. "Voila," she said.

He eyed it suspiciously. "Well, what is it?"

"The money I owe you," Paula answered. "That I sto— er, borrowed."

Eyebrows raised, Tony opened the envelope and thumbed through the multicolored stack, astonished. "There's got to be — how many times have I told you not to carry around — where'd you get this kind of cash?"

Paula laughed. "Relax, Pop. I didn't burglarize any more restaurants, if that's what you're worried about. I'm turnin' over a — Well, let's just say my leaf is on its side. I sold my car to Marella."

Her father's eyes popped wide. "My mother's drivin' a Camaro?"

The waiter returned with their drinks. With a glare at the meager tip, he hurried back indoors, where all the sane people were. The cappuccino steamed in the cold air and the whipped cream was firm and speckled with little bits of chocolate sprinkles. *Ah, just the way I like it.* She scooped off a dollop of cream and delicately licked it from the spoon.

Tony cleared his throat. "I got something for you, too," he said and tossed a package across the bistro table.

Paula picked it up, intrigued. It was heavy. "What is it?"

"Think of it as a late birthday present," he suggested.

She tore at the paper. Then, she looked at her father. "This is Karl's book," she said stupidly.

"So you can read," he approved.

Paula opened the thick tome and leafed through the crisp, clean pages. She stared at the water colors and ink sketches on page twenty-five. "This is my illustration," she exclaimed. "And this one, and this one."

"Yeah. I guess that's why your name's on the cover."

Speechless, she looked at the cover. Then she looked at her father. Then, she looked again at the book, and became teary eyed.

"Hey, come on, Paoli." Glancing around uncomfortable, Tony gave her his handkerchief. "You been runnin' like a faucet with a broken spigot for weeks. What's goin' on?"

Paula dabbed her eyes and blew her nose. "Oh, I don't know," she sighed miserable. "Maybe its hormones. Or maybe, it's a reaction to everything. I still feel like I knew Karl, you know? And poor, poor Jorgi . . . I shoulda guessed. How could I have missed Mueller-Morrow being such a disguise genius? He was SO perfect at it."

"Hmph," Her father said and drank his beer. "There really was no way you could have known. I even had no idea how bent he got."

She really looked at him, this time. When had his hair greyed? She didn't remember that. And that tiny scar over his right eye. When did he get that?

"Maybe, I should go home," she ventured. "Marella's not gettin' any younger, you know, and —"

"Sure," Tony agreed. "I mean, if you don't like being' alone. . . ."

Paula stiffened. "Who says I don't like being alone?" She snapped. "I love being alone. I'm having a wonderful time my own."

Tony smacked the foam off his lips.

"Don't get me wrong," she hastily amended. "I meet all kinds of men. I mean, lots of them. As it is, I hardly have time to paint. Don't worry about me; I'm having a great time."

"Yep. Life is great," Tony repeated and picked up his paper. "So, okay, fine."

Paula wished she'd ordered a beer. Okay, so maybe things weren't so great. They'd get better. Sooner or later, she'd quit comparing every man who asked out with the one picture she had in her head.

A hand touched her shoulder. By the waft of cologne, she knew who it was before she even looked up, so she was able to keep her jaw firmly shut. Her eyebrows lowered to a straight, belligerent line. "What are you doing here?" She challenged.

Larsonnier's eyebrows rose in surprise. "Why, your note, of course. I only found it just now."

Paula gawked at him. He wasn't wearing a coat. "What note?" She demanded. "I didn't write any note."

"But, of course you did," he said impatiently. "Wait — here it is."

She snatched the piece of paper from his hands.

I am so sorry; I cannot express it enough. I beg you to meet me at Maison Kammerzell at two o'clock today.

Paula guffawed. "You've got to be kidding," she scoffed disdainfully and stuffed the paper back into his palm. "I beg YOU? You've *got* to be kidding."

Frowning, he replied, "So you didn't write it?"

"I most certainly did NOT." She tried not to look at him and how handsome he looked with that curl just over his eye and the way the cold was pinking his cheeks. *He really should be wearing a coat.*

"It says two o'clock at the Kammerzell," he insisted. "And here you are."

She set her cup down hard in the saucer. "If you're implying —"

"Sit down, for cryin' out loud," Tony complained. "You're blockin' the light."

"He isn't staying" Paula declared.

Larsonnier sat. He was looking at her with those either-or eyes. They were brown right now, the color of the cappuccino, minus the chocolate sprinkles, of course. His fingers tapped the table top.

He really believes I wrote that stupid note. This is ridiculous. I'd never write a note like that, even if I — er, would like to hear his explanations. She squirmed in her seat.

"I've been out of town, actually," Larsonnier explained. As if she'd asked, which she hadn't because she already knew from Yasmine.

"Oh, really?" Paula couldn't help asking. "Spy business . . . or off on field exercises?"

He found his cigarettes. "I believe I told you — repeatedly — that, I resigned from the service years ago," Christian irritably replied.

"Oh, then, it must be 'army business'", she sweetly said.

"Tell me, how do you keep them all straight — from the roster . . .or do you list them by the Dewey Decimal System?" *Ha! Score one for the dumpee.*

His cigarette snapped in half. "I told you —"

Paula interrupted. "That's the problem, isn't it? You're used to *telling* the babes what to do and they do it, don't they? 'Oooh, Christian!" She squealed in falsetto. "Lord, if I live to be a thousand, I'll never understand the attraction."

"You seemed to understand it well enough," Christian countered. "That is, until something was expected of you — adult behavior, for example."

"You mean like letting you run my life?"

"If you two are going to browse through the photo album," Tony put in. "Do it someplace else, would you? I'm tryin' to read here!"

"Damn!" Christian exploded, jumping to his feet. "What is it you want from me?"

Matching his decibel, Paula shouted back, "I want you to quit telling me how to live, that's what! How dare you order me to quit!"

Tony lowered his paper and opened his mouth to speak. She flashed a glare — **don't you dare!** Message received, he closed his mouth and retreated into the sports section.

"Hell, if I want to strip naked and dance on a table like Mata Hari, I'll do it! I don't have to live by your rules."

He leaned on the palm of his hands.

"And that's the true crux of the issue, isn't it? You aren't used to playing by any rules at all."

Tony stirred uneasily. "Hey, do you mind? You're makin' a scene."

"That's okay, Pop," Paula assured him, leaping up. "I'm goin'. I don't have to take this crap." She grabbed her knapsack. It caught the table and she pulled at it angrily, uselessly, till Christian courteously lifted the table leg.

"Running away again?" He asked politely.

"No! I have to go. I. . . . I have a date."

"Oh?" His voice was neutral "Rouget, I suppose? I hear he's finally out of the hospital."

"You suppose wrong. But then, you always do. Marc was out last night. Tonight, it's, uh, Gaston. He's a bass at the opera. Really broad chested. Great guy. Never once wipes the water drips from under my glass."

"Sounds as if you've settled in quite nicely," Larsonnier observed through his teeth.

"Oh, hell, yeah, I'm havin' a great time."

Tony took his cue. "Yeah, great," he said from behind his paper.

Paula opened her folio. "Here's your damned sketch," she spat and tossed the canvas onto the table between them.

"So-o-o nice to see you again. Do stop by the flat sometime. It's a five flight walk up, but a nice view of the cathedral. Only, call first, will you, so I can LEAVE! OH, and before I forget—we never did have that ORDAINED conversation, did we?"

Christian stared after her as she stalked off through the crowds, the Stetson, a bobbing red exclamation point. "Just maybe, we didn't need to." He whispered under his breath; his eyes wide in disbelief.

Giordano put down his paper. "You know, Laronneer, mebbe I lack your expertise in these matters, but I don't think she's comin' back to the table."

"The woman is *impossible!*" Larsonnier vowed. "She lies, she steals, she . . .she drives me to distraction!"

"Yeah, that's my girl."

"Why won't she resign?" He demanded. "Why must she be so obstinate?"

Giordano refolded the newspaper perfectly.

"I shouldn't be tellin' ya this, but . . . Paoli quit months ago."

Christian whirled, stunned. "Months ago? But . . . but, why didn't she say so?"

Tony's eyes were all blue innocence. "Well, you know, women." He shrugged. "Who knows what they're really thinkin' . . . And actually, I had no idea myself until a few days ago. Why don't you look at the sketch?"

Curiosity with mingling confusion, the Frenchman lifted the onionskin covering. La Maison Blanche rode the crest of its hill like a ship on the sea. The faintest wash of color softened the boldness of its lines and there on the roof, barely visible, the nest.

"C'est Magnifique," Christian breathed. "She has captured it, perfectly." In his mind's eye, he saw the label, proudly displayed among the other great wines of Alsace.

Tony took the print from his hands and examined his daughter's work. He grunted admiration. "She's definitely got some talent."

"Yes." Christian took the sketch back. He mused, "do you know, I've never taken another woman to La Mason Blanche."

"So why are you telling *me* this? Why don't you tell Paula?"

Larsonnier looked at him, his expression bemused. "I believe I will," he decided.

Giordano watched as he put the sketch under his arm and strode away, quickly disappearing into the crowds surrounding the cathedral.

"Superbly done."

Giordano looked up. Maurice Larsonnier was seating himself in the chair his son had just vacated. His coat, cashmere, his scarf, silk. The Frenchman opened his gold cigarette case and extracted a cigarette.

The American shrugged, a grin getting away from him. "A little paper, a little ink . . . They'll drive each other nuts, but it's better than driving *us* crazy."

Larsonnier smiled. "The heart has its reasons, which reason knows nothing of.' Pascal," he added by the way of explanation. "I find Molière far too cynical in the matters of the heart." He sighed. "A great pity, these ideas you Americans have about retirement and old age. You would do well as an ambassador . . .or a matchmaker, perhaps! An ambassador of love." Maurice laughed this own joke.

Tony tossed a few coins onto the table and struggled out of his chair.

"And while I'm thinkin' about it, what is it with your son's so-called ordination? Frankly, he's hardly the type."

"Actually, he's been considering that for years—naturally, against my wishes and his mother's as well. But, I believe he managed some kind of special permission between the organization he sometimes works for and the diocese. I am not sure of the details and he won't tell me anything."

"Ahh. Well, my bet is that he'll soon forget all about it."

"Let's hope."

"Thanks all the same, Moritz, but who needs the indigestion? I'm outta here. I got my first pension check waitin' to be endorsed and a mother drivin' around in a sports car in New York." He let out a deep sigh. "And if you don't mind, keep an eye on my kid, will ya?"

"Always, Monsieur," Maurice rose too, and gripped the engulfing hand with all the respect it deserved. "Was it not my old friend Jorgi's last request?"

Yeah, well . . ." Tony chuckled. "Mebbe it's best if you never bring that up."

Maurice watched the American stride across the square as the awed crowds parted.

"I saw him, I saw him with my own eyes," he quoted softly. Something touched his cheek, piercing the cold. He looked up and smiled. It was starting to snow.

**Michèle Milano**, native New Yorker, children's book author, life-long artist and retired music teacher, enjoys art in a variety of forms! A classically trained and degreed musician, singer/jazz pianist, painter, photographer and jewelry metalsmith, who has performed as a Classical Pianist and Singer and as a solo Jazz Musician in various venues including Notre Dame Cathedral Strasbourg, Cathedral of Augsburg, Germany.

Army Wife to her military career husband where Ms. Milano travelled extensively in Europe as well as Coast to Coast in the US. As an absolute book-a-holic, Michèle wrote for various military affiliated publications and has always been known as a great story teller of some of her most amazing experiences.

Rook to Strasbourg, co-authored with her best friend, Michele J. Olson captures both author's love of France and travel.

Michèle's academic background started in English/Communications at the former Briarcliff College in New York. She holds a BS in French, BA in Music and attended Graduate School at The Catholic University of America, studying Vocal Pedagogy. Having learned Jewelry Metalsmithing at the Corcoran School of Art and Design, Michèle has shown her jewelry and photographs in a variety of art galleries in Northern Virginia and New York.

Currently, she is working on her next children's book.

 **Michele J. Olson**, the adventurous author *of **Rook to Strasbourg***, fell in love with Strasbourg in the 1980s while residing in Germany during her husband Ed's service with the US army. Captivated by all things French, Michele and her best friend, Michèle took many day trips to Strasbourg and the French region of Alsace.

She lived a life as captivating as her novel. A lifelong lover of reading and France, Michele J. Olson lived by her passions.

After growing up in Terre Haute, Indiana, Michele went to Northern State University in South Dakota where she met her lifelong husband, Ed.

Eventually Michele and her husband settled in Minnesota, where she instilled a love for stories to her children and grandchildren. She passed away in her sleep in 2019, and is fondly remembered by her friends and family.

Rook to Strasbourg stands as a posthumous masterpiece, a testament to Michele's indomitable spirit, imaginative storytelling, and the cherished presence of her four amazing children.

Made in the USA
Middletown, DE
12 May 2025

75471435R00188